Praise for
*The Book of the Film of the*
*Story of My Life*
and William Brand

"Thank goodness for William Brandt's sly English-Kiwi voice, because it sets the love story on its ear with perfect pitch . . . With the wise heart of a Nick Hornby and satirical echoes of a Terry Southern or J. P. Donleavy, Brandt delivers stingingly fresh observations on love in the age of Gender Wars that will make both male and female readers feel they've won . . . Brandt's writerly jewels—truth and humor—shine through with giddy clarity. I've seen the new face of literary humor and its name is William Brandt."

—Chris Gilson, author of *Crazy for Cornelia*

"This is that rarest of literary commodities: a truly hilarious novel that has something interesting to say about men, women, and New Zealand. With surprising plot twists up to the last page, laugh-out-loud one-liners, and a lovably bitter midlife narrator."

—Stephen McCauley, author of
*True Enough* and *The Object of My Affection*

"A dazzling piece of writing . . . Brandt's prose would be funny almost regardless of content, but it's his ability to create well-observed, complex, and believable characters you care about—even when you want to wring their necks—makes him stand out."

—*New Zealand Herald*

"Sophisticated, stylish."
—*Dominion Post*

"Outstanding, hilarious . . . the feel-good of the year."
—*Christchurch Press*

"Enjoyable and thematically tight . . . The energy and invention recall a tender-minded Thom Jones, but the integration and roundedness of the narrative voices suggest Richard Ford or even Raymond Carver. Brandt is an astute and natural writer."

—*Times Literary Supplement*

*Also by William Brandt*

Alpha Male

*The*

# BOOK

*of the*

# FILM

*of the*

# STORY

*of My*

# LIFE

William Brandt

**WARNER BOOKS**

NEW YORK   BOSTON

This book is a work of fiction. Names, characters, places, and incidents are the product of the author's imagination or are used fictitiously. Any resemblance to actual events, locales, or persons, living or dead, is coincidental.

This Warner Books edition is published by arrangement with Victoria University Press, Victoria University of Wellington, P.O. Box 600, Wellington 6001, New Zealand

Warner Books

Time Warner Book Group
1271 Avenue of the Americas, New York, NY 10020
Visit our Web site at www.twbookmark.com.

Printed in the United States of America
First Warner Books Printing: February 2005
10 9 8 7 6 5 4 3 2 1

Library of Congress Cataloging-in-Publication Data

Brandt, William, 1961–
  The book of the film of the story of my life / William Brandt.
      p.   cm.
  ISBN 0-446-69381-2
  1. Motion picture producers and directors—Fiction. 2. New Zealanders—England—Fiction. 3. Birthday parties—Fiction. 4. London (England)—Fiction. 5. Runaway wives—Fiction. 6. Prostitutes—Fiction. 7. New Zealand—Fiction. 8. Islands—Fiction. I. Title.

PR9639.3.B665B66    2005
823'.914—dc22                                                        2004041574

Cover design by Beck Stvan
Book design and text composition by Ralph L. Fowler

*To Cecile*

*Acknowledgments*

I would like to thank the following people: Fergus Barrowman, Caroline Dawnay, Dan Franklin, Eirlys Hunter, Bill Manhire, Deborah Panckhurst, Lourdes Pangelinan, Stella Spencer.

I gratefully acknowledge the assistance of Creative New Zealand.

*The*

# BOOK

*of the*

# FILM

*of the*

# STORY

*of My*

# LIFE

*To make the truth more plausible,*
*it's absolutely necessary to mix a*
*bit of falsehood with it.*

— DOSTOYEVSKY

## Chapter 1

". . . FREDERICK? Are you there? Dear?"

"Yeah, I'm here. I'm just . . ."

I brace my arm against the wall. I change weight, I try to breathe. My forehead is prickling.

"Or even if it was just for a holiday, just for six months."

"Yeah, that would be nice."

"How long has it been now?"

"How long? Oh, must have been a while."

"It must be three or four years, dear."

"Yeah, probably about that."

"At least."

"Yeah."

She pauses. It's one of those crystal-clear lines you get sometimes and I can hear the catch in her voice. "We do miss you, you know."

"Oh, yeah, of course, I mean hell, I miss you too. You know, it's just, you know how it is, I'm up to my eyes out here. Otherwise, wild horses, I mean, like a shot." I put my back against the wall, lean on it and slide.

"Well, think about it."

"I will. I'll give it some serious thought. I'll think about it. Seriously."

"Just for a holiday."

"I could do with a holiday, that's for sure."

"I hope you're not working too hard."

"Don't worry, I'm fine."

"I saw Sophie in the paper this morning."

"Mm-hm." I dig my fingernails into the wallpaper. I don't want to hear about Sophie being in the paper.

"She looked quite thin, I thought."

I don't want to talk about her.

"Do you think she's eating properly?"

"Gee, I really don't know."

"Have you seen her at all lately dear?"

"Well, she's in the States right now, but we keep in touch, sure. We see each other when we can. You know. It's fine, it's cool, we're mates. We're just both pretty busy, so, you know, we don't, that often . . . but when we can yeah. For sure."

"If you did come back we could take the boat up to Russell."

"That would be nice."

"Dad's getting the transom rebuilt."

"Oh, that's good. He never did like that transom."

"Well . . ." She sighs, and I can hear her fingernails drumming on the receiver. Tappity tappity. Here it comes. The clincher. This is the part where she offers me money. I then refuse, breezily. She then offers again, vaguely, we let it drop, then just before we hang up we agree on a sum and it turns up in a few days. Then I go to Selfridges and buy clothes. I go to Jermyn Street and buy cheese. I take taxis everywhere. I go to restaurants and cafes. I buy watches, electronic goods, shoes, knickknacks and gewgaws. I sit in parks. I take train rides to nowhere.

"So . . . did you get the card?"

"I got it. It's great. The socks are great too. They . . . just great socks. Great."

"I hope you're having a happy birthday."

"It's great. It's great." When I woke up this morning I was forty-two. That's when it hit me. *That's* when I realized I was forty. I'd always suspected that forty went over a little too easily. Now it's kicking in.

"So you're sure everything is okay, dear?"

"Oh, sure. Great. Couldn't be better." I resolved a long time ago to protect my parents from my life. After all they've done for me, it's the least I could do.

". . . Are you all right for cash, dear?"

Normally, a forty-two-year-old man doesn't need money from his parents. A forty-two-year-old may well not *have* parents. Instead, he has his own money. He has children. Responsibilities. A career. I'm sweating bricks. "Oh, yeah, I'm fine, I'm fine. I'm just fine."

Another pause. I can hear my dad's voice rumbling in the background. "Dad says do you want him to send some money over?"

"No. No, I'm fine. Don't bother."

"The exchange rate is murder nowadays."

"Well, that's what you get."

"Sorry, dear?"

"That's what you get for devaluing."

"Yes." She sounds a little unsure. "Still, it's good for the farmers, isn't it?"

"And what's good for the farmers is . . . good for the farmers."

"Sorry, dear?"

"What?"

"What do you mean?"

"I don't know, what do I mean?"

"So, do you want Dad to . . . ?"

I hang up a few moments later. I hang up and sit and I try to breathe. I've done an insane thing. I said no. I said love to all, I said take care, I said thanks for the card. I said I'd really think about that holiday, seriously. Then I said no, three times. And the last one did it. She actually believed me. They aren't going to send any money. I really think they aren't going to send it. I told them not to send it and they aren't going to send it. She was waiting for me to change my mind and say, Oh, send it, and *I* was waiting for me to say it, but I didn't. I didn't say it and she believed me, she believed that I actually didn't want it. We said good-bye and she said happy birthday one more time, and we hung up.

What really rocked me was when my mother suggested that it's time I go home. She said a holiday, but she didn't mean that. I know what she meant. They want me to come home. There are only two reasons for going back to New Zealand to live. One, you've got kids. Two, you've failed. I don't have kids.

If my mother is suggesting that I have failed, it's serious. My parents are pathologically supportive. Despite overwhelming evidence to the contrary garnered over the last forty-two years, they still think I'm wonderful and can do no wrong. Heartbreaking. That's why I am the way I am. It's not their fault. They just backed the wrong horse, God bless them. How were they to know? How was I to know? How was anyone to know? But sometimes I think, if they'd just made it a bit tougher, deprived me of a few things now and again—money, opportunity, love—I wouldn't be in the mess I'm in now. Still, you have to be philosophical. These things happen. Lives turn out wrong, or they don't turn out at all. It's no big deal, it happens all the time, for all sorts of reasons. God almighty, people *die*. Entire families are crushed by falling masonry. Men are tortured, women are raped, and vice versa. We won't even start on the children. No one is doing any of those things to me. I'm not dead, I'm not even hungry. Christ, I need to lose a few kilos. I should be grateful. Life is a strange and wonderful gift and today is the first day of the rest of it. There is no such thing as failure, only opportunities to learn. I should be jumping for joy. I should be over the moon.

But I'm not. I don't know what's wrong with me, I've gone all limp, I've gone all gutless. I lack ambition and drive. I've become soft and passive and weepy and sentimental. Anything can set me off. It's got so bad I can't go to the movies anymore. And the children, oh, God, the children. An ad for nappy cream is enough to reduce me to tears. I walk past playgrounds and I have to cross the road. Maybe it's a natural part of the aging process.

BEEP BEEP BEEP.

I have ten seconds. I sit on the edge of the bed, rest my left arm on the bedside table, and keep still.

POCKETA POCKETA POCKETA.

The pressure cuff hidden on my left biceps begins to fill with air. A prickly feeling on my forehead. I force myself to relax. I look around the room. Flowery wallpaper. A small window with a view of a chimney pot forest against a gray sky. A light drizzle falling. A 747 inching its way across the windowpane. In one corner a bed. In the other a hand basin. Next to that a tiny fridge with an electric jug on top.

In the fridge, I happen to know, is a bottle of Stolichnaya. By now the cuff has tightened until it's almost painful; it hesitates, inflates a little more until it is, then deflates slowly in increments. My hand throbs as the blood floods back. My fingers tingle.

BEEP BEEP.

All done. I glance at the LCD display on the cigarette-packet–sized apparatus attached to my belt. Up a couple of points.

But now, to work. I open my Foster and Sons leather satchel. I pull out three original screenplays. I take up the first, which consists of 120 A4 pages bound with three brass studs. Plain and unpretentious, the cover page is blank except for the title, centered and typed in twelve-point Courier: *Blood Count.* So far so good. I get myself comfortable, inhale deeply through my nose, clear my mind of all extraneous influences, and begin to read. About ten minutes later I put it down. I reread the end of the last scene:

. . . SUDDENLY THE CLEANING LADY DROPS HER MOP AND PULLS AN UZI OUT OF THE BUCKET.

                    Cleaning Lady

            Fuck you, mother fucker.

**SLOW MOTION**: THE UZI SPITS LEAD, BUT THE CLEAN-
ING LADY IS SHOOTING WIDE. THE PRICELESS STAINED
GLASS WINDOWS DISSOLVE INTO A MILLION SHARDS
BEHIND BAKER'S HEAD AS HE CARTWHEELS, DRAWS HIS
WEAPON AND EMPTIES ALL SEVENTEEN ROUNDS OF THE
NICKEL-FINISHED HECKLER AND KOCH P7M10 SPECIAL
INTO THE CLEANING LADY'S FACE.

**TIGHT ON**: CLEANING LADY'S FACE DISSOLVES INTO A
BLOOMING FOUNTAIN OF BLOOD AND BONE.

**ANGLE ON**: CLEANING LADY'S BRAINS SPLATTER ACROSS
THE RECENTLY-CLEANED LINOLEUM SURFACE.

                    Baker

            Mop that.

BAKER CHUCKLES. MAYBE IT'S NOT GOING TO BE SUCH
A BAD DAY AFTER ALL.

Now, Baker is the good guy. I don't know, I guess I really am getting old. I sigh. I return to the script. After another hundred-odd
pages, six violent deaths, two maimings and an extended torture
sequence, I lay the script aside and stare at the ceiling to give my
stomach time to settle. I make a few notes for future reference and

turn to the next script. This is an entirely different kettle of fish. It is elegantly spiral-bound. Centered on the glossy black plasticized cover is a color reproduction of the part of the Sistine Chapel roof depicting God and Adam fingering each other. The title is discreetly embossed: *The Eternal Round.* There is a subtitle too: *A Pseudo-Shakespearean Romance.* I flip through the pages. The paper is heavy, one hundred grams at least. Laser-printed. Everything bespeaks enormous effort, attention to detail, and great care. My spirits rise. This is more like it. I breathe deeply, clear my mind of all preconceptions and begin to read.

It is subliterate. It is sub-subliterate. "Their" and "there" are treated as alternate spellings. Every time a word ends in "s" it has an apostrophe. Furthermore, the characters speak in a ghastly parody of Elizabethan English, with frequent lapses into nineties vernacular. It is set in a sort of science-fictionized seventeenth-century Venice, observed by little invisible green men who have floated down from the sky and are, I think, supposed to be cute.

Blakensop

Antonia, Antonia, I beg thee, just don't do this
thing that you are thinking of, okay?

Antonia

Blakensop, I wouldst that I could not but
consider it for thou art passing spunky
in those tight's.

SHE GRIN'S IMPISHLY, KISSES HIM IMPETUOUSLY,
FLASHES HER BUTTOCK'S AT HIM AND DISAPPEAR'S
OVER THE BALCONY RAILING. THE CUTE LITTLE MART-
IAN GIGGLE'S IMPISHLY AND FOLLOW'S BLAKENSOP TO
THE MARBLED BATHROOM WHERE HE SIGHS AND BEGINS
TO WASH HIS GENITAL'S.

I stare at this passage for several minutes, trying to project myself into the mind that wrote it. I fail. I do not believe that a mind was involved. I wonder if it has perhaps been computer-generated. Or maybe it's a terrorist plot. Script number three is simply bound. It is entitled *Jacko*. I open a page at random.

```
JACKO HOVERS IN THE DOORWAY. HE WATCHES SAL'S
DEFT FINGERS AS SHE WORKS ON THE WALLABY.

                    Sal

                 You orf?

PENSIVELY SHE GLANCES OVER HER SHOULDER, HER HEART
POUNDING WITH REGRET. HE LOOKS BACK AT HER,
THOUGHTFUL BUT DISTANT, FINGERING HIS BROW, A
FLICKER OF SPENT PASSION PASSING ACROSS HIS FACE
EVERY NOW AND THEN LIKE THE LAST RUMBLES OF A
THUNDERSTORM AS IT DRIFTS ACROSS THE PLAINS AND
VANISHES OVER THE HORIZON. BUT THE MOMENT HAS
PASSED AND A BLEAK SENSE OF SEPARATION SETTLES
HEAVILY BETWEEN THEM. SILENCE FALLS IN THE CRAMPED
HUT. TURNING BACK TO THE SINK, SAL CONTINUES TO
SCRUB THE WALLABY'S LIMP SCRAWNY CORPSE, WITH
SLOW, HOPELESS MOVEMENTS. CAMERA TRACKS AND ZOOMS
AS THE DEAD WALLABY'S PAWS FLOP TO AND FRO LIKE
THE PATHETIC CAPERINGS OF AN AGING CLOWN. THIS
THOUGHT STRIKES THEM BOTH AT THE SAME TIME, AS
JACKO STANDS IN THE DOORWAY, UNMOVING, AS STILL AS
ROCK. SHE SEEMS TO HIM SO LIKE HIS LONG LOST
MOTHER AT THIS MOMENT EXCEPT FOR THE COLOR OF HER
HAIR BUT THIS IS A THOUGHT HE ONLY HALF FORMULATES
EVEN TO HIMSELF AND WILL NEVER EVEN BEGIN TO FIND
THE WORDS TO THINK ABOUT EXPRESSING.
```

Jacko

Reckon.

SAL TOSSES HER HEAD MOURNFULLY, AND CATCHES HIS
EYE.

ZOOM IN TO **EXTREME CLOSE-UP** OF JACKO'S EYES. THE
PUPILS FILL THE SCREEN. THE BOTTOMLESS DEPTH OF
HIS PUPILS EXPRESS A SENSE OF LOSS, A LOSS SO
DEEP, SO INEXTRICABLY WOUND INTO THE CORE OF
HIS BEING THAT NONE BUT SHE CAN TRULY UNDERSTAND
WHERE AND HOW IT CAME TO BE THERE. BUT EVEN SHE
CANNOT REACH HIM NOW. SHE BEGINS TO SKIN THE
WALLABY.

Sal

Yeah?

JACKO TURNS TO LOOK OUT THE WINDOW AT THE LONE
TREE. ITS BRANCHES DEAD AND BARE, IT HAS NOT
CHANGED, THERE IS NO FLICKER OF GREEN ANYWHERE
ABOUT IT, IT IS JUST AS BLACK AND BARE AND HOPE-
LESS AS IT HAS EVER BEEN. THE HILLS TOO ARE
UNCHANGING, THE RED EARTH BAKING IN THE HARSH
GLARE OF THE PITILESS SUN. THEIR DEEP TECTONIC
SHIFTS, INVISIBLE, UNGUESSED AT, UNSEEN, FAR FAR
BELOW THE SURFACE, SEEM TO REFLECT AND COMMENT
IRONICALLY ON THE GRIM HAGGARD LANDSCAPE OF
JACKO'S IMPASSIVE FACE. IT IS AS IF THIS MAN,
THIS MOMENT, THIS TIME AND THIS UNIVERSE WERE
BORN THE ONE FOR THE OTHER, AS IF ALL TIME AND
ALL CREATION HAS BEEN DIRECTED BY THE GREAT
UNSEEN HAND OF NATURE TO THIS ONE INDESCRIBABLE
MOMENT.

<u>Jacko</u>

Yeah.

On balance I think I prefer *Blood Count*. At least it has a story. I'm constantly coming across scripts in which either nothing happens at all, or anything that *does* happen has nothing to do with anything else that happens. My job is to read them anyway. It's hard work and thankless, the pay is shit and I can't get enough of it to survive, but someone has to do it. Someone has to read this stuff so that others will never have to. Yes it's a war we're fighting down here, protecting the innocent. Not perhaps the reason I got into the film business. My reasons for getting into the film business were more Olympian. Right up to my thirty-seventh birthday I believed, passionately, that I was destined to change the world and that I was destined to do so through the medium of film. The articles of incorporation of Godzone International Proprietary Limited actually include the phrase "development, production and exploitation of cinematic works of a seminal and world-changing character." So it's right there, in black and white. On my thirty-seventh birthday, as a matter of fact, I was riding through Paris with Sophie in a sports car when I realized I was never going to change the world. It came to me, quite suddenly, waiting for a red light on the Champs-Elysées. It just wasn't going to happen. Okay, I said to myself at the time, no need to panic, I'll just change my strategy. I won't change the world, I'll make the most of it as it is instead. No problem. I'll screw the bastard. This morning I woke up and I was forty-two and I realized something else. I haven't changed the world. I haven't even made the most of it as it is. I certainly haven't screwed the bastard. And now I get this uncomfortable feeling—now it's the world's turn.

But first, a bathroom stop. I let myself out of my room, and into the potato-smelling staircase. A couple of flights down there's a new family. For some reason their doormat is always thickly strewn with potato peels and children's shoes. It looks like something you'd see at the ICA.

And this morning it's even more surreal than usual because someone is waiting for me on the landing. Someone in red leather, top to toe, a bright red helmet on his head. He looks like one of Satan's little helpers. Under his arm is a package. How I wish I was a motorcycle courier. Someone who actually *does* something. "Can you help me, mate? I'm looking for a Mr." — he squints at the package — "a Mr. or Ms. Case-Carlisle."

"That's me. I'm Frederick Case."

He looks at me, then back at Mrs. Traversham's door. The two or so square inches of face visible behind the helmet appear to be suspicious.

"I'm the boarder. That's my address too. This is my room. I live on the landing but that's my address." I get out my key to demonstrate, eyeing the package. It's about the size of a duty-free pack of cigarettes. It's wrapped in brown paper. "Also, for your information, it's my birthday."

"Sign here."

I sign with unseemly haste.

"Happy birthday." The courier clumps away down the stairs. I take the package back into my room. I shut the door and rip off the wrapping. It's a wooden box, the proportions of a tiny coffin. It's wrapped in about a mile of shiny red ribbon. There's an envelope taped to the outside. I open the envelope. Inside is a card, and a tiny pair of golden scissors. Inside the card is a message: *Cut the red tape.* I take the scissors and cut the tape. I open the box, which has hinges. Inside the box, in a nest of tissue paper and straw, is an old Coke bottle. Looks to have spent some time in the sea — it's clouded and abraded. It's very heavy, thick glass.

There's a message in the bottle, rolled up. I pull it out. It's a piece of paper, burnt around the edges in traditional ye-olde-pirate style. It's been photocopied, with our names written in by hand:

EXPERIENCE THE LAND OF FIRE AND MAGIC!

*Dear Frederick and Sophie,*

*Charles C. Menard would like to take this opportunity to heartily solicit your participation in celebrating the occasion of his fortieth year here on planet Earth.*

I note the split infinitive, but read on anyway.

*The festivities will take place on the Pacific island paradise of Makulalanana. Makulalanana is a sacred volcano. Smoke rises mysteriously from the summit. Witness for yourself the glowing lava-filled crater.*

*Nestled like a jewel inside its protective coral reef, this tiny completely uninhabited island forms part of the Guelep archipelago, a little known group of islands approximately two hundred and fifty nautical miles north of Vanuatu and accessible only by seaplane or boat.*

*Charles will be celebrating throughout the week of November 14, 2002, and you are welcome to join him for part or all of this time in the luxury tent-town of Makulalanana, erected especially for the occasion.*

*Please come prepared for a fancy dress gala event dinner on the Sunday night.*

*All amenities will be provided. (And we do mean all, darlings . . .)*

*RSVP to Karl Bell of Bell and Beauchamp Ecstatic Experiences, Ltd.*

*PS: It is Charles's great pleasure to offer you this entire island experience as his guest.*

I blink. This is ironic. Charles C. Menard is offering to fly me all the way around the world and back, to celebrate his birthday. Not my birthday. His birthday. Plus, it's all a mistake anyway. He's really inviting Sophie. Must be a glitch in the system somewhere. He has yet to update his database. I suppose I should let Sophie know, but I'm fucked if I'm ringing her on *my* birthday. She'll probably find out anyway. She'll probably go in fact, which means I'd better not. I can think of better ways to spend a week than hanging around sad and single in a sandy confined space with my estranged wife and her film-star boyfriend.

I run my hands through my hair. I feel primal. I feel dizzy. I sling the box under the bed and climb the half-flight to Mrs. Traversham's flat, knock lightly and let myself in. Mrs. Traversham has returned from her morning constitutional. I know this because of the yapping.

"Ah, Mr. Case, is that you?"

"Yes, Mrs. Traversham, it is indeed I."

"I wonder could I possibly prevail on you to render me a moment's assistance?"

She's in the kitchen with a jar of Branston Pickle that won't open. Freddy, her King Charles, is jumping around her feet. He adores Branston Pickle. Can't get enough of it.

"I'm most terribly sorry but I simply can't seem to induce this lid to budge."

"Allow me."

Mrs. Traversham is ninety-six. She's thin as a bird, covered in large brown liver spots, hunched over, small, white-haired, and dresses exclusively in tweed with enormous wrinkles in her support stockings. She has the plummiest accent I've ever heard in my life. She's worse than the Queen. She can see about twenty-five feet, which is just enough to get you across the road if you trust the signals. As far as I know, Mrs. Traversham has no relatives, no friends and no acquaintances. She has lived alone in this small flat off the Edgware Road for the last sixty-odd years with a succession of King Charles spaniels ever since Mr. T was crushed, along with their two small children, by a collapsing building in 1941, which is ironic because he was a bomber pilot at home on leave. She still has his uniform hanging up in the hall closet in a dry-cleaner's bag with a handful of mothballs. Every single one of her King Charles spaniels, except for one who was mauled to death by a cat, has died of heart disease. She says it's congenital. I say it's Branston Pickle.

I've been here for about four months. I came here almost straight from the split-up with Sophie, after a short stint at Tamintha's. I was a mess when I got here. I was manic. I kept going on and on about nothing at all. Then I'd suddenly become silent and black. Mrs. Traversham wasn't too sure at all at the interview, but when she discovered I have the same first name as her dog she cheered up enormously. Then she found out I was a New Zealander and that clinched it. "Oh, that explains it," she said, greatly relieved. I think she meant the ponytail; I'm not sure.

I open the jar and hand it back with a flourish. Freddy is by now going berserk. He slips on the linoleum and almost brains himself on my kneecap.

"Mr. Case, you are a constant source of delight and amazement."

"Mrs. Traversham, it is, as always, an inexpressible pleasure." It is too. It's the most useful thing I've done all day. All week. All . . . no, stop. That way lies madness. "Oh . . ." I reach into my back pocket and pull out a hundred and fifty quid. "I owe you for this month."

"Very kind of you, Mr. Case, thank you so much. I'll make out your receipt directly."

After relieving myself in Mrs. Traversham's 1942-era bathroom, I make the classic mistake. I stop to look in the mirror. For some little time now I have been aware of pressure building in my upper lip. I was right. It's an enormous blind pimple the size of Hawaii, pushing out from the corner of my mouth. It changes the shape of my entire face. I look like a spawning salmon, one of those doomed hook-jawed monsters fighting their hopeless upstream battle. Forty-two years old and erupting all over the place like a teenager. Happy birthday.

I went to a Chinese herbalist once for my skin. He was all the rage. He had this tiny little practice in Soho. He was wearing Hush Puppies. I remember that bothered me. I believe that clothes maketh the man. He looked at my eyes, at my fingernails, my neck, my earlobes. He told me no bread, meat, whiskey, beer, wine, orange juice, eggs, potatoes, corn, breakfast cereals or flour. Which left rice, raw vegetables and lentils. For alcohol I was allowed vodka. I ignored most of his advice but I did go straight out and buy a bottle of Stolichnaya. I've drunk nothing else since. Everyone tells me it's stress. It's just *stress*. "You're under a lot of *stress*." Well, it's not stress. It's acne.

Back in my room there's a message on my cellphone. My pulse instantly goes to two hundred because I get this insane idea that it's Sophie calling for my birthday. It isn't. It's a call from Mee, the mad Singaporean–New Zealander. He wants to know if I've read the manuscript he sent me and when he can expect a contract. And he wants to remind me that the contents are copyright. That's classic, a sure sign. The less valuable the idea, the more obsessed the author is with protecting it. When you're a producer, you get a lot of phone calls. Calls from mad, bad people who have written mad, bad scripts, people full of fear and anger, people obsessed with betrayal and copyright and fees and stars and let me tell you I might bitch about these three scripts I'm reading today but they're Shakespeare compared to what I've seen. I'm reading these scripts professionally, for Biscrobus Film, an established production house that actually, incredibly, gloriously, *makes* films. Yes, these scripts already have a producer. Sure, Biscrobus doesn't want to make them, but there are actually people who want to. They're Nobel quality compared to what's out there. The stuff I get, at my bottom-hugging, below-radar, hedgehopping level, is beyond belief. All you have to do is say the word "producer" and it comes at you from all over, like flies to a corpse. Dross, crap. Sub-dross. Just say the word "producer." You'll see. Film is a world of big fish and little fish, sure, but it's a world where the little fish chase the big fish.

BEEP BEEP BEEP.

I sit still, rest my arm on the bedside table.

POCKETA POCKETA POCKETA.

I try to relax and think neutral and low-pressure thoughts. On the bedside table at my elbow is the birthday card from my parents—*Birthday Thoughts and Love to a Special Boy*. Sheesh. Next to that is a photo of me and Sophie on our wedding day. I keep it by the bed. Just my little joke. I have a very postmodern sense of humor. Sophie is gorgeous in black leather, black lipstick, fuck-me-now stilettos. However, I—frankly—in my Workshop suit, barefoot, with long blond hair drawn back in a flowing ponytail, and delicate, chiseled features, am equally gorgeous. Damnit, I am *more* gorgeous. Even my *feet* were attractive then. I was a demi-god. Tall, graceful, athletic. Not, in fact, an athlete, I couldn't run to catch a bus, but I *looked* athletic. That's what counts. I sit and stare at this photo and I just can't understand where it all went. I just don't get it. Of that wonderful creature in the photograph all that now remains is the ponytail. And that's thinning.

Still, that really was some wedding, best damn wedding I ever had.

BEEP BEEP.

A hundred and sixty-five over a hundred and eight. Must calm down.

Okay. Time to get out of here. Time to go down those stairs and get out there and hustle. I put on my Bundeswehr boots. They make me feel brave. Big black shiny fuckers, sixteen holes. Bought them in a place near Seven Dials. Nonslip rubber soles. Treads the size of truck tires. I put on a long-sleeve thermal vest and an orange T-shirt over that. On the T-shirt is a message. The message is: BEWARE. Next, a pair of Desert Storm pants, and over the lot my sheepskin-lined Swedish border-guard's greatcoat, which reaches all the way to the top of my boots, stands up by itself and would stop a tank round. If I had a steel helmet I'd wear that too. I stick the scripts in my briefcase, stick the briefcase under my arm, and I'm ready.

"Mrs. Traversham?"

"Yes, Mr. Case?"

"I'm just going out, now. I may be some time."

"Carry on, Mr. Case, and God's blessings go with you."

---

Bayswater Road and it's cold and the traffic is blasting past and the air smells like popcorn and there she is, plastered across the news-agents on the corner. *Shag City*, it says, in furry pink lettering. She has one finger on her lips. Shhhh. She's in a flak jacket and a helmet. The polish on her fingernail is pink, bright pink. That's the only splash of color—the fingernails and the lips. *Shag City*, starring Sophie Carlisle and Matt Chalmers, is the first main-stream film ever to depict an erect penis being sucked. It has won, already, a Critics award in Canberra, the Golden Stag at Monte Carlo and an adult film industry nomination for best blowjob. It's been reviewed, well, all over the world, it's sold in sixty-five coun-tries, it opens in the States today; and it is plastered all over Lon-don six inches thick. You can't move. She's on the backs of buses, on billboards, newsagents, the underground. You can't get away from her. As I ride the down escalator I pass another two Sophies on the way.

The fact is that Sophie is way too famous for comfort. Before, even six weeks ago, she was a *bit* famous. That was okay. Now she's a lot famous and I'm seeing her all the time and it's a pain in the arse. Being haunted by the past is one thing, but when the past is on *billboards*, all over town, that's something else, believe me.

And frankly, I have to confess I don't even get it. I mean, I've seen all her stuff—except for *Shag City*, which I'm saving up for a quietly suicidal winter's afternoon—and I have to say I just don't get it. All I ever seem to see somehow is Sophie. I sit there in the dark with everyone else, looking up at the silver screen, and there's Sophie, clumping around, saying her lines, snogging strange guys, laughing, shouting, roaring, weeping, being chased by deranged killers, chasing deranged killers, buying, selling, falling in and out of love, whatever, it's just Sophie. Oh, it's probably just me. It's *definitely* just me. But there is one thing I'd like to know: in the planning stages of this supersaturation publicity campaign, did anyone stop just for one moment to think how all this was going to make me *feel*? Of course not.

I get off at Piccadilly Circus and start down Haymarket. My phone goes. Without thinking, I answer it.

"It's Mee."

"Sorry?"

"Mee. It's Mee."

"Oh, Mee, of course, hi, I'm glad you called as a matter of fact . . ."

"I was wondering if you'd had a chance to read the manuscript yet." His voice is cold.

"I'll probably get to it this afternoon. It's in my briefcase now, as a matter of fact."

"Let's meet this evening. After you've read it. I'll come round at six."

"I'm sorry I can't tonight. I have a meeting."

"Tomorrow morning."

"I'll be in Brussels." This is a barefaced lie.

"When do you get back?"

"Thursday week."

"All right. It'll have to be tonight. After your meeting. At your place."

"But I . . ."

It's a vicious circle. You're at a party in a warehouse near Kings Cross. You don't know anybody. You get talking to a pale-faced guy in a black coat and clumpy shoes. He has this script. But doesn't know how to get started, he doesn't have any contacts. He doesn't want to send it to a film company. What if it got stolen? How do you protect your ideas? People in this industry are such arseholes. They never answer your letters; they never return phone calls. You get excited; you know just exactly what he means. You know how it feels, you've been there too. You're still there, in fact. But it doesn't have to be that way. You can be the human face of the industry. I'm a producer, you say, I've got contacts, I know them all, the Irish Brothers, everyone. I'll read it. I'll give you some tips. I'll get you started. I'll protect your ideas. I'll return your phone calls. You exchange phone numbers. You're feeling terribly excited. This guy actually thinks you're important and useful and you can help him. And besides, you tell yourself, this really could be it. Sure he appears to be ill-educated, frowsy and dull, but who knows? This could be that once-in-a-lifetime brilliant script. This could be the next *Muriel's Wedding* or *Reservoir Dogs*. This is what producing is all about. Energy, taking a punt, following up on opportunities, networking. You're over the moon. You stagger home.

At eight o'clock the next morning, you're in the middle of a very beautiful dream in which, inexplicably, preposterously, everything has just turned out all right after all when the phone rings. It's him. He's coming around. You try to tell him tomorrow would be more convenient because you're terribly hungover and you need another twelve hours sleep and a transfusion but he won't listen. He has to see you. It's urgent. All right, you say, come at

twelve. He comes at eight-thirty. He sits on the bed in your tiny
evil-smelling room while you stumble about feeling nauseous and
making coffee and he goes on and on and on about how this is
only a first draft and it needs work and he's not sure about the
third act and what about copyright, and what an arsehole everyone is and Syd Field and Linda Seger and how he's thinking
about doing a course but everyone says he should do a short film
first but he can't be fucked and Hollywood movies suck and
they're all so formulaic and he wants to do something different
but at the same time mainstream because all those art films suck
too and he's amazed at the crappy scripts that actually get made
into films and Steven Spielberg is an arsehole and Peter Jackson is
just mainstream and if people are willing to make crap like that
then any idiot can and he's working in a government agency that
has some arcane ancillary function in relation to the Westminster
Council Drainage Planning Unit.

By now you are wrestling with negative feelings toward this
guy. A leaden weight settles on your soul. You realize the truth.
He has no idea whatsoever and his script is going to be terrible
and when you've read it you're going to have to say you don't like
it and when you do he's going to get all defensive and blame you
and force you to explain why you don't like it and no matter what
you say it just won't help because the more you explain the less he
will understand and the more hostile he will get and the more you
will realize that you yourself don't have any idea what's wrong
with it, beyond the fact that it's crap and you never want to see this
guy again and you will have one more person who hates you in
this world.

And all of this for nothing. There is no money in it for you.
There never was. There is no possible reason for doing this except
that you're doing him a favor because you felt sorry for him and
now you don't even like him anymore. At least with Biscrobus you
can read a better class of crap—and get paid for it too.

And then, just when you thought it couldn't get any worse, you remember also what you were saying last night at the party to this very same person and you realize just what an arsehole you are. You're just like all the others, maybe even worse, you've been spouting utter steaming bullshit, you don't have any contacts at all beyond an ex-wife who doesn't talk to you anymore and through whom you met a lot of famous people who don't want to know you and you don't have any money or energy or drive or even really any idea how to get a film made beyond how to write a bullshit letter to the European Film Commission and the only substantive difference between you and the person sitting on your bed waiting to drink the first cup of coffee, is that *he* has no dress sense.

By now you've finished making the coffee. The ill-bred lumpen prol is sitting behind you waiting arrogantly for his coffee. The first cup, the cup that was meant for you. You give him the coffee. You look at the script, which is sitting on the bed. Sitting on top of the script is a little piece of paper.

"What's that?" you ask, innocently.

"Oh," he says, "that's a confidentiality agreement. I mean, let's face it, we don't really know each other that well."

Now, you hate him. So you roll up your sleeves, you sharpen your pencil, and you sit down and get started on not-getting-around to reading that script. And he starts phoning. And you start coming up with excuses. And it goes on and on. And there is really no way that you can get out of it. Eventually, sooner or later, you will read it. You will have that conversation. You will take your rightful place in the pantheon of arseholes, and only then will it be all over. Until the next time.

That's my life.

Oh well, time to face the music. Time to skim it at least fully enough to be able to sound like I've read it. "I'm sorry but I'll be out after that. I won't be home till eleven at the earliest."

There's the slightest pause. "All right. Eleven." He hangs up and I pocket the phone. By now I'm outside the sports bar and there's that sickening smell of chips in stale oil, and a racing car in the window. BEEP BEEP BEEP. I put the phone away and lean my hand on the plate glass. The hostess at the desk stares at me, like she knows I'm shit but she can't quite figure out what flavor. POCKETA POCKETA POCKETA.

I walk another half block and turn in at the automated double-glass doors of the net-curtain nightmare, the giant licorice all-sort that is New Zealand House. I wave to the security guards and cross the marble floor. I take the lift to the third floor. I walk down the long narrow avocado-green corridor. At the end of the corridor is a door. Beside the door is a brass plaque: GODZONE INTERNA-TIONAL, LTD. I unlock the door, cross several thousand square feet of empty open-plan office space and sit at a tiny desk in the far corner. I am the sole occupant of the entire floor. I won't be here much longer—the rent holiday runs out in August. I did my company tax return last week. The biggest item of expenditure for the year was the accountant's fee, and the biggest item of income was the tax refund on last year's loss carried forward. I like that—*carried forward*. Sounds so professional. I am in fact very professional in the way I run my business. I have an excellent accountant, I keep up to date on all the paperwork, which I find kind of sooth-ing. I have a registered office, a business card—three colors, exquisite print job, cost a fortune—I have letterhead, I have a fax machine, e-mail, a network hub (no network as yet, but I'm future proofed). I even have my own website. Only problem is I have no employees and I'm losing money hand over fist. Not my money, obviously, I have no money. My parents' money. Last week was the AGM. I met myself in the lobby, adjourned upstairs and sat and stared at the beige carpet for an hour. I decided that Godzone would have to go. Then I accepted the minutes, elected a new secretary, resigned as chairman, re-elected myself, jerked off on the carpet, had a little weep and went out for a hamburger. Kinda sad, huh?

I fire up the PC, check there's enough paper in the printer and start to type.

```
TITLE:       BLOOD COUNT
GENRE:       HORROR
PERIOD:      PRESENT DAY.
LOCATION:    NEW YORK—PRAGUE
DIRECTOR:    Klaus Smith.
DRAFT:       2
READER:      F.C.
```

SYNOPSIS: JACK BORMAN, a jaded New York cop, haunted by the serial murder of his wife and young child (revealed in minute detail in a series of flashbacks), is on the trail of their killer. He meets and falls in love with a young East European prostitute, who, he has reason to believe, will lead him to the killer. He also fears she could be the next victim, and there-fore trails her to her place of employment.

However what he is at first given ample reason to believe a brothel, turns out in fact to be a Manson-like sect, led by the killer of BORMAN's wife and child. The sect members are all vam-piresses posing as prostitutes and drinking the blood of their clients. At first BORMAN thinks it's just another New York thing, but when he is himself attacked by his erstwhile girlfriend (in the course of lovemaking), he quickly realizes that she possesses supernatural powers. He is forced to eviscerate her with a wooden stake.

When he reports his findings however, BORMAN is suspended and booked for psychological evaluation. Taking the law into his own hands, he lays in a large supply of own-build nine-millimeter soft-nose silver tips and goes vampire hunting. After a series of indescribably bloody encounters he has almost rid the city of the vampire menace, but is now himself pursued by half the NYPD. He tracks the leader of the sect—Dracula himself—to a seedy tenement block, only to be confronted by his own wife and child who are both vampires. He hesitates, and the Prince of Darkness escapes, taking BORMAN's wife and child with him.

BORMAN tracks DRACULA to Prague, where he finds and is forced to terminate his erstwhile family. At last they have been laid to rest. However his last silver bullet has his name on it. Bitten by the prostitute-vampiress, he knows that the suppurating wound on his shoulder will inevitably claim him. He lies down beside the peacefully resting corpses of his family and blows his own brains out.

COMMENTS: A blood-spattered orgy of overtly sexualized violence, with cardboard characters and a no-brand storyline. Director Klaus Smith already has a solid box-office success under his belt (*Eviscerator*) and there seems to be no reason why *Blood Count,* which is more or less indistinguishable, should not follow suit.

Structurally, first and second act turning points are clear and strongly marked, and the

action rises steadily to an action-packed climax. Unencumbered by considerations of motivation, credibility or taste, the action is
relentlessly paced throughout, and remains both
unremittingly violent and ceaselessly inventive.
     Looking toward another draft, a disorientating
third act relocation to Prague could perhaps be
substituted, in the interests of budget if nothing else (and what else matters with stuff like
this?), for Lower East Side or similar. Also,
central character BORMAN needs to be more sympathetic. A subsequent draft should look to
inserting more wisecracks and lighter moments.
A Mickey Mouse tie? A pet hamster? Dopey side-
kick?

READER'S RECOMMENDATION: PLEASE, GOD, DON'T
MAKE IT.

I move on to *The Eternal Round* and *Jacko*. By early afternoon I'm
finished. I decide to walk around to Biscrobus to drop them off.
Hopefully they'll have some more for me, and if I'm feeling especially bold I can hit Tamintha up for a full-time job. Plus maybe
I'll think of a subtle way of mentioning it's my birthday. I go out
again, wave to the security guards, who smile and nod. God I love
the smile of a security guard. It's like water to a drowning man.
     I cross Haymarket. The day has turned grayer, a light drizzle
falling, a fitful wind blowing fragments of dead leaves up my nose.
I withdraw fifty quid from the hole-in-the-wall across the road, cut
through to Leicester Square then on up to Soho and so to the hal-
lowed precincts of Biscrobus Film, behind Oxford Street. I say hi
to Tracy at the desk, which is not really a desk but a giant fish tank
with a slab of granite across the top.

While Tracy phones through to see if Tamintha's free, I pick up a copy of *Empire* and flick through. The Irish Brothers are being interviewed about their latest. I glance through but don't read the article. Reading the articles is never worth it. They never actually capture the inner essence of the person. I'm telling you, I know. There's a nice picture, big toothy grins, arms around each other's skinny-kid shoulders, stripy T-shirts and crazy hair. Seamus and Sean. Indistinguishable. They do it on purpose. They could easily get contrasting clothes, color-coded haircuts, something. Sophie says she can always tell them apart but I never can. I've met them plenty of times—they hang out with Sophie when they're in London. I've met them all, at one time or another.

I turn the page. There's Sophie with the Irish Brothers. She's laughing. You can see all her teeth. The Irish Brothers are laughing. That's nice. Everyone looks happy. According to the caption, Sophie may be starring in the Irish Brothers' next movie. That's nice. That's really nice. I put the magazine down. I look around the room. Tracy smiles at me. She's very nice too. This room is nice. Everything, everyone here, is so *nice*. The phone rings, Tracy picks it up. "Tamintha says to go on through."

I stand.

"Hey, like your boots."

"Thanks. They're German."

I thread my way through the bustling open-plan office: computers and photocopiers and people on phones, all busy, all needed, useful, employed, getting something done. Reach out. Touch a wall. You can feel it. Everything here is real. A real film company with real money, real films, real employees and a real tax situation. I get to a glass-block wall and a door, which is ajar. I tap on it and push.

Tamintha has the phone cradled on her shoulder, laptop open on an enormous game of Minesweeper. She raises an eyebrow and jerks her chin at me and I sit. I'm happy. I like this office. I think I could sit here forever watching Tamintha on the phone. She seems to be talking to LA about New York. New York is trying to close London and open in Berlin. London is trying to close New York and open in Paris. LA is either trying to stay right out of it or planning to close them both and open in Brussels. No one's sure. I was talking to Tamintha about it the other day. I thought New York and London should close LA and open in Auckland. She laughed. I like Tamintha. For a start, she's slightly older than me. People who are younger than me seem to be taking over entirely. Not that I have anything against younger people. I just think they should wait until they're older. Also, Tamintha is a New Zealander. "Always hire a New Zealander"—that's her motto.

She hangs up, smiles, lights a cigarette. I push the assessments across and she puts her feet up on the desk and tilts her reading glasses on her nose, squinting through the smoke. Her hair falls forward and she has to stop to hook it behind her ears, which is extremely cute in a killer exec. She is perhaps a little on the dumpy side, I suppose, technically, but people in glass houses and who cares anyway? The older I get the more attractive women get. Soon I'm going to be walking down the street in a haze of constant but generalized physical attraction. Then I'll probably start on the men. In fact maybe I already have. Mind you, this is all strictly on-paper attraction. When it comes to the actual hands-on, forget it. I'm just not interested. I am a cloud in pants.

Tamintha is skimming my assessments. She grunts and turns a page. I hope it was a good grunt. She pulls a face. "Yuck." She makes it all seem so easy. Sometimes I complain to her that I don't know what the hell I'm doing. "Just say what you think," she always says. That's fine for her, she obviously *knows* what she thinks. I've been reading scripts for her for several years now and the more I do it the less of a clue I have. It was supposed to be temporary, just until Godzone really took off. It's that sort of job. A foot-in-the-door job, for people who want to be film execs or producers or script doctors or film execs or screenwriters or film execs or directors. And did I mention film execs? But for me, it's become something else. Not so much a foot-in-the-door as a fingernail-on-the-cliff. The bottom rung of the slippery pole.

I have to say I do worry about the quality of my assessments. I started to worry when I noticed that the ones I trashed were always the ones that ended up winning prizes at film festivals around the world, whereas the ones I praised to the skies were never heard of again. I tried adjusting my style. I tried trashing the ones I liked and praising the ones I hated—it didn't seem to make any difference at all to my hit rate. Recently one of my assessments came back from LA. The big boss had scrawled something in the margin: "What's this guy on?" I thought they were going to tell Tamintha to fire me but she said not to worry. The guy's just an arsehole. He's been sleeping with New York and now he's trying to destabilize London. She said the scripts she was giving me they pretty much knew about, anyway. They were all bottom-of-the-barrel stuff and it was mainly just a question of creating a paper trail.

But I do suspect my criteria are all out of whack. I can't see the films as films. I keep judging them. I keep forgetting they're not real and it doesn't matter. I want to punish them for having bad things in them, for having villains and violence and infidelity and short-changers and unhappiness and unfairness and undernourishment. I want to expunge evil from the face of filmmaking. I want to impose strict rules of cinematic hygiene, high standards of moral behavior and messages of goodness and truth. Let's face it, I'm a Stalinist.

It's ridiculous. I'm in the wrong line of work. I suspect that Tamintha only gave me the job as a favor to Sophie. She's Sophie's friend, really. We met her because Biscrobus put money into *Bonza, Mate.* Sophie and Tamintha really hit it off—Kiwi girls together, etc. Hanging out in The Sanctuary, stuff like that. Apparently it's really amazing in there. Steam rooms and steam baths and naked

Amazons wandering around getting massages and sitting on swings over the pool. Sophie was telling me all about it.

If it isn't because of Sophie then Tamintha probably only keeps me on because she's sorry for me. Don't believe what they say about film execs, it's just not true, they're people too. Tamintha has a very soft spot. Once she made friends with this mad panhandling junkie who used to hang out on Old Compton Street. She started inviting him around to use the office shower and have a croissant and coffee with the girls. The staff put around a petition and she got really mad at them, called them uptight Pommie wankers and fascists. Then Tracy noticed the goldfish were going missing. When challenged he said fish oil is good for the skin. But she's like that, Tamintha. Tenderhearted, natural, unconstrained by convention. A collector of strays. So naturally enough when I moved out of the flat, Tamintha put me up for a couple of weeks while I "looked for somewhere else."

Probably that was a favor to Sophie too, although I actually suspect sometimes that she is secretly hot for me. It's not so unreasonable. It's hard for women at her level to get a guy. Apparently the guys are intimidated by the status. I sure as hell am. But then for me that's just the beginning. I'm intimidated by women at *any* level. I have no desire ever to be inside a woman again—and that includes the Statue of Liberty. Sure, I find women attractive, but I find trees attractive too. Doesn't mean I want to go rubbing myself all over one.

Even back in the old days, before my mojo headed West, I was always very selective. It was only ever actresses who did it for me. I don't know what it was exactly but that's just the way it's always been. Maybe it was the mercurial, elusive, ineffable quality of their personalities, the mystery within a mystery, the riddle within the riddle. Maybe it was the leotards.

Tamintha has finished skimming. She slings the assessments in a pile. "Want some more?"

"Sure."

"Anything in particular?"

"Got any romantic comedies?" Romantic comedies are really all I'm good for. God I love a good romantic comedy. Not that I've actually found one yet. Even the bad ones, I weep buckets. Tamintha reaches across to a huge stack of scripts piled four feet high beside the desk, pulls off the top ten and fans them. "There you go: couple in there, I think."

"Ta." I stash them in my satchel.

Tamintha looks at me, slightly askew. "You're not looking for a job are you?"

"At Biscrobus?"

"I mean I know you probably won't be interested, you've got your own business and everything, but we've got a full-time vacancy coming up, so I just thought I'd mention it." She's very tactful, Tamintha. She knows perfectly well what the score is with God-zone.

"What, er, sort of vacancy?"

"Assistant Vice Director of Acquisitions. Basically full-time on script-reading, and there'd be some liaison work too. We might even send you to Cannes next year. Also you'd open the mail." She pulls out a great stack of papers. I realize with a lurch that it's all my past assessments. It makes a hefty pile. "I've been looking over your stuff. It's all fine," she says, leafing through.

"But?"

She holds up an assessment and reads from the back page. " 'Reader's recommendation—recommended to be shot.' " She picks out another. " 'Recommended to be hung, drawn and quartered' . . ." Another. " 'Don't even think about thinking about this one.' " One more. " 'The existence of this script is proof of the existence of unintelligent life from other planets.' " Tamintha puts the scripts down. She looks over her glasses. "You know, we do have to show these to people sometimes."

"You do?"

"Think you could cut the stylistic flourishes?"

"Well . . ."

"There's no immediate hurry. Have a think." Tamintha takes her glasses right off. She looks more askew than ever. "Have you . . . spoken to Sophie lately?"

"No, now that you mention, not lately."

Tamintha hesitates. She opens her mouth to speak, but she is interrupted.

BEEP BEEP BEEP. I rest my arm casually on the chair and smile. POCKETA POCKETA POCKETA.

"What the hell is that?"

"I'm having my blood pressure monitored."

"What for?"

"Oh, just a routine test."

"Routine?"

"I'm borderline hypertensive."

"God, Frederick, is that serious?"

"Lord, no. It's just a routine test."

"You must be stressed."

"Yeah, that's probably it. Stress."

Her eyes flicker to the pimple on my lip. "Are you looking after yourself?"

"Absolutely."

She purses her lips. "I spoke to Sophie this morning as a matter of fact."

"Oh, yes? Is she back in town?"

"No, she's still in the States. With Matt." She glances at me.

"How is she?"

"Oh, I think she's good."

"I saw her in *Empire*."

"Oh, that, yeah. Nice photo."

"Yeah, very nice."

"So what did Sophie have to say for herself?"

"She's planning to ring you, actually."

Clearly there's something going on. Tamintha's eyes stray to the Minesweeper game. She taps a key. Clearly she's experiencing some sort of conflict of loyalties.

BEEP BEEP.

Luckily for her, subtlety and tact are two of my strongest suits. I stand. "Well, I guess I better get going. Say hi to Sophie if you talk to her again."

"How do you do it?"

"Do what?"

"You're just so *nice* about it all."

I shrug and smile. "You've got to let these things go in the end. Life's too short." I turn to go but she stops me again, in the doorway. "Oh, Frederick, I almost forgot. Happy birthday!" She gets up, comes right across and kisses me. "What are you doing tonight? Come round for a drink later on, if you like."

"I will. Thanks."

"I'll be up till late. I have to call LA."

Outside there's a light drizzle falling. I make my way through Soho, moving fast, my Bundeswehr boots striking hard, punishing the English pavement, the scripts swinging heavy in the bag on the end of my arm. I hit Oxford Street, turn left. The foot traffic thickens and I'm reduced to a crawl. I'm heading for Selfridges. Matt Chalmers. I want to kill Matt Chalmers. I want to kill him, I want to kill him dead. I want to throttle him, slowly. I want to erase him from the face of the earth. I want to destroy him, and all his ilk. His kith, his kin. His seed. The seed of his seed. The seed of the seed of his seed. I want . . . I want a hot salt beef sandwich. I want it now.

I look at my watch. Hell, damn and blast. I'm supposed to be at the doctor's.

| | | |
|---|---|---|
| 0700 | 155/102 | *On tube.* |
| 0800 | 150/103 | *Breakfast. Feel like shit.* |
| 0900 | 155/103 | *On telephone to mother.* |
| 0930 | 148/105 | *In flat, sitting. Reading scripts.* |
| 1000 | 160/98 | *In flat, sitting. Reading scripts.* |
| 1030 | 155/100 | *In flat. Sitting. Cup of tea. Reading scripts.* |
| 1100 | 166/101 | *Lying down. Reading scripts.* |
| 1130 | 168/103 | *Sitting. Reading scripts. Sitting up. Cup of tea.* |
| 1200 | 170/106 | *Tube. Sitting.* |
| 1230 | 150/106 | *Walking. Arguing on phone.* |
| 1300 | 144/97 | *Sitting in office. Working.* |
| 1330 | 150/100 | *Walking. Soho.* |
| 1400 | 167/108 | *Sitting. Ex-wife is going out with Matt Chalmers.* |
| 1430 | 150/99 | *Walking.* |
| 1500 | 155/103 | *Walking.* |
| 1530 | 160/104 | *Walking.* |
| 1600 | 155/103 | *Walking.* |

| | | |
|------|---------|-----------------------------------------|
| 1630 | 160/104 | *Walking.* |
| 1700 | 155/106 | *Home lying on bed. Staring at ceiling.* |
| 1730 | 158/102 | *Home lying on bed. Arguing on phone.* |
| 1800 | 159/106 | *Walking.* |
| 1830 | 162/107 | *Dinner. Spaghetti.* |
| 1900 | 160/104 | *Walking.* |
| 1930 | 154/90  | *Home, lying on bed. Reading script.* |
| 2230 | 170/98  | *Walking.* |
| 2330 | 177/100 | *Walking.* |
| 0000 | 175/107 | *Walking.* |
| 0100 | 180/108 | *Walking.* |
| 0200 | 150/99  | *Walking.* |
| 0230 | 187/109 | *Asleep.* |
| 0300 | 150/90  | *Asleep.* |
| 0330 | 150/95  | *Reading. (Dostoyevsky.)* |
| 0400 | 140/88  | *Asleep.* |
| 0730 | 160/77  | *Eating breakfast. Feel like shit.* |
| 0800 | 166/105 | *Tube.* |
| 0830 | 168/106 | *Waiting room.* |

Dr. McVeigh looks up from her desk. "And this is a normal twenty-four-hour period?"

"In essence, yes."

"You often go for a three-and-a-half-hour walk between ten thirty and two a.m.?"

"I find it clears my mind."

"And you sleep about four hours a night?"

"Off and on."

"And while you're awake you read Dostoyevsky?"

"Could be Kafka."

"No wonder you have trouble sleeping." Dr. McVeigh looks back down at her notes. She has a faint Scottish accent. Her hands, like her face, are narrow and lightly freckled. She clasps them loosely on the desktop. She is younger than me, probably in her mid-thirties. Under her white coat, she is wearing a simple cotton dress. Her wedding ring is a plain gold band. This is my third visit to the St. Mary's Hypertension Clinic, and Dr. McVeigh has not smiled once. Not when I smile at her, not when I make self-deprecating comments, not even when I tripped over the rubbish bin. Not so much as a sympathy smile. I'm not unreasonable. An insincere smile is fine. Just so long as it's a smile. Everyone knows you smile. You come in, you greet the person, you smile. It's just so basic. I want to jump and sing. I want to run around the office. I want to scream. *Smile, bitch, smile!!* It's true what they say about Western medicine. You'd think that at some point in her ten years or more of intensive medical training someone would have mentioned sometime that, oh, by the way, it's a good idea to smile at your patients from time to time. Wouldn't you think that?

"How many units of alcohol do you consume a week?"

"Ten. I counted them last week."

"And that's normal consumption?"

"Yes." This is a little white lie. I got to ten units by Tuesday. But then I stopped counting, so I did count ten units.

Dr. McVeigh nods. "And you don't smoke, do you?"

"Never."

"For a hypertensive patient who smokes, the risk of heart attack, stroke or thrombosis rises dramatically." She looks up, severely.

"Absolutely. I never smoke."

"I'd strongly advise you not to start." She looks down again at the chart lying on the desk in front of her. Suddenly I'm very, very scared. My heart is hammering. Sweat in my hairline. She knows I'm lying. I *am* lying. I smoke other people's all the time. I just never buy them. Dr. McVeigh unclasps her hands and lays them flat on the table. "The results of the twenty-four-hour test show that your daytime diastolic pressures are consistently high."

I'm going to die.

"Normally, blood pressure drops during periods of sleep. Some people, even though they have abnormally high diastolic levels during the day, drop to more normal readings at night. In the long term, this reduces the cumulative stress on the vascular system to acceptable levels."

I'm going to live.

"Unfortunately, in your case the diastolic pressures remain abnormally high during sleep periods as well . . . such as they are."

I'm going to die.

Dr. McVeigh looks up. Her eyes are windows on a midwinter sky. "My diagnosis is therefore moderate to mild hypertension. By this I mean that, taking into account the various risk factors such as weight, lifestyle, current age . . ." She opens a file, finds the chart she's looking for and runs a finger down a column of figures. Her finger pauses. She has found the figure. She looks up. ". . . your risk of death by stroke or heart attack before the age of fifty-five is currently running at six percent." She closes the file. "Which compares to a population average of less than one."

The chair I'm sitting on is tilting slowly backward. She catches the expression on my face. "That doesn't mean that you're going to drop dead the minute you walk out of here."

"How long have I got?"

"All we can say is that you belong to a statistical group with elevated risk. We're saying nothing about you as an individual. Even in the absence of treatment, you could quite conceivably live a long and healthy life. But, *statistically*, you are less likely to do so than the average person."

"I see."

"Some people tolerate high blood pressure perfectly well. However, there are associated risk indicators we can look for. Vascular damage can show up early in the retinas or the feet, for example. Another thing we look for is thickening of the heart wall. This indicates the heart is having to work harder than it should. In your case an echocardiogram you took last month has shown a definite thickening of the heart wall. Although, looking on the positive side, you have the retinas of a young man."

"Couldn't I just happen to have a thick heart?"

"Once again, it's all statistical."

"But . . ."

She reaches into a drawer and lays a small white-and-pink cardboard box on the desk. "I'd like to put you on a course of beta-blockers. Beta-blockers work by slowing your heart, and thereby reducing the force with which it pumps the blood around your body. This is a relatively low dose, of five milligrams. We'll start there and see what effect that has."

"How long will I have to take them?"

"As we age, we tend to get more hypertensive, not less. It's a natural process."

"You mean I'll be taking these for the rest of my life?"

"Most likely."

"What about side effects?"

Dr. McVeigh talks more rapidly. "Some people experience dizziness, tiredness or loss of libido, however in the majority of cases . . ."

"Loss of what?"

She pauses. "Libido."

"Oh, man. Can't I just relax more? I mean it's all just stress, isn't it?"

She shakes her head. "'Stress' is a much misunderstood term."

"What about bleeding? Couldn't you just bleed me from time to time?"

She shakes her head. "I'm afraid that wouldn't work."

"But there must be something I can do. Maybe if I stop drinking entirely."

She glances at the clock. "Mr. Case, I think the solution for you is medication, but there's no great hurry. Take the pills with you. We'll give it a month. If you decide to start the medication, fine. Or if you want to give yourself another shot at bringing your pressure down by cutting dietary salt, alcohol, and losing more weight, you can do so. Make an appointment to come back and see me in a month's time and we'll talk it over."

Dr. McVeigh lays both hands on the desk. She smiles.

It's getting raw and dark outside St. Mary's, traffic loud in the damp air. A light drizzle falling. A young black woman in a track-suit walks by, singing quietly to herself. She doesn't see me. I wonder if perhaps I'm a ghost. I feel weak and cold. I pull my Swedish Army greatcoat closer. I want to believe that somehow, some-where, someone has made a mistake. But there is no mistake. It's all over. I'm finished. I stagger in what I think is the general direc-tion of Paddington Station. I'm going to have to get serious about this. I'm actually going to have to stop smoking and drinking. Out-rageous. A great sense of loss wells up inside me. No, more than that. Fear. No, more even than that. Existential terror. Cigarettes, alcohol and stylistic flourishes—without them, what else remains?

## Chapter 3

Hi, Frederick, how the wether in London?

Light drizzle, low cloud base. How's Helsinki?

I've been playing a lot of Internet chess lately. E-Heaven on the Bayswater Road has become a second home. Friendly faces, reasonable coffee, almost comfortable chairs. I make my moves — a Scotch game, a Sicilian and something indescribable — and check my e-mail. I've already eaten at the nearest Stockpot and soon it'll be time to think about getting on to Tamintha's. There's a message from my mother, but it turns out to be a photograph of a Palestinian sniper victim. My mum has been doing a lot of this lately. She's on a number of mailing lists. Aged sixty-eight, she's still trying to change the world. There are also a few birthday messages from friends wanting to know where the hell I've got to. If I ever find out, they'll be the first to know. There's one from Russell and Ella, which is very sweet. Lots of different fonts, which shows they really do care.

I've done the e-mail. I've done the chess. This is the time to close it down. But I don't. Instead, I run a search on Sophie. I shouldn't. It's a kind of a bad habit. Humiliating. There's the usual swag of reviews, filmographies and the like, all of which I've seen before. But since *Shag City* came out I notice a different element is creeping in.

Like:

**Sophie Carlisle in the Nude!**
**We are the only site to carry this**
**shocking explicit material!**

Or:

*Sophie Carlisle: Nasty Pics!*

I'm here to tell you that Sophie in the nude is neither shocking nor nasty. What are these people on? And then if you really want a laugh, there's always Sophie's fan site. It's run by a guy called Brad somewhere in Ohio. It's not official. Appalling design. Illegible mauve font on a violent green background with expanding star clusters and a stupid little revolving smiley. Music too. "Greensleeves." Sophie doesn't even wear green. It makes her look bilious. He wrote to her once. I read the letter. The guy is completely mad, and he can't spell "passionately." In the letter he claims that when she smiles at the camera in the last scene of *Transcendental Punishment,* he felt that it was "specially for him."

She gets mail all the time. Mainly it's handwritten scrawls from adolescents, which is sort of forgivable but the ingrown adults, they're scary. We used to read them out for fun but they just kept coming and coming and it very quickly got depressing. For a while she wrote replies (*For God's sake, get a life/Your suggestions are sick and disgusting and you need help/Never write to me again,* etc.) but we quickly figured out that that was a bad idea. It doesn't matter what you say, it only encourages them. Now she never replies. She just bins them.

Hi and Welcome to the Official Number One Sophie Carlisle Web Site, the web site for everyone who thinks Sophie Carlisle is the most amazing chick on the entire planet!!!!!

Biog
Pics
Filmography
Links

Got any Sophie Carlisle updates or anecdotes? Don't keep it to yourself, guys!!! E-mail me!!! Now!!

I haven't visited the site for months. The last time was a few weeks after the big break. I was in a bad way. I logged on and I e-mailed the guy.

TO:   brad@bradbradbrad.com:
RE:   Marital Status.
      She's split up with her husband.

He e-mailed me back: *How do you know?*
*Because I'm the husband.*
Guess what the reply was? *Dream on, buddy.*
You know you're in trouble when mad, sad, fan site operators think you're a crank. Still Brad missed a golden opportunity there because I've got the dirt all right. I've got it all, the inside story. I could tell him stuff that would make his creepy little toes curl. Yes, indeedy. I click on the *Biog* page. It hasn't been updated.

> Born in 1972 in the peace and quiet of Auckland, New
> Zealand (that's in Australia, for you folks who don't know
> your geography), Sophie has come a long way since then.
> Her first ever professional stage appearance was at age four
> in a Christmas pantomime. She played one of Santa's elves.
> Lucky Santa!!!!!!!

It's a good thing for Brad that exclamation marks aren't carcino-
genic. It goes on like that for pages. And pages!!!!!!! As for the thing
about New Zealand being part of Australia, all I can say is, if I ever
meet you, Brad, I will do my very best to make *you* part of Australia.
I click on *Recent News*.

> Hey Guys! The best of all possible news! Sophie is single
> again! As you are no doubt aware, until recently she was
> living in London with her kill-joy husband (boo . . . hoo . . .
> hey, no fair, come on guy, share and share alike!!!) . . . but
> no longer! She's dumped the guy!!! Yeah!!!!! Way to go,
> Sophie!!!!! Queue from the right fellas!!!!!!!

Arsehole. I wonder where he gets his information from.

> Sophie now with new boyfriend Matt Chalmers.
> (Awwww!!!!! Come on Matt, share and share alike!!!!!)

Up to date, I see. Although in fact if you really want to know, Brad,
she was with Matt Chalmers *before* she left me.
The next one, I read, and reread. And read again.

> Sophie is pregnant!!! (Lucky baby!!!!! Come on, hey no fair,
> queue from the right . . . ) That's right, guys, Matt Chalmers
> ain't shooting no blanks!!!!! Hey, way to go Matt, name it
> after me . . . !!!!!

You know you're feeling good about yourself, if, when you sit on the tube, the people around you look good. You sit there and everyone glows, their faces alive with hope and simple dignity. The courage of a daily life lived, hope for the future, love of family, the belief that somehow in some way it all adds up to something and is worth it. It shows.

Other times it isn't like that. This is one of those other times. Everyone looks like I feel: yellowish-greenish, blank-eyed, spotty, lank-haired. Misproportioned, broken people, all of us, sinners and castoffs. It shows.

This is the last train on the Central Line. I'm sitting with a romantic comedy on my knee but I can't concentrate. There's a guy sitting across from me trapped in semi-sleep, his head drooping with the rocking of the train, lower and lower, until he begins to fall and pulls himself up short. But he never quite wakes up, and so he never really sleeps. Next to him is a sick-looking girl. Farther down the carriage is an Eastern European refugee begging for change, her baby in her arms. They're very well organized. You can see them gathering in an alley off Oxford Street to arrange the shifts. In my pocket are the pills, rattling quietly with every step. I'm finished. An unsmiling doctor has taken away my youth. I am a dried-up sexless drone, a clapped-out pump feebly fluttering in my passionless chest. They're right, all of them. I should go home. I've had it. I'm finished.

I've always been able to rise above it. Whatever it is. I've always been known for my unflappability, my sangfroid, my perspective on things. I've always seen life as the greatest adventure of all. That was the spirit I always tried to communicate to Sophie too. But I've lost it now. I've lost the spirit. I've lost the drive. I've lost the perspective. I just feel old and tired and useless and even afraid. I've always had the courage to look life right down the barrel, with a little smile. Not anymore. I'm shaking in my shoes. This is beyond a joke. This is serious stuff.

My Bundeswehr boots are truly in blitzkrieg mode now. Coming out of the Oxford Street tube I've hit my stride and I'm moving on through. It's late. Shops all shut and the place has shut down. No cars, no one on the footpaths. London like this reminds me of downtown Auckland any weeknight.

**EXT. LONDON STREETS—NIGHT.**

HIS BUNDESWEHR BOOTS POUND THE LONDON PAVEMENT. HE'S HIT HIS STRIDE NOW AND HE MOVES RAPIDLY ALONG EMPTY DARKENED STREETS. A NAKED MANNEQUIN STANDS POSED IN A SHOPWINDOW. THE FOOTPATH GLIS-TENS IN THE LIGHT DRIZZLE THAT FALLS, DROPLETS GHOSTING AROUND THE STREET LAMPS. HE PAUSES TO HITCH UP HIS UNDERPANTS.

I spend so much time in other people's half-baked screen fantasies the boundaries tend to dissolve. Sometimes I feel like I'm not living my life at all, I'm in the straight-to-cable movie of it. And indeed, if life does imitate art, it imitates the bad scripts, the ones that don't add up, that make no sense, bristling with dei ex machinis, unmotivated action and arbitrary events. Help, help, oh, help. Am trapped in endless Wednesday-afternoon screening of cliché, which happens to be my life with only half a bag of peanuts and no interval in sight. The story so far: clapped-out stressed-out fucked-over midlife disaster, lost and alone, blunders into furniture with fly undone. We all larfed.

**FLASHBACK:**

SOPHIE LAUGHING, HER HEAD FLUNG BACK, HER THROAT EXPOSED. FREDERICK TAKES HER IN HIS ARMS.

<u>Frederick</u>

Darling, let's have a baby.

SOPHIE STOPS LAUGHING. HER FACE GOES COLD.

Actually it wasn't quite like that but that captures the essence.

Yes, indeed, we've just had a major plot development, a real biggie this one. Ex-wife of our hero has become pregnant to Hollywood überstud. A plot development that will probably fuel the action for goodness knows how long, flinging our hapless hero into yet another round of nerveless spastic behavior masquerading as a plan of action. But—but, but, but, here's the wisdom of the script reader: we've just had a major plot development, but will it actually *lead* anywhere? In art, yes. But for Life itself, as for the fourth-rate bottom-of-the-barrel script, the answer is the same— we just can't say yet. And there's another thing we don't know. This is the one that sends chills down my back. Something that, in art, would be well established by now: what's the genre? I'm hoping for romantic comedy, but there are other, darker, possibilities after all.

HE SWINGS LEFT INTO UPPER REGENT STREET, KEEPING A
WEATHER EYE OUT FOR VIOLENT CRIMINALS. STOPS AT A
QUAINT (GEORGIAN?) BLOCK OF FLATS AND PUSHES THE
BUTTON FOR NUMBER TWO. HE CHECKS HIS WATCH. HE SHUF-
FLES NERVOUSLY. THE INTERCOM CRACKLES INTO LIFE.

<u>Frederick</u>

Hi, it's me, Frederick.

THE DOOR BUZZES IN PLACE OF REPLY. HE SKIPS UP
THE FOUR MARBLE STEPS AND SHE'S WAITING IN THE

DOORWAY IN JEANS AND T-SHIRT, HALF-LEANING ON
THE WALL.

"Hey, come on in." She turns and heads for the kitchen. I follow,
closing the door behind me. It's a great flat. Big and well
appointed. Tamintha explained once how it really belongs to a
friend, but he spends half the year in Hong Kong. It's complicated. I forget exactly. She has shares in his business. They're married. He's gay. Immigration. Accommodation. Something like
that. Anyway, it's a nice flat. In the kitchen, Tamintha waves a
slice of bread triumphantly. "Vogel's!"

"Wow, where'd you get that?"

"Sainsbury's. Honey?"

"Ta."

She rolls a joint while the toast is toasting. While she rolls, I
watch her eyebrows. You could imagine them propping up a cathe-
dral somewhere. She has her good features. She flicks her hair off
her forehead. The toast pops and Tamintha spreads honey, lazily,
in thick golden circles. Nice executive wrist action.

After Sophie left, Tamintha put me up for a couple of weeks. I
didn't want to stay in the flat. I didn't want to be alone. I stayed in
the guest room just down the hall. We'd smoke a joint, eat some
toast, talk. I didn't leave this place for days on end. I'd read scripts,
read Empire, read Cinema Papers or Vanity Fair or FHM or Vogue
or Harper's, or Dostoyevsky. I'd go for long walks in my Bundeswehr boots. Then I found Mrs. Traversham and gradually I
began to pick up the threads of my old life. I'd go to movies. I'd
ring Channel Four. Daydream. Have meetings with other no-
hopers in cafes and pubs and bars, discussing projects no one had
any real interest in, least of all me. I'd ring Channel Four again.
I'd think about getting a real job, like maybe taxi driving. Those
black-cab guys are amazing. Imagine it: a whole city in your
head. I'd get drunk. I'd run out of money. I'd ring my folks. I'd ask

them for more money. They'd send more money. I'd buy more clothes.

That's my life. Horrible but true. A lot of people think it's easy having rich parents. Let me tell you, it isn't. It can seriously stunt your growth. Not that I'm complaining, you understand. I mean, I know I can't complain. In fact that's the hardest thing of all. You can't complain. What sort of a life is it when you can't even complain? I *want* to complain. But who's going to give me the time of day? Who's going to listen to a forty-two-year-old rich kid complaining, in a world of child poverty and war and drugs and disease? No one. Even *I'm* not going to listen. Which, speaking cinematically, is the kiss of death. Here I am, the unwilling hero of the film of my life-of-undetermined-genre, and I'm not even a sympathetic character.

I have to give it up. This is the thing. If I were poor and struggling and somehow getting by, at least I'd get some sympathy. And God knows, we all need sympathy. Yes, I don't know where or how exactly but somehow I know I'm looking at a new life. Today is the first day. Etc. No more handouts. From now on I take control.

*Sophie is pregnant. Sophie has a child.*

We take our toast and tea through to the lounge. I sit on the pastel-blue sofa, which is comfortable but almost impossible to get out of. It's very low and very soft and my view is blocked by my own knees. My Bundeswehr boots feel like overkill now, but I don't want to take them off. Tamintha puts on a CD. I think it's Miles Davis. Uh-uh. The honey and toast is on the coffee table. I take a bite.

"Careful, it's heads." She hands me the joint, curls up at the end of the sofa, feet tucked under, facing me.

"Careful? At my age?" I cough violently.

"There, there, old man, have a sip of tea."

I settle back and look at the ceiling. I know this ceiling well. During those three weeks I spent a lot of time staring at it. There's a crack along the center line and to one side a very faint stain that looks like Australia. Why do stains always look like Australia and never like New Zealand? It's so typical of Australia to hog the limelight like that. I hate Australia and all things Australian. It's so unfair. It's just like Canada and the US. I love Canadians. I also love the Irish and the Scottish and all other peoples of small countries who are condescended to and made the butts of jokes by large neighboring arrogant countries that sometimes even invade and occupy them and cause terrible social dislocation that they then have the temerity to turn around and poke fun at them for. (Sometime in the next five hundred years I just *know* that Australia's going to have a crack at us. The kangaroo-skin jackboot of Canberra will descend.) I'm also reasonably fond of the Scandinavians although some of them are a abit right wing. I also, incidentally, have enormous postcolonial guilt, but that's another story.

Tamintha holds out her hand for the joint and I pass it. She inhales, holds it, passes it back and watches me closely. "Have you had any thoughts about the job?"

"Actually, no. But I have a question for you."

"Shoot."

"Is Sophie pregnant?" I inhale, pass and hold.

Tamintha sighs. "So she rang you at last?"

"No, she didn't ring me."

"Damn. She's such a naughty, naughty girl. I *told* her to ring you. I told her you'd find out. I wanted to tell you, really I did, but she swore me to secrecy, and I thought it would be best if you found out from her, direct. She said she wanted to call you herself. She wasn't sure how to break the news."

"It's no big deal of course. I was just curious." My boots now feel way too big. They take up half the room. I stand up. With difficulty.

"Where are you going?"

"I'm just going to the kitchen." I start to move. My Bundeswehr boots are Bundeswehr boats and the corridor seems longer than I remember it. But I get there. I roll up my sleeves while the water runs. I stand facing the sink. It's a very nice kitchen, this. The brass pots on the wall glow in my peripheral vision. The sink seems to be taking a very long time to fill. I realize I haven't put in the plug. I put in the plug. She was right about this dope, it's very strong. The thing is, I've had a little shock and I need time to think. I need to formulate a concrete policy and make a plan of action. One thing we know now, for sure. Sophie is definitely pregnant. There's now no room for doubt. Sophie is with child.

Tamintha pokes her head around the door. Her eyes widen in horror. "No! Frederick, please, no, stop!"

I ignore her. They say no, but deep down they always mean yes.

Tamintha folds her arms. "Well, I'm not helping, that's for sure."

"Nobody asked you to." I turn off the tap. A lone soap bubble rises, bobbling gently, then bursts. I pick up a plate.

"So, how *did* you find out? If Sophie didn't ring you?"

"From Brad."

"Who's he?"

"A mutual friend."

"I don't think I've met him."

"Very few have. Er, did I just wash this?"

"Oh, leave 'em, for Chrissake." Tamintha reaches over and takes the plate from my hand, puts it on the bench. "Frederick," she says.

"Tamintha," I say.

Sophie is pregnant. I lean toward Tamintha. Her face is getting bigger. Her eyes are dark, bottomless pools. Sad pools. I'm sad. She's sad. We're all sad. Our lips collide slowly, enormous, dry and rubbery, two bouncy castles. A click of tooth on tooth. Two sad faces, striving for purchase. Well, that settles it. I am now kissing Tamintha. I don't know why I'm doing this. This is insane. Sophie is pregnant.

The bedroom is blue. There's a blue lampshade, and blue covers on the bed. Tamintha leads me to the bed. I can't do this. She is holding my hand. I feel dizzy. I feel hot and cold and greasy all over. Tamintha has led me to the bed. I sink, slowly, slowly, to the blue covers. Her eyes are two pools of sadness. Huge globes, empty and dark and sad. I see nothing.

"Frederick? Are you okay?"

"Tell you what, I'm just going to use the bathroom."

The corridor is now doing distinctly unpleasant things. It just can't settle on a length and stick to it. Just when you think it's over, it adds extra feet, and then just when you think you've got yards to go, you're standing in the bathroom.

I lock the door. Bathrooms are safe places. Hygienic surfaces, locks on the doors, and a window overlooking the truth. I place my feet thus and thus, taking position. I'm going to do it. I'm going to do it again. That really dumb thing. I look in the mirror.

I want to go home. I feel about six inches tall and I want to go home. All the way home. Sophie said that once. "I want to go home." That was during her year in the wilderness. The year she didn't get any work. Her annus horribilis. We all have them, even the common folk. That year, Sophie depended on me utterly. I was her rock. I was her foundation. Without me she'd never have made it. I'd come home and there she'd be on the couch in T-shirt and socks, watching daytime TV. Day after day, daytime TV. What a terrible thing is daytime TV. One thing I have never done in my life and will never do is watch daytime TV. But that's how low she sank in that year. It was the year she hit rock bottom. I'm not really naturally a bottom-dwelling type, I tend to float, but Sophie has a lot of lead in her pencil. She's a sinker. When she goes down, she goes down. I remember the night that she bottomed out. I remember it very clearly. I came home, it was about ten o'clock. I found Sophie on the couch. She had a bottle of gin in her lap. Tears, T-shirt, socks. The TV was on.

"Oh man," I said. "You watched it, didn't you?"

She didn't say anything. She didn't have to.

"I told you not to watch it. Did she win?"

She nodded.

"Oh, shit. I *told* you not to watch." I switched the TV off. She'd been watching the Academy Awards. That year a young, naïve, slightly overweight Australian actress trying to make it in Hollywood had been nominated for her performance as a young, naïve, slightly overweight Australian actress trying to make it in Hollywood and she'd just been awarded best female. (She subsequently went on to a meteoric career across the Atlantic.) It was the part Sophie had turned down the year before. They offered it to her first, and she turned it down.

"I want to go home." I hardly recognized her voice. And I have to admit I was shocked. I'd never heard talk like that before. For nine months, nine long months of silence, no interviews, no jobs, no auditions, no nothing, she'd stuck it out. But that was the last straw.

The mistake most people make about pep talks is they think they have to vary them. They keep looking for fresh ways of motivating and encouraging. You don't need to do that. Find the formula and stick to it. But what you do need to work on is delivery. The delivery is all. Passion, commitment and sincerity. That's what counts.

"Sam Neill," I said. "Jane Campion. Lucy Lawless. Russell Crowe. Peter Jackson. Kerry Fox. Temuera Morrison. Cliff Curtis. Lee Tamahori. Lots of other people I can't think of right now but whom I would certainly mention if I could. What do all these wonderful people have in common?"

She sighs.

"Tell me. Look me in the eye, and tell me."

Sophie rolls her eyes. "They're successful New Zealanders in film."

"Do you think these people ever had moments of doubt or uncertainty in their lives?"

"Probably."

"Do you?"

"Yes."

"And in those moments of despair, do you think they gave up? Do you think that's how they got where they got? Because they gave up?"

She hangs her head. "No."

"I'm sorry, I didn't hear that."

"No."

"Now say it like you mean it."

"No. No, they didn't."

"What do you think people said the first time A. J. Hackett ever suggested it might be a good idea to jump off a bridge with a piece of elastic tied to your legs? What do you think people said when Sir Edmund Hillary said he was going to climb Everest?"

"There are some New Zealanders who fail, you know."

"Name one. Name just one."

"I can't, they're nameless. That's what failing is. Being nameless. They're just failed nameless faceless tiny little lost New Zealanders floating like scum on the surface of the planet. Like me. Nameless New Zealanders like me. I'm going to end up a tired old nameless bitter New Zealander with no money and no career."

"Well, okay." (Now, here comes the crunch. Pay close attention. You have to be realistic. You have to include an admission of the possibility of failure.) "What would you rather be? Fifty years from now? A tired old nameless bitter New Zealander with no career who never tried, never gave it her best shot, or a tired old nameless bitter New Zealander with no career who gave it her best shot? Who can, at least, stand in front of the mirror, look herself in the eye, and say, 'Sophie, you gave it your best shot'? Well? Which would you rather be?"

She sniffs. I hand her a box of tissues. She blows her nose. "I had a call from Simon today."

"Yeah?"

"I've got an audition."

"But that's great! Why the long face?"

She shook her head. "No, it's not great. It's an *audition*. Up until now it's always been *meetings*. A meeting with the director to discuss the role. Now it's *auditions*. I've been downgraded." She chucks a script, which has been lying on the coffee table, across the room and bursts into tears. "And besides, I just can't do it. I can't, I can't, I can't. I can't do it anymore, I've lost all my drive and confidence and I can't face an audition and I want to go home."

The script was *Flagrant Consequence*. I read it. Then I sat up with her until three in the morning. I told her that it was a good script, a brilliant part, and it suited her perfectly. And indeed, it was quite a good script, the part was at least average, and it didn't suit her too badly at all. I told her she could get this part. I told her this could be the moment she remembered for the rest of her life as the moment it all turned around. She did the audition. She got the part. The rest is history. Sophie has joined the pantheon. It actually happened, just the way I said it would. I saw it all, I was there. *I* shaped the course of events, even. If Sophie was Hillary, then I'd be Tenzing. Only in this case, Hillary arrives at the summit, turns around and gives his faithful Sherpa a good hard shove right off the North Face. I served my purpose. My work is done.

I look myself in the mirror. The window of truth. "Well, Frederick," I say, "what's it going to be?"

"How did that go?" Tamintha is about two thirds asleep.

"Better than I expected, thanks." I sit on the edge of the bed. She puts a hand on my arm. "Tamintha, I'm not ready for this."

"So I gathered."

"I'm sorry. I feel really bad."

"No, God, *you* don't have to feel bad. *I* feel bad. I shouldn't have pressured you."

"Don't *you* feel bad."

"But I do. I do feel very, very bad."

"But you're good. Don't feel bad. I'm bad."

"You're not bad, Frederick. You're not bad." She squeezes my arm. "You're good."

"Maybe another time then."

"Sure, another time. Listen, I'm sorry about the news. I know it must have rocked you."

"What the hell. It could have been worse. At least she waited a little while."

There's something close to panic in the look on Tamintha's face, which pulls me up.

"How long has she been pregnant? Tamintha? How long?"

"I don't know exactly how long."

"Roughly how long?"

"A while. Months. Maybe six."

## Chapter 4

PICCADILLY CIRCUS. Selfridges is closed, so I've come here to think. It's about ten-thirty and the place is packed, swarming, teeming with life. We have new information. We have a twist, a development. I have to see Sophie. I have to see her in person, and in private. Soon.

We had a day's shooting here, at Piccadilly Circus, for *Bonza, Mate*. We stood in front of the neon signs over there and kissed for the camera. That was how we met; kissing for the camera. In the original script of *Bonza, Mate* I had about twenty-five scenes. In all of the scenes my character exchanged two words of dialogue with Sophie's character, then they kissed passionately. That was pretty much it. The first time I met Sophie was in rehearsal the week before shooting began. It was a Tuesday. I was a little nervous. The first day of rehearsal is generally a pretty tense experience for everyone, but I was mainly worried about the kissing. In rehearsal, would we just do the lines, or would we actually do the actual kissing as well? If it was just the lines, it was going to be a short rehearsal. If it was the kissing as well, how far should we take it? Tongues or no tongues? It was a long time since I'd had to worry about *that* one.

The Tuesday morning I found the right warehouse and went

upstairs. There was Janine waiting for me. Janine was the director. She didn't look at all tense even though this was her second film, which is generally a very tense-making experience. Her first film was really good. It was all about this guy who hitchhikes around New Zealand in bare feet. I was expecting to sit down with Janine and talk about the backstory and character arc and deep motivation but Janine only had one question: "What do you think about glasses for this guy? I think he'd look cute in glasses."

The only other person in the room was a girl sitting cross-legged on the floor over in the corner. She had very long slightly stringy hair hanging down so you couldn't see her face. In front of her was a script, a big fat notebook, a big plate of jelly donuts, and next to the donuts a packet of Marlboros and an overflowing ashtray. She was going for it. She was shoveling down the donuts two at a time. Naturally I assumed she was the first assistant.

"All righty," said Janine, "come and meet Sophie."

We went over to the corner, to the face-stuffing girl. I couldn't believe it.

"Frederick this is Sophie. Sophie this is Frederick."

The girl looked up. Her mouth was full of jelly donut. She didn't particularly look like anything much. Sort of hippyish, maybe. No makeup and a wide mouth. Spiky black hair. Her voice was drawled out and her eyes were light brown and narrowed against the light from the window. She swallowed, licked her fingers and lit a cigarette. She looked straight at me. A very direct gaze.

"Hi," she said.

"Hi," I said.

She held up a donut. "Want one?"

"Maybe later," I said.

"All righty," said Janine. "Now you kids know each other, let's do it."

This was it. I was almost in trouble.

"Oh, just one other thing," said Janine. "For these scenes, don't worry about the dialogue, I'm cutting it all. Just go for it."

"All righty," said Sophie. She stood up. She was almost as tall as me. There was a small dollop of ersatz cream on her cheek. Now, I *was* in trouble. I was in trouble because I realized I liked her and my nerve was failing. Once your nerve fails you've had it. I needed to do something bold and active. I needed to take the initiative. I reached out and I brushed away the spot of cream. I said nothing. I looked Sophie right in the eye, and I kissed her. Quite hard. She tasted of sugar, Marlboros, and future happiness.

"Wow," said Sophie.

"Can you guys try that up against the wall?" said Janine.

"All righty," I said.

I don't remember a lot after that, mainly just Janine's voice going, "Try cupping her breasts," or, "Can you get that from the other side?" or, "How about more leg?"

It was a special sort of freedom. It wasn't me and it wasn't her. But at the same time it *was* us. Of course actors do that kind of stuff all the time. They get used to it. It's just a job. Finally, Janine had had enough. We rolled apart, gasping. Then Janine took me down to wardrobe and we tried on some glasses. We settled on a nice thick pair of horn-rims.

So that was my part.

The kisses had to take place all over the world, in the world's most romantic places. So we had Sophie kissing me in front of the Eiffel Tower, in front of Nelson's Column, the eighty-foot statue of Christ in Montevideo, St. Basil's in Moscow, the leaning tower of Pisa, etc. So that meant that although ninety percent of the film was actually shot in a warehouse in Auckland, lovingly re-creating the interiors of the backpackers, pensiones and B&Bs of low-rent Europe, they flew me and Sophie and Janine and the cameraman to Paris, Rome, Pisa, London, Amsterdam, Moscow, Berlin and Prague. At each city we would get off the plane, drive to the local romantic monument, kiss passionately, get a night's sleep, jump on the plane and do it all over again. It took us six weeks. Now if that's not a romantic way to meet someone, I don't know what is.

Naturally, Sophie and I spent a lot of time together and we got to know each other quite well. In Paris we went to the Pompidou Centre. In London we went to the National Gallery. Sometimes Sophie dragged me to a nightclub. As it happens I'm a gifted dancer, so that went off fine too. Anyway, we hit it off. We shared points of view. We walked and talked. And talked. And talked. Sometimes we held hands. We put pencils up our noses. We kidded around quite a lot, which was healthy and fun and doesn't cost anything.

For quite a while things stayed on that kidding-around level. For some reason I was reluctant to make the first move. Sophie was definitely a live wire and maybe I was even worried that she might be a little too much to handle, but in actual fact I discovered I could handle her no trouble at all. I had her right around my little finger. She adored me—and with good reason. I was extremely good-looking, fun, outgoing, even a little zany, yet at the same time steady and mature, a moderating influence. I didn't have moods. I didn't get hung up on things. I wasn't flighty or extreme. I did dishes. I washed. Plus, being older, I had perspective. I knew that this too shall pass. She looked up to me. In fact she believed every word I said, right down to the "I believe I was born to change the world for the better" part. Extraordinary, really. I mean, hell, Christ and goddamnit it all *I* believed it too.

Sophie, on the other hand, while being extremely focused and ambitious, not to mention talented, was young and not particularly stable. She was only twenty-four. She was likely to do foolish things, to drink way way too much, to get viciously depressed for twenty-four hours at a time, to succumb to sudden waves of fear and doubt, to throw rubbish bags off apartment buildings or even claim insurance on a stereo she hadn't lost. This stuff can be embarrassing. It can come back. I was exactly what she needed, and she knew it too.

When we got back to New Zealand things took a more serious turn. She took me to meet her folks, and they liked me. They loved me. They adored me. What wasn't to like? I was rich, handsome, comparatively young, yet respectful, considerate and helpful. Mature. On my very first visit I did the dishes, helped clear the leaves out of the guttering and deplored violence in the Middle East. I liked them too. The handshakes were firm and the coffee was hot. They were solid people, you could tell that right away. Her dad is from South Africa and her mum is from Upper Hutt. I think they met on safari.

I took her around to meet my folks too. They adored her. They absolutely adored her. She was young, sexy, almost famous, dry-witted, ambitious—and she could cook. She even called my dad Kev. He loved it. Loved it. She had them eating out of her hand in about thirty seconds. She adored them too. She thought my dad was a scream. She was right, my dad *is* a scream. He's a self-made scream. He made his fortune manufacturing light fittings for the Japanese, which is not so easy. He retired years ago, and he still uses the words "quality control" about three times in every sentence. My mum, well everyone adores my mum. She's just one of those people.

So, yes, we were riding high, we were on a roll. In Auckland we were like royalty. Everybody thought we were just amazing. We'd just been in this really cool film, we were almost famous, people hung on our words. We were solid. Rock solid.

*Bonza, Mate* did extremely well. It played a number of festivals, it won a couple of prizes and Sophie really took off, almost instantly. The New Zealand press went absolutely nuts, as soon as she'd won a couple of overseas awards. (This is pre–Peter Jackson. Nowadays you have to get an Oscar at the very least if you want to impress anyone back home.) Speaking of the press, I even got a couple of mentions myself: "Haunted by erotically charged visions of a bespectacled fantasy lover . . ." ". . . pursued by a mysterious incubus in glasses." That was me. The fantasy lover. *Erotically charged.* I like that. *Erotically charged.* Has a ring to it, huh?

There was a phone call from Janine. She was delirious. She was in London. "You've got to get over here," she kept saying over and over. She'd been talking to some people. There was a guy at ICM. He'd seen Sophie, and if Sophie was considering relocating he'd love to represent her in London. There was no real question. We were going, of course. We'd been working up to that from the very beginning. We got married in Las Vegas on the way over. I've got dual citizenship but Sophie hasn't, so this way it would be easier with work. But that wasn't the only reason. We were in love. I'd like to stress that. It was real. We were really in love then, and whatever has happened since doesn't make it any the less real. We were in love. That's why we got married.

Sophie called Simon at ICM the first day we were in London. She went around to meet him. A strange guy. Spends his entire working day pacing up and down his office wearing a headset, waving his arms and talking to people who aren't even there. He seems to have an eye problem too. On the rare occasions when I would be in his office, whenever I said something he would look vaguely troubled and glance around the room like he could swear he just heard somebody say something but he couldn't tell for the life of him where it was coming from. Simon took Sophie on. There was never any question of him taking me on. Christ, I knew that. I had *erotically charged*, but that was about it. I was optimistic, though, I was buoyed up by success. Only problem was, the success I was buoyed up by was Sophie's.

We found a flat in West Hampstead, bought a bed, settled right in. Sophie almost instantly got a small part in *The Bill* in which she played a cheerful overweight Australian hitchhiker who gets incinerated in a backpacker's fire. Then nothing for a few months, then a run of small TV parts playing large Australians: a walking tour of the Lake District, living in a houseboat in Regent's Canal selling drugs, a budding journalist. I got no jobs at all. I met a couple of agents, mainly friends of friends of Sophie who explained that their books were very full and if they thought they could realistically do anything for me they would take me on like a shot, but . . . So after bumming out with ICM and PFD and all the others I ended up with ACA: Actors Cooperative Agency. A sad setup indeed. We all took turns at representing one another. I'd spend a couple of days a month manning the phones. Which were running hot. Not. I did once score a job as Ernest Rutherford's father in a BBC radio docudrama and another time I got to do a voice-over for a TV ad for New Ziland lemb. For a while I thought I'd found a niche in the market but in the end I was undercut by an Australian. They told me they thought he sounded more authentic.

Meanwhile, Sophie was getting worried. She was still getting work, but she felt she was being typecast as an overweight antipodean. We talked it over. If she was ever going to bust through, she decided she would have to take drastic action. She turned down an offer to play the lead in a film about a young overweight Australian trying to make it in Hollywood and went on a diet. She was re-branding. She lost six kilos. Then another two. She lost her Kiwi accent. She changed her lipstick. Instantly, the work stopped. There was nothing. Nada. And thus began the year of pain. The year which ended in *Flagrant Consequence*.

There's a light drizzle falling. I've been carried along, a microbe caught in a mass of foreign bodies, stirring slowly like cake mix, borne along by the madding crowd, crushed shoulder to shoulder back to front with Pommies. Pommies, Pommies everywhere, and not a drop to drink. What a time to give up alcohol. I can't believe this is happening to me. I have no vices. Help, help, I need a vice.

We seem to be moving in the general direction of Soho. Pommies are nothing like New Zealanders. They're polite but unfriendly. They let their dogs crap just anywhere. They don't even smell the same. Actually, we're a lot more at home in California. It's not that we're any more like Californians than we are like Pommies, it's just that in California it doesn't matter what you're like. They're all so soothing. We feel right at home. Anyone feels right at home. Home. Home! A great wave of homesickness picks me up and dumps me on the shores of despondency. I want to go home.

"Looking for a girl?"

She can't be more than twenty-five. She's standing with her hands in the pockets of a green coat, belted tight. She's got masses of thick curly hair and babyish skin and she looks a bit like the lady doctor off *ER*. She has a bright professional smile. Good teeth. She's a New Zealander. I recognized the accent instantly. Oh, that accent. It's a real New Zealand accent. One hundred percent pure. I have to hear it again. I just have to, one more time. It's making me go all trembly and teary-eyed, like when the Maori cultural group does a haka. They practice in New Zealand House just down the hall from me on Thursday nights. Chokes me up every time. The girl smiles again, seductively, and touches my arm, lightly. "Come on, it's not far. See that doorway over there?" She smiles. She waits. She's very polite. "I take Visa," she adds. I guess that's supposed to be the clincher.

"You're a New Zealander."

She blinks. "Well, yeah."

"So am I."

"Oh, yeah, right! Where are you from?"

"Auckland."

She rolls her eyes. "Yeah, figures. But I won't hold it against you. You coming?"

"How do you like it here?"

"London?" She shakes her head. "It's a hole."

"Really?"

"Unbelievable." She holds a hand out, palm upward. "It's been weeks now. Weeks. And it's not even proper rain. It's just this pissy gutless drizzle all the time. No wonder they invaded the Pacific. I would too, if I lived here. And as for the *traffic*. Oh, the traffic. You know it took me an hour and a half just to get to work this evening? I could have walked it in twenty. And the tube, it's so *dirty*. And everything's so *expensive*. And you can't even get decent food. And everyone walks around looking like they've got a poker stuck up their arse. Which half of them have. Believe me, I know what I'm talking about. And the TV is so *boring*. Really, it's just a hole. The whole place, it's just a great big dirty, dark, wet hole. As a matter of fact, if you really wanna know, it sucks, real bad. The whole place. Sucks. And as for the beer . . . actually, I have to admit I quite like the beer." She pauses for breath.

"What about the art galleries? The museums? The libraries? The wonderful parks, the architecture, the sense of history, of access to the rich fascinating tapestry of European culture, thought, art and philosophy?"

"Nah, I'm not really into that, eh. I do like the movies though."

"The shopping?"

"Yeah, the shopping's not bad. But the shop assistants, God, they're all so up themselves. And electronics are cheaper in Auckland. Nah, the whole place sucks. Badly."

"I see."

"Although, sorry, I have to say this, Auckland sucks just as badly as London nowadays. Worse than London. It's so humid. And the traffic is just as bad. And they're all such wankers. They all think New Zealand ends at the Bombay Hills."

"So where are you from then?"

"Oh, I'm from Levin." She straightens up with pride. Levin is a small, one-car-dealership town in the middle of a cold, flat, windy, featureless plain. It's about as exciting as Monday morning and has been voted New Zealand's most boring town ten years running.

"You must be really homesick."

She sighs. "Yeah, I really miss it, eh. Really miss home."

We share a trembly moment. "Why don't you go home then?"

She shakes her head. "Can't go home."

"Why not?"

She shrugs. I think I know why. I think I understand.

"So how long have you been here?"

"Oh, not that long, eh." She puts on her professional voice again, lowers it an intimate octave and leans in close. "So, are we doing anything tonight or not, honey?"

"Sorry, I have an urgent appointment. I mean, it's been very nice to meet you though."

She shrugs. She's remarkably polite and professional and I can't help thinking she's been well brought up. "Well, if you change your mind, come on up and see me, any time." She hands me her card. It's a flimsy piece of green card, photocopied. MISS MELISSA, it says. There's a picture of a woman half in and half out of a bikini. It doesn't look anything like her. Below it is a headline and a phone number. FRESH OFF THE BOAT! BE FIRST IN TO PICK MY LUSCIOUS AUSSIE PEACHES!

"There's something I don't understand. It says here you're Australian."

"Oh, yeah, I know. People don't really respond to New Zealand. Australia is more sexy."

"What's so sexy about Australia?"

"Sun, sand, surf. You know."

"But you're a New Zealander."

Melissa shrugs.

"Have you no *pride*?"

She rolls her eyes. "Tell me, what do people think of when they think of New Zealand?"

"Er . . ."

"Right: sheep-fuckers. That is our international image. Like it or not, if you say, 'New Zealand,' most people will say, 'Sheep-fuckers.' So where does that get me? I'm not even a sheep."

"How about 'Fresh New Zealand Lamb'? or 'One hundred percent Virgin Shagpile'?"

"Nice try but I don't think so."

"But, *Australia* . . ."

"Look, it's just like anything, it's like soap powder. People need something they can identify with. My clients are getting something they recognize, something they relate to—buns on the beach, bronzed surfy chicks. All that."

"But . . . *Australia*. What about the South Pacific? You could be a maiden of the South Pacific."

"Dusky maiden, fine, but I'm the wrong color, bud."

"I know, bungee jumping! 'New Zealand' says bungee jumping! How about 'Plunge into the Land of Adventure' or better still, 'Taking Rubber to the Limits'?"

She shakes her head. "We're downplaying the risk aspect of the industry right now." She grins, suddenly. "But keep coming with those ideas."

She waves a saucy little good-bye. The poor thing has no idea. Talking to me she might as well be a liquor wholesaler cultivating Saudi connections. Still, I am moved to stop and turn back and watch her go. And I feel sad. I feel such sadness. That a young woman like that, so full of promise, bright and perky, her whole life ahead of her, has sunk to such a terrible deluded, degraded existence. Pretending to be an Australian. It's enough to make you weep.

I sigh, and hitch my Swedish Army greatcoat closer around my shoulders. The air is raw and a heavy mist hangs in the air, muffling the pitter-pat of the light drizzle as it falls on cobbled streets. I stagger away into the London night.

## Chapter 5

ON THE WAY UP TO MY ROOM I notice that someone has swept up the potato peelings and replaced them with fresh ones. They've arranged the shoes neatly too, in pairs, in order of size. Nice to see a bit of neighborhood pride.

There's something arranged on my doorstep too. It's Mee. He's huddled on the doormat, fast asleep in his greasy black coat, his clumpy black shoes sticking out of his slightly black trousers. This whole black clothing thing is a plague sweeping the New Zealand nation. It started in Wellington. Now it's got as far as the newsreaders. I've seen it. Sometimes my mother sends me tapes. Everywhere, New Zealanders are in black. Black ties, black suits, black shirts. They must be in mourning for their standard of living. Mee stirs, and yips like a dreaming dog. A delicate scent of old rubber and peanuts rises and envelops the landing. I look at my watch. It's one a.m. While I've been out pounding the streets of London he's been here, waiting. And waiting. Clinging to me like a drowning man. Clinging to hope long after all grounds for hope are gone. I feel sorry, and sad. But not that sorry. With infinite care I step over his sleeping body, let myself into the room, ease the door shut and lock it.

I'd like to trace it all back. I have that trace-it-all-back feeling coming on. Of course you can never trace it all back. Back to what? Back to when? I remember the day quite clearly. It would be about eighteen months ago now. I remember sitting in the kitchen in the flat we had then, which was quite nice but I didn't want to keep it afterward. I didn't want anywhere quite nice at all. I was sitting with my head cradled in my palms. I was thinking about Godzone. Sophie was in the sitting room. She was in her T-shirt and socks but it was a Saturday morning so that was okay. She laughed. I went through to the next room. She had a script propped on her thighs.

"What's so funny?"

"It's this script Janine has sent me. She wants me to suck a guy's dick."

". . . She what?"

She holds up the script. "It's from Janine. It's got a dick-sucking scene in it."

"Well, bin that one."

She looks annoyed. "It's a good script."

"Wait a minute. You're going to do what? Suck a guy's dick on film? Because it's a good script?"

"Don't be silly. I'll just tell her to cut it. She's just trying it on. You know Janine."

"I *do* know Janine. What sort of a script is this anyway?"

"You can read it after me."

"Who's up for it?"

"Some good people."

"Whose dick?"

"Forget the dick. I'll just tell them to cut it."

"Sounds painful."

She went back to it, and I went to the bedroom. I lay down on the bed. A little later I heard Sophie on the phone. She was talking to Simon. ". . . I mean, don't get me wrong, I happen to enjoy sucking dick, so no problem there . . . but . . . yeah . . . it would be more from that quarter, yeah . . . well I can talk to him . . ."

I rolled over on the bed. I waited. Sophie appeared in the doorway. "I've been talking to Simon."

"Uh-huh."

"He says Janine's pretty set on the dick-sucking scene."

"Meaning?"

"Meaning . . . whoever plays the part is going to have to be prepared to do the scene."

"I see."

"I said I'd talk to you about it."

I know the score already. It's crystal clear. Sophie's going to do it. She's made up her mind and there's nothing I can say or do to stop her.

She takes a tentative step toward me. "It's just a dick."

"My God. You're actually going to do this, aren't you?"

"Not if you don't want me to."

"Whose dick is it anyway?"

"Matt Chalmers."

"Matt Chalmers, perfect."

"He hasn't gone firm on it yet."

"He'll go firm all right. He'll firm up very smartly, I'm sure."

"Why don't you just come right out and tell me how you feel about it?"

"About you sucking Matt Chalmers's dick?"

"It wouldn't mean anything."

"It would mean you would be sucking Matt Chalmers's dick."

"Just for a job."

"Is that supposed to make me feel better? Because if so . . ."

"You're responsible for your own feelings. I'm just trying to tell you how it is. How it would be."

"Is he married? Matt?"

"I think so."

"What does his wife think about it?"

"I don't know."

"We could start a support group."

She sighs. "Look. If you don't want me to do it, just say so."

I clear my throat. I sit up. "I don't want you to do it."

"You haven't even read it."

"No, I haven't read it."

"You could at least read it before you decide."

"I think I know enough already."

"It's just one scene. One little scene. It's not like I'm turning into a porn star or something." She sighs. She pleads. "It's a really good script. At least read it."

I always used to read Sophie's scripts. She used to rely on me completely. But this time I didn't. I couldn't see that reading it was going to do me any good. Either way it would just make my position harder. Janine, who was based in LA nowadays, had this stupid idea that we could all talk about it, the five of us, and sort it out and there wouldn't be any problem. She took us all out to dinner at the Ivy. I didn't want to go but I couldn't see how not going was going to advance my cause any.

Matt was this big Californian guy, slow-talking, blue eyes, just the way he looks on screen. It's the little things. The teeth. The eyelashes. How do they do it? How much does it cost? Should I do it too? He actually seemed like a perfectly nice guy even if there was something a little unpredictable about the eyes if you watched him watching someone else. But he was dripping with charisma. Loaded with it. Anne-Marie, his wife, was very blonde, very tanned, very open and very charming. A huge amount of eyeliner, tons of gold and only minimal cosmetic surgery. She had the most amazing eyes. They were deep, deep brown and the size of a horse's. They were huge. She had this habit of opening them very wide when she listened to you talk, so you could see the whites all the way around. She was wearing a formfitting cotton/ Lycra jumpsuit with flares. She had biceps bigger than my thighs, and thighs bigger than my waist. All muscle. She had muscles in all those places you never even realize people can *have* muscles. Her neck, her jaw, the bridge of her nose. Arnold Schwarzenegger with breasts.

She was about my age, as was Matt. As indeed was Janine, so Sophie was the odd one out there. I hadn't seen Janine for a while. She was wired and she kept saying how excited she was. Which I'm sure she was. Janine, I don't know. She has this way of looking at me. Sort of not exactly hungry, but like she was looking *at* me. Like she was never saying what she was thinking. Or thinking what she was saying. That was the way she *used* to look at me. Now, she seemed to have caught the same disease Simon at ICM was suffering from.

Things started out the way you might expect. Sophie and Anne-Marie were so nice to each other it was frightening. Matt and I shook hands firmly and looked each other in the eye. Someone said something about the weather. Sophie and Matt ignored each other.

We all sat down and ordered, and we all got to know one another. Matt and Anne-Marie had three children. They lived in California. They loved London, except for the weather. They had a flat in St. John's Wood so they could come over whenever they wanted. They wanted to send their kids to study in England. They absolutely loved New Zealand, and they already knew that it wasn't part of Australia. In fact we had an entire discussion about New Zealand without mentioning Australia once. They understood that it was a very green country with many sheep and the people were friendly and they planned to go skiing there some-time soon.

They told us how they met. Anne-Marie used to be a wardrobe artist, but then she met Matt on set and they got married and she stopped working to devote herself to the kids. This was fifteen years ago now, when he was still doing soaps. They touched each other a lot. She'd stroke his arm, or he'd stroke her leg. I noticed that whenever Sophie and Anne-Marie were talking to each other, Matt was looking at Sophie. Whenever Sophie was talking to Matt, he was looking at Anne-Marie. Whenever Janine was talking to Sophie, she was looking at Anne-Marie, and Matt was looking at her. Whenever I was talking, everyone was looking at Janine. No one was ever looking at me.

We talked about all sorts of stuff. We talked about kiwis, atomic bombs, the former Soviet Union, granola, globalization, clothes, golf, cheese, celery, interplanetary travel, sauerkraut, hyperthy-roidism, inflation, taxes, ancient Babylon, caffeine, drug-resistant flu strains and Lake Como, and all the time all I could think about was something else. Matt Chalmers's dick. It was there, lurking under the table. I spent the entire dinner fantasizing about it. I might as well have ordered Cumberland sausage. Size, shape, color, consistency, smell. Taste. Oh, God.

After dessert, I stood up. "I'm going to the men's," I said. I was half cut.

"Yeah, I think I'll join ya." Matt stood up too.

The men's room in the Ivy is actually quite cramped. It has two porcelain urinals, side by side. I froze. I locked up completely. I just couldn't do it. I stood there trying desperately to pee while Matt chattered away about this and that, gushing like a fire hydrant. Don't look down. I was saying to myself, don't look down. He'll see. He'll see you looking down.

I looked down.

It was enormous. It was horse-sized. It was thick and hairy and covered with snaking purple veins. It was a pendulous, pachydermous, Brobdingnagian horror. We washed our hands, and just before we went through the door, Matt hitched his trousers, put a hand on my shoulder and said, "So listen, Fred, you're cool about this, right? This scene. No big deal, right?"

"Scene?" I said.

"Yeah, you know, the scene. Sophie and I have that scene. That one scene where she . . . y'know, she goes down on me."

"There's a scene where she goes down on you?"

"Ah . . . yeah."

"Oh," I said, "yeah, okay."

Matt shifts weight. "I mean, it's just a scene, right?"

"Oh, sure, just a scene. Hell."

He patted my shoulder. We went back to the table. Anne-Marie and Sophie were nodding and smiling at each other, very very vigorously, and Sophie's eyes were shining in an insincere sort of way. She had one hand laid loosely on the table, palm half upward, half-reaching toward Anne-Marie. Janine was looking rapidly from one to the other with a fixed smile. All her teeth showing. "All righty," she kept saying. Sophie turned to us. She was showing a little color high on the cheeks. She looked straight at Matt. Straight down the barrel. "I was just saying to Anne-Marie, if she has any questions or anything at all about this scene, she only has to ask."

Anne-Marie smiled. Janine nodded furiously, her teeth flashing like piano keys in a dim lit room. Matt looked very, very serious. "Yeah. I think, you know, like, Fred and I were just saying in the john, we should all just feel free to say whatever it is we're feeling, and, you know, communicate about it. And just stay open."

Now, everyone looked at me. All of them. It was all on. The blood drained from every part of my body simultaneously. Where it actually went, I don't think I will ever know. "Right," I said.

"Good." I could see it. I could see as plainly as if I were there and it was happening. I could see Matt Chalmers's enormous throbbing dick plunging in and out of Sophie's rosebud mouth. I could see nothing else. I felt for the chair, blindly. I felt ill. I sat down.

"I mean, hey, after all," said Matt, "it's just a scene, right? We're all friends here, and that's all that it is, it's just a scene in a motion picture. And it's gonna be one hell of a motion picture." Janine ordered port and when it arrived Matt proposed a toast. "To *Shag City*," he said.

"To *Shag City*." We all drank. Deeply. As I put down my glass I looked across and caught Anne-Marie's eye. We'd hardly said a word to each other all evening. I tried to read her expression, but with all that mascara it was hard. She was doing the wide-open thing with her eyes. I think she thought it gave her an open, caring, listening aspect. I wasn't sure, but I thought I'd caught a little glimpse of distress.

"Say," said Matt, "you know what I feel like? I feel like a big fat cigar. Who's for a cigar? Frederick?"

"I don't smoke."

"I'll have one," said Sophie.

On the way out, Anne-Marie took my arm. "Listen, Frederick, if you ever want to talk, give me a call, okay? I'm going to be in London right through the whole shoot. The kids are gonna be on vacation." She gave me her card, and she gave my arm a little squeeze. "You just give me a call, huh?"

Sophie and I went straight home and had a big fight. It was our best and biggest. Normally we didn't have fights at all, we'd just go silent, but this time we did. We really went to town. We did everything, we shouted, we stormed around the room, and then I picked up a plate and with incredible ease I frisbeed it across the table. It sailed through the air, wobbling slightly, and there was that magical motionless silent interval that always occurs when you've gone too far and you know it, when it seemed as if it would never arrive and time had stopped entirely. Then it exploded against the wall in a million pieces.

A golden silence fell as we stood and admired our handiwork. "Look," I said, "you know what? You just go ahead and do whatever you like. I don't think I actually care anymore." Then I went to bed.

———————

Tea's made. I pour the tea and I take a sip. I'll just sit it out. Only take a minute. Then I'll wash those mugs. I think that's actually what pulled me through the whole thing. The drinking and shouting and throwing things, while exhilarating, was completely useless. Instead I did dishes. Always respond to a bad thing with a good thing. Doesn't matter how small. Just do some small, useful, good thing. Like, the morning that Sophie did actually leave, I went to the kitchen. All the way down the hall I was thinking about one thing, I was thinking about the vodka in the fridge. If I can just make it to the vodka. Seemed reasonable. It was traditional. But when I actually got to the kitchen the first thing I saw was the chef's knife with the green handle. Eight-inch blade. I had had many thoughts over the last two days. It's fair to say that a number of those thoughts did in fact center on the green-handled Zwilling chef's knife with the eight-inch blade. That very morning, just before, just after Sophie had gone to phone Rebecca, I'd actually said to her, "I'm afraid."

"Of what?"

"I'm afraid I might hurt myself."

She took a breath, a long one. She was in the bedroom. She had an open suitcase on the bed. "We've been through this. I've phoned Rebecca," she said. "She's coming over. I'm going to pack." She then went to the drawers and started emptying them. It was very clear to me that if I was going to hurt myself, that was my problem now.

"Forget it," I said. "Forget I said that."

She didn't say anything.

"Can I help you with anything?" I said.

She shook her head and carried on with her packing and I went back to the lounge. I thought, hell, I can always hurt myself later. Which is the thing to remember about self-mutilation and suicide. There's never any hurry, you've always got it as an option. I prefer to keep it that way, in reserve, as a fallback position. I turned on the TV. This was daytime, but I was watching a video so that was okay. I was watching Kubrick's 2001: A Space Odyssey. A strange feeling of contentment crept over me. Sophie hadn't gone yet. She was still here, she was in the house, packing. The TV was on. Something would come up. I felt increasing certainty that she wouldn't leave. A quiet inner confidence. She hadn't left yet. She didn't leave last night. She wasn't going to leave this morning. Something would happen. An eleventh-hour reprieve. Sophie would change her mind.

Rebecca came around; they got the suitcases down the stairs. I could hear them whispering in the hall and banging the suitcases on the stairway. That was really my job, to be carrying suitcases. When Sophie changed her mind I'd help her get them back up. I turned up the TV so I didn't have to listen. HAL was dying. "Daisy, Daisy, give me your answer do . . ."

Then I realized Sophie was standing right in front of me.

"I'm going," she said. She had to raise her voice above the TV.

"Okay," I said. Ha, that got her, I thought. She won't do it. I was utterly convinced she wouldn't do it. I turned off the TV. I listened. There was nothing. The house was empty. I went to the kitchen, my footsteps accelerating as I walked. I had a sense of impending doom, of horror and unstoppable menace.

But now that I was here, in the kitchen, alone, now that I was in complete privacy and freedom with plenty of time on my hands and no particular thing to live for that I could think of at the time, what I saw with total clarity was that I absolutely did *not* want to hurt myself. I saw that very clearly. What I most wanted was to treat myself with the utmost sensitivity, care and respect. I think this is where upbringing really comes into play. So when I looked at the green-handled Zwilling, what I focused on was that it had dried cheese on the blade and greasy fingermarks on the handle.

And that led me to observe that there were other dishes also. They were all over the damn place, they were stacked to the roof. No one had been thinking about things like dishes for the last couple of days — absolutely not. The conversations over the last couple of days had not been kitchen conversations. Take it from me. Sophie had gone, but the dirty dishes remained.

Then I remembered the vodka, which was in fact the whole reason I was here in the first place. The vodka was in the fridge, keeping cold in the freezer. The fridge was on my right, and the dishes were on my left, and the knife was in the middle. I had a world of choice, right there in an abandoned kitchen.

I took a step into the room. The fridge must have heard me coming because it started up. It was an old one and it made a sound like a V8. It had fins too. I was going to have a vodka. I was going to have too much vodka. But there was something I had to do first. I washed every single dish in that kitchen. I scrubbed the pots, I soaked the casserole, I even did the gas grill, which was solid with melted cheese and toast crumbs. I got the kitchen clean, and then I opened the fridge door and poured myself a large glass of cold vodka.

I told myself, Frederick, you have done well. You have shown the self-control, the maturity and strength of character to do all the dishes *including* the gas grill prior to getting badly and completely wasted. And if you can do that, the very day that your happiness walked out the door, you can do anything. This can augur nothing but good. I predict a bright future. I predict a long and happy life, full of successes, friends, and all good things.

I then drank the entire glass. And the rest of course is history. I woke up many hours later shoeless in the stairwell. But the first thing I thought to myself as I lay there was this: *At least I did the dishes.* I clung to that knowledge as I crawled up a flight. I cradled that knowledge as I dry-retched in the bathroom, as I crawled toward that lonely double bed, as I discovered that Sophie had taken the sheets. As I wrapped myself in the curtains and lay down to attempt fitful dreaming sleep. That knowledge sustained me. No life, no matter how desperate the circumstances, is without hope, just as long as you do the dishes.

Yes. Learn from me. Do the dishes. Brush your teeth—twice a day—shave, daily, wash your clothes. *Don't* watch television during the day except for brief snatches in airports and the windows of appliance stores. Be kind to animals. Change *all* underwear *every* day—*regardless of apparent necessity.* Cook your own evening meal at least four times a week. Never drink before six o'clock. Use the vacuum cleaner. Get up in the morning. Go to bed at night. These are the things that will see you through. Things that will *not* help include (but are not limited to): talking to seemingly sympathetic people you don't really know, especially while drinking, drinking, breaking small objects, flinging yourself against walls, punching bricks, failing to forward mail, kicking cats, raving wildly at friends, staring at photographs, staring out windows, staring at walls, cars, gutters, hungry people, women, the swirling waters of the Thames, electrified rails. Staring is generally not a good idea. Leads to eye strain.

———

It's a nice cup of tea. In a minute I'll do those dishes. I become vaguely aware that for a long time now I've been aware of yapping.

Freddy frequently yaps, but never for this long and never at this time of night. I look at my watch. It's three. I ease open the door. Mee is still there. He's snoring gently. I step over him and go up the half-flight to Mrs. Traversham's door. I can see Freddy through the frosted glass, a dark batlike shape leaping, scrabbling, leaping again.

I knock. "Mrs. Traversham?" No reply. I get out my key and slip inside. Freddy prances around my ankles, yapping like mad. He's done his business on the carpet. "Mrs. Traversham? Might I intrude?"

The bedroom door is open and from the hall I can see her feet, both shoes on. She's lying on the bed. She's fast asleep. Freddy yaps. I tap on the door and stick my head around the corner. "Please do forgive me for intruding at such an hour . . ."

She's lying down, fully dressed. She's on her back, arms at her sides, perfectly still. But it's all wrong. She's too still. The stillness of her body is unnatural. It fills the room. Her hands are wrong. They're at the wrong angle. So is her head. When I touch her hand it's so cold it gives the impression of hardness, of stone. I take a step back. It's the stillness. It's unbearable. It rises off her, a miasma of immobility.

"Oh, God, Mrs. Traversham." I stare and I stare. I know what this is, but I can't think of the word. Not yet.

So still.

I keep thinking I can see her chest rising and falling, but it's an optical illusion. It's like the road going backward when you stop the car. Actually, there's nothing. There's not the slightest breath. I take another step back.

Her eyes are slitted as if she's watching me slyly from under her lashes. Her mouth is slack, her cheeks caved inward, her jaw falling open toward her chest.

God, someone help her.

Freddy is yapping, yapping.

They arrive about the same time, an ambulance and a pair of children disguised as constables, one male and one female. The female listens to the story and takes down my details. The police don't want her moved until she's been seen by a doctor, so the ambulance crew go away again. The WPC offers to make me a cup of tea, which I accept. We all three sit at the kitchen table.

"Did you know her well, then?" asks the WPC.

"Not so well, really, I guess. I've only been here a few months. I mean, I really liked her."

"Poor old duck." The male constable is back from the hall. He's been looking through Mrs. Traversham's address book by the telephone. "How many numbers do you think she had in there? Hardly a one."

"Still," says the WPC, "she was lucky, really. I hope to God I go like that. Quick and quiet, at home in bed. My granddad, he lingered for months. We all just had to sit there and watch him waste away, slowly, before our very eyes. Every day, he was a little thinner, a little weaker. And he suffered. God, he suffered."

"What did he die of?" I ask.

"Cancer."

"Yeah," says the MPC, "but to die all alone like that. That's sad. I'd hate to die alone. I don't think there could be anything worse than to have your last moments alone."

"She had the dog."

"There's no comfort in a dog. Not at a time like that."

I'm beginning to think Mrs. Traversham is better company. The doctor arrives. He goes into the room alone, comes out twenty minutes later and sits down with us at the kitchen table. He's fifty, fattish, with white hair and amazing eyebrows.

"Are you Mr. Case? The boarder?"

"Yes, I am."

"How are the filmmaking activities?" He smiles. "She mentioned you from time to time."

"Oh."

The WPC looks interested. "Are you a filmmaker?"

"Yes, I'm a producer."

"What do they do? Producers?"

"We handle the money." They both look at me disbelievingly. "What sort of films do you produce, then?"

"We have a number of projects in development." I turn to the doctor. "How did she die?"

"A stroke, without a doubt. She was hypertensive."

"Really?"

"She probably felt unwell, perhaps a headache, she would have gone to have a lie down, and most likely she died very suddenly, as is suggested by her failure to remove her shoes. She probably didn't feel a thing." He shakes his head and his eyes moisten. "She was a dear old soul. It's a shame she never got home. She often talked of it but she never got there."

"How do you mean?"

He looks at me in surprise. "Didn't you know? She was a New Zealander."

He declines the offer of a cuppa, pats my shoulder, and leaves.

The ambulance crew come back. They go into her room, come out moments later carrying a stretcher. I stand at the door as she is carried away. It's about five-thirty. Mee, on my doorstep, down a half-flight, is yawning and stretching and looking around. I close the door quickly. Freddy looks up from his bowl, Branston Pickle smeared over his muzzle.

I go to the window. It's still dark outside. I try to imagine tracer bullets arcing across the darkness, flashes of light, searchlights waving to and fro, the crump of artillery, ack-ack, the drone of bombers, fighters, the glow of fires. Maybe that's what I need. A good war. Something to get me going.

I'm trapped in Mrs. Traversham's for another hour while Mee

knocks, and waits, but eventually he gives up, and I nip downstairs to get my phone.

"Darling! How are you?"

"I'm fine."

"What are you up to at this moment?"

"As a matter of fact I'm just planning a holiday. I was wondering if I could change my mind about the cash situation."

"Of course you could darling."

This is not a backward step, I tell myself, when I've hung up. I have to have the money. I have a purpose. I have a mission. I have a place to be and someone to see. I glance at my watch again. Hell, damn and blast. It's now six. I have to be in prison in a couple of hours.

## Chapter 6

I'VE NEVER BEEN TO PRISON before so I'm not sure what the dress code is, but I've gone for tweed. It's an exquisite three-piece in pale green with a mauve check. Genuine Scottish. Cost me seven hundred quid. I bought it for the premiere of *Consequential Damage*, which came after *Flagrant Consequence*. *Consequential Damage* established Sophie as a serious actress, capable not only of looking good in underwear but of looking *intelligent* in underwear. I'm wearing my Church's brogues. I can see myself in the toes: I have to say I'm looking less than calm. My palms are sweaty and I have a fluttery feeling in my chest. I keep thinking my heart has stopped. The pills from Dr. McVeigh are in my top pocket. They come in blister packs of seven, one for each day of the week. They're tiny, round and white. They look like tiny skulls.

WELCOME TO HISTORIC SITTLEBURY

We're out of the cutting now and blasting past a huge Park-n-Ride, then we're racing along the platform of a sleepy suburban station. There's a Goth girl on a bench seat. I catch sight of her as she flashes by. Raven-haired, she's dressed all in black. Black leather, black platforms, black lipstick. Her face made up dead white. She's slightly hunched over, her hair falling slightly forward. Her mouth gapes wide, black lips stretched tight across white teeth. She's yawning. The train begins to slow.

––––––––––

Down the hill the sleepy town of Sittlebury. Before me a giant brick wall, twenty feet high. The bricks old, the mortar crumbling. Rusty razor-wire coiled haphazardly along the top. Set in the wall a set of double gates, and set inside the gates a small postern, with a Plexiglas spy hole. On the wall a sign with a list of "don'ts" for visitors. No drugs, no weapons, no alcohol. I now understand the true horror of prison. It is more dreadful than anything I could ever have guessed. It's exactly like school.

Waiting with me are the other visitors. A relaxed crowd, chatting amongst themselves, chewing gum, the occasional low-key joke. The dress code is mixed—a few shell suits, a smattering of fake fur and imitation leopard, and one ultra-ultramini in red plastic. I stick out like a spare prick, especially in view of the fact that I'm the only male. More than one glance comes my way.

The spy hole rattles open, then shut, and a moment later the postern opens. Silver buttons glint on a dark uniform. "All right, one at time please." We line up. When it gets to my turn, the postern is so low I have to duck to get through. I'm inside the gatehouse. I queue again, with the women, in front of a reception desk guarded by a thick Plexiglas window. I'm panicking already. I try to copy the women, who assume an air of detached nonchalance. I wish I had some gum. When it's my turn at the window I slip my passport through the slot and state my business.

"Frederick Case. I'm with the Artists in Prisons program."

"The wot?"

"Artists in Prisons."

"Got a name? Someone I can contact?"

"A Dr. Bartholomew Higgins. I think he's with the Secure Unit."

He shakes his head, wanders over to a phone. There's a long pause involving repeated telephone calls. The guard comes back to the window. "Wait over there, please." I go to the bench indicated. I wait. One by one the women go through, leaving me alone. Cheap perfume still hangs in the air. I look at my watch. It's been half an hour already. I can feel my heart. It's unnaturally heavy. I'm already wishing I hadn't come. They didn't actually ask me, they asked Sophie, but she was busy so I suggested she suggest me. I think I had some insane idea that it would be an ego boost. I wanted to go to Brixton but they got Glenda Jackson. Sittlebury Secure Unit got me.

Another guard is standing over me. He's about twenty-five, his neck is thicker than his head and his pants are way, way too tight. "You for the Secure Unit?" I nod. He takes me through the metal door to security. The door slams shut behind me and locks. A female officer with exquisite skin, a tight shirt and piles of gorgeous hair gestures to a metal table.

"Put your bag on the table please, sir."

I put my bag on the table while the guard with the tight pants approaches from the rear. He frisks me, thoroughly, while the female goes through my bag. Tight-pants finds the pills in my top pocket, while the female with exquisite skin finds my pocket knife, my Walkman and some books. All these items go on a tray and the tray goes in a locker. They walk me through a metal detector, pass me the key to the locker and push me into a small annex with an iron-barred door looking onto a tiny, grim courtyard.

I stand by the bars, staring into space. I feel oppressed and tearful. I look at my watch. If I'm like this after forty minutes, what would ten years do?

"Mr. Case?" A tiny scruffy man in a corduroy suit is in the courtyard on the other side of the bars, squinting up at me. He can't be more than five feet tall. He has a graying wispy beard, thick black plastic glasses held together with sticking plaster, a nose dotted with blackheads, and a fruity Oxbridge accent. "I'm Dr. Bartholomew Higgins. I'm the Secure Unit probation officer." He smiles. "But you can call me Bart." When he smiles his whole face crumples. That smile, in a place like this, is a drink of water. It's a ray of sunshine, a flower in the desert. It's one hell of a smile. I grip his hand through the bars and I never want to let go. Tight-pants wanders over, pulls out a bunch of keys, lets me through.

I follow Bartholomew Higgins, toting a huge bunch of complicated-looking brass keys, through a gate in the fence down a narrow barbed-wire alley and through another gate that opens onto the main prison grounds. Dr. Higgins points out the administration block on one side and the main prison block on the other. It's a huge five-story Victorian brick building, row upon row of tiny barred windows staring sightlessly down on us. Rusty water weeps slowly down the blackened walls.

Dr. Higgins walks fast, head down, chatting all the way. "It's not often we get visitors like yourself. The boys are all dying to meet you. They love to meet people from outside."

"Is there anything in particular you want me to say?"

"No, not really. Just talk a bit about yourself, answer any questions. The main idea is to remind them that there is a world beyond these walls, widen their horizons. So good of you to give up your valuable time like this."

"I see it as a chance to put something back in."

We walk past the corner of the main block and there, before us, is an old, neglected, low-lying building painted dull yellow. Sprouting out of it, one toadstool on the back of another, is a much newer building of pink concrete with slit-like windows. It looks like something you might have at a missile test facility. Dr. Higgins gets out his keys. He stops and looks back at me suddenly. I notice for the first time a gold crucifix around his neck.

"Do you read the classics?"

"Well, yes, I do."

He looks at me penetratingly. We pass through another double fence. There is no blade of grass, no tree, no plant of any description. I breathe deeply. There doesn't seem to be enough air. We enter the old building. More keys and locks as Dr. Higgins leads me on, and on, down a long wide blue corridor, across ancient liver-colored linoleum. There's a powerful smell of disinfectant. At the far end of the corridor we come to a new-looking door controlled by a guard's post. There's a sign above the door: SECURE UNIT. Dr. Higgins waves his ID at the guard watching from behind bullet-proof glass. The electric door slides back. My heart is pounding. I feel as if I'm under water. The door slides shut behind us.

"Welcome," says Dr. Higgins, "to the Secure Unit." I look around. We're in a brand-new concrete corridor, wide and spacious, with delicate lemon-painted walls, clean denim-blue linoleum, and tasteful pink bars on the windows. Cell doors down the corridor are also pastel pink. There's an overpowering smell of bacon fat.

At one end of the corridor, milling around the bottom of the stairwell, is a group of youthful louts. These must be the criminals. They look to be average age of about eighteen. Ditto for the IQ. They're shouting, laughing, ragging each other like school-boys, each of them clutching an enormous bacon sandwich. The government-issue jeans are all four sizes too big and slung too low—way, way too low. Arse crack exposure must be averaging 40 to 50 percent. T-shirts this season are white, again massively over-sized. Cigarette packets are worn Brando-style in the right sleeve. Trainers are unlaced and many have opted for no laces at all. We're getting quite close here to my personal vision of hell.

One of them lopes toward us, Quasimodo fashion, his sand-wich spattering gray watery bacon fat down the linoleum as he comes. He's short, pale and skinny. There's a pathetic attempt at a mustache on his upper lip and a red bandana around his head. By now Quasimodo is right up close. I grip my briefcase tightly, tense all my muscles and prepare to defend myself, but he ignores me and dances around Dr. Higgins like a brain-damaged puppy. I can now see the reason for the attempted mustache. A badly repaired harelip.

"Hey, guv . . ."

Dr. Higgins puts him in a headlock. "Don't call me guv!"

The kid squirms. "Sorry."

"Never call me guv!"

"No, sir."

"Call me Bart."

"Yeah, awright. Bart."

"Who am I?"

"Bart."

Dr. Higgins releases him, and the kid shakes himself all over. "What can I do for you, Rickie?"

"Tha' 'im?" He jerks a thumb at me. "Tha' the film geezer?"

"Yes, Rickie, this geezer is Mr. Case and, Rickie, Mr. Case can speak for himself. Can't you Mr. Case?"

I open my mouth. Nothing comes out.

Rickie gallops ahead as I follow Dr. Higgins to the staircase at the end. We climb, the mob behind us. I'm waiting for a forearm to close around my throat but it doesn't.

Dr. Higgins's office is a slightly big room with a view over the prison walls to some blue hills, far away. Arranged around the walls of the room are shelves, ceiling high, crammed with books. In front of the bookshelves are chairs. Armchairs, broken-backed and threadbare, straight chairs, spindle backs, cushions, an old love seat. The room fills as Rickie does the rounds with a jug, pouring out instant coffee.

The room is full. It's warm and stuffy, criminals stacked two high. I look around me. I don't get it. They're all tiny, scrawny.

Not a single one would give me the slightest concern in a dark alley. That kid over there in the corner with the curly hair and glasses. What could he possibly have done to end up in here? Cheated on his A levels?

Dr. Higgins stands up and taps the table. "Now then, boys, this is Mr. Case, of Godzone International. Mr. Case is a well-known and successful film actor and producer, so as you can well imagine he has a fascinating and exciting life, and many stories to tell. Today he's going to talk to us about employment opportunities in the film industry."

All faces are turned my way. Long faces, short faces, fat faces and thin faces. White faces, a couple of black faces. They're all waiting. I have to say something.

"Well . . . it's good to be here today."

Silence.

Dr. Higgins coughs. "Before we start, perhaps you boys could introduce yourselves. Rickie?"

Quasimodo kid jumps to his feet. "Me name's Rickie. Rickie Lunt."

Someone mutters the obvious.

"That's quite enough of that, thank you. We have a guest. Go on, Rickie. How long have you been here, now?"

"Been in four years now. Three to go." He pauses. "Oh, yeah, and my crime was rape. Of a little girl, like."

"How old was she, Rickie?"

"She was only seven."

"And how do you feel about your crime now?"

"It were wrong." He looks baffled a moment, sits down, sighs, then looks around to see who's next.

They're all sexually violent deviants. The whole roomful. Rape, rape and murder, sexual assault, molestation, rape and arson, rape and abduction of minors, family members, and in one case a horse. The curly-headed kid in glasses knifed and raped his mother, then locked the door and set fire to the family home. We work our way right around the room.

". . . Mr. Case?" Silence. All faces are turned my way. This is all wrong. There should be howling and wailing and gnashing of teeth. Not instant coffee and a chat. "So, Mr. Case, perhaps you'd like to tell us about yourself. What led you to film?"

My gaze travels wildly around the room. Behind the murderers are the books. I take a deep breath. I fixate on a handsome leather-bound volume of *Crime and Punishment*.

"Well, I was always interested in film . . . I . . . ah . . . I used to go to the movies when I was a kid. I worked as an actor for a while and then I got into producing. And when I came to England a few years back I started my company, Godzone International. And here I am."

A rather good-looking black kid puts up his hand. "You made a lot of films, then?"

"We . . . have a number of projects on the slate."

"What sort of films?"

"Well, all sorts." I have a proposal with Channel Four for a documentary on the history of the G-string, called *G-String Century*. I have a projected television series on first aid for dogs, imaginatively entitled *First Aid for Dogs*, and last but not least I have a drama about a kid who takes his goldfish with cancer to Disneyland. Originally it was the kid who had cancer but the programmer at Channel Four thought it was a bit of a downer so we changed it to the goldfish. Also we thought this way it could easily go to a series, with different pets and different diseases. Of course when I say "on the slate" what I really mean is I haven't got the rejection letter yet.

Dr. Higgins nods thoughtfully. "What films have you acted in, Frederick?"

"Just the one, really. It's called *Bonza, Mate*." I look around hopefully. Blank faces. "It was quite successful."

"What's it about?"

"Well, it's about a young Australian hitchhiking her way around Europe."

"Do you do your own stunts?"

"There are no stunts."

Mystified silence. A thin, red-faced boy puts up his hand. He broke into a house and strangled two nine-year-olds. He was just starting on his third when they got there. "What sort of car 'ave you got?"

I look at Bart. He shrugs. "Ah . . . a Toyota Corolla."

"What year?"

"1989."

There's an incredulous hush.

"Do you know Sylvester Stallone?"

"I haven't actually *met* him, no. Although I have been to Planet Hollywood."

"Bruce Willis?"

"Most of the stars I know are more . . ."

"Steven Seagal?"

"Bruce Lee?"

"Nah, he's dead, stupid."

Disappointment hangs in the air. Dr. Higgins smiles and rubs his hands together. "So, Mr. Case, say I want to get a start in the film business. Say I want to hobnob with the stars myself. How would I go about it? Would I need to start at the bottom and work my way up?"

"Yeah, that would be best."

"And what skills would I need to have?"

"Well you need a lot of interpersonal skills. There's a lot of networking. You have to be able to communicate your ideas with energy and passion. You need a lot of determination to succeed."

"And would I need to be able to *read and write*?" He looks pointedly around the group.

"Ah, well, yeah, I would say you would need to be able to do that."

Dr. Higgins nods, significantly. "I would need to be able to *read* and *write*. Does anyone else have any questions?" There are no more questions. "Well, let's all give Mr. Case a round of applause to thank him for coming along today."

As the others are filing out the door, one of the prisoners comes up to me. "Hey guv, you know about the Corolla?"

"Yes?"

"Get a steering-wheel lock. Dead easy, is Corollas."

Dr. Higgins brings another one over himself. He looks a little older than the others. His jeans are done up tight around his ribcage. He's wearing a shirt with long sleeves and a button-down collar, done up at the wrists and neck. His hair is slicked down flat, gleaming with oil, parted perfectly down the middle. His skin is incredibly pale. His eyes are a washed-out blue.

"This is Gerard," says Dr. Higgins. "Gerard is a fellow countryman."

"A New Zealander?"

"He's from New Plymouth. Aren't you, Gerard?"

Gerard shuffles his feet. He's obviously very shy. I'm trying to remember what he did.

"Hi, Gerard."

He mumbles something.

"Gerard has written a film script," says Dr. Higgins, significantly.

"Oh . . . really?" Oh, Christ. Just what I need.

"Well," says Dr. Higgins. "I'm sure you two have a lot to talk about. Gerard, you can take Frederick down to your cell if you like. Just come back to the office when you're finished." He winks at me as I follow Gerard down the corridor. He is wearing grandpa slippers and he shuffles along like an old man.

Gerard's cell is a tiny concrete slot with a two-tier bunk, a stainless-steel hand basin and lavatory, a high narrow window and spread-eagled pinups all over the walls. Gerard offers me a small chair. I take it. He sits on the bed.

"So," I say, "have you been here long?"

"Oh, not really." Gerard starts to roll a cigarette. He moves very, very slowly, as if he has all the time in the world. Which he probably has. "Just a year. Most of that on remand. I'm going to serve my sentence in New Zealand. They're going to fly me back."

"They're going to fly you back? To New Zealand?"

"Yeah, that's what they do sometimes. I'm really rapt, eh. Gonna be going home."

Gerard reaches under the bunk and pulls out a sheaf of pages. He hands it to me shyly. It's a screenplay all right. The layout appears to be more or less standard but it's handwritten. A tiny neat scrawl, dead straight, strong backward slope. One of the most basic rules of the trade is this: never read anything written in hand. Just don't do it. "Well, this is certainly weighty." It looks to be a good couple of hundred pages. Even allowing for the writing it must be well over-length. "When did you write this?"

"Oh, I've had lots of time, eh."

"What's it about?"

"It's the story of my life."

Of all my most unfavorites, prison scripts are absolutely the worst. They're generally all about how tough it is being in jail all the time when you could be out there having fun. There'll probably be a kid in it too. The kid will be in need of a father figure and suffering from a terminal disease and the criminal will end up doing one last job to save the orphanage. "Well, that certainly looks very interesting."

"I've put everything of myself into that. I've tried to trace the origins of my crime right back." And then he does something quite extraordinary. He blushes. He blushes right from the roots of his hair down to the neckline of his oversize white prison-issue T-shirt. He goes bright red and he hangs his head. "I killed the only woman I ever loved. That was my crime. She was the only one I ever loved and I killed her."

What do you say in a situation like this?

"And her kid too. Her unborn kid. It wasn't mine."

"It wasn't?"

"It was someone else's."

"Right."

"And then when I realized what I'd done I tried to kill myself."

"I see."

"It was heavy metal music. They put messages in it."

"In heavy metal music?"

"Yeah. They put these messages in the music, telling you to do things. You know, like telling you to kill people. It's actually the work of the devil."

"Oh really?"

"Yeah. It's actually the devil. People don't know, but it is. And that's where it all started to go wrong for me."

"I see." I stand. "Well, I'll certainly be glad to give it a read and . . ."

"And then there was Ted."

"Ted?"

"Yeah. He was in the SAS but he wasn't really. He only said he was. It was all lies, and that blurred the boundary between fantasy and reality still further."

"I see. That would be a problem."

"I've worked it all out. I've traced it right back. Right back to the very origins."

"Well, ah . . . well done."

"It took a long time, because when you follow it right back, it actually all traces back to the beginning of the world, and the birth of sin." He taps the screenplay. "It's all in here. I've put it all down."

"Well, I'll certainly look forward to . . ."

"'Cos it's in all of us, eh?"

"What is?"

"Sin."

I want to leave. I don't like it in here, I feel mildly insulted and I want to leave.

"Even in you." He looks up when he says this. It's the way he looks at me. His eyes are extraordinary. They're burnt-out blue with black exploded centers, like bomb-sites. "Yeah," he nods, slowly and definitely as if confirming something to himself, something he'd always suspected. "Even in you."

I look at my watch.

"But if I can figure it all out, then when I get out, I'll be okay."

"And when do you get out?"

"Ten years. So I need to be ready."

"Yes."

"Because I need to do something good. I've done a terrible thing, I've done a lot of terrible things and I need to do all I can to make up for it. And this is the only thing I can do. The only good thing." He blushes again and falls silent. He seems overcome. "Dr. Higgins said you could make my film."

"Did he indeed?"

"'Cos I really think I can save the world."

"You think so?"

"He's made his plans, you know? The devil. He made them a long time ago. He's been plotting and planning for thousands of years. The big takeover. He's taking over the world, he's twisting our minds. All of us. Even you. But this film is going to make the difference. It's going to win the war. Because that's where this war will be fought. In the minds of humanity. Can you help me? Can you help me save the world?"

---

Dr. Higgins finishes early on Thursdays. He walks me down the hill to the Sittlebury station and I buy him a pint in the local, which is a real, genuine, ye-olde place. You can tell the real places easily enough: they're the ones where you're constantly braining yourself on the ceiling beams. They never think of that when they're building the pretend places.

"Yes, the classics. It was the classics that did it for him. I put him onto the classics and he didn't look back. Brought him right back from the brink. He had such a thirst for learning." He sucks on his beer, perhaps by way of demonstration. I'm buying, by the way; I've just found out that he's Catholic, he's got six children, two at university. And you wouldn't believe how little a probation officer makes. Anyway, I've got a small fortune coming through in the next few days. It's like this, always. Like a drug. Reluctance, fear, the resolve to kick the habit. Then capitulation, self-disgust, followed by shameless gloating and anticipation. Ah.

"There's one thing I don't understand."

He looks up. There's a line of foam stuck to his whiskers. He looks like a stoat.

"I can't believe somehow that those guys are as dangerous as all that. They just seem so . . ."

"Dangerous?" He laughs. "They're not dangerous."

"So why are they in the Secure Unit?"

"The Secure Unit is for *their* protection. If they were on the main wing they'd be mincemeat." He sees my look of incomprehension. "They're the most vulnerable prisoners: the young, the small, the immature, the damaged. They're all guilty of sexual crimes, which makes them prime targets for the other prisoners. Robbers and thieves come over amazingly moral when confronted by a weedy rapist. So we separate them from the main population."

"Oh."

"We've got the other sort too, in A wing. The animals. I'll take you through some time. Some of those fellows, you don't go in the cell."

"It's hard to imagine those weedy little guys doing those terrible things."

"Yes. But that's so often the way of it. Of course the vast majority of them you could let out tomorrow. They'd be a danger only to themselves. There are others, however. Such as Gerard."

"Oh?"

He shakes his head sadly. "Gerard will never be released."

"Never?"

"Gerard's been with us for three years. Two of them on remand. He began his sentence last year. Once he's stabilized he'll be extradited back to New Zealand. We had a psychiatrist examine him only last week."

"So, you're going to move him?"

"Yes, he'll be going back to New Zealand. He'll spend the rest of his life in a maximum-security institution there."

"How will you get him there?"

"Fly him. A psychiatrist and two policemen will fly with him. He'll be heavily sedated."

"What do the flying public think of that?"

"They don't know. It happens all the time."

"God."

"Oh, yes. The airlines don't like handcuffs because it makes people nervous, so they do it with drugs: a chemical straitjacket. They dope them up, sit a policeman on either side, the psychiatrist to monitor the medication, and away they go."

He goes to get another round. I think about Gerard, about his hopes for the future—all illusion. He has no future. I think about his eyes. His bomb-site eyes. Dr. Higgins slides back into his seat, puts a full pint in front of me. "Yes, he's a very severely damaged personality, Gerard. Poor chap. He'd end up killing again, or killing himself. No doubt about that."

"But he seems so harmless and so . . . so sorry."

"Oh, he is. He's terribly, terribly sorry. He's haunted by what he did. He's horrified by it. He always has been. He's tortured by it. For the first year he woke up every night, screaming. Every night."

"Good God."

"He's been through torments you and I could never imagine. We had him on suicide watch for twelve months. He still isn't allowed shoelaces." I think of the grandpa slippers. Dr. Higgins pulls on his pint. "He's made a lot of progress lately. In prison he's in a controlled environment. Low stimulus. No decisions, no responsibility. But out in the real world he'd spiral down into the same delusional behavior that led him to offend. He'd meet someone, he'd become obsessed, he'd become paranoid and dangerous. It would happen all over again and he'd be utterly powerless to stop it. I could time it almost to the day." He sucks again on his beer.

"But he told me he'll be out in ten years."

"If I told him now that he'll never get out he couldn't take it. It would destroy him. He'd be lost in a permanent nightmare, he'd never stabilize again. It's vital to choose the moment to tell him the truth. There's plenty of time, after all. Once he's adapted to imprisonment, once he's established some sort of a life for himself, become institutionalized. The day will come, maybe five, six years from now. Maybe longer. One day, he'll be strong enough to face the truth." He looks at me keenly. "That screenplay. That's all he has, you know. That's what's got him this far. He's pinned all his hopes on it. All his dreams."

"Mm."

"A few words of encouragement, it would mean all the world to him."

"Well, I'll see what I can do."

Dr. Higgins sucks on his beer. "My job, you know, is very simple. It's my job to care." He glances at his cheap digital watch. "I'm so sorry, I'm going to have to dash. My wife is expecting me." He drains his beer, shakes my hand and is gone. I stay behind for a while. In my briefcase I carry the work of a man without a life. Dead but unburied, buried but undead.

## Chapter 7

I CHECK THE ADDRESS ON THE CARD. Sixty-nine Bishop's Prick Lane. Looks like the place all right. I approach the white-haired grandmother in the ticket booth. "Excuse me . . ."

She speaks without looking up from her knitting. "Yes, dear, that'll be six pounds, live sucking and fucking, on stage starting in five minutes, all right darling?"

"I'm actually looking for Melissa . . ."

"Six pounds, love, includes a free drink, up the pink staircase, starts in five minutes. There you go sweetness-heart, enjoy the show."

The pink staircase is very steep and narrow. Melissa said to come by any weeknight between seven and eight, which is happy hour. She didn't say anything about the six quid. The pink staircase seems to go on forever. It's very narrow and the steps are steep. I have to stop for a moment on the pink landing to catch my breath. My heart is heavy and hot in my chest, and it's making a different sound. Every time it beats there's a sort of squelching and then immediately after a squeak. It feels as if it's swollen. I'm still in my tweed suit and the pills are still in the top pocket.

After the pink landing, the painter seems to have given up. We switch to peeling black wallpaper. No more lurid posters either. I

drag myself up the last steps to the door, push it open. I'm standing in a long narrow room, about the size and shape of a railway
carriage. It's dark. Windows along one side have been painted out
with black paint. You can hear the rustle of the street below. Along
the other side is a bar. The surface is thick with grease and dust.
There's a row of spirit bottles on the back wall and a stack of
greasy glasses.

The room smells of bodily fluids, whiskey and hairspray. There's
a cracked mirror ball hanging from the ceiling. Bob Marley is
playing faintly from a hidden loudspeaker.

There's an entrance, covered with a black curtain, at the back
of the bar.

"Hello?"

No answer.

At the far end of the room are a few hard-backed seats. Between
me and the seats is a greasy, stained mattress. It takes up the entire
width of the room. It squelches as I walk across it. The carpet is so
sticky I can hear my shoes peeling away with every step. I sit for a
long time. It's getting hotter. The tweed is getting prickly.

There's a quiet noise and I look up. A man is standing behind
the bar. He seems to have appeared as if by magic. He's small,
pale and wiry, with a ginger mustache drooping either side of his
mouth like a seventies porn star. Watching me without looking at
me, he carelessly splashes a little Seven-Up into a clear plastic
cup and pushes it my way.

"Hi, I'm actually looking for . . ."

He doesn't answer. He doesn't even look at me. He leaves the
drink on the counter and disappears through a curtained doorway
behind the bar. I go over to the bar, ease myself into a stool. Time
passes. It's getting hot. I sip the Seven-Up. It's warm and flat. I feel
fidgety, then drowsy.

A woman, perhaps in her fifties, ginger-haired, overweight, with
a drooping face, comes out from behind the black curtain. She's

wearing a black toweling dressing gown. I glimpse leopard skin. Ignoring me, she looks around the room, sighs, then stumps back toward the curtain.

"Excuse me," I say.

She is gone. The man comes out again. He pours another Seven-Up, pushes it toward me. "That'll be seven pound."

"Sorry?"

"Seven pound."

"But I thought the drink was free."

He rolls his eyes and grits his teeth. "First drink's complimentary. You gotta buy at least one drink after that."

"Seven pounds for a glass of Seven-Up?"

"It's in the rules."

"Rules? What rules?"

"They're hung up in plain view for all to see."

"Where?" By now he is looking at me with passionate hatred, shaking with rage. I put the money on the counter. "I'm actually just looking for . . ."

He goes. Another twenty minutes passes. The reggae stops. By now it is really getting hot. I get up, squelch around the bar and put an ear close to the curtain. Not a sound. "Hello?"

No answer.

"Anybody there?"

The ginger-mustached man sticks his head out. He gives me such an evil look that I step backward. "Inna minute, all right? Just 'ang on a minute."

I go back to my table. I'm boiling hot, irritable and nervous. I don't know what the hell I'm doing here. I should leave. I really should leave. Suddenly the lights go out. I'm in complete darkness. I fight an urge to shout. My sense of smell sharpens and a thousand terrifying odors flood my senses. I am about to start feeling my way for the door when a spot snaps on, focused on the bed. The reggae comes back, much louder. Bob Marley is saying he's going to give someone some good good lovin'. The ginger-haired man and the ginger-haired woman saunter out from behind the curtain, both in G-strings. The man is flatfooted, small and wiry, with a tiny bottom. His skin is dazzlingly white, with such enormous ginger freckles on his shoulders, back, and upper arms that he could best be described as piebald. The woman is at least twice his size, roughly walrus-shaped, with a gigantic leopard-skin bra to go with the G-string.

The ginger-haired man glances at his watch, as the ginger-haired woman yawns, climbs out of her G-string and bra, lies down on her back, spread-eagled on the mattress, the top of her head pointing toward me. She needs her roots done.

The ginger-haired man yawns and casually flips off his G-string. He is already three-quarters erect. He coughs, spits on his hand and kneels between the ginger-haired woman's legs.

"No!" I squeak. "Stop!"

The man squints in my direction. The woman twists around to look at me, raising a hand to shield her eyes from the spotlight.

"You wanna show or dontcha?" says the man.

"I don't."

"What's your problem, then?" says the woman, in a nasty tone of voice.

"I'm . . . from New Zealand."

The man wipes his hands on the mattress and stands up. The woman gathers up her things and stumps out, muttering. The man goes over to the wall and flicks some switches. The room lights come back. He pulls a dressing gown out from under the bar, puts it on, and looks at me with folded arms.

"I could 'ave you arrested, you know."

"What for?"

"Wod'yer want?"

"I told you. I'm here to see Melissa."

The man scratches his pubes.

"Melissa. She said to ask for Melissa."

"'Ang on." He disappears.

More waiting. Finally he comes out again. "Follow me."

He disappears behind the curtain. I take a deep breath and follow him down a narrow corridor, painted black. A dressing-room door is ajar to one side. The ginger-haired woman is sitting at a makeup table. Then a flight of stairs, even narrower and steeper than the entranceway. Another door, another corridor, this one back to pink, with red lightbulbs and doors to either side.

The man gets chatty. "What's your name, anyway?"

"Frederick."

"Melissa, was it, Frederick?"

"That's right."

"All right Frederick, 'ere we go, Frederick, that'll be a hundred pounds, please, Frederick."

"But . . ."

Instantly he is trembling with rage. I pull out my wallet. I give him his money. He puts a hand on my shoulder and gently shoves me toward the last door in the corridor. "'Ave a nice time then, Frederick." He walks off.

It's a small room. The lighting is yellow. The ceiling is at an angle. There are batik cloths hanging on the walls. The air is sweet with cleaning products. New Age music. There's a bed: low, double and hard-looking. Beside it is a hand basin, a bidet and a tubular steel chair. On the chair is a lava lamp, a pump action K-Y jelly dispenser and an economy pack of condoms. Cross-legged on the bed, wearing a dressing gown, is the girl from the street. She smiles, a little cheesily. "Hi, Frederick, you made it, come on in." I step into the room. "Okay, so this is how it works. With Ernie, that was room hire. So for thirty minutes, you have a room. Now if you want something to go with the room . . . me, we can talk about that." Then, more gently, "Would you like to talk about that?" She lets the dressing gown fall from her shoulders, revealing some very spectacular underwear. She's perfect for what I have in mind. "Let me run you through the options. Option one, you can have the straight suck and fuck. That'll cost you a hundred. For another fifty you can have doggie. That's option two. Option three—that's another fifty—you get the works."

"Mind if I sit down?"

"Oh, sure, sit down."

"I really just wanted to talk for a couple of minutes. If that was possible."

She spreads her hands. "Cost you a hundred, in advance, but sure, no problem at all. If you change your mind, that's fine too. But do please remember: the clock *will* be ticking, and when the time's up, the time's up. And Ernie *will* come knocking. What would you like to do?"

"That sounds fine."

"Would you mind paying in advance, please?"

"Certainly." I pay the hundred. She thanks me politely, puts the money away, looks up brightly. She has much the same bed-side manner as Dr. McVeigh, only with smiles. "Would you like me to stay like this, or . . . ?"

"No, no. I've seen all I need to see, thank you."

She shrugs back into her dressing gown, takes out a cigarette, lights it and makes herself comfortable. She purses her lips to blow a thin stream of smoke in the direction of the tiny ventilation window. "So." She smiles. "What's on your mind?"

"I have a business proposition to put to you. I'm looking for a woman to accompany me on an all-expenses-paid holiday, to the South Pacific."

"I do do escort work, yes." There's now a cautious note to her voice. "If that's what you're asking."

"To an extent."

She shrugs.

"But I do have a number of specific requirements. It's a birthday party. Whoever accompanies me on this trip will be mixing with the film world's elite — film executives, actors, actresses, directors, producers. I need a companion who can plausibly play the role of my girlfriend in front of these people, many of whom are known to me personally, some of whom are close friends. In other words I need someone who can play the role of a reasonably well-educated, intelligent, socially adept young woman, who happens to think the world of me personally — and play it convincingly." I pause to let the point sink in. "I immediately thought of you, because I thought it would be a nice touch to bring a New Zealander."

She nods. "Anything else?"

"No sex."

She shrugs. "Sure, no problem — but no reduction."

"In public we'd have to pretend to be lovers. Kissing, cuddling, the odd peck on the cheek. Holding hands. No tongues."

She nods briskly. She certainly has a can-do attitude.

"Think you can do it?"

"I do it all the time. You happen to have come to the right person. I'm a part-time actress. Just part-time, but I've got big plans."

"An actress?"

"That's right. I'm working with Ernie."

"Ernie?"

"Guy that let you in. That's his wife, Mara. You would have met her too. They've been doing that act for thirty-five years."

"My God."

"Yeah, kinda sweet isn't it?" Melissa tips her head back and blows smoke at the windows. She thinks for a bit. She blows more smoke. "When do we leave?"

---

She waves good-bye at the door. I find my way down the pink corridor and down another flight of stairs marked EXIT, which take me down to a seedy nightclub. From the seedy nightclub I emerge in an empty cobbled alley at the back of a possibly Georgian structure. A light drizzle is falling. It's dark and raw. I notice a blue plaque on the brickwork by the doorway. KARL MARX FREQUENTED THIS KNOCKING SHOP. You've got to give the English this. They do have a sense of history.

## Chapter 8

**EXT. PLAIN OUTSIDE CITY—DAY.**
THE ELEPHANTS SHUFFLE RESTLESSLY, BRIGHTLY-
COLORED HOWDAHS PERCHED PRECARIOUSLY ON THEIR
BACKS. CLAD IN LION SKIN, THE PRINCE SHAZAMAN
LOOKS OUT ACROSS THE VALLEY TO THE CITY OF GRUZ.

<u>Prince</u>

Burn the houses. Kill the men. Kill the women.
Kill the children.

THE HORSEMEN ASSEMBLED ON THE HILL CHEER AND
CLASH THEIR SWORDS AGAINST THEIR SHIELDS. THE
ELEPHANTS TRUMPET IN FEAR. SHAZAMAN RAISES HIS
SWORD AND CHARGES DOWN THE HILL ON HIS WHITE
STEED. THE ARMY FLOWS AFTER HIM LIKE A BLACK
TIDE OF DEATH.

**EXT. CITY OF GRUZ—DAY.**
THE SOLDIERS OF SHAZAMAN RAMPAGE THROUGH THE
STREETS OF THE CITY, IMPALING, BURNING, SLASH-
ING, DESTROYING. CHILDREN ARE FLUNG INTO THE

FLAMES. WOMEN ARE DISEMBOWELED. MEN ARE CHOPPED
INTO PIECES. SHAZAMAN RIDES THROUGH THE MIDST OF
THE CARNAGE. HIS EYES ARE BURNING WITH THE LIGHT
OF BATTLE, WITH THE THIRST FOR BLOOD.

I have to say, Gerard's script is not quite what I expected. I've
skimmed through the first ten or so pages on the plane, while
waiting for my tomato juice. So far there's been no mention of a
boy at all, and certainly no terminal diseases, although there's
been plenty of terminating going on. I put the script away and
stretch.

———

We met at Heathrow. She was standing under the arrivals board in
her long green plastic mac, high boots and a red hat. My heart
sank as she gave me that same saucy little wave. I'd been half-
hoping maybe she wouldn't show; but there she is, relaxed, confident, fresh. Me, I'm a mess. It's six in the morning, I haven't had
time for coffee and it has now been over a week since my visit to
Dr. McVeigh. I haven't had a drink or a cigarette since. It's turning out to be extraordinarily difficult—not so much the with-
drawal symptoms, which, while pretty bad, are nothing compared
to the terrible waves of clarity that sweep over me suddenly and
unpredictably. It's awful. Outlines are becoming sharper. I hear
what people say. I understand. When I wake up in the morning, I
*wake up*. I see the whole day, laid out before me like a tube map.
I have perspective and insight. Ghastly. Like for instance, this
morning I sat bolt upright in bed at two o'clock. I'd only been in
bed for thirty minutes after an extended pedestrian tour of inner
London. I thought to myself, I'm going on holiday with a prostitute from Levin, whom I'm going to try to pass off as my girlfriend
in front of my pregnant ex-wife. It came to me, in a sudden blinding Apollonian burst, that this was not normal behavior. Yet only

last week it seemed, under the circumstances, like the obvious thing to do. I thought about calling and canceling, but I didn't quite have the guts to do that either. I couldn't face turning up alone. I just couldn't. I was damned if I was going to do that.

Despite appearances, when I come up to her she's complaining. "Christ, this is murder. I can't feel my legs. I've never been up this early in my life."

"I thought you were a country girl. Weren't you up at sparrow-fart every morning to milk the cows or something?"

"Levin is not the country. It's a town. A built-up area. There are no cows."

"Whatever. Let's check in, then we can find some coffee."

Checking-in is the usual business, except I notice immediately that people are looking at us. Us, a couple. Guys, sure, but not just guys, people in general. God, I exist. I remember that from when I'd walk down the street with Sophie. Glances, looks. You can feel them, casual glances sliding by, sticking for a moment, moving on. No big deal, but it's a nice feeling, a caressing people-are-noticing-you feeling. Gives things a boost. This morning I am, incidentally, apart from the size twelve eye-bags, a dead ringer for the guy with everything. Steerhide coat, slightly square trousers, nice shirt, hot girlfriend. You'd never guess, never, the seething turmoil on the inside. Who knows? Maybe you've already seen me. Maybe you're looking at me right now.

We go upstairs, pick out a franchise and find a table. Melissa is full of ideas. "We need to discuss our story."

"What did you have in mind?"

She holds up a finger. "First things first."

"I beg your pardon." I pull out the money. The terms have already been agreed. It's cash, in advance, one thousand pounds per week, plus per diems. No physical contact except in public, for the purposes of deception. All reasonable efforts to be made to establish pretense of genuine romantic involvement, as deemed necessary by the party of the first part (me). All expenses, including but not limited to travel, accommodation, incidentals and medical, to be my sole responsibility. In the event of travel delay, all additional costs to be my responsibility. She keeps her air miles.

She counts the money, puts it away and sits back, sucking her teeth. The money from my folks, by the way, came through like clockwork. I went into the bank and there it was, a nice fat little bundle of zeros. My heart sank and beat faster, all at the same time.

Meanwhile, Melissa pulls an exercise book out of her cabin bag, smooths it on the table. "Okay. Now. You want romance, right?"

"That's what I want."

"I've got some great ideas here. Fox hunting."

"I beg your pardon?"

"We met at a fox hunt. We were both protesters. One of the fox hunters attacked me with a riding whip. You leapt forward and dragged him off his horse, but he turned out to be the cousin of the local . . ."

I hold up a hand. Time for a hose-down. "People actually need to believe this, you know."

She waits.

"A lot of these people have met me before. Some of them even know me. I've never been near a fox hunt in my life."

"Sometimes people do unexpected things."

"No fox hunting."

She puts the paper away in silence. I've hurt her feelings. She sighs. "Okay, what do you want? What's the story?"

"Something simple. Direct. Credible. Boring. I don't know . . . Selfridges. The garden furniture section. We met there."

She looks puzzled.

"I go there all the time." Sophie knows that. She'll believe that. I go there to read scripts.

"What was I doing there?"

"Buying garden furniture, I suppose."

She spreads her hands. "All right. What else? Who am I? What am I?"

"What work experience do you have?"

"Apart from what I'm doing now? When I left school I worked a year in Kentucky Fried. Oh, and I nannied for a few months when I first arrived in London."

"But that's perfect."

"Kentucky Fried?"

"Nannying. It's perfect."

"I thought maybe I could have a wealthy background. You know, like my dad could be a shipping magnate or maybe an aircraft designer . . ."

"What does your dad actually do?"

"He runs the Toyota dealership in Levin."

"You're kidding!"

"No, why?"

"I know that place. On the corner just before you leave town?"

"That's the one."

"I used to drive past that place all the time. I lived in Wellington for a year."

She shakes her head. "Takes all types, I suppose."

"Anyway, that's perfect. Keep your dad, keep your mum. Keep everything. Just wind the clock back a couple of years. You're nannying in London. Use the same kids, the same family, everything. Make nothing up."

"Okay, smart-arse. What's a nanny doing buying garden furniture?"

"You were on your way to the CD section. You have to use your imagination sometimes."

"Where *is* the CD section?"

"Carry on straight past garden furniture and take a right at the donut outlet."

She makes some notes in her exercise book. I have to admit she's professional, even if her lips do move when she writes. "Now. How serious are we? As a couple?"

"We've only recently met."

"When?"

"Six weeks."

"So we're holding hands, we're staring into each other's eyes?"

"Yep."

She nods, and writes down "insatiable," if my lip-reading is up to scratch.

"But without being gross or tasteless."

"No tongues."

"Exactly."

"So when do we start?"

"I'm sorry?"

"Holding hands and staring into each other's eyes. You want to start now, or what?"

"Oh, God, no. Let's wait till LA at least. I couldn't face it this early in the morning. I haven't even finished my coffee. Anyway that'll do for now."

"I have a suggestion."

"Yes?"

"Lose the ponytail."

"Why would I want to do that?"

"Because it is completely and utterly noncredible that a girl like me is going to be attracted to a guy with a ponytail."

"Let's get one thing straight now, shall we? The tail stays."

She shrugs. "Your funeral."

"Anyway," I say, gruffly, "I have to work." Interview over. I pull out a romantic comedy. The hook of this one is a husband and wife who end up falling in love and making secret assignations with their respective chatroom e-pals. They don't know it, but they're actually chatting with each other. It will never work because it's basically a story about two cheaters. Cheaters can never win. When was the last time you saw a film about a woman who met some nice guy and left her nice husband for him and lived happily ever after and didn't get chased all over the place by some arsehole with a knife?

Seeing what I'm doing, Melissa retaliates by reaching into her cabin bag and pulling out a big fat crime thriller. I get a glimpse inside the bag; it's stuffed with paperbacks. "How many books have you got in there?"

"Oh, heaps. I read them so fast I need to bring a stack whenever I travel." She peers into my bag. "What have *you* got?"

"Christ, between the two of us we'll be lucky if we get off the tarmac."

---

Melissa groans in her sleep, tries to turn over and kicks me in the chest. I push her foot out of the way and try to read some more. We've been in the air for six hours. Future generations of intergalactic travelers are going to look back from the shopping malls of their vast intergalactic space liners in pity and horror at the conditions endured by late twentieth/early twenty-first-century travelers. The queues for the toilets, the lack of legroom, the appalling food. There's really only one way to do it. Start drinking early and keep drinking. The added advantage of this technique is that it enforces regular leg stretching exercise in the form of lavatory trips, thus reducing the chances of deep vein thrombosis. The mistake people make is not that they drink, it's that they *stop* halfway through the flight—and then they wonder why they feel terrible. Keep going, no matter what. That's my advice . . . Although there is another way. You could do what I do. Fly business. The first thing I did when I got the tickets from Charles was upgrade.

The first leg takes us London–LA direct. We spend a few hours in duty-free. Melissa buys makeup. By the time we find a hotel we're completely whacked. It's now four in the afternoon in LA and midnight in London.

After a vast meal of Hawaiian chicken legs with hash browns and onion rings, followed by three flavors of ice cream and a gallon of weak brown coffee, we retire. I take the first shower, then sit in bed reading a script, while Melissa disappears into the bathroom and reappears in a puff of steam, rosy-cheeked, hair falling around her shoulders. She sorts through her things, looking for underwear. I observe surreptitiously.

It has been said, by someone, that beauty is the promise of happiness. I wouldn't know. I approach happiness the way some people approach cigarettes: strictly other people's. If that is the case, however, I would say that Melissa promises happiness of a very specific kind. Big-breasted, wide-hipped, narrow-waisted, with flawless skin and masses of shiny, bouncy, curly chestnut hair, she's a walking male fantasy of the mainstream, mass-consumption, centerfold kind. Charmingly, she has one defect. Slightly plump knees. Also, without makeup, her eyes have all but vanished, and her chin is surprisingly pointed. She climbs into bed looking defenseless, like a small laboratory animal. She looks across at me, as if waiting for instructions, eyebrows raised. I cough and concentrate on my script. It strikes me that this is the first time I've shared a bed since Sophie split. For a moment I'm close to panic. Then I relax. It's okay. I don't have to do anything. I'm in charge. I am the customer, and the customer is always right.

"So," says Melissa, "this is it? Right?"

"This is it."

"No sex?"

"None whatsoever."

She shrugs. "Okay. I just don't want you to feel, like . . ."

"Like what?"

"Just feels a bit weird, that's all. Taking your money like that." She pulls out a paperback. "But we start tomorrow morning?"

"Start what?"

"Acting like a couple in public."

"We'll start tomorrow."

"Can I ask you one question?"

"Sure."

"Just out of curiosity. Why the no sex?"

"I happen to be a married man." I'm tired. I roll over.

"You're kidding?"

"Not at all. Does that surprise you?"

"Not that you're married, no. Where is your wife?"

"Probably on a plane."

"Does she know about this?"

"Certainly not. But she'll be on the island when we get there."

She scratches her head. "I'm sorry, I'm really not getting this. It's no sex because you're married. But you want me to pretend to be your . . ."

"We're estranged."

"Ah."

I put down my script. "Perhaps I should explain. I'm hiring you purely as a courtesy to others."

"Come again?"

"I'm going to a party where I'll be seeing my estranged wife and her boyfriend, plus a number of my friends and acquaintances. I don't want to go, but it's imperative that I see my wife, in person, as soon as possible. For reasons which I'd rather not discuss. If I turn up alone on the island, not only will my estranged wife be suspicious, and make it difficult for me to have access to her alone, but her boyfriend will most probably be territorial and aggressive, and all my other friends will feel obliged to be sorry for me, to give me special attention because I'm all by myself and Sophie's there and Matt's there, and so on. You know how people are. It would make them uncomfortable. It would make them feel they had to give me advice about my life and eye contact and hugs and pats on the shoulder and all sorts of other things I'd much prefer to avoid. But if I bring someone, like you, someone young and attractive, and I can give them the impression that I'm having a whale of a time, we can all just forget about it and get on with what we're doing."

"But don't you have anyone else you can bring? Like a normal regular girlfriend for example?"

"Well, there is someone, as it happens, but she'd expect me to sleep with her."

"So why don't you just sleep with her?"

"Because I'm married. Do try to keep up."

"So you've hired a hooker because you *don't* want to have sex?"

"That's right."

There's a pause. "You want me to put the light out?"

"No, that's okay. I've got a blindfold from the plane."

"I won't read for long."

"Well, good night, then."

"G'night."

I put on the blindfold. Melissa's fingernails scrape on paper. A page turns. I can hear her breathing. I think she breathes a little harder when she's concentrating. Another page turns. She seems to be turning pages every twenty seconds. "What are you reading?"

"Just another thriller."

"Another? You only started one yesterday."

"I only ever read thrillers."

I take a peek from under the blindfold. Her eyes are scanning vertically, barely tracking sideways at all. "I've never seen anyone read that fast."

"I took a speed-reading course once."

I slip the blindfold back in place. Melissa's fingernail scrapes on paper. I wait. I count. Twenty seconds later, her fingernail scrapes on paper.

I wake about eight the next morning after a long and complicated dream in which Sophie was trying to teach me to fly. I lie disoriented for a time, thinking I'm at home. Melissa is already in the shower. She's clearly a very clean person. She emerges in jeans and T-shirt. She looks bright and radiant. I take my turn and we go down to breakfast. Just before the lift doors open, Melissa turns to me. "Okay, big boy, ready?" She twines her fingers between mine and leads me casually out of the lift and across the restaurant floor. I'm a bundle of nerves. It's all I can do to keep from bumping into the tables. We pick a place near the bar. Melissa kisses me on the cheek and slips into her chair. She picks up a menu. "What are you having, sweetheart? Hungry?" She looks at me over the menu and bats her eyelids. Incredible.

After a rousing breakfast of hash browns, eggs over easy, sausages, bacon, toast, fried tomatoes, three gallons of very weak coffee and a glass of orange juice, we're ready for a day's sightseeing. We decide to hire a car and just drive around. The courtesy shuttle drops us at the car hire place, where Melissa picks out a huge Dodge saloon. It's far more than we need, and it's going to cost a fortune. I put it on the card.

We pull out of the hire garage, take a right, a left, change lanes, accelerate wildly, take another left, slam on the brakes, accelerate wildly, take a right, a left, two more rights, accelerate still more, and we're on the way to Disneyland. Melissa says that every New Zealand kid longs more than anything else to go to Disneyland and this is her chance to fulfill that dream. You grow up with Disneyland. Disneyland on the back of your cornflakes packets, Disneyland in the comics you read. A free trip to Disneyland for the lucky kid who sends in the right coupon. And then at school some rich kid shows up back from the Christmas holidays in a pair of Mickey Mouse sunglasses talking about Space Mountain, and you just die with envy.

I was that rich kid. I don't *want* to go to Disneyland—I've already been, three times. I'm hanging out for the La Brea Tar Pits. Throughout my childhood I was haunted by an image, from *The*

*Children's Illustrated Encyclopedia of Fates Worse than Death*, of a life-size model mother mammoth up to her knees in tar, her helpless baby bellowing from the bank as Mum disappears into the morass. I wanted to go, but we never got to the pits because every time we went through LA we naturally went to Disneyland. This is a perfect opportunity to reconnect with some childhood fears and I'm in exactly the right frame of mind for some gratuitous pathos but Melissa's mind is made up, it's the Magic Kingdom or bust. In all conscience, I feel I cannot deny her. Besides, she's driving.

Melissa holds out a small square of blotting paper. It has a Mickey Mouse face printed on it. "Want one?"

"Oh my God. You took those through customs?"

She shrugs.

"Where did you hide them?"

"A safe place."

"Jesus. Promise me you won't do that again."

"Do you want one or not?"

"We're going to Disneyland as it is. Isn't that enough for you?" The last time I dropped a trip I remember spending several hours watching neon Mickey Mouses crawl across the walls. I don't even like Mickey Mouse.

Melissa shrugs. "Whatever. I've already taken mine."

We drive in bruised silence. I wonder if I'm getting on Melissa's nerves. Young people can be very difficult. They have no idea, really. They *sound* like grown-ups, they have the vocabulary, they *look* like grown-ups, but in actual fact they aren't. I actually think that having a real girlfriend this age would be unbearable. My absolute most unfavorite story cliché of all time is the one the French love to death. You know the one: the clapped-out fucked-over-by-life middle-aged mojo-less guy like me who ends up, by some colossal unlikely concatenation of contrived events, stuck in close proximity with an incredibly hot spunky young gamin with spiky hair and nose rings and way too much attitude. She, utterly inexplicably, finds him sexy, reaches out and touches him in some deep and amazing and mildly pornographic way and then either fades away into the ether or dies of a drug overdose while he rises up, throws away his hairpiece and walks, wiser and happier. Of course "wiser and happier" is an oxymoron, anyway. This is generally just after the scene where he takes her to the opera and she gets through two boxes of Kleenex before the interval that is supposed to prove that she isn't just some hard-hearted slag.

"So listen. How old are you?"

"Old enough, granddad."

"You don't find me sexy, do you?"

She looks at me. "Professionally speaking, you're a big turn-on."

"But personally speaking?"

"So where is *this* leading?"

"Relax. I just need to be sure you don't have some sort of sick secret thing for forty-two-year-old balding fattish guys. Reassure me, here."

"Be reassured. Be very reassured."

"That's all right then." I have a morbid fear of cliché. I also have a morbid fear of death. Which is the ultimate cliché, after all. Surely. "Just to be on the safe side, remind me never to take you to the opera."

"Consider it done."

I look out the window. I love driving in America. The freeway is big and fast, if a little lumpy at times. But it's the cars: they're big and fast and not at all lumpy. They're fantastic. They're huge turbo-charged supersonic lounges. The perfect car for the man who dislikes driving. You're hardly there at all. Everything is electric. There's cruise control and climate control and every other sort in between. Yes, everything is under control.

Let me just point out here too that I love Americans. I really do. I didn't think I would, but I do, and this is even from *before*

September 11. Those Americans, they're okay. Doesn't matter what sort of an arsehole they've got for president, person-for-person I like them. It's endearing too that the nation which invented jeans has such trouble looking good in them. I think they must be the worst jeans-wearers on the planet. And I respect that. You look around you and you realize you're surrounded by ordinary, honest, bad jeans-fitting folk who are just as much the victims of rampant American imperialist capitalism as anyone else. Hell, more so—they're closer to it than anyone else. Me, I may not be able to hide but at least I can run.

Nonetheless, despite all these feel-good vibes, as the what-me-worry landscape of suburban LA slides by the window I'm starting to feel maybe just a little somber. A little mellow. "Do you ever get the feeling that we're all living on borrowed time?"

"Well, we *are* all living on borrowed time."

"So you do get that feeling?"

"No, never."

"You know, last time I was out this way I was getting married."

"Really?"

"Yeah, we drove to Las Vegas."

"Oh, that's nice."

"Yeah, it was nice."

"Did you have one of those theme weddings?"

"Well, we wanted satanic but they didn't have that so in the end we settled for the no-frills version because we were running short on time."

It was really very sweet. The celebrant said a few things like Frederick are you into Sophie, and Sophie do you really dig Frederick, and we said we did, and we exchanged rings, then it was congratulations, you kids are married. We kissed and signed on the dotted line. I've got the video somewhere.

There's a silence while Melissa concentrates on her driving; we're being squeezed between a sixty-foot limo and something straight out of Monster Truck Madness. "Just think," she says. "Bruce Willis could be in that limo, and we'd never know."

"They all take helicopters nowadays."

She shakes her head. "It's true what they say. This really is the land of dreams."

"Do they say that?"

"Of course."

"Maybe we should have gone to Universal Studios."

Melissa changes lanes and the limo speeds past. "So what happened with you two, anyway? Why did she leave you?"

"It's kind of complicated. Infidelity, I suppose you could say."

"You were unfaithful?"

"Why do people always assume that? *She* was unfaithful."

"So you left her?"

"No. She left me. First she was unfaithful, then she left me. I did try to be unfaithful, immediately after finding out that she had been unfaithful. But I failed. And then she left me so I didn't really have the opportunity to try again."

"That's pretty sad."

"We all have our stories to tell."

"You know, infidelity in a relationship is really only a sign that other much more fundamental stuff isn't being addressed. She was probably seeking to end the relationship for other reasons but unable to take the first step."

"Thank you for that stunning insight. I'll treasure it always."

"Have you seen *Shag City*?"

"No, I haven't."

"You should go and see it. It's brilliant. And that's what it's all about, exactly that. It's about this woman, she's married and she's a highly successful . . . well, I won't tell you the story. It'd spoil it."

"As a matter of fact my wife is Sophie Carlisle."

"You're kidding!"

"I'm afraid not."

"Your ex-wife?"

"My estranged wife."

"The one we're going to see?"

"That's right."

"*The* Sophie Carlisle?"

"That's the one."

"She's the one that we're going to be seeing? On this island?"

"Correct."

"But . . . she's my personal hero!"

"Possibly you mean heroine."

"She's a genius."

"How so?"

"She's finally achieved what sex-filmmakers have dreamed of for generations. She's broken down the artificial distinction between pornography and art."

"I thought you weren't interested in art."

"I'm not, but I'm interested in pornography. I've seen *Shag City* four times. It's brilliant. It's absolutely brilliant. I dream of making films like that—well, sort of like that, only hotter."

"Hotter?"

"More sex."

"Well, I'm glad you enjoyed it."

"And it's supposed to have many parallels with her own . . ." Her face falls.

I clear my throat tactfully. "It's true that there are some superficial similarities between the character of the husband in the film and me, but no, it is not based on me. Nor is it an accurate account of my life with Sophie. Nor was it ever intended to be." Melissa falls very silent. She stares at the road. "The auto-castration scene, for example, is entirely fictional."

"Right."

"As are the multiple infidelities. In real life there was only one. Although on the other hand it is true that I own a green-handled kitchen knife. It was a wedding present in fact. The script was written by a personal friend so little details like that are bound to pop up. And I guess it is true that my career has yet to take off."

Melissa's eyes are still on the road.

"Also, I never tried to drop a piano on her. Nor did I trash the apartment, torch the car or strangle the dog. And I would *never* do that with a cigarette butt. I don't even smoke."

"I thought you hadn't seen it."

"I haven't. But you pick up bits and pieces."

"So . . . what *did* you do?"

"When I found out?"

"Yeah?"

"I did the dishes."

"Wow, that's fairly fictionalized."

"As I say. That's the magic of Hollywood. Oh, hell, give me the tab."

"You sure?"

"Sure, I'm sure." She hands me the tab, then pounds the steering wheel. "Wow. I can't believe it. I'm going to meet Sophie Carlisle! Outta sight! What's she like?"

"A lot shorter than she looks on screen."

"What else?"

"She can seem aloof and distant at first. But then if you dig deeper you'll find that at heart she's cold and unapproachable."

"Maybe I'm asking the wrong person."

"I'm just kidding. She's fine. We're best mates, really." I look at the tab. I put it in my mouth, chew and swallow. Anyway, I've never heard of LSD giving you hypertension. "But here we are talking about me. I'm sure you must have a story or two of your own."

"Oh, not really."

"Come on. I bet you meet all sorts of weird, fascinating characters, plucked straight from the pages of fiction."

"Oh, it's pretty routine really. They come in, they climb on, they get in, they get off, they get out."

"Well, what about you, then? Did you have a terrible childhood and a broken home and all that?"

"No, it was totally middle-class, eh. I suppose my brother was a bit of an arsehole."

"What did he do?"

"Sometimes he used to call me names, and once he drowned my guinea pig. He said it was an accident and he was just trying to give him a bath, but I don't believe him."

"Were you abused as a child?"

"I don't *think* so."

"So why do you do it?"

"The money's good and the hours are short."

"But how can you touch the flesh of a stranger? Repeatedly? Experience physical intimacy with someone you don't even know? Someone who may not even shower regularly? Not to mention the risk of disease?"

"I'm not squeamish. And of course you take precautions."

"God. I can't imagine it."

"But I won't be in the game much longer. I'm just doing this to tide me over."

"Isn't that what they all say?"

"Isn't that what *everyone* says?" She has a point. "What I really want to do is get into porn."

"Don't aim too high, will you?"

"I've already made a couple of movies. Ernie says if they come out all right I might get a contract."

"The very best of British to you."

"What's the matter? Can't deal with it?"

"I'm just amazed that you aspire to be a porn actress. You might as well aspire to . . . well . . ."

"To be a hooker?"

"Well, yeah. You've got a brain. Get a real job."

"Ernie says it's like the circus. We're all freaks and outcasts. Plus you have to run away to join."

"Ernie may have something there."

"Anyway, you think I'm weird, what about you?"

"Excuse me, I think you're forgetting something."

"What's that?"

"The customer is always right."

She shakes her head. "You're right, I do meet all sorts of weird characters."

We drive in silence for a while. There is no turnoff that says "Disneyland." I think there should be. Instead, however, we're looking for South Jubilee Drive. As chief navigator I'm reading the signs as they flick by but I still haven't seen what we're looking for. I look at my watch. It's been an hour and a bit since we left LA.

"Don't you think we should be there by now?"

"Relax." But Melissa sounds tense.

Another twenty minutes go by. "Are you feeling anything yet?"

"I'm fine." Definitely very tense.

"Because we really need to get off the freeway before it starts."

"I know that. Just watch the signs." Melissa lights a cigarette.

"Isn't this a no-smoking vehicle?"

"Just watch the signs." I watch the signs. They're green signs. Large, flat, round edged. There's writing on them. White writing. I watch the writing and the signs but I feel that there is something else I should be doing. I realize I haven't been reading the signs. I've just been looking at the signs. I look across. Melissa is staring at the road, hunched forward. A huge 4x4 blasts past. There's a GOD SAVE AMERICA sticker on the bumper and the stars and stripes flutter stiffly in miniature from the aerial.

A horn blares.

"Was that us?" Melissa glances at me and back to the road.

"I don't know. I think maybe it was."

"We have to pull off."

"Which lane are we in?"

"I don't know."

"Is there anything to the right?"

"No, nothing. Wait!" A long low white sedan cruises by on the inside. It's unbelievably long. "There's Bruce again. I think he's following us."

"The lane, Frederick, the lane!"

"Yes. Now."

"Now?"

"Go!" Melissa swerves right, hits the shoulder, corrects and recovers. God, this is the life. Irresponsible driving in LA! Fact and fiction merge seamlessly. "There! There! The exit! Go! Go! Go!" Melissa takes the exit, edges through a ninety-degree spiral and starts to pull over. My momentary exultation evaporates.

"That was it? South Jubilee?"

"I don't know. I forgot to read the sign. Actually I don't think I can *read* anymore."

Melissa stops the car. "I don't think I can *drive* anymore." We sit in silence. "Wow, that stuff comes on fast, doesn't it?"

I look around. My face feels large and reddish, like one of those giant Doris plums. Wherever we are, it isn't Disneyland. On the passenger side, right outside my window, is a chain-link fence. On the other side of the fence is waste ground for a few hundred yards, and then the freeway overpass. On Melissa's side, across the road, is a Red Roof Inn. "Let's ask at the hotel over there."

"I don't want to drive."

"We can't leave the car here."

"I'm not driving."

Where is the reckless overconfidence of youth when you need it? "All right, shove over." It's simple, I tell myself. I put the car in gear. I start the engine, I . . . no. I start the engine, *then* I put the car in gear . . . "I can't do it either."

"Oh, shit."

"Maybe we should just sit here."

"For six hours?"

"We could listen to the radio."

"We're supposed to be going to Disneyland, not sitting in an empty lot listening to classic hits for six hours." We lock up the car and cross the road on foot. Fortunately there's not much traffic.

I don't know if the hospitality industry is permitted to Jehovah's Witnesses, but the guy behind the desk at the Red Roof Inn sure looks like one. He has a white shirt, a name tag and a very short haircut. I can't read the name tag. I decide to let Melissa do the talking. It's uncanny how normal she sounds. She sounds so normal I want to scream. She's asking for directions to Disneyland. The guy comes to the door with us and points down the road. There's something sinister and wrong about all this. About five hundred yards away is a huge roller-coaster structure silhouetted against the skyline. It's so huge and obvious I can't believe we didn't see it before. I find myself concluding that it must have been built between the time we entered the Red Roof Inn, and the time we left again. How long were we in there?

"Over there," says the guy. "Can't miss it, folks."

"Thanks," says Melissa.

"You're welcome, have a nice day." They actually do say that here. They say it all the time. It's the worst thing about cliché. The cliché *is* the reality. The guy goes back inside.

"Shouldn't we tip him?"

"Don't be silly. Come on."

Still, neither of us wants to drive so we decide the car will just have to be okay where it is. It's very big and blue and it's hunched over on the side of the road tipped at a crazy angle. Will we ever see it again? We start to walk toward Disneyland. The footpath is wide and safe. The sky is a stonewash-denim blue. At the end of the block we come upon a sign. I can't read it, but Melissa says it's the way. We cross the road, turn right and keep walking. There's a huge wall on our right and from behind comes the sound of bag-pipes and snare drums and the hissing of a billion snakes, although I could be wrong about the snare drums.

We walk on. I look at my watch but I can't read that either. It seems to be telling me a mystic tale of ineffable significance. At long, long last we come to a gate. There is no gatekeeper. That seems to be significant too. We pass through the gate, joining a thin but steady stream of foot traffic. We follow the crowd. They're all headed the same way. Suddenly it hits me. This is a pilgrim-age. People come here from around the world in ritual headgear, thronging to the Happiest Place on Earth. It is here that the essence of the Western dream is realized, that the spiritual and the commercial become one.

We pay our money at the booth.

We pass the turnstile.

We have entered the City of God.

Melissa looks around. Her eyes are shining. "Oh, man, this is so cool. Let's go on Space Mountain." Perfect happiness floods my entire being. I hold Melissa's hand as she leads me through the ranks of the blessed. We queue. We shuffle. We queue some more. Again we shuffle, again we queue. At length, we enter a long brightly-lit corridor. It seems to be some sort of space station. The people around us are all in baseball caps. They're younger than us. Their jeans don't fit and their T-shirts are too big and the girls have too much makeup and they're spotty, but that's okay. Everything's okay. This is the Land of the Free. These people are not American. They're Polish, Irish, Russian, Lithuanian, Korean. You can see it in their jeans. They're making the dream happen.

We shuffle forward, past illuminated panels depicting space flight. Space, the final frontier. One day, far in the future, when population pressure is high enough and the commercial incen-tives are in place, vast ships will spread out across the galaxy in search of new worlds and cheap real estate.

We emerge on a high mezzanine-floor looking down into the

launch bay. The cars arrive, the passengers disembark, the cars move forward, the passengers embark. We shuffle forward, the line moving faster and faster the closer we get. I follow Melissa into the front car. We sit on hard curved plastic seats. Ahead of us is blackness. From somewhere out of the blackness comes the sound of wailing. Just as a solid metal bar clamps down on my shoulders, locking me helplessly in place, I realize with a sickening lurch of sheer terror, I've been tricked.

Horror.

The car lurches forward with a violent jerk, stops abruptly, starts a long clanking climb up a near-vertical slope. It is dark. Smoke curls from hidden vents as we pass. Higher we climb, and higher.

Torment. We are whirled and buffeted by terrible winds in the darkness. There is no up, no down, no left, no right. There is only suffering and a profound sense of separation from God, from light, from one's internal organs. My spine is broken in at least three places. My head slams against the headrest. Strange moons flash past. The souls of the damned wail in my ears. I'm going to throw up.

The car slows, violently, emerges from darkness. I climb out after Melissa and stagger down the exit tunnel and out into the dazzling light of day. Waves of nausea travel from the soles of my feet to my scalp. I want to find a bush and crawl under it. Young people in baseball caps and ill-fitting jeans are everywhere. They are talking. They keep glancing at me and whispering.

"Wow, that was so cool. What did you think?"

"That was the worst experience I've ever had in my entire life."

"I thought it was good."

"Pure, unadulterated suffering."

"So you don't want to go round again?"

"I would rather be hung, drawn and quartered."

"Well, I'm going to go again."

"You're not going to leave me here alone are you?"

"You'll be okay. Go get a hot dog. I'll meet you back here in an hour, then we can do something else."

**EXT. DISNEYLAND—DAY.**

SEEMINGLY UNCONCERNED SHE WALKS OFF AROUND THE
CORNER TO REJOIN THE QUEUE. HE SITS ON A NEARBY
PLASTIC BUCKET SEAT AND RESTS HIS HEAD IN HIS
HANDS. HE'S ALONE IN DISNEYLAND. SOMETHING
APPEARS TO BE RESTING ON HIS LEFT SHOULDER. HE
TWISTS AND TURNS TO LOOK BUT HE CAN'T SEE ANY-
THING. HE CLOSES HIS EYES.

**INSERT:**

ROBES FLAPPING IN THE DESERT WIND.

**INSERT:**

EYES. THE EYES OF THE PROPHET. BLUE, BOMB-SITE
EYES: BURNT OUT. BY SIN. THE EYES OF THE
PROPHET. BLUE BOMB-SITE EYES: ZEROING IN. ON
SIN.

<u>Frederick</u>

God, the eyes.

HE OPENS HIS EYES. PEOPLE IN BASEBALL CAPS AND
BADLY-FITTING JEANS ARE HUDDLED TOGETHER IN COR-
NERS, WHISPERING AND POINTING. SINNING.

I get to my feet. The something, which weighs heavy on my left shoulder, which has been sitting there for all this time, I know at last what it is. It's Death, not any old death, either, but my death. I get up and walk, Death perched as easily on my shoulder as a parrot on his pirate. Death is real. The cliché is the reality.

I look around me. Death looks around too. The confections in plastic and steel, the people queuing, in baseball caps and ill-fitting jeans, to ride the mini-motorway over there to my left, to zip along in tiny cars, nose-to-tailing under a baby overpass just exactly like the monster freeway they all took to get here; the hot dog stands, the vast domed structures, brightly-colored, the old-world vehicles, Pluto over there signing autographs with a giant white-gloved hand: it strikes me with such force that I stagger backward. I clap my hand to my forehead. Light pours into all the hidden spaces. Blinding, hideous clarity, more clarity than a human heart can stand. Death has to cling on tight as I fall to my knees there in the bright courtyard outside Space Mountain, passers-by looking on, curious. Christ, God, Jesus, all the saints and blessed martyrs. The most appalling fiendish twist of all. The truth about Disneyland, about its mystique, its strange attraction is that Disneyland is REAL.

*Chapter* 9

TAMINTHA HAS A PLACE IN THE COUNTRY. It's an old nine-teenth-century rectory, with a twelfth-century wing. The main building is big, gray, square and solid. Slate roof, stone floors, mullioned windows. Freezing in winter. There's a tennis court, several acres of fields, a defunct orchard, a trout pond half-choked with pond weed; home to a family of ducks and six trout—all called Simon. You can't tell them apart anyway. Over the dry stone wall at the back of the house is the graveyard of a medieval church. Jumbled headstones, eroded gargoyles and hanging festoons of dark glossy-green ivy. Crows call from the oak trees and wheel heavily in the cold air, flocking, black against the steel-gray sky.

Come with me now, as we vault the dry stone wall (easy does it), and approach the ancient church. Noseless knights gaze down serenely from the portico. There's an old yellowing sign pinned to the door advising that the Bosnian Children's Relief Fund is still looking for items of warm winter clothing in good condition, especially in smaller sizes. Pinned above it is a newer sign advising that the Afghan Famine Relief Fund is still looking for tins. The interior of the church is surprisingly small, like a child's church. Slanting shafts of bejeweled light strike the stone flags from the high narrow stained-glass windows. The air is cool. There is quiet and peace here, total separation from the hurly-burly of contemporary life. It's whole, untouched, and maybe just a little bit sad. Let us take a pew. Let us sit in peaceful contemplation.

The fourteenth-century wing of the rectory is the same age as the church. It abuts the Victorian wing to form the short stroke of an L. It is Tamintha's personal obsession. It took her six years of labor, red tape and unthinkable expense to transform it from what it was when she bought it—a roofless pile of very old stones with a sign saying DANGER KEEP OUT—to what it is now: a rabbit warren of odd-sized rooms, turrets and basements, a beautiful winding stone staircase, a second-story doorway opening into thin air, and a magnificent banquet hall complete with rush-and-hound–ready stone floor and a high ceiling supported by massive beams in genuine French oak—there was a particularly vicious round of continental storms that year and it was cheaper to import. You know it's real—real stone, real oak. It's the original building, rebuilt. It's real, but it isn't.

I'm in a four-poster bed with a lumpy mattress and a three-foot pile of duvets and blankets. As long as I don't move, I'm warm. My breath is steaming around me. It's eight-thirty a.m. I'm feeling peaceful but dejected and soon I'm going to be hungry. Time to be getting up. I put one foot on the floor. Good God almighty. It's a stone floor and it's so cold it burns like hellfire. I pull my foot back in, lie still, and listen. I can hear nothing. No footsteps, no voices. No dogs, no cats. No lowing cows, no babbling brooks, no jets overhead. I'm at the very far end of the medieval wing, in the turret room. I could scream my head off and no one would hear me. I could starve up here, and who would know? Who would care? I am lonely and bereft. I crave human company. I need food, sympathy. But the first thing is to wash and dress. The en suite bathroom hasn't been connected up yet and the nearest shower is a thousand miles away, next to the kitchen. The logical thing is to stay here and starve to death. I wrap my feet in a duvet, hop across the room, gathering up clothes and shoes.

I pause at the top of the stone spiral staircase. I can hear nothing. There's a charming little window set in a deep stone sill and I can look out through the sinuous thorned curve of a climbing rose onto the orchard. Downstairs people will already be in the kitchen, rugged up in big woolly oatmeal cable-knit sweaters and Timberland shoes, smoking drugs and drinking coffee and eating poached eggs on toast and planning walks that they will probably never take. I breathe deeply.

Tamintha hails me chummily from over by the Aga. "Have some porridge."

"Maybe in a bit. Hi, guys."

The film types wave and smile. There's an unshaven one, a shaven one, and an in-between. Also, there's Ella and Russell over by the fire, and I go over. Ella and Russell are our best friends. Ella has their two-month-old baby in her arms, Russell is sitting next to her, bending forward and making coo-coo noises. It's very nice. They don't seem to be aware that there's anyone else in the room. The baby's name, for some reason, is Brian. Sophie and I are the godparents, something which was arranged just last night.

Some babies have an ancient, wise-beyond-their-years look, a sort of Buddha-like calm. Brian doesn't really have that look. He has more of a middle-aged harassed-dope look. He has the body of a sumo wrestler with two tiny bright blue astonished eyes drowning in a massive head. Bluish veins crisscross his skull. He looks like something from *Beneath the Planet of the Apes*. His fist is in his mouth, up to the wrist. Russell and Ella gaze at him with rapt admiration. It's true what they say. Even the ugliest baby in the world is the most beautiful baby in the world.

"Hey, Brian."

I want one. I've known this for some time, actually. I didn't realize this happened to men. It does. I see a baby, and I want one.

It's a little bell, ringing, back of the head. Ring-a-ding-ding. Every time.

Russell grins. "I think he recognized your voice."

"What makes you say that?"

"He was looking around, sort of." Russell wants me to have a baby too. He really wants me to have a baby. He's desperate for me to have a baby. If Sophie and I have a baby, now, then we can stay pretty much in step and be couples with babies together. We can hang out at the playground, spell each other with babysitting, share a world view. Otherwise, and Russell senses this keenly, we're on divergent paths.

"He seems very alert this morning."

"It's the country air. It stimulates him."

I breathe in. It's the smell, isn't it? It's the smell of those babies, it's just incredible. Like fresh-baked bread. You just want to eat them. "Anyone seen Sophie?"

The unshaven film type looks up from teasing the dog with a piece of bacon. His name is Rufus. He's huge, yellow and shaggy. That's the dog. The film type is called Boris. He has something technical to do with coordinating the marketing of prerelease publicity campaigns. He's obsessed with Sophie. He invites her to lunch all the time and keeps dropping by on Wednesday mornings around ten-thirty in the hope that I'm at the office. It's okay. He doesn't stand a chance—I'm never at the office. Besides, he's too short and he wears his jeans too tight and his shirts too loose. Sophie likes him though. She's being mates with him. He and I go out for a beer too from time to time and he surreptitiously pumps me—about Sophie. I don't mind.

"Sorry, haven't seen her this morning." Boris goes back to the dog. He makes a point of never knowing where Sophie is. Sort of a courtesy to me. Instead, Tamintha answers. "She's checking the orchard, I think."

"What for?"

"Trees?"

I put on a Barbour and a pair of gumboots from the communal store near the backdoor. I slip out, closing it quickly to keep out the cold. Rufus slips out too, and lopes ahead. He's a great lolloping hound, half Irish setter, half cow. I put my hands in my pockets to keep them warm and schlep across the courtyard.

Sophie has just got back from shooting *Shag City*. She flew in from LA just last Thursday, and for those two days she's been quiet and distant. Withdrawn. Jet-lagged, tired out, wrung out. She's always like this when she gets back from a job. She'll recover.

I have a plan. It's over, I'm telling myself. The whole thing is over. I'm going to draw a line under it. I tried drawing a line *at* it, but that didn't work, so now I'm shifting the line. I'm going to put the whole thing behind me and I'm going to start again. I'm going to tell Sophie that, and I'm going to tell her that if she's willing to put the whole thing behind her, then I'm willing to put the whole thing behind me. I'm going to tell her I'm willing to quit the film business and get a proper job. Whatever it takes. The time has come. I want us to have a child. "I want us to move forward." I'm going to use that phrase. I'm going to drop it in at the right moment. I can feel it on my tongue, smooth and heavy.

I come around the corner of the dry stone wall. I stop. Straight ahead is the entrance to the old orchard: a gap in the wall and a wrought-iron arch. A crow croaks. To my left, over the dry stone wall, is the graveyard. I lean against the wall. I run a hand across the stone. Rufus comes lolloping back to check on me. He tosses my hand on the end of his nose.

I take a couple of breaths. I'm not scared, not exactly, but I'm pretty excited. This is going to be a big moment. This is going to be a moment to look back on. I know that already, whatever happens. I'm going to say it again. Let's have a kid. Kid. I'm going to lay down an ultimatum. I go on through the arch and cross the orchard. Apple trees all over the place. Shiny bark. She's right

over the other side, sitting on the dry stone wall, swinging her legs.
She's looking out across the valley. It's a peaceful view: rolling
green hills, the odd cow. One of the big shocks I got when I came
to England was that they do actually have grass over here. Grass,
cows, trees, everything. You could walk a whole day out here, and
not a single dark satanic mill in sight. I'm walking up behind her.
She still hasn't heard me approaching. She's just sitting there,
swinging her legs, looking out at the countryside, and coming up
behind her I'm the future. I'm the juggernaut future, I'm
progress, I'm coming up behind and I'm going to change everything forever.

---

After the big fight, we pretended nothing had happened. We didn't
talk about it. We didn't even say sorry. We couldn't. We'd taken
positions. We'd dug in. It was trench warfare. The script went
through a few more drafts and I didn't read any of them. I never
asked how it was going. I never asked anything. She never told
me. Sometimes she'd get phone calls: Matt would call, or Janine
would, or someone. Janine I could stand, even Matt ("Hi, Frederick, howya doin'?"). Matt was always insufferably cheerful and
friendly. But it was the Someones, they were the ones I couldn't
stand. I never got used to those Someones.

"Someone on the phone."

"Who?"

"Didn't say."

They call, the Someones, any hour of the day or night. You
might be eating, you might be sleeping. "Is Sewphie there,
please?" Always this impeccable plummy accent. Tens of thisands
of pinds in public school education and they haven't even got the
basics of telephone etiquette. I mean, *what* do they think? *Who* do
they think?

Six weeks later she has her bags packed, the door is ajar and a black cab is coming in ten. I have that long to say something. She's going to be away for three months shooting in Australia and I know I have to say something. I want to say something, I just don't know what. I get up and I head straight for the dishes.

Sophie comes in. She stands behind me. There's a long, long silence.

"If I kiss someone for a role, do you have a problem with that?"

"With or without tongues?"

She ignores this. She waits.

"I've never liked it. I put up with it, sure."

"What's the difference?"

"The difference?" This is my chance. This is my chance to say something. I know that. "What's the difference? You're asking me what's the difference?"

"Yes."

"The difference is obvious."

There's a toot outside.

"Look," she says.

"Taxi's here," I say.

There's a respectably long pause. "Yeah," she says.

"See you."

"See you."

I heard the door shut. I heard the taxi drive away. I really didn't like that last "see you." It was barren and windswept, a place where nothing can grow.

For the three months that Sophie was away on the shoot, I became a porn fiend. Seemed like the thing to do. Just my way of taking an interest in her work. I went to a little place in Soho. In the end I got to know the guy behind the desk quite well. His name was Gary and he wore a lot of silver. He was tall and slender and pale-looking and he had very fine features. Big eyebrows, arching. I liked him. I remember the first time I went into the shop, he smiled. That was a shock, for a start.

"Wot you lookin' for then?" Startled, I looked around. The instant before he spoke I'd been staring, open-mouthed, at a great wall of pink. Pink, of course, is a soothing color, and strangely, despite the admitted seediness, the shop had a quiet contemplative air, rather like a small country church. Gary was in a corner, hemmed in by a tiny counter. The black curtain behind him was still swaying.

"Well, I'd like a movie to rent."

"What sorta fing you lookin' for?"

"Well, er . . ."

"Straight? Bi? Gay? Group? SM?" He looks me up and down with a practiced, sizing air, like he's a suit salesman. The question has caught me off-guard. What do I want?

"Something nice. Lyrical, if you have it."

He nods. It's just as he thought. "Straight couple?"

I nod. "Yeah."

"Yeah, all right." He waves me away from the shelf. "Don' worry about all that rubbish over there. Yeah got just the fing for ya, mate, got it right 'ere." He reaches under the counter, slaps a video cassette, coverless, on the scarred wood surface. "Get a load a' that. You'll love it. That's really 'ot, that is." He pats it affectionately. The cassette has no identifying marks of any kind, beyond a small white adhesive label with the legend "3/44." "Tenner for that, oright?"

I pull out a tenner.

"You wanna bag for that?"

I took it back to the flat and put it in the machine later that night, after a home-delivered lamb vindaloo and a half bottle of white burgundy. I'm feeling extremely nervous. After some white noise and some bars and tone, the scene opens abruptly. A real estate agent is showing a client around a clifftop pad overlooking the sea. The agent, who looks almost exactly like Al Bundy and keeps saying things like "definitely a lot of potential," or "the view from here is really excellent," leads her to a patio looking out over the ocean. Suddenly, for no reason whatsoever beyond the fact that she has just been cued by the director, the client lunges forward and begins to undo the real estate agent's shirt. The real estate agent, looking slightly embarrassed, delivers a lame ad-lib—"Shouldn't we get to know each other first?"—then lunges back. They kiss. Tongues are in evidence. Poppy lounge music starts as we now cut away to a close-up of a passing US Coast Guard patrol boat. For a moment I think I must have accidentally switched on the TV, but abruptly we cut back to the action. In a pretzel-like flexion, if not outright violation, of the rules of continuity, the real estate agent is now pantless and more or less erect. The client is on her knees, giving a solid if uninspired performance. Yes, Jim, it is an art form, but not as we know it. The words that spring to mind are "diligent" and "workmanlike." Neither of them looks as if they're enjoying it, exactly, but they don't look as if they're *not* enjoying it either. They're concentrating, hard. The real estate agent groans once or twice, and says, "Yeah, oh, baby," although he sounds distinctly self-conscious; his expression is inward-turned, he's concentrating on maintaining his erection. Sex is the last thing on his mind.

I put the video on pause. I stare at the frozen, blurred image on the video screen. This is real. You can see that. The woman's face, distorted by the penis in her mouth, has a vacant, slightly horsey expression. How do these people *do* this? *Why* do they do this?

I rewind to the kiss at the beginning of the scene. I've seen Sophie do that a hundred times. That's how I met her, kissing for the camera. I met her and I said hi, and about five minutes later we were kissing. I kissed her and kissed her and kissed her and she kissed me and said wow. I was in trouble already and I knew it. I'm still in trouble. When I kissed Sophie, it wasn't real. But actually, later, it turned out it was. I look again at the screen. The blowjob in *Shag City* will have no patrol boats or continuity violations.

There will be sophisticated lighting, skillful camera work, believable performances and a storyline. But it will be real. It isn't supposed to be real. Taste dictates that it not be real.

I turn off the video. I pick up the phone. "Hi, Anne-Marie, it's Frederick Case speaking, of Godzone International, I don't know if you remember me." I can hear my own voice. I sound nasal and pompous. I can't believe I said that about Godzone. I sound like I'm about to offer her a job.

"Oh," she says, cautiously, "of course, Frederick. How are you?"

"Er, is this a good time to call?"

"Sure, kids are in bed, what can I do you for?"

"Well, I don't know, I mean I hope you don't mind, I mean I . . . I thought I might drop round. If it was convenient."

"Well, Frederick, sure, you wanna stop by, just stop on by, it'd be great to see you."

"Great."

Another pause. "Okay, well, come on over."

---

"It's the blokes I feel for," says Gary.

"The blokes?"

He leans on the counter, pulls a cigarette out from behind his ear, plays with it, and puts it back. "Yeah, it's hard for the blokes. They gotta perform, know wot I mean? There's gonna be all these people watching, director, cameraman, lighting, makeup, wha'ever. Maybe they know the girl, maybe they don't. Maybe they fancy 'er, maybe they don't. But none a that matters. They gotta get up, get in, get out, every time, on cue, on time, on budget. There's easier ways of makin' a livin' let me tell yer. There's not many blokes what can do it, as a matter of fact. Like the best ones, they can keep it up for hours and hours. And then when you need the cumshot, there it is, bang, on cue. They can time it to the second. Give 'em a few minutes and they're ready to go again. It's a gift, really."

"I never thought of it that way."

But, like, the girls get all the attention. It's really about the girls, innit? The blokes tend to be more secretive. They come and they go. The girls, there's never any shortage of girls, know wot I mean? They all want to get in on it. They all wanna be the next porn queen. But the blokes, they're harder to find. You find a good bloke, you 'ang on to 'im."

"You've obviously worked in the industry yourself."

"Oh yeah," says Gary, "I've been in the business for years now."

"You perform?"

"No, not me. I 'aven't got the gift, know wot I mean? I do all sorts. Bit a' camera work, bit a' lighting, script supervisor, directing, wha'ever." He leans on the counter again, gets out the cigarette and taps it on the counter. "Of course it goes right back, dunnit?"

"What?"

"Porno."

"You mean the Greeks and their vases?"

"Oh, well, yeah, there was that. But I meant more like on film. Like they started makin' porno same time as they discovered film at all, know wot I mean?"

"Oh, really?"

"Oh, yeah. They got right on it. Then you got the stags, over in America, like."

"The stags?"

"Yeah, in the thirties and the forties and the fifties, used to make these little short films, right. Called 'em stags. Little porno films. Used to show 'em all over. Private screenings. And then you've got your golden age. The golden age of porn." He sighs sentimentally.

"Let me guess. The seventies?"

"Yeah, late sixties, early seventies. Got your big-budget porn round then. The classics, like *Behind the Green Door, Opening of Misty Beethoven,* all that. Them were the days, really. People put money into it then. Nowadays it's all just gonzo. Just a geezer and a girl and a room and a video camera. Bang bang bang, thank you very much darling there's a tenner, know wot I mean? No lighting, no script, no story. That's the thing I miss. No story at all. Back in the seventies you had a real story—humor too. Some very funny moments in porn, sometimes. Really amusing."

"So what happened after the seventies?"

"Well, you got your feminist-orientated porn o' course. That's the eighties, early nineties."

"Really?"

"Oh, yeah, a bunch of girls got together, all in the business, made their own production company. Called it Femme Productions. They made a few in'eresting films. Not very 'ot though, not really, not from a bloke's point of view, anyway. Not enough closeups. See that's the fing, innit? Porn's gotta be 'ot, or what's the point? Yeah?"

"Absolutely. And what happened after that?"

"Well, people just lost interest really. You got the Net and all that, now. I mean it's huge, the industry, it's vast. It's bigger than 'ollywood."

"It's not."

"It is."

"It isn't."

"Yeah, it is, it's a fifty-billion-dollar industry, the porno industry."

"Good God."

"Yeah, but it's all just low budget nowadays, see? Instant gra'ification, know wot I mean? Nobody wants to make any effort. They just want to see the business, know wot I mean? Well, ask me, you can keep it. No story, no characterization. That's the fing. See, that's what you're after, innit, Frederick? I can tell. You want a bit of a story, a bit of character." He taps his cigarette one last time, holds it to his lips, stares into space, sighs, and puts it away, unlit. "See, nobody cares about that anymore. No setting, no lighting. No . . . what was that you said the other week? No lyricism. Yeah, that's it. Course you got your *Wild Orchid*, 9 1/2 *Weeks*, stuff like that, but that's just soft, innit? It ain't the real fing, it ain't 'ard. Know wot I mean?" He shakes his head. "Nah, it ain't porno. Nah," he sighs, "it's a kind of a rebel fing. But who knows? Maybe fings are gonna change again. You ask me, what we need is a really big star to come along and make a big budget porno film, with a story and everyfing, like the old days. It'll 'appen. Mark my words. Like, nowadays, it's all remakes innit? Well, they're running out of fings to remake, in't they? I mean, if they can do a remake of *Spider-Man*, they can do a big budget porno." He pauses. "It's just another genre, see—like dance films, well, you don't see them anymore, do you? But one day, you will. Really, it's just a very misunnerstood genre, is all."

The next time I went into the shop, Gary wasn't there. Instead there was an old man with one eye and a hunch and no smile. I didn't see Gary again.

---

It's one of those enormous, square, ivy-clad brick mansions on Avenue Road, just a few doors down from the discreet, high-class knocking shop on the corner of Allison Road. Rachel Hunter has a place a bit farther along and on the other side. I cross the forecourt. There's a Mercedes four-wheel-drive parked outside, and the coach light at the front door is on. The door opens after a stomach-churning wait of a few seconds, during which I almost lose my nerve and make a run for it.

"Well, hi Frederick, come on in." She stands back, smiling relaxed, breezy. It's a relatively warm evening in late spring, and she's in T-shirt and jeans. She's got the same makeup mask, the same wrought-iron hair, the same biceps. "You want something to drink?"

"Thanks, that'd be great."

She takes my steerhide coat and we sit in an unspeakably pleasant little sitting room near the back of the house. I don't know what the interior of the house was like when it was first built but there's probably hardly a wall in its original position. Everything is white, and light, and airy and halogen-lit without being harsh or barren. From where I'm sitting the kitchen is visible through an arch and I can see kids' drawings magneted to the fridge.

I sip my crystal whiskey bucket. "I'm sorry to barge in on you, like this."

"That's okay, Frederick, don't be sorry, it's really good to see you."

"Could I ask you one thing?"

"Sure."

"What do you think about all this?"

"About the filming? About Sophie and Matt? If you really want to know, Frederick, I don't like it."

"Right."

"I don't like it at all."

"Well, *I* don't like it either."

"Have you told Sophie that?"

"I think she knows."

"But, you know, Frederick, with Matt, I've learned over the years, that if you really love someone you have to accept them as they are."

"Mm."

"You have to look at the whole deal. I think that's what you have to do."

"Uh-huh."

"I know with Matt, he's not the average person. I can accept

that. Or not. That's my choice. But it's no good just burning up
about it. You know, the fact is, if you're gonna make movies, if
you're gonna be a Hollywood actor, you gotta play by different
rules. It's another world out there."

"But . . . what about Paul Newman?"

"The exception that proves the rule."

"But . . ."

"You don't like it. Sure. Neither do I. But that's how it is."

"Yeah. But . . ."

"Look. I don't know Sophie. I don't know you. But I know Matt
and I know that over the years, I mean I've been through so many
issues with Matt over the years, and I've been up against it before
now, and I've just learnt that if I want to be with Matt, I have to
accept certain things. I don't have to like them. And I don't have
to pretend I like them either. And, in fact, I don't. Like them. But
it's my choice. You know?"

"Wow."

Anne-Marie flips her hair to the other shoulder and caresses
her left biceps absently. "I think you have to look at the whole
deal. Matt is such a wonderful guy in so many ways. He's given
me so much. Because he is just such a wonderful, amazing guy.
You know? So I just look at what I have, I mean, I have so *much*. I
have three wonderful children, and I have a wonderful life here,
and elsewhere, wonderful friends, and so much freedom, and you
know, you have to do that, look at the whole deal. You can't be
with someone who is special, and different, with this very special
career, and expect him at the same time just to be a regular ordinary guy. 'Cos he just ain't. And I wouldn't love him the way I do
if he was."

"The whole deal . . ."

"That's what I do."

"So what you're saying is . . . ?"

"I'm not saying anything about how you should handle it because I don't know you. But that's how *I* handle it. It's like, if you love something, let it go." She releases an imaginary dove.

"I never thought about it that way."

"Hey. I'm glad you stopped by."

"But I mean, this scene . . ."

"The blowjob."

"Yeah. That scene."

"Crazy, huh?" She shakes her head, then tosses it back and laughs. "I know, I know . . . just about drove me crazy."

I mean. I just . . ."

"Yeah?"

"I just can't . . . cope."

"Well, hey, Frederick, they're pushing boundaries here. In not many years, the rules about what you can and can't show in a mainstream movie have changed, dramatically."

"Yeah but I don't mean that."

"You mean, like, why should we put up with it?"

"Yeah."

"You know what I say? I say to myself, she's giving my husband a blowjob. Okay. But what it means . . ." She taps her head. "It's all in here. Right? It's up to him. It's up to her. It's up to me. It's up to you. Matt said to me, if you say no, I won't do it. He said that to me. So, I thought about it. And I decided, okay. I'm gonna trust you with this. If you say that you can handle it, and you can be clear about it in your own mind, then hell, if we can put a man on the moon, surely we can be okay about a little onscreen blowjob?"

---

I'm standing in an English garden. An orchard. She's sitting with her back to me, looking out across the valley. She's wearing a sky-blue coat and her hair is tangled across the back. It's very fine hair and it tangles easily. I have all these phrases heavy on my tongue,

I have it all worked out, and I never get to say any of it, because when she turns I don't even recognize her face and I'm getting that zooming-in dollying-out feeling and I realize that something bad and unexpected is about to happen.

"I had an affair with Matt." She starts to cry.

The ground tilts. Well, I think to myself, that's it. The worst has finally happened.

And suddenly, just like that, I was free. I put my hands on her shoulders. "Listen," I said, "I don't care. Don't get me wrong, I'm not happy about what you've done. But I understand how it could happen. You're under pressure. Pressure to perform, every day. You're in an emotionally charged situation, you're spending all your time—twelve, fourteen hours a day, maybe more—with this small tight-knit group of people, you're thrown together with this guy, you're spending all day playing make-believe, you're drawing on your own feelings. You're fooling your own feelings, and you're getting paid to make it real. I know, I've been there. The two of you are in the same boat. You rely on each other. You have a lot in common. He's a good-looking guy. A fun guy. It's only natural that the lines are going to get a bit blurred, a bit fuzzy. It's totally understandable. And there you are, away from home, you're lonely. You want comfort. I can understand that." I felt a fierce pride. It was something bright and beautiful. I was not a jealous guy. I was a loving guy. I took her hand. "Look," I said, "things have been bad for a while now between us. I know that. There's a distance between us. I'm as responsible for that as you are. But we can work it through. We can do it. We can turn it around."

I think somewhere about now I expected Sophie to look at me with gratitude and love, and maybe to say something. But she didn't, she just kept crying. She was getting distinctly puffy.

"Hey," I said. "It's okay."

"No." She shook her head. "You don't understand. It's not okay. I'm in love with him."

**EXT. ORCHARD—DAY.**

FREDERICK TURNS. STUMBLING ON FALLEN APPLES HE
HEADS FOR THE HOUSE. SOPHIE CALLS AFTER HIM
SOFTLY, BLINDLY.

**INT. KITCHEN—DAY.**

BORIS LOOKS UP FROM THE DOG.

<u>Boris</u>

Find her?

<u>Frederick</u>

Yeah, I found her.

<u>Boris</u>

In the orchard?

<u>Frederick</u>

No, actually she's gone for a walk down
by the river.

THERE IS A HUGE ZINC SINK BENCH UNDER THE WIN-
DOWS OVERLOOKING THE CHURCH GRAVEYARD. FREDERICK
CROSSES TO IT AND TURNS ON THE TWO MASSIVE BRASS
TAPS. THE WATER QUICKLY RUNS HOT. STEAM RISES.
TAMINTHA STROLLS BY.

<u>Tamintha</u>

Don't know what we'd do without you, Frederick.

<u>Frederick</u>

Get a maid?

On the road again. Feels good. It was easy—finished the dishes, nipped upstairs, grabbed my wallet, a pair of boots, nipped back downstairs, over the dry stone wall, through the churchyard and away.

Scot-free.

A new life.

Around the bend is a right-of-way that cuts across the fields, down the hill and into the village. There'll be a train later this afternoon. I can walk it in forty minutes. I follow a huge well-tended hawthorn hedge to the entrance to the right-of-way, climb the stile and slip through. The path leads through a farmyard. Chickens, a couple of outbuildings, what looks like a cucumber frame and behind that a dirty glasshouse. A girl in overalls is working on a tractor. She doesn't look up although I pass within ten feet.

I climb another stile behind the glasshouse and the track starts up a smooth, steep, rolling hill. It's muddy underfoot. Twice I slip but I don't fall. At the brow of the hill I cross another stile, and start across a field of burnt stubble. I pick my way until I come to a lone tree standing stark against the rounded crest, a lone crow hunched on one wandering branch. I stand under the tree, breathing heavily. Looking ahead, I can see the church spire from the next village jutting like a lighthouse above a tangle of bare limbed trees fringing the next hill crest.

Looking behind me, the way I've come, I can see the whole picture. The rectory, the church, the country lane, the farm. The tractor is a bright red Matchbox toy, the girl in overalls a blue speck. The old orchard is a brownish fuzz behind the rectory, bordered on two sides by the dry stone wall. A tiny figure in a sky-blue coat is crossing the courtyard, heading from the orchard to the house. Blue smoke drifts from the chimney. The tiny figure is intercepted by an enormous leaping dog.

I look around for somewhere to sit. There's nowhere, so I stand, my hands in my pockets, wriggling my toes to keep them warm. A couple of minutes pass, then the figure comes out the door again, looks around, goes back to the orchard. It's as good as TV.

I'm in the village before lunchtime. I go to the station and buy a ticket for Glasgow. The man behind the window smiles as he hands me the ticket. I step out onto the platform. The rails begin to sing.

I'm sitting on the train. I've got ten minutes. I'm full of confidence. I'm doing it. I'm gone. Glasgow. I'll go to Glasgow. I could be happy in Glasgow. I'll find a B&B. I've got the credit card. I'll be all right for a week. I'll find a job. There must be some sort of a job in Glasgow. I don't care. Any job. A real job. Dishwasher. I'll find a room. A half a room. I don't mind. I'll be a dishwasher with half a room in Glasgow. I'll gladly do that. I'll leave the past behind. I'll drink Guinness. I might even start to write poetry. A red-haired Scottish lass will take pity on me. Her name will be Morag. People will get to know me. Maybe they'll take pity on me too. You can never have too much pity. I'll be a local character with a nickname. That mad old Kiwi booger. They can call me that. They'll talk about me sometimes when I'm not there. Not often, but sometimes, just enough. They'll speculate about my past. Some will say I killed a man. Some will say I was unlucky in love. But no one will know, because I won't talk about myself, ever. I'll just be this mysterious, broken, foreign guy in a chef's hat and a dirty apron, washing dishes at the back of an old Glasgow pub drinking Guinness. And no one will ever hear of me again.

I look at my watch. Three minutes to go.

Glasgow. It'll be beautiful. The fogs, the cold. I'll need a heavy coat. There's all my stuff back in London—but I'm not going back to London. It really hits me now. I'm not going back. I'm never going back. And this is the thing about being grown-up. If you're ten you can go and sulk in your room and they'll come looking for you. If you're forty, you can go to Glasgow—and they won't. One minute to go. Okay, I'm starting to sweat it. There's a poem going through my head. And I don't even *read* poetry.

*Rage, rage against the dying of the light.*

Who wrote that? I can't even remember who wrote it. What's it doing in my head? At thirty seconds, I can see it, a black wall coming straight at me. I know what it is. It is a moment of decision. Coming right at me here. Ten seconds. I'm watching the hand. I hear a whistle blowing somewhere.

Here it comes.

It's here.

**INT. TRAIN CARRIAGE—DAY.**

THE TRAIN MAKES AN INCREDIBLY LOUD BLATTERING
NOISE FOR ABOUT FIFTEEN SECONDS THEN IT STARTS
TO MOVE.

**SLOW MOTION:**

FREDERICK GETS OUT OF HIS SEAT. HE MAKES HIS WAY
DOWN THE AISLE. THERE'S A GOTH GIRL IN THE LAST
SEAT, HER FACE WHITE, STARING STRAIGHT AHEAD OF
HER. HE STEPS LIGHTLY DOWN TO THE PLATFORM,
STAGGERING SLIGHTLY, AND STANDS TO WATCH AS THE
TRAIN GATHERS SPEED.

———————

Eventually, Melissa finds me, huddled on a bench somewhere near the whirling teacups. It's mid-afternoon. My head no longer feels like a Doris plum, ripe-to-bursting, so much as a giant wizened prune. I'm desperately thirsty, and querulous. She drags me back to the car, slides into the driver's seat and starts the engine.

"Where to now?"

"A phone."

We pull into the parking lot of the Red Roof Inn. The nice man in the white shirt has been replaced by a bored but cooperative woman in a lilac pullover, who points us in the direction of a pay phone that is squeezed in between two soft-drink dispensers and an ice machine that makes a sound exactly like my fridge at home.

"Anne-Marie?"

"Hello?" Above the roar of the ice machine I can hear a kid in the background, talking, the clash of dishes, the blare of a TV, and possibly the clink of jewelry. All the intimate realness of a real Californian family, uncensored, raw, direct, down the line. "Frederick, is that you? Are you in LA?"

***

It's a big square place in Santa Monica, on the beach. It's unreal. I've seen this beach so many times on TV I feel like I must have been here. We park and ring the bell. The door is opened by a skeleton. Gaunt, her eyes so huge they seem to weigh down her head.

"Hi, Frederick," she whispers. "And you must be Melissa. Nice to meet you. Come on in."

We follow her shuffling figure to a large lounge flooded with bluish light from the huge plateglass windows looking out across the beach. The Pacific is opaque and gray and foaming.

She makes us coffee and we sit on the edge of a big sofa. I drink a huge glass of water without stopping. She sits before us on a little footstool, her arms clamped between her knees, her hands dangling nervelessly. "So you guys are together, huh? That's nice.

That's real nice." She smiles a desolate smile. Melissa puts a hand on my arm. I feel sick. Anne-Marie stares out the window. "So you'll be seeing him, huh?"

I nod.

"Say hi from me." She frowns. "You know I never thought he'd actually leave. I never thought he'd do that."

"I'm sure he'll come back."

She shakes her head. "I really don't know." She stands and goes to the window. She stares out at the angry Pacific. "He won't communicate. I haven't had a word from him, since he left. He won't come to the phone. He won't write. It's not fair on the kids."

"It's not fair on anyone."

There's a noise in the doorway. A girl is standing there, maybe she's twelve or thirteen. "Mom?"

"Come and say hello, honey."

The girl mutters a greeting, but she doesn't look at us and she stays hovering in the doorway. "Mom?" Anne-Marie excuses herself. She goes to the kitchen.

Melissa and I go to stand at the windows. We look out at the angry sea. We can hear Anne-Marie and her daughter talking. We can't hear what they're saying but it's low and urgent and pleading.

When Anne-Marie gets back she comes and stands with us at the window. "Tell him something from me? Tell him, 'Your children need you.' Just tell him that. Will you?"

"I'll tell him, Anne-Marie. I'll tell him that."

**INT. COUNTRY CHURCH—DAY.**

THE INTERIOR OF THE CHURCH IS SURPRISINGLY SMALL, LIKE A CHILD'S CHURCH. THE AIR IS COOL. THERE IS QUIET AND PEACE HERE, TOTAL SEPARATION FROM THE HURLY-BURLY OF DAILY LIFE. FREDERICK TAKES A PEW NEAR THE BACK. THE PLACE IS EMPTY. A NOSELESS KNIGHT STARES SIGHTLESSLY DOWN. BEAMS

OF SUNLIGHT STRIKE THROUGH THE STAINED-GLASS
WINDOWS THROWING SPLASHES OF GOLD, RED, GREEN
ACROSS HIS FACE. HE IS SUNK IN THOUGHT.

Sophie is quite simply wrong. She doesn't love Matt Chalmers.
You can't love Matt Chalmers. An affair, okay. Lust—well, unpal-
atable, but credible. Love? Never. It's a serious case of genre mistake. It just doesn't sit with the story. One thing is clear. I owe it to
her and to me and to the narrative integrity of both our lives to
make every conceivable effort to disabuse her of this crazy, misguided notion.

I find her outside the old stables next to a potted geranium on a
flight of stone steps to nowhere. They used to lead to the loft, but
Tamintha hasn't rebuilt it yet. She looks remarkably calm and collected. She looks beautiful and majestic and tragic. I feel like I've
never seen her before in my life. She's some beautiful, significant
stranger. I don't say a word. I sit on a lower step. I look out across
the valley. The cloud cover is breaking fast. The hills are glowing
green, bright and dark, shadows racing. My heart leaps with hope.
The sun breaks through and it's warm, instantly. Sophie takes off
her coat. Her arms are thin and pale and she has gooseflesh.

"Where have you been?"

"Glasgow."

She doesn't seem to find this surprising at all.

"So, listen." I look around. Sophie is listening. The hills are listening. The whole world is listening in the thin bright sunshine.

## Chapter 10

ISLANDS ARE SCATTERED ACROSS the silver sea like offcuts of shagpile. The plane drops, staggers, steadies. We skim across red dirt roads, tin roofs, palm trees. There is no sign of an airport anywhere. No sign of anything. We're dropping straight down into a forest of palm trees. At the last moment a runway rushes up out of nowhere to meet us. We bounce once and we're down. Melissa, jolted awake by the landing, looks around, rubbing her eyes, which have become small and red. "Are we there?"

"I think so." I've lost count. For the last fifteen hours we've been island-hopping: a few hours in the air, then land, deplane, wander for an hour and a half around a tiny airport building constructed from woven palm fronds, wearing a flower necklace, dripping with perspiration, searching for an unlocked lavatory while an old gray-haired guy without teeth plays the ukulele in front of a duty-free section that sells nothing but straw hats, ceremonial masks, Johnnie Walker Black Label and bumper packs of insect repellent. Then back on the plane, another flight, another South Pacific airport.

We deplane directly onto the tarmac. It's about five in the afternoon and it's as hot as an oven. The first drops of sweat are trickling down my forehead before I reach the bottom of the steps.

Melissa is walking in front of me. Just as I reach the bottom step there's a shout. I turn just in time to catch a falling woman; she cannons into me and we both sprawl on the tarmac, me underneath. Staring as I am up her left nostril, I get an overpowering whiff of whiskey. We struggle to our feet. She looks to be in her late twenties, peroxide hair, unfocused eyes. Her face lacks tone — the flesh is strangely puffy. She looks like a human mushroom. She puts out an arm and I catch it to steady her. Although she's quite thin seeming, when I grab her arm my fingers just sink right in and keep on going. There don't seem to be any bones in there at all.

She looks at me fuzzily. Two guys come up, looking worried. They're tanned, handsome and muscular, with square jaws and straight noses. One has long hair, one short. They take her arms, one on each side. "Sorry about that, mate. Hope you didn't break anything."

"That's okay."

They hustle her away across the tarmac. We follow. The sun is low and red and huge, the hot wet air closes around us and squeezes like a sweaty palm. In the airport building we collect a flower necklace, change some pounds into an incomprehensibly large number of vaatu and head for passport control.

On the pavement outside the airport building there are a few battered taxis and people standing everywhere in floral shirts and flower necklaces. Everywhere you look, people are smiling. Someone is playing the ukulele. No one seems to be in a hurry to go anywhere or do anything.

Melissa jogs my elbow: a little way off is a sign saying CHARLES MENARD BIRTHDAY GROUP. We go over. There's a young woman standing at a folding table with a clipboard and a huge smile, dropping flower necklaces around necks and ticking off names. Guests are piling into a minibus as we approach.

"Welcome to Vanuatu." A pungent flower necklace slips around my neck. "Your names please?"

"Frederick Case."

The girl's head bends over her list. Her smile flickers for a moment. "Sorry, what name did you say?"

"Case, Frederick Case."

"That's funny, I've already ticked you off." She turns to Melissa. "Sophie Carlisle?"

"Melissa Witherspoon."

She looks back at her list. Her brow furrows. I step in. "I'm not with Sophie. I used to be."

She shrugs. "Sorry about that."

"Is she here?"

"No, she came through yesterday, I think."

We climb aboard a minibus, smelling hot vinyl, road dust, flowers, sweat and perfume. Others pile in after us, chattering in the dark, until we're jammed shoulder to shoulder. The van starts up and careers through the sweet-scented night, under overhanging trees, past sleeping houses.

---

Melissa comes in to use the hair dryer while I'm shaving. She's all ready for bed, in T-shirt and boxers, damp hair combed, cheeks scrubbed.

"What are those for?"

"Blood pressure."

"My dad takes those."

"Thanks for that completely unnecessary information." I slip the blister pack back into my toiletries bag.

"Aren't you going to take one?"

"No. I don't think I will."

By the time I get out she's already in bed, a cigarette smoldering on the ashtray, reading her thriller. It's a new one. She finished another two on the plane, both of them violent and forensic and Bible-length. I climb into bed with a fresh romantic comedy but I find myself staring at Melissa instead. She reads incredibly fast. If you watch closely as her eyes track vertically, you can catch a slight left-right shimmy. She turns a page. "So, what's happening?"

"What's happening where?"

"The book."

"They're onto him."

"Oh, good."

"No—bad."

I look around. The room is shabby. The walls are brownish and there's a transparent lizard on the picture rail. The air conditioning sounds like a lawn mower. Smoke from Melissa's cigarette climbs, hits an eddy and throws a sharp left. I listen to my heart. Ka bump. Ka bump.

Melissa turns a page.

"What's happening now?"

She grunts and flicks ash.

"Are they still onto him?"

"They've got him."

"Oh dear, oh dear, oh dear."

She turns the page. Scritch-scratch go her long fingernails.

"So what are they doing to him?"

"You don't want to know."

"Nothing dental, I hope?"

"Dental doesn't even come close."

"Why do you read that stuff?"

"It's soothing."

"Torture and mayhem is soothing?"

"It always gets sorted out in the end."

"I see. Catalyzing event, first act turning point, second act turning point, rising action, climax, resolution."

"Eh?"

"Nothing." I'm really not in the mood for romantic comedy. I suppose I could read some of Gerard's screenplay. It's just down there in my bag. I could skim a few pages.

Melissa turns a page. "I still can't believe someone else is paying for all this."

"I think he could have done better with the hotel."

"This is probably the best in town." She yawns loudly. "Who is this guy, anyway?"

"A film producer."

"Same as you?"

"Except he makes films."

"So what do you do?"

"I *try* to make films."

"So, what's he like?"

"Charles? Fun, or possibly a ratbag. Depends on your point of view."

"I think I know the type."

"He's very interested in boundaries."

"Definitely know the type. You do realize what's going to happen?"

"What?"

"The whole thing, it's such a classic. The guests, the island. You'll see. We'll be washing up on the beach one after the other."

"You've got to stop reading that stuff."

She sighs, puts down the book. "It's kind of a habit." She turns out the light. It's pitch black. I lie on my back listening to the rattle of the air conditioner. Melissa takes a deep breath. She smells like fresh hay. She rolls over. "G'night."

"Yeah, sleep well and everything."

The sheets tighten and settle against my skin.

I wake in the night. This is what happens. I fall asleep. I wake up an hour later, my heart going like a jackhammer. No chance of sleeping. I'll probably be like this for hours. Black dread. All the worse things. And there's Melissa sleeping next to me, sleeping the sleep of the innocent. I'm envious. It's true what they say, youth is wasted on the young. Money is wasted on the rich. Happiness is wasted on the happy. Life is wasted on the living. Only one thing to do when it gets like this. I slip out of bed, find the key on top of the television, fumble around for some clothes.

The driveway winds back up to the main road, which leads through deep shadow under trees. There's a street lamp every hundred yards. No footpath. No traffic. It's still hot but there are sweet night smells on the air; flowers, grass, water. Stars glitter through the overhanging branches.

I've been walking about twenty minutes when I hear voices around the bend. Kids' voices. And strange noises too. Thunka-thunka. Plink. A roar. Laughter. A rattle of chains. I round the bend and I'm looking down a steep embankment onto a basketball court. Floodlights blazing on the broken tarmac. Kids of all ages, little black kids, from five to twenty, playing basketball. I stop to watch. I guess this is what you do on a Saturday night if you don't have TV.

I'd make a great dad. I know that because everyone tells me so. Frederick, you'd make such a great dad. I have to say, I am always the one that the kids pick out. That's true. It's always Uncle Frederick who has to feed the teddy bear or drive the fire engine. I always sort of assumed that I would be one. I always assumed that it would just come along, like wisdom and maturity and money and everything else that *doesn't* just come along. I always assumed Sophie and I would have kids. I kept waiting for Sophie to say something. I thought she'd turn to me one day, somewhere romantic, maybe Hyde Park in autumn in her chocolate-brown deerskin coat with the tartan collar and look up into my eyes and say, Darling, let's start a family. But time went by and she still hadn't said it, so in the end I did.

It was a romantic setting, all right. We were standing in front of Karl Marx's grave. It doesn't get more romantic than that. We were standing there in an alley of gravestones, long grass growing. Some council housing just over the fence at the back, which I thought was a nice touch. Postmodern. The sky was leaden gray, the trees were bare. A little mud underfoot. Sophie was looking pale and serious. Her skin tones are great under a gray sky. She goes all luminous. It was cold and the air was making that sort of hollow roaring sound. She was in the deerskin, I was in black and gray and a big scarf. Ideally I would have been barefoot but the weather ruled that out.

Anyway, there we were, and I was getting some strong sensations. I could feel many strands of history meeting. It was the perfect opportunity. I put an arm around her shoulders. "Let's have a kid, kid," I said.

Sophie had an answer all ready. "We can't." She shook her head.

I really hadn't expected that. She sounded so definite. I'd always just assumed we'd be doing it some time. We'd talked about children of course the way you do. We'd made up imaginary children. We'd discussed names. We'd imagined what children of ours would look like. We'd tried different combinations of features: for a girl we thought my chin and her nose, for a boy my nose and her chin. In any case, her eyebrows—but never her ears. She has slightly sticky-out ears. I think it's cute but she hates it. My ears, on the other hand, are perfect. There's nothing wrong with them, which is rare in an adult.

"Don't you want to have children?"

"Of course I do."

"What is it then?"

"We can't afford it."

"We'll get by."

"I don't want to 'get by.' I want certainty."

I'd always suspected a traditionalist streak in Sophie's character; funny little habits she had, like budgeting and life insurance. But this was getting scary. It was like one of those conversations at a party where you meet a nice person and you're chatting away and suddenly they're telling you the Holocaust was just a media beat-up.

"I didn't realize that sort of thing was so important to you."

"What sort of thing?"

"Well, money."

She shook her head. A light drizzle began.

"I mean, God, it's just money. Right?"

Sophie lit a cigarette, tossed the match away amongst the headstones. "You have to get *real*."

"I am real."

She gave me such a look I began to wonder if maybe I wasn't.

"All right," I said, "what do you suggest?"

She sucked on her cigarette. She shrugged. "Get a real job."

A cold trickling feeling down my spine. This was worse than the dinner-party fascist. This was *Invasion of the Body Snatchers*. This was *Night of the Living Dead*. "Look," I said, "I can always get money. You know that. Mum and Dad will . . ."

Sophie snorted. "You're thirty-nine years old, Frederick." (That seemed like a lot at the time.)

"I'll stay home. I'll look after the kid. I can do that. I'd like to do that. You can keep working. We'll be fine."

"If I have a child, I don't want to work." She turned on her heel. "It's raining. I'm going to wait in the car." The drizzle increased. I watched Karl's headstone getting wetter. I wonder if anyone ever said anything like that to him. Get a real job, Karl.

---

Breakfast is complicated. Melissa is overacting terribly—she keeps putting small pieces of food in my mouth and giggling. I really do not approve of giggling. And every time I turn around she's *touch-*

*ing* me. People keep looking. I'm going to have to talk to her. Also, I think I've spotted the Irish Brothers, over behind a potted palm on the other side of the restaurant. They can't see me, but I can see their T-shirts. I should go over and say hello, but I'm too scared. Plus, my facial muscles are getting tired.

"How's that?" It's the waitress. I had to send the first coffee back. It was instant. People around here seem to think of instant coffee as a delicacy. She smiles as she puts a bucket of espresso in front of me.

"Thank you so much, that's great. That's just perfect." I smile.

"Tank yu too mas." Melissa's decided to learn Bislama. She smiles.

The waitress smiles. "Is alraet."

Melissa smiles again.

I smile again.

The waitress smiles again. She wanders off, swinging her tea towel and whistling. Truly, this is the land of smile. I feel right at home.

I look around. I suppose half the people in here are party guests, but I don't recognize anyone apart from the Irish Brothers. There's a heavy preponderance of young well-cut guys in tight T-shirts and chunky shoes, well-cut women in sundresses and spangly sandals, and a few older couples in Hawaiian shirts and sensible shorts. It seems I don't have to worry about Sophie until we get to the island. Thank God for small mercies. It'll give me a chance to sort Melissa out.

There's another movement behind the potted palm across the room. I catch a glimpse of a long thin nose, a mop of curly hair and a flash of stripy T-shirt. Yes. It's *definitely* the Irish Brothers. There can't be three noses like that on the planet.

"Here, try this." Melissa reaches across the table and pops a piece of pineapple in my mouth. She giggles.

The lobby of the Meridien Port Vila is basically a huge thatched roof on poles. The ceiling must be thirty feet away. Fans hang from the rafters, spinning, some slow, some fast, some oscillating alarmingly. I make a mental note to watch where I'm standing. The sunlight in the entrance door is dazzling and it's getting hotter. Every so often a trickle of sweat scampers down my ribcage like a scared mouse. A small mountain of luggage is being loaded into a waiting truck by a couple of smiling young men in grass skirts and headdresses. Rivers of sweat pour down their backs.

We've been told to assemble here after breakfast, with our luggage, and await instructions. There are little knots of guests here and there all over. I don't know anyone. Then, over by the reception desk, I spot a tiny blond woman in denim overalls cut off at the knees. She's talking forcefully to the receptionist, who is looking worried. This is Ella. Standing at a slight distance, pretending it's nothing to do with him, is a very tall, beaky guy with glasses and fluffy hair, an enormous pink-and-green Hawaiian shirt, baggy shorts and Timberland sandals. He looks terrible. He's got enormous shadows under his eyes. He's lost weight, he's lost hair. It's Russell. I nudge Melissa. "Okay, here we go . . . good friends at twelve o'clock . . . hey, Russell!" I stride over.

Russell turns. When he sees me his face riffles through a complicated succession of emotions, and settles on pitying affection tinged with nostalgic regret. "Hey, Frederick!"

"Russell, this is Melissa. Melissa, this is Russell."

Melissa smiles at Russell, and slips her arm through mine. She giggles. These giggles are driving me nuts. It would never have crossed my mind in a million years that Melissa could be a giggler. Russell blinks, glances rapidly from Melissa to me and back again. Melissa looks down. "And who's this little fellow?"

Sitting in a pool of saliva at Russell's feet is my godson. Since I last saw him, Brian has got bigger. And uglier. And hairier.

"Oh," says Melissa, "he's gorgeous. How old is he?"

"Almost nine months now."

I kneel down. "Hey there, little guy. You've grown since I saw you."

Brian removes his hand from his mouth. This takes a while because it's inserted up to the elbow. When his fist at last appears it's clutching a small sodden scrap of carrot stick. He holds the carrot stick out to me. I steel myself. I take the carrot stick. "Thank you, I will treasure this always."

"I think he remembers you," says Russell. Brian looks at me. He opens his mouth. He begins to cry. The sound is unbelievably loud. "Quick, give him the carrot stick!" screams Russell. He doesn't even *try* to look amused. I remember last time I was around their place, Brian screamed for an hour and half without stopping. I give Brian the carrot stick. He takes it, but he keeps on crying.

"The duck, the duck!" It's Ella, shouting from the reception desk. "For Chrissake, the duck!"

"I haven't got the duck!" shouts Russell. "You've got the duck!"

"Oh, fuck!" Ella comes running, patting her pockets, cursing, waving a small yellow plastic duck. Seen up close, she looks even worse than Russell. She's got the same raccoon eyes, she's lost even more hair than him and she has a complete new set of forehead wrinkles. Russell takes the duck and gives it to Brian, who instantly stops crying and tries to cram it into his mouth.

Ella turns to me. "Hi, Frederick." She hugs me, holds me out at arm's length. She's about to tell me off. I can just tell. I shiver with anticipation. "You've lost weight," she says, accusingly.

"Me? *I* haven't lost weight, *you* have."

Ella shakes her head. "You have *definitely* lost weight."

"No way."

"And where have you been? We haven't seen you for ages."

"Yeah, sorry, I've been snowed under. You know how it is."

Truth is I've been on a couple-free diet the last little while. Russell and I hung out a bit when Sophie left, but he was pretty stuck with the baby and it was hard to meet up. Besides, he got so emotional. One look at me and he'd crack up. Russell and Ella were both hit very hard by the split. I went around for dinner once, but it was a complete failure. The first few hours were all Brian, and then when he finally decided to go to sleep we all just sat around a dried-out chicken dinner staring at our plates. Every once in a while Russell or Ella would say, "I just can't believe it," or, "How could she do it?" or, "Do you think there's any hope at all?" I snapped. Suddenly I drank about sixteen cans of Elephant beer and started raving. Ella went to bed and Russell fell asleep on the tabletop. I can't even remember how I got home.

Also, I'm fairly sure they're still seeing Sophie. It isn't that I resent it, but it feels kind of weird. We divided everything else up. It seems strange to keep friends in common. I'm probably better off with the CD collection anyway. I don't have a lot of use for friends. I like them just as much as ever, I just don't know what to *do* with them. All that happens is I end up raving. I suppose it's the rogue elephant phase.

Ella is now eyeing Melissa with a hint of hackle. I introduce them. Melissa hits the right note immediately. "Is he your first? He's so gorgeous." Ella strains every muscle in her body to heave Brian onto her hip and staggers across to a sofa near a group of potted palms. We all sit down. She and Melissa get straight down to a very macho conversation about childbirth. I listen, trying not to wince. Russell is right in there, with comments like "and there are only eight pints in the entire human body," or "a tear heals better than a cut anyway," or "you should try shitting a pumpkin sometime!"

Then Ella gets out the photos. I've seen them before. There's one of her sitting up in a hospital bed with a vast blob of baby in her arms. Frankly, it's hard to tell if Brian is the right way up even. Ella, well, she looks just exactly like a dead person. I know, I saw one once. There is no blood in her face at all. She's smiling, but her lips are white. Russell, still in surgical greens, hair all over the place, is leaning over her, grinning wildly like some mad experimental brain surgeon.

Melissa turns to Russell. "So you were there for the birth?"

Russell nods. "It was the most important experience of my entire life."

"I think that's really sweet." She looks across at me. "Taking notes, pumpkin?"

*Pumpkin?*

Ella and Melissa carry on with the photos. Russell turns to me. He puts a hand on my shoulder. "It's great to see you, Frederick. We've haven't been in touch much lately." His eyes fill with tears.

I pat his knee. "It's good to see you too, Russell."

"We must *talk*."

"We must." What Russell means is we must go over it all again, in the search for a rationalization that makes the whole thing okay after all. As far as I'm concerned the whole thing isn't okay and I don't really want to go over it all again, but for his sake I guess I'll have to.

"You're looking good."

"Well, hell, I'm *feeling* good."

Ella puts the photos away and Melissa changes seats. She sits right next to me, leans against me, and runs a hand delicately up and down my inner thigh.

Russell coughs. "So how long have you two known each other, now?"

"How long have we known each other, now?"

Melissa mock-frowns. "Don't you remember, pumpkin?"

I turn to Russell. "A little while now."

Melissa grabs my hand. "It's our anniversary on Saturday. Our first month together." Melissa crosses her legs high. Russell swallows hard and averts his gaze.

"And how did you meet?" Ella is brightly interested.

"We met in Selfridges. Didn't we, bunny?"

Ella blinks.

"That's right, as it happens we did." I put on my most serious voice. I'm starting to get a prickly feeling down the back of my neck.

Melissa turns to Russell. "It was in garden furniture." Russell nods, seriously. "He was sitting in a swing seat. He was reading a book and he just looked so cute and adorable that I *had* to talk to him. I went right up to him and I said, 'Have you got the time?' And he said—tell them what you said, pumpkin."

"That's okay, you tell them."

"No, you tell them."

"*You* tell them."

"He said, 'Sure, if you've got the money.' Isn't that *hysterical*?"

Ella and Russell glance at each other.

"She's just kidding," I say.

Ella smiles and shifts Brian on her knee. Brian removes the duck from his mouth. "Dah," he says. He rotates the duck and reinserts it. Russell coughs. Over Russell's left shoulder, moving among the potted palms, I spot the Irish Brothers. They're walking slowly, heads down, discussing something. Seamus is wringing his hands.

"So, Melissa," says Ella, "at a guess I'd say you're from New Zealand."

"That's right, how did you guys know?"

Ella smiles, sweetly if condescendingly. "What are you doing in London? Are you nannying?"

"Actually I'm a nuclear physicist."

While I'm swallowing my tongue, Ella looks at Russell. Russell looks at Ella. "Ah, really?" He can't keep the incredulity out of his voice.

"Well, I'm studying to be one."

"You're studying nuclear physics?"

"That's right."

"Gosh. Where are you studying?"

Melissa squeezes my arm. "Tell them, pumpkin."

"*You* tell them."

"No, you tell them."

"Cambridge. She's in Cambridge."

"So you're not living in London?"

"I . . ."

"She commutes."

"Well . . ." says Russell. "That's . . . wow, I mean, it must be really hard."

"Oh, not really. It's just a knack. You've got it or you haven't."

"Wow." I clap my hands together. "How about Charles, eh? Forty years old! Some birthday party, huh? What about that? I mean this must be costing, what, half a million, easy." Ella smiles. Melissa picks a piece of fluff off my shirt. She giggles. At this moment I happen to look up. There's someone standing on the other side of the lobby, watching me with a stricken expression on her face. It's Tamintha. Oh, God, no. "Excuse me," I say, "I've just seen someone I know."

"Don't be long, sugarbunny."

I extricate myself from Melissa and head over that way. I'm not feeling very proud. Tamintha meets me with a tight face. "Hello, Frederick."

"Hi. I didn't know you were invited."

"Obviously. I didn't say anything because I didn't want to hurt your feelings."

"Well, it's nice to see you."

Tamintha doesn't smile. "Who's that woman you're with?"

"That's Melissa."

"And who's Melissa?"

"She's, well, she's a friend of mine."

"You could have just said so at the start."

"Yeah, I'm sorry about that. Actually . . ."

She turns on her heel and walks away. I wonder what her policy is on firing New Zealanders. Feeling about two inches tall, I head back to the couches. Just as I arrive, a tall patrician-looking guy in a very floral shirt who has been standing around near the entrance for some time holding a clipboard now puts the clipboard between his knees and claps his hands together loudly. "Charles Menard birthday group!" he calls in a loud and lisping voice. "Could I have your attention, please, darlings?"

"Who's that?"

"Oh, that's Karl."

"Of Ecstatic Experiences?"

"That's the one. He's the camp organizer."

"He certainly is."

Karl the Camp Organizer claps his hands again and waves his clipboard. "Okay, everyone," he says, "your minibuses are waiting. Remember we've got a long drive ahead of us, so now's the time, children. Last flushable toilet for two and half hours."

"That's me," I say. "I'll meet you guys outside."

I head for the men's. When I get Melissa alone I'm going to give her a serious dressing down. I may even be forced to fire her. I'm just about to get started when the door opens. The Irish Brothers come in, talking heatedly. "They must have satellite on the boat."

"Come on, they're not going to have Sky."

"They might."

"Frederick!" says Irish One, who is either Sean or Seamus.

"Oh," I say, keeping it breezy. "Hi, guys."

"How y'doin'?" says Seamus or Sean.

"Can't complain." Breezy, breezy. Seamus or Sean takes the left, Sean or Seamus takes the right. They unzip in perfect time. These guys are everything I ever wished or hoped I could be. Young, cockney, scruffy, but wildly successful. Casual, friendly, unaffected, universally loved. The films they make are irreverent, naughty, funky, clever, uncooperative, and brilliant. These guys are *it*. And there are *two* of them. When Sophie and I were together I used to hang with these guys. Really. *Me.* I used to drop in at the edit suite in Soho whenever I felt like it, no appointment necessary.

*Fred, come on in, have a lager.*

*What do you think, Fred? Should we cut it this way or that?*

They used to drop around the house. We used to watch football. We'd go to the movies. We'd play pool. I haven't seen them once since Sophie left me. Not a phone call, not a card, nothing. But then, they're busy, and they're too young and cool to be considerate. It's still possible that they do actually like me for myself and not merely for my connection with Sophie. I think if they would only still be my buddies everything would be all right for the rest of my life. I think my self-respect, my sense of belonging to the human tribe, my essential optimism, my belief in the goodness of human beings and the ultimate justice of the universe would survive unscathed. But I mustn't appear desperate or overeager. If you love something, set it free.

"Saw you guys in *Empire*."

"Oh, that. Crap photo."

"I thought it was good."

About eight weeks ago (and counting), I woke up in the middle of the night. I had a *brilliant* idea for a film. It was *stunning*. It was so unbelievable that I couldn't believe it. I dashed to my office (i.e., switched on the laptop at the side of the bed), and did something I, as a film producer, never do. I wrote an outline for a film idea. I printed it on one hundred gram eggshell wove, I did a covering letter on Godzone letterhead, slipped it inside a proposal folder, paper-clipped a business card to the top corner, scrawled in casual, chummy longhand *Hi guys!! How's it hanging? Let's do lunch. Cheers, Frederick*, and mailed it off to the Irish Brothers the next day.

I was on the moon. I was on Venus. I was on Mars. I was transfused with ineffable joy. I was scared that my head was going to explode. This time, I said to myself, *this time* I've struck gold. My true genius has at last shone through (tears filled my eyes). With an idea like this, I just can't miss. I mean, I *really* can't miss. The Irish Brothers cannot choose but love it. No one could choose. They will be my slaves. Welcome, Frederick, they will say, to your own. They're going to phone any day now and fly me out to LA and give me a fantastic job and Sophie will be sorry and love me. This state of euphoria lasted a day. I went to Selfridges and had a hot salt beef sandwich and watched the Jewish princesses go by. I was so happy it hurt.

The next night, I woke up again. I sat bolt upright. A bucket of ice water flooded my bowels. I was overcome by a terrible wave of total, pitiless clarity. It was an *appalling* idea for a film. It was so, so utterly fucked and embarrassing and stupid that I couldn't believe I had ever thought for a moment that it was worth even writing down just for the pleasure of ripping it to a thousand shreds, dousing it with lighter fluid and ritually burning it as a symbolic cleansing of all fucked ideas from the surface of the globe.

The Irish Brothers wouldn't get past paragraph two. I could see them now. Irish One turns to Irish Two: "Poor old Frederick. He's really lost it now." "Yeah," says Irish One, "he's finally exposing the complete lack of creative ability and feebleness of imagination he's always suffered from without any of us being impolite enough to tell him so to his face." "Yeah," says Irish Two, "for Sophie's sake we never said anything, but in a way don't you think it would have been kinder to tell him before now, before he makes such a total and utter pillock of himself in our eyes by sending us this utterly completely inadequate piece of dog shit? I mean, look at the way he's scrawled across the top of the letter in a fake casual-chummy longhand, 'How's it hanging?' I mean, really, only a seriously inadequate individual with no understanding of how truly cool and creative people like ourselves think and behave could possibly ever have written such a pathetic, childish comment."

Irish One thinks. "I think you're right, Sean," he says. "I agree with everything you say."

"You're Sean," says Irish Two. "I'm Seamus."

"Oh, yeah," says Irish One. "Sorry about that."

It's an old story, from here on in. They didn't phone. They didn't write. In a nutshell, they didn't communicate. And now, here they are.

Yes.

There is something I have to do. There is a tiny, tiny possibility that they didn't get the outline. That it went astray in the post or something like that. If that happened, I want to know. That way I can relax. They never read it. I can forget it. I can send them another outline another time. If they did read it, however, that I also need to know. "Not what we're looking for." I need to hear it. So I can put it to bed. So I can lay it out, cold and stiff. Pay my last respects.

But if I want to know, I'm going to have to ask. That's not going to be easy.

Meanwhile something is becoming apparent. It's happening again. I can't get started. I'm as dry as the Sahara. This is becoming monotonous. I'm going to have to give up urinals altogether. With Sean/Seamus and Seamus/Sean gushing like a pair of frisky young stallions either side, I force myself to relax. Think watery thoughts. Nothing.

"What about Saturday, then? What about that?"

"Oh, yeah."

"Tossers," says Sean/Seamus.

"My granny could kick better than that," says Seamus/Sean.

I don't actually know anything about football, beyond the fact that they have to use their feet, and I find it mind-numbingly boring to watch. Doesn't matter. If I could do it with these guys, I'd watch back-to-back reruns of *The Love Boat*. I'd watch paint dry.

"Are you all right, then, Frederick?"

"Oh, sure, you know, same old same old."

Still nothing. I picture waterfalls, cataracts. I can feel it. If I could just get it started I'd be all right. But I can't get it started. *Pee. God, pee.*

"You've lost weight, mate."

"Yeah, you have."

"And hey, who's that chick I saw you with?"

"Oh, that's Melissa. We met at Selfridges. In garden furniture."

"She looks all right."

"Yeah, she's all right." I'm going for breezy-casual, but it's impossible to sound convincingly casual when you're standing over a dry urinal with the breeze caressing your nethers. There's an edge of hysteria that can't be masked.

Irish Two finishes, shakes off and zips up. Irish One zips up too. I'm now standing here alone, with my dick hanging out, trying to have a casual conversation. It's worse than impossible. "So, you guys have a project going with Sophie?"

Irish Two chuckles. "Don't believe everything you read."

Irish One slaps me on the shoulder. "See you around, Fred."

"Yeah, see you guys on the island."

The door swings shut.

The sluice gates open.

They didn't even wash their hands. How's that for cool?

---

A convoy of minivans drives out of town past plantations of coconut trees arranged in rows with large exceptionally clean red-and-white cows grazing underneath. What is wrong with this picture?

There's something about that combination, cows and coconuts, that just doesn't go, like pictures of cavemen hunting a dinosaur.

The scenery is amazing. The greens are so green they're unreal, supersaturated. It reminds me of this time I had a black eye (long story) and my eye was shut for three weeks. When it finally started to open the colors were so bright and vivid it was like being in a cartoon. We climb a hill, then wind down a near-vertical metaled road with vines and creepers and jungle on all sides, banana trees, mangoes, pawpaws, bright splashes of bougainvillea, purple and red, and hanging bell-shaped white flowers that might or might not be datura.

Melissa and I are in the backseat. Her behavior is frankly embarrassing. She's cornered me against the window, draped herself across me. She keeps trying to stick her tongue in my ear. Russell is having kittens, Ella is looking incredulous.

The road is getting worse with every mile. It's like a turbulent river of tarmac poured through the jungle. The minivans pick their way, lurching dangerously. The drive takes three hours. We stop once along the way, in a widening of the road, just to stretch our legs. Dust hangs in the air, it's hotter than ever, and the noise of the cicadas is deafening. I think I'm getting a headache. People don't walk far. They stand around in the shade, sipping water and sweating. Melissa is asleep in the back. Russell gets me aside. "So what's the story with Melissa?"

"How do you mean?"

"Well, I mean . . . nuclear physics. Wow. Don't you feel intimidated?"

"Not at all. It's nice to have found my intellectual equal."

"She seems to be very fond of you."

"We hit it off okay."

Russell puts a hand on my shoulder. "Frederick, you deserve this. You deserve to be happy."

"Thanks, Russell, I think so too."

He squeezes my arm. He doesn't say any more. He's too choked up. I help him back to the van.

Around midday we climb slowly, painfully, up the steepest section of road I've ever seen in my entire life, including Space Mountain. Then we descend a terrifying dirt track. Some of the ruts are so deep you can't see the bottom. Every so often the thick overhanging vine-laden trees part on a bend and we catch a glimpse of the solid, supersaturated implacable blue of the sea.

At the bottom of the hill the track ends in a dusty turnaround. The other vans are already parked. We all climb out and walk a few yards through the bush. We come out on a small beach of blinding white sand. It's so bright, if I take off my sunglasses I can't see. Behind us crouches the bush, a green wave rolling to meet the blue. Around us is the buzz of cicadas, the call of parrots. A small marquee has been erected on the beach, staffed by several smiling ni-Vanuatu in white printed T-shirts. On the front: HOW IS YOUR DAY? On the back: HOW CAN I MAKE IT BETTER? On the sleeve a monogram: CM. Melissa helps herself to champagne.

"So where's Charles?" I ask.

"On the boat," says Ella. "Ah, there's the cocksucker now."

This is a fairly impolite way to refer to one's host, and I have to say I'm a little shocked. It must show on my face because Ella laughs. "Look." I follow Ella's pointing finger. Coming slowly around the point is a boat. A beautiful boat, a long, white, floating dream, a luxury oceangoing motor yacht with graceful, sweeping lines. Must be a good thirty meters. Stenciled along the bows in flowing elegant copperplate is the boat's name: COCKSUCKER.

Melissa and I are in the last boatload, with Russell and Ella, an elderly couple from New Zealand, the drunken woman who fell on me on the way off the plane, whose name is Denise, Ken and Ramon—her bodyguards—and a couple of good-looking gay boys. Ken has a close-trimmed beard, and obviously works out.

Denise is barely compos. She sits slumped in the bows, a scarf fixing her hat to her head, fifties-style sunglasses awry on her nose, a glass of champagne in one hand and a sausage roll in the other. Apparently she is an heiress and considers herself to be a terrorist target.

"Don't worry about her," says Ken. "She'll be sober by March."

The boat is drawing nearer. As we run up alongside the boatman kills the motor and grabs the railing.

"Gidday, gidday, welcome aboard, one and all!" There he stands, grinning, larger than life, a nut-brown teddy bear in a black G-string and a cowboy hat, champagne cocktail in one hand, the other held out to hoist us aboard.

## Chapter 11

"WELL, FOR GOODNESS SAKE: do you want a sexual relation-ship, or don't you?"

"Of course I do. I want the sex, I want the attraction. But it has to be subtle, suggested. Back there on the bus, that was a practical demonstration. It's a question of taste."

"Men with ponytails shouldn't talk about taste."

I've hurt her feelings. I can tell. "Don't work so hard at it, that's all I'm saying. You can afford to leave a little more to the imagina-tion. It's sexier like that anyway. People don't want it shoved in their faces."

"They do sometimes."

"Well it's not what *I* want. And something else. This nonsense about nuclear physics. That's worse than fox hunting. What are you trying to do?"

She looks embarrassed. "It just slipped out. I don't think any-one noticed."

"Of course they noticed."

"Look. You don't impress people like this with a nanny from Levin."

"The aim is not to impress. The aim is to blend."

"Okay, you want it that way, fine. But there's something I want to say to you."

"By all means."

"You say I'm over the top, fine. But you—you're a cold fish. You never say anything warm. You don't touch me, you don't show affection, you're not spontaneous or even friendly. You just stand there like a stiff. It's embarrassing. If you don't loosen up, people are going to think there's something wrong."

"Okay, I'll try to be more demonstrative."

"That would help."

"I just hope to God nobody asks you anything about nuclear physics."

"Relax. Who wants to know anything about nuclear physics?"

"I'm going to get an orange juice." I push off from the rail.

"Whoa. Hold it right there!"

"What?"

She throws up her hands in exasperation. "See? That's exactly what I mean. You just walk off, head down, with a depressed, worried look on your face. You don't smile, you don't pat my arm, you don't kiss me or cuddle me—where's the romance? Where's the fun?"

She's right. I lean down, close. I'm looking into her eyes. Eyes. What is it about eyes? I look into someone's eyes nowadays, all I ever see is—eyes. I remember staring into Sophie's eyes. I remember spending entire days staring into Sophie's eyes. It was better than TV. I take a deep breath. I can do this. I brace myself. "Another champagne? . . . sweet . . . heart?"

Melissa smiles, almost maliciously. "Gee, thanks, pumpkin. And another couple of tuna rolls would be nice." She pecks me on the cheek.

"Do you *have* to call me 'pumpkin'?"

She lowers her voice to a venomous hiss. "Oh, I'm sorry, would you prefer some other vegetable?"

She gooses me as I turn to go. I make for the champagne, which is set up under an awning erected over a horseshoe-shaped seating arrangement just forward of the wheelhouse. I catch sight of Ella, sitting with Brian on her knee, keeping him under the shade. Brian is done up with a huge frilly hat and sun cream. His face is white. He looks like an aging clown. Ella gives me a little wave. She's watching Melissa and me, I know. Every time I turn around, there she is. Trying to appear relaxed, I pour a champagne flute for Melissa and an orange juice for me.

I look around. The *Cocksucker* is big, absolutely gorgeous, and designed for comfort. Teak decking, brass fittings, varnished wood everywhere. Everywhere you look there are smiling dark-skinned staff in white T-shirts carrying trays of canapés. There's a light but insistent breeze blowing, and we're just clearing the harbor mouth. The first Pacific rollers are lifting the bow. I feel that familiar old surge under my feet.

The birthday boy is in the middle of the group under the awning, keeping up a nonstop patter routine. He can't blink without getting a laugh. Tamintha is in the crowd, laughing politely, looking miserable. I've noticed a few more people I know, more or less, but no one I feel compelled to go and talk to. For example, over there, leaning on the port-side rail and talking to a designer called Mark, is Rebecca. She catches sight of me over Mark's shoulder. I give her a little wave and a smile. She shakes her head and looks away. She says something to Mark. Mark gives me a grin and a wave.

I haven't seen Rebecca since that time she came around to pick up Sophie. She was Sophie's support person. Sophie was very supportive of her when she was leaving her husband, who by the way is a guy by the name of Enoch. He used to own a farm although I think he sold it recently. Nice enough guy. Tweedy but clean. Red-apple cheeks. They had three hundred acres, three children, two dogs and a cow called Bessie. When it all fell apart

Sophie went around with Rebecca to pick up the cow and the dogs. The breakup was especially long and messy and Rebecca used to come around at all hours of the day and night to sit with Sophie at the kitchen table and tell her all the reasons he was an arsehole and unreasonable and demented and self-centered and vicious and uncooperative. I have to say I was shocked. To meet the guy you would never have known. But then it's true that no one ever really knows what goes on inside a marriage — least of all the ones who are in it. Not that I'm cynical about marriage. Some of my best friends are married. I'm just cynical about *my* marriage.

Anyway, when Sophie was leaving me, Rebecca was the natural choice for a support person — obviously she had Matt, who left Anne-Marie and flew straight over to London and lived with her in the exact same house on Avenue Road I'd visited Anne-Marie in — but she also had Rebecca. There wasn't too much for Rebecca to do, as our breakup was not drawn out or nasty or anything other than extremely civilized and postmodern at all times, but you do need someone anyway, and she was always on hand with tissues and glasses of water and helpful suggestions whenever Sophie ran out of horrible things to say about me. I know Sophie was saying horrible things about me, because it's just one of those things you have to do. I know what she was saying too, because she said it all to me first. I don't think she meant any of it. It's just one of those things.

Russell, as my support person, didn't really work out so well on account of his being so busy with Brian and so tired all the time, and besides he was trying to stay friends with Sophie too, which made him next to useless when it came to saying horrible things about Sophie. Which, naturally, I needed to do just as much as she did about me. Russell didn't actually object, but every time I got started, he'd kind of hunch down and stare into his cup of tea and look embarrassed and sad and forlorn. I didn't want that. I wanted enthusiasm, I wanted *suggestions*. We'd usually end up doing Matt instead. That was pretty easy.

For her part, Sophie came up with some amazing stuff. After she told me about Matt, that weekend at Tamintha's, we went straight home, and we locked the door and for forty-eight hours we were in there, hard at it. Hammering it out, toe-to-toe, trading bald assertion for bald assertion, denial for denial and attribution for invective. We said it all. We said it, loud and clear. It was domestic hardball, and no mistake.

Sophie explained to me, in some detail, how I'd become a deadening and uninspiring person. I'd become a cipher. There was nothing there anymore. I never did anything. I had nothing to offer. I was going nowhere with my life, all I did was hang around and drink vodka and spout bullshit. I was psychically dragging her down to my own level. I was a black hole of despair. Further, Sophie said, *even if I didn't realize it,* deep down I wanted her to fail. (That was smart, that, *even if I didn't realize it.*) She said deep down in my heart I'd never been comfortable with her success and I wanted her to fall flat on her face so I could pick up the pieces and be powerful in the relationship again. She said I simply couldn't cope with a successful woman. She said the real reason I didn't want her to do *Shag* had nothing to do with the sex scenes, and nothing to do with Matt Chalmers and everything to do with my fear of her continuing success.

Of course none of this was remotely true. I've always been very comfortable with Sophie's success. I've always been very comfortable *because* of Sophie's success. It was my failure I was uncomfortable with. And the same went for Sophie: she just couldn't cope with my failure. Not at all. She was so scared of failing herself that she was scared of even being around failure. She was scared that I'd taint her, that I'd drag her down. But as I pointed out to her, if she gave in to that fear, and ditched me merely because I was a failure, something inside her, something bright and tender and real, would die. She'd be forever just that little bit less a human being, that little bit more a calculating machine.

Furthermore, I said, that's all Matt Chalmers was to her. He was a symbol of success. In deluding herself that she was falling in love with Matt Chalmers, what she was really falling in love with was her own success, her own career—with herself. Thus she was doomed to become involuted, dehumanized and closed off from the real world of compassion, humanity and feeling. And as for *Shag City*, her willingness to do such a cheap, low-down, exploitative piece of rubbish was an indication of the danger she was already in.

In the end we had to agree to disagree. Although in fact we *did* agree on most things, on questions of fact. We agreed that I'd failed. We agreed that she'd succeeded. We agreed that she'd had an affair with Matt. Where we differed was over the more complex question of causality. For Sophie, there was a clear stream of causality, flowing strongly in one direction: everything *I* did made her do everything *she* did. For me there was no stream. It was more a swamp of causality. Everything was in there, floating around, smelling less than wonderful, bumping into everything else. Things had been caused, that was clear enough, but by what and by whom, I had no idea.

Also, there was the crucial question. Sophie claimed to have fallen in love with Matt Chalmers. I rejected that utterly. It was sheer madness, sheer folly. A daydream.

"*Mark my words.*"

It was two in the morning of the second day and only hours before her final departure. We'd finished the last bottle of wine, the bread was stale and we were starting to run low on assertions. I stood on the table. "Mark my words," I said. "He means nothing to you, and you even less to him. *Even if you don't realize it now.*" I think that was probably my finest moment. I kind of went downhill from there.

I drain my orange juice and pour another. Rebecca is at this moment leaning on the rail and staring out to sea and telling Mark what an arsehole I am. I can see her lips moving from here. Fact is, Rebecca and I have a past.

Rebecca always hated me. I couldn't understand it. She really, really seemed to hate me. It was like we'd been implacable foes in a past life. The first time I ever set eyes on her, she gave me a look so evil I crossed myself. And that's the way it stayed. Monosyllabic replies, averted eyes. The odd evil glance.

At first I tried to win her over. I made jokes, I made cups of tea. I took an overt interest in her personal life. I addressed her repeatedly by her first name. I put her at ease by giving her lots of private time with Sophie and yet at the same time cheerfully accompanying them on clothes and cosmetic shopping expeditions to help carry the parcels. *"You know, Rebecca, I think that lipstick really goes with your eyes."*

No dice. Nothing.

Then I realized what it was. She *didn't* hate me. She was, secretly, incredibly hot for me. She couldn't trust herself even to look me in the eye for fear she would betray her true feelings, break down and throw herself at me, thus betraying her friendship with Sophie. Beneath that barren cinder cone of dislike lurked the seething lava of passion. How she must have suffered, so close and yet so far from the object of her passion. And then of course she broke up with Enoch, and that clinched it. It was all clear. She'd left him because of me. There was no other explanation. I even began to feel sorry for the kid.

Then, when Sophie finally left, I went into my revenge phase, which lasted about six hours. I decided to seduce Rebecca. I decided to wreck things between Sophie and her best friend, just when she needed her most. Wicked, huh? I went right around to Rebecca's place with a bottle of wine and a Miles Davis CD. Turned out I was right the first time: she wasn't secretly incredibly hot for me at all, she really, really hated me. She told Sophie all about it later. I denied everything. Sophie said she didn't know what was more pathetic, trying it on with her best friend or denying it later. I think probably the denial, although admittedly it's a close-run thing.

I've drained yet another orange juice and I pour what I think is my third. Pretty soon I'm going to have to go looking for the head. As for Melissa, I'm worried. She has "loose cannon" written all over her. Although she's right about one thing. I haven't been showing enough affection. It's *hard* to show affection. A drink would help, but I can't drink. If I drink I die. I don't think I've ever been this sober in my life. It's terrifying just how sober you can get. It's been several weeks now, and *still* I'm getting more sober. Every morning I wake up a little soberer. I don't see things anymore, I see *through* things. It's terrible. And as for the LSD, that was no help at all. I bitterly regret taking it and I'll never take it again. It has to be the most useless drug ever invented. I mean what is the point of a drug that *increases* your level of insight?

I must relax. I must show affection. I must find the head.

"Frederick." Now it's Ella. Looks like she wants a piece of me too.

"Great boat, huh?"

"Listen, what's the story with you and Melissa?" This is Ella's style. Some might say she's blunt and tactless but she prefers to think of herself as direct and no-nonsense.

"Well, there's not a lot to say really. We met in Selfridges. In garden furniture, actually. She said have you got the time, I said . . ."

Ella gives an impatient wave of her hand. "She obviously thinks the world of you, Frederick."

"Oh she does. She's wild about me. Wild."

"She seems really nice."

"She is."

"Very affectionate."

"Yeah, oh yeah. Very affectionate."

"She seems like a really lovely girl."

"Lovely. Charming."

She looks at me fixedly. "Are you serious about her?" There's something about the way she's looking at me that's making me nervous. I don't know what the right answer is.

"Well, sure, I mean we are serious, of course. Why?"

Ella is still looking at me. "I don't know, I just . . . you're not still on the rebound, are you? Because I think she's better than that. I think she deserves better."

"Oh, of course." I'm beginning to feel slightly sweaty.

"Tell me it's none of my business, but . . . I just wonder if you're ready for this. Do you really think you're ready for this?"

"Ready? Am I what? Of course I am. I've never been so ready in my life."

Her tone softens. "I assume you've heard about Sophie?"

"What about Sophie?"

"That she's pregnant."

"Oh, that. Yes, yes. Great isn't it? Is it a boy or a girl? Does she know?"

Ella looks at me disbelievingly and pats my arm. "Take care, Frederick. Take care of yourself. And take care of Melissa." She's suspicious I'm sure. She's on to me.

When I get back to Melissa, I find her chatting to the captain. He's wearing a white hat, white shoes and white suit, but he looks distinctly rough trade—*Querelle* twenty years on. The uniform is crumpled, a little greasy. He's around fifty, weather-beaten, seamed and lined, tangled blond hair, big broad shoulders. A white scar down his forehead, across one corner of his eye and down his cheek. Not too clean. I notice a Tahitian tattoo on the back of one hand, and more tattoos crawling up the back of his neck.

"Gilles," says Melissa, smiling unpleasantly, and caressing my cheek, "this is Frederick. Frederick, this is Gilles. Gilles has been telling me all about himself."

"And I'm sure you've been telling Gilles all about yourself, too."
She looks blank.

"Here you are . . . darling." I hand over the champagne.

"As a matter of fact," says Gilles, "Melissa has been telling me all about you. You are the estranged husband of the famous actress who performs oral sex on camera?"

"I am."

Melissa takes my hand. "Gilles has been teaching me how to say 'oral sex' in French."

"That should come in handy."

Gilles steps toward me. "And you are a New Zealander?"

"Yes."

He puts a hand on his heart. "Then allow me to apologize to you, personally, and to all New Zealanders, for the sinking of the *Rainbow Warrior* in New Zealand's national waters. It was an act of state piracy of the worst kind."

Melissa steps in again. "Gilles used to live on his own yacht. He used to spend all his time sailing from island to island, all over the Pacific."

"Sounds like paradise."

Gilles shrugs. "Yes, but paradise—what is that? You sail from island to island. You catch fish, you eat bananas. Once a year you stop somewhere, you work, you make a little money, you fix up the boat, you stock up on beer, you sail off again."

"Idyllic."

"You forget. The so-what factor."

"The who?"

"You wake up one morning, you're anchored in a perfect little bay somewhere, the parrots are fluttering about the coconut palms, the water is so clear you can see the bottom five meters down and you think—so what?"

"Yeah, good point. That would be a problem. I can see that. So what did you do?"

"I got this job."

There's an uncomfortable pause.

"So, Gilles. Where's the head?"

He beckons to us. "Come."

I force myself to hold Melissa's hand as we follow Gilles to the wheelhouse, which looks like the cockpit of a 747. There's Internet, e-mail, sat-phone, real-time weather information with downloadable satellite photos, GPS, radar, depth sounders, autopilot. There are depth alarms, fire alarms, fuel alarms, weather alarms, leak alarms. "And," says Gilles, proudly, "every system is backed up. We even have backups for the backups."

"Let me guess," I say, "even God couldn't sink this boat."

Gilles looks at me. "Not even the *French* could sink this boat."

Below decks it's a palace. From the wheelhouse we come out in a mahogany-paneled library. There's a galley to put to shame any kitchen, a dining table to seat ten, separate lounge, showers, stereo, TV, electric toilets, works of art on the walls. Melissa is round-eyed, but I'm bored. I know about boats but I don't really like them. I think it's mainly just the fact that I'm such a terrible sailor. I took a couple of Sea Legs before we left this morning, so I'll be okay, but then I can never stay awake much past lunchtime.

Melissa turns to Gilles. "How much would a boat like this cost?"

Gilles shrugs. "Several millions."

"In what currency?"

"Any currency."

Melissa whistles.

"Voilà!" With his eyes on Melissa, Gilles flings open the door to a magnificent stateroom. The bed is enormous, with a tiger-skin spread. Erotic art on the walls, an Exercycle and an en suite bathroom with bidet. "What do you think of that?"

"Very nice." Melissa sits on the bed. She pats the cover. "Nice and firm." There's a slightly pregnant pause. Gilles appears to be breathing heavily. "Anyway, I must go back to the wheelhouse. I'll leave you two to make use of the facilities. Feel free. Take your time." He leaves, discreetly closing the door.

When I come out of the head, Melissa is lying on the bed. "I thought of something we could do. I thought it might help."

"Help with what?"

"With the relationship." She's looking at me in a way I don't quite like.

"What?"

"Why don't we just do it, stud? Right here and now."

"I thought I made this clear. No sex."

She sighs. "You really are very screwed up about your body, did you know that?"

"Of course. It's a natural part of the aging process."

"You're actually incapable of showing physical affection. Aren't you?"

"I am not incapable. I just choose not to."

"How in the world do you expect to convince people that you're having a normal physical relationship with me if you can't even touch me?"

"I can touch you."

"Go on then. Touch me."

"All right. There."

"Not like that."

"I just touched you, didn't I?"

"You prodded me in the leg with your index finger. I'm talking about sensuous contact. Sexual touching."

All of a sudden it seems strangely hot in here. "I'm sorry. What exactly is the problem here? I've asked you to do a job, and . . ."

"Look," she says. "Tin tacks, okay? You want me to shut up, I'll shut up. No skin off my nose. I could take your money, I could say nothing about it. We can go back up on deck and we can continue just the way we are. But I don't like to work that way." She sits up, cross-legged. "Do you want me to continue?"

"Continue."

"I know what you want. You want intimacy, right?"

"Simulated intimacy."

"The fact is, the way things are, no one is going to believe for a moment that I'm your girlfriend. They are all going to see right through it, and they're going to guess what I am, and there is nothing I can do about it."

"Why?"

"Because you just don't have 'it.' "

"Have . . . what?"

"Call it whatever you like. Fact is, to put it bluntly, you don't look like someone who's getting it regular. You have an aura of chastity. You carry it with you wherever you go."

"I do?"

"Every time I go near you, you freeze up, you look embarrassed and you look the other way. You see what I'm saying? Your body language is telling everybody that you hardly know me, and know even less what to do with me."

"Well, I suppose maybe I could be a little out of practice . . ."

"Let me ask you this: when was the last time you did it?"

"Well . . ."

"Was it with your wife?"

"Of course it was with my wife."

"Mm. That's what I thought."

Ah yes. I remember it well. It was a sympathy fuck pure and simple and I treasure the memory. After all it's not every day you get *that* much sympathy. And you can never get too much sympathy. It was the last night. The night I stood on the table. I had my finest moment, up there on the table, and Sophie heard me out. There was a moment's silence. Then she said she was leaving me. That very minute. She went and phoned Rebecca. I was still standing on the table. It was like *The China Syndrome*. I was Jack

Lemmon. No one would listen to me. She just kept on doing what she was doing, making plans and arrangements, packing, calculating her share of the phone bill. I suddenly realized that this was real. She might really, actually leave. Tonight. That had never occurred to me before.

I got down and I begged. I got down on my hands and knees, and I begged. It wasn't so bad, not really, not once you get going. Actually it came to me quite naturally—not that I have no pride. I have a deep innate sense of self-respect and pride. This is the product of my privileged upbringing and caring background. I was taught to value myself, and I do. Yes—I'm proud, and proud to be proud. But I wear my pride on the inside.

*Please. Please don't leave. Please don't go. Oh, please, oh please oh please. Not tonight. Not now, don't leave me. I am begging you not to go. Just one more night, please please please.* I didn't cry. I would have, but she hates it when I cry. If I had cried it would have been all over. I did wring my hands, but only a little. I kept the delivery straight, and I just said it, quietly, humbly, with dignity. I remember the scene. I have perfect recall. It was about two in the morning. We were in the bedroom. There was a candle burning. The blue coverlet of the bed glowed unnaturally. Sophie was standing. I was prostrate, the sweet earthen taste of carpet on my tongue.

"Christ," said Sophie.

I could well understand her frustration. She didn't want to leave me like this. She wanted closure. Ideally I suppose she wanted *me* to leave *her*. We'd just spent forty-eight hours failing to find agreement. We'd agreed that there was no possibility of agreement. And *still* I wouldn't leave her. I was a rock. I was a stone. An albatross. What was she supposed to do?

She sighed. I knew that sigh. I jubilated. "Tonight. Then tomorrow—no fuss. Okay?"

"Okay."

She went to the phone. She picked it up and called Rebecca and told her not to come. I could hear Rebecca begging her to reconsider. Begging her to leave me now. To leave me for dead.

She sat on the side of the bed, her back to me as she took off her shoes, the knuckles of her spine pressing against the skin. I lay on my back. I felt completely normal and utterly at ease and safe. Tomorrow Sophie was going but it wasn't tomorrow yet. It was tonight and tonight was forever. Then a wave of sorrow washed through me and carried me clean across the bed, right into her arms. I didn't give her a chance, I just clamped on. I was a barnacle, a limpet, a cattle tick. I burrowed right down into her, all the way under her tobacco-and-salt–tasting skin. We wrestled. I didn't care. She hit me. I didn't care. I didn't care about anything. She clamped me between her legs and grabbed my hair. She held my face like that. I looked in her eyes. I was as open as a flower.

"Wait," she said, harshly. "Wait."

I waited.

She sighed. "In the bathroom. In my bag."

This was it. First time for a long time and the last time forever. I went to the bathroom, I fumbled for the light switch. I found her toilet bag and tipped the contents out. The condoms were there: a choice of Excite Vibra SuperPlus with ribs or Stimulomatic Three Regular. Sophie keeps all sorts of stuff in her toilet bag. I sorted through. Disprin, spare batteries—needle and thread. I looked at the needle, and I looked up and caught sight of my face in the mirror. And it was there that I read the true extent of my own intentions.

It was a sympathy fuck, pure and simple. I made the most of it. I gave it my all. I carved colors in the dark. I melted down into white-hot energy and went spiraling out and away into the blue night. I'm not sure about Sophie. She was probably doing mental crosswords.

A little later, Sophie was asleep. I lay wide awake listening to her breathe. It was four o'clock. It was the darkest hour. I thought of Jack Lemmon in *The China Syndrome*, and how he died, gunned down in the back as he made for the button. I thought of the blood in his mouth, the sadness and waste, and in his eyes the desire, the living desire that never died, even when the eyes died—how, even in the process of dying, you could see the intention, you could see him reaching with his heart and mind for the switch. He never got there. I watched the numbers flip over on the clock by the bed. I didn't miss a single one.

Melissa touches my arm. "Are you okay?"

"Oh, I'm fine."

"I'm not judging you, you know. I never judge my clients."

I wipe my forehead.

"Maybe you're not really ready to . . ."

"Oh, what the hell. Let's do it."

"Are you sure?"

"Absolutely. Gotta get back on that horse sometime."

"Okay." She settles herself. "But first I want you to do something for me. Shake your hands. Let it all go. Shake it off the tips of your fingers." She shakes her hands to show me, like shaking water off your hands. I shake my hands. "Now breathe deeply a few times. Relax. Let it all go. Ready?"

"Ready."

"Now. What do you like about my body?"

"Well, obviously, I like your body."

"What specifically do you like about it?"

"It's nice."

"What part?"

"Oh, all of it."

"But what's your favorite part?"

"Do we have to do this?"

"It'll help. It will."

"I . . . like your legs."

"Legs, huh?" She uncrosses her legs. She smiles a slinky and obviously put-on smile. "Okay, what *exactly* do you like about them?"

"Um . . . your knees."

"Yes? What do you like about my knees?"

"You really want to know?"

"Oh, yeah."

"They're a little fattish."

Her gaze is level. Her tone is calm, absolutely uninflected and nonjudgmental. "That's what you like?"

"That's what I like."

"That's the thing you like best about my entire body?"

"You asked."

She glances briefly at the heavens. "Okay. Now, I want you to touch my knees. I want you to use your open palms and I want you to stroke my knees."

I reach out with one hand. I can't help noticing that it's trembling. I don't feel well. I don't feel well at all. I put one hand on her knee. It's a warm knee, it gives a little to the touch. Nice knee. Pretend it's a pussycat. A bald pussycat. Without a tail.

"How's that?"

"I can't breathe."

When Sophie and I first got together the sex was great. Everything was great. We'd go for hours, days. We'd romp all night, a couple of carefree little critters, there in the tiger-striped half-light of the bedroom of my little Auckland flat, below the street lamp, as the traffic whispered and shushed past the window and the drunks called to one another in the distance. We'd go and go, head out to eat, come back, go all over again. We never did anything else. There was nothing else worth doing.

But then, after the flush of those first rapturous, heady, four or five years, I began to wonder. And you know what they say. If you're wondering, you ain't doing it right. I mean, hell, really, I've never been what you would call a specialist. I've always been more of an all-rounder. You know—a bit of this, a bit of that, a cuddle, a kiss, a few shared interests, a bit of a laugh, a bit of whiteware, and Bob's your uncle. That's the way I've always seen it. But I began to wonder if that was really how Sophie saw it.

"Sophie?" I said. We were lying awake at night in bed and it was dark and there were no points of reference. London was throbbing in the distance and all around, calling like a wounded beast. She didn't answer at first and it was silent and scary and I began to float. I lost all points of contact. It was the scariest question you could ever ask that I was nursing in my head and I didn't know what the future held.

"What?" She knew. Oh, she knew.

My head began to grow. It just kept getting bigger and bigger and less and less dense, as if it was filling with gas, and the rest of my body except my teeth disappeared and I was nothing but a great round inflated gaseous head the size of Jupiter, with teeth, floating in black space. "How is it . . . for you?"

"How's what?"

I now left my body entirely and I could feel her body receding too, flying away into space at the speed of light, as I expanded still further and she expanded and we both cooled and became tenuous and partly nonexistent and I thought this is what they mean by entropy. I thought if I reached out now to touch her hand she wouldn't be there at all. I'd pass right through her.

"Because, I mean, for me it's good." I could hear the sincerity in my own voice.

"Good." From somewhere way out there in the darkest coldest deepest reaches of outer space she put forth a hand all the way across the universe and touched my arm, once, briefly, with a forefinger, the way you'd tap a map to show someone where you live. There, right there. X marks the spot. "Anyway, I'm tired."

She rolled over and I came slamming back down into my body and I rolled over too. She went to sleep and I didn't and London howled and screamed and whistled and moaned in the distance and all around.

"Are you okay?" My hand is still on Melissa's knee. Melissa is looking concerned. Her eyes are large and close. What is it with eyes? All I ever see in eyes, is eyes. I used to see whole constellations.

"I . . ."

"You've gone all pale and trembly."

"I'm sorry, I don't seem to . . ."

"Hey, don't worry. I see a lot of this sort of thing."

"You do?"

"You'd be surprised. Anyway, I think that's probably enough for today."

In the doorway Melissa grabs my arm. "Wait." She ruffles my hair, then her own. She pinches her cheeks and starts jogging on the spot.

"What are you doing?"

"We might as well make it *look* like something's been going on."

"Good thinking! Try star jumps."

Suitably tousled, we emerge on deck via the aft companionway. The crowd on deck has scattered, people standing in ones, twos and threes, looking out at the sea, the sky. Melissa pours herself another champagne. The mainland is out of sight. The sun is beating down like a stick. We're out on blue water now: the Pacific is dark and deep as the evening sky and the swells are real swells; an endless, slow-shifting landscape of small blue hills. The bow rises and falls in long arcing swoops. Spray flies in rainbowing sheets from the bows. Ella is watching from over by the hors d'oeuvres. I take my courage in both hands.

"Hey, follow me." I grab Melissa by the hand and lead her forward to the bowsprit. We stand in the pulpit on the very tip of the bow. Clutching the railing, we're ahead of the whole boat, ahead even of the bow wave, and we can look straight down between our legs to the smooth blue water, rushing past, dizzyingly fast, first close, then far away. I lean forward, into the motion of the boat, brace my legs, and for just that second as the bow plunges I'm weightless, I'm flying.

"Look!" Melissa is pointing. In the water below are the dark rushing torpedo shapes of dolphins. Occasionally they break surface, their long muscular bodies mottled gray, black and white. She laughs. I wonder how she gets her teeth that white.

For all I know, she's doing it now. Somewhere, out there, across the blue sea, on a white-sand–ringed Pacific island she is right now, at this very moment, perhaps, turning into white-hot energy and they're spiraling away, together, the two of them, into the blue night.

Goddamnit. Ella is watching. I can see her, sitting in front of the wheelhouse, cradling Brian in her arms, watching.

"Melissa. I'm going to kiss you."

"Go for it. I'll be right behind you all the way."

"But no tongues."

"Perish the thought."

I lean forward, I shut my eyes, I think of Paris, and I kiss her. She's warm, soft-but-springy, and she tastes of salt, fish and future happiness.

I straighten up. I feel dizzy, but okay. I actually feel okay.

"Hey, tiger."

"For future reference, I prefer 'tiger' to 'pumpkin.'"

"You gotta earn it."

I glance back at the wheelhouse. Ella is no longer watching. But Russell is.

———————

Later in the afternoon, the island begins to emerge. First a dark smudge, it grows to a round-shouldered peak, broadening suddenly to a woolly, bush-clad base. Another island emerges as we approach, lower but larger. Gradually the islands get closer, until we can make out cliffs, palm trees, a bright line of sand at the water's edge. The sun is starting to drop in the sky as we slip through the pass, breakers foaming on the reef on either side, and enter the still, cyan waters of the lagoon. Everyone crowds the railings. To our right is Makulalanana, the sacred volcano: a singed bald head jutting above hunched bush-clad shoulders, dark, brooding and mysterious. Bands of sulfurous yellow and pink on the summit, lower down mottled patches of dark green and white on sooty black. To the left is the volcano's wife, Pakulalanana: green, fertile and bush-clad.

We glide silently between man and wife and anchor in a sheltered bay beneath the slopes of the volcano. The rattle of the anchor chain echoes from the hills. Tall, graceful palms and larger, spreading, white-trunked trees line the shore. Parrots call from the branches. A shoal of fish ruffles the surface of the lagoon.

It looks like paradise.

So what?

## Chapter 12

A SEAPLANE IS APPROACHING. Flying low, it clears the shoulder of the volcano, drops into the bay, the morning sun flashing on the leading edges of the wings. It skips once, leaving a white scar in the sea, skips again, and once more, then settles to plowing a long white furrow from sea to shore.

"Ah, that'll be the croissants." The elderly gentleman from the tent next door grins across at me, rubs his hands in anticipation and saunters down to the sea, accompanied by his wife.

I'm at the open door flap of an orange tent. Behind me Melissa is dressing in orange light. I'm looking out across a perfect bay. It's seven o'clock in the morning, maybe even earlier. The beach is still in shade, although the light is dazzling out on the water. I feel a little shaky and I've slept but little. There's not a breath of wind. Behind me, smoke from the volcano rises in a vertical column. The air is heavy, hard to breathe; the waves are lifeless, as if coated with oil. The palms droop their heads. In the light of dawn they seem alien, prehistoric. We even have a couple of dinosaurs; slipping silently into the water, the elderly couple glide out to neck level, cutting a V-shaped wake. A fish jumps.

Melissa appears behind me. "Morning, tiger. Sleep well?"

"No, not particularly. You?"

"Like a log."

The old couple wave and smile from the water. We wave back. Melissa snuggles her head on my shoulder.

"Feel like some breakfast . . . sweetheart?"

"Sure."

We stroll along the beach to the main encampment, hand in hand. I'm trying to put my memories of last night in order.

I remember climbing down the side of the *Cocksucker* into the motorboat. As we approach the shore I can make out orange tents ranged along the beach, sheltering just under the leafy fringe of the bush. There must be about fifty of them. We glide closer, across tiny turquoise ripples. The water is unbelievably clear. It's as if the boat is flying above sand, rocks, stones. Here and there are patches of coral. Blue, pink, red. A school of transparent fish scatter.

There's a pair of totem poles stuck upright in the beach, looming larger as we approach—stylized human figures, a male and a female, with feather headdresses and round staring eyes. There's a banner slung between them, and now I can read the words on it: ABANDON ALL INHIBITIONS YE WHO ENTER HERE.

"Fuck off!" The boat lurches violently. Drunken Denise has just tried to jump out. Ramon and Ken grin, but they're looking a little tense.

Very close now. I notice something in the water: a bunch of black dots grouped near the beach. Heads. There are twenty of them, lolling neck deep in the shallows, chins just clear of the tiny wavelets. An arm's length from each head is a glass of champagne. The heads give an ironic cheer as the boatman cuts the motor. We glide the last few feet and then the bow crunches on sand and we all lurch forward.

I climb over the gunwale and wade ashore with the others. The sand is as fine as talcum powder and we sink in right up to our ankles. The water is body temperature. You can hardly feel it at all. We walk right between the two totems and up the beach to where tables and chairs are arranged under the broad spreading trees. Staff are running. There's a scent of perfume and food and wine and the clink of glasses. Music is playing. A champagne cork pops.

Charles is waiting for us. He stands on a chair, with Karl on one side to steady him. "Ladies and Jellybeans, welcome one and all to Camp Paradise. You'll find that no effort has been spared to ensure your total comfort and pleasure at all times." He pauses to allow the cheers to die down. "Our policy here is to provide twenty-four-hour food and drink. If at any moment of the day or night you feel hungry, thirsty, dizzy, bored, sober, flatulent, hung-over or lonely, you have only to make your way to the bar/buffet area where staff are waiting to serve you in any way possible." More cheers. "Accommodation is under canvas but you'll find that the luxury tenting we have provided is . . . luxurious. Your luggage is waiting for you in your tent. Finally, while it is our policy at Camp Paradise to cater for all reasonable needs . . . please remember that unreasonable ones take precedence at all times."

Tents are allotted. We're in number twenty-five. We start along the beach, to unpack before dinner. The sun is falling, heading for a small gap of clear sea between the neighboring island and the end of the isthmus. Everything is going red. The clouds are going crazy. The sun is falling so fast I'm waiting for the splash.

There's a pregnant woman in a black bathing suit wading toward shore. She's sheltered by a huge straw sunhat, stabilized with a silk scarf, and swathed in a huge wet silk sheet that trails behind her in the water as she comes. Her belly is a perfect sphere, like a beach ball. Her head is down as she approaches, a loose twist of wet black hair falling across her collarbone, one arm swinging, an empty glass in her hand, her sharp shinbones cutting the water like catamaran hulls. It's a picture all right: the sea, the islands, the heat, the setting sun, the light on the waves. The woman lifts her head. She's all cheekbone. She's wearing a tight almost-smile behind her chunky black sunglasses, a let's-get-this-over-with sort of smile.

I remember her being taller. How can I have forgotten how tall she is? "Frederick." She doesn't remove her sunglasses.

"Oh, Sophie, hi." I sound as if I'm on helium. "I didn't know if you'd be here."

The shiny black surfaces of her sunglasses swing around. They lock onto Melissa. They scan, down and up. I happen to know that the eyes behind the glasses are light brown. She's a pale person, that's the look. Pale skin, black hair. She used to be more into earth tones. This holiday is going to cost her a fortune in sunblock. I should grab Melissa's hand. I should reach right over now and grab Melissa's hand, nice and casual, and say, "Oh and this is Melissa by the way."

Can't move. Can't even lift my arms.

"You must be Sophie, right? I'm Melissa."

The sunglasses don't move.

"Look, I really have to say this so I might as well just say it. I've seen *Shag City* four times and I think it's absolutely brilliant. I just loved it."

"Thanks." Still the sunglasses don't move.

And here he comes. Six-foot-something, tanned white-blond hair cut short. Six-pack. Narrow temples, wide jaw. Strong chin. Slightly crooked nose. A pair of little round wire-rimmed sunglasses halfway down his nose. Rugged, lined face. Around forty. Your thinking man's superhero. His eyes are narrow and green, almost khaki. Army-surplus eyes. He stops just outside my reach, ready to smile, ready to block and counterpunch. "Hey, Frederick, how ya doin'?"

"Hi, Matt."

"This is Melissa," says Sophie.

"Hi, how ya doin'?"

Four gunslingers, we stand facing one another. The sun slips below the surface of the sea, throwing out frantic distress signals in all directions, beacons of red, pink and yellow.

"Well," I say. I swing my arms.

Sophie's stomach is enormous. It's enormous and so round it could be a giant balloon. I'm not looking at it. I'm looking at everything else. I'm looking at the sky, at the sea and the waves. I'm not looking at the belly. "Have you guys been here long?"

Matt coughs. "We came over yesterday."

"Nice boat, huh?"

"Oh, yeah. Nice boat."

"Nice place."

Sophie is carved out of rock.

I throw out my arm, a stiff, jerky gesture, like I'm trying to lose a piece of sticking plaster. "So, ah, we better go and unpack. See you guys round."

Melissa follows reluctantly.

"Yeah, see ya round." Matt smiles.

Sophie says nothing. She rests one hand on the front of her stomach and takes off her sunglasses to watch us go. Her eyes are slightly bloodshot.

The tent is everything the hotel in Port Vila should have been. There are towels and soap, bottles of moisturizer and sunblock and mosquito repellent. Special lamps for bedtime reading and a thick foam rubber mattress with crisp freshly laundered sheets. I lie on the mattress. Everything is very far away. I feel tired, gritty and salty. Melissa is excited.

"She's a lot shorter than I expected."

"Five-two-and-a-half."

"She's got an amazing presence. And him, he's gorgeous. I mean, wow. He looks even better than he does on film. I can see why she left you for him."

"Hmm."

"God, I can't believe it. Sophie Carlisle and Matt Chalmers, in the flesh!"

"Incredible."

"Do you think she'd mind if I asked for an autograph?"

"I'm sure she'd be very happy to oblige."

Melissa's weight sinks onto the mattress next to me. "Wow. I'm so glad I came. This is going to be fantastic. What time's dinner?"

I close my eyes.

---

The seaplane is nosed up to the beach as the pilot lugs a huge wicker basket across the sand. It really is very impressive what they've done. The undergrowth has been cleared out from under the large spreading trees by the beach, to form a sort of a large shady central square, with tables dotted around. Arranged around the edges of the central clearing are the amenities: to one side a fully equipped bar, its roof thatched with palm leaves. Behind the bar is the kitchen tent. Smells of cooking and the clatter of saucepans drift on the breeze. Every so often a harassed-looking cook or waiter emerges to add another item to the laden buffet. There's fruit, pastries, cold meats, croissants, coffee and tea, cereals, three sorts of muesli, juices — you name it. On another side is the hairdresser's *fale*. There's a queue halfway to the beach already. A fattish blond woman with her head in curlers sits reading *Cleo* magazine against a backdrop of jungle creepers. Behind that is the massage hut. Groans of pleasurable abandon compete with the plaintive whine of the hair dryers.

On the opposite side of the square from the bar, under the boughs of a massive spreading tree, is a raised stage, with a movie screen behind it and a sprung dance floor in front, made of marine-ply. A couple of technicians are still working on the sound system. There's a young white guy in an old black baseball cap going CHUH CHUH into the microphones and an old black guy in a new white baseball cap twiddling knobs on the mixing desk. They're both wearing Hawaiian shirts. There are big fat black cables all over the place and the speakers are stacked three-high either side.

We choose an empty table, sit down. Already there are heads bobbing in the shallows. Drunken Denise is there, with Ramon and Ken to keep her mouth clear of the waves. An enormously fat woman wades in to join them, toting several bottles of champagne. Here and there people are sprawled on deck chairs with drinks and cocktails, books, magazines. Out on the bay a speedboat is towing a parasail. The *Cocksucker* rides at anchor in the bay, a wet, white dream. In the space of a few minutes, the sun clears the shoulder of the volcano, the still of the early morning burns off like fog, the temperature rises by about five degrees, and a gentle land breeze picks up. We're in business.

Charles wanders by in G-string, cowboy hat and flip-flops. He has the build of a middle-aged construction-site foreman: he's all stomach. He has an elegant crystal champagne flute in one hand and a bacon-wrapped quail in the other. He's munching it like an apple. I glance at my watch. It's eight o'clock in the morning. He's looking flushed and unsteady. "Hey, Freddy boy!"

"Charles, hi. How are you?"

"Having fun?"

"Great, thanks. Great party. Thanks for inviting us."

"Seen the toilets yet?"

"Not this morning, no."

"Check 'em out. They're bloody amazing." He approaches, crabwise, frowning. "You've lost weight, mate."

"Oh, everyone says that."

"Looking good." He pats my tummy, grins obscenely at Melissa, who grins back. Charles laughs like a drain and empties his champagne glass.

"How about some fruit juice and muesli, pumpkin?"

"Thanks . . . dear heart."

Charles's eyes go round. Melissa turns to him. "Refill for you?"

Charles goes to hand her the glass, then snatches it back. "On second thoughts just bring the bottle."

Charles watches her go. "Christ, mate, you haven't wasted any time." Charles is a high-flyer in the stratospheric world of film production. He spends almost all his time in LA and probably visits New Zealand about once every ten years for family funerals. His Kiwi accent gets stronger every year. "Where'd you pick her up?"

"We met in Selfridges. In garden furniture."

Charles nods thoughtfully, watching Melissa wiggle across the sand. She's in a minuscule tan-colored string bikini. "Bet she fucks like a weasel, eh?"

"I wouldn't know."

Charles looks puzzled.

"I've never fucked a weasel."

He grins. On his breath I can smell beer, champagne, marijuana, whiskey, chicken and something old and unidentifiable. Possibly seaweed. "What's her name?"

"Melissa."

"Fuckin' dynamite, mate. Where'd you dig her up?"

"Selfridges. In garden furniture. She was just going by and she said have you got the time, and I said . . ."

"Little minx, mate."

"I thought she was a weasel."

"Fuckin' polecat, mate." He lurches.

I nod, smiling, and look around, hoping for a tidal wave or an eruption. He can go on like this for hours. But don't be fooled. He may be drunk but he's as sharp as a tack. In fact the drunker he gets the sharper he gets. This, incidentally, is the sad truth about the elite: they are the elite because they are better. Not one of the elite on this island got where they are today merely thanks to their wealthy and privileged backgrounds. After all, I have a wealthy and privileged background and look at me. Privilege and wealth are only two of the requirements: you also have to be smart, motivated and disciplined. Good-looking doesn't hurt, either. Yes, they're better than us. Pure and simple. Smarter, richer, better-looking. That's why I prefer my geniuses dead, poor, unappreciated in their lifetime and preferably misguided. Karl Marx is good, Van Gogh, people like that.

Charles is looking sideways at me. "You know Soph's here?"

"Oh, yeah." I try for breezy. "Yeah, I saw her last night, when we came in. She's looking good. Good to catch up. Haven't seen her for a while."

He nods. "Matt's here too."

"Yeah, I saw him too." I smile and look enthusiastic.

Charles raises a finger. "Watch him, mate, watch him."

"How do you mean?"

"Oh, he's insatiable, mate. Fuckin' tomcat, mate." He gestures with his chin in the direction of Melissa.

"You don't seriously mean . . . ?"

Charles shakes his head. "He can't help himself. Can't help himself, mate. He's a rabbit, he's a snake on heat, he's a little . . . fuckin' . . . fucker. Mate." Charles eyes me narrowly.

"I see."

"Watch him. Watch him."

"I will."

"Watch him like a hawk. Like an eagle. Like an owl. Like a fuckin' . . . ah . . . watch him like a fuckin' . . . watcher."

"Thanks for the advice."

"So, how do you guys get on nowadays? You and Soph?"

"Oh, fine. We're best mates."

"That's good."

"Oh, yeah. It's all in the past now. You know how it is. Water under the bridge."

"Yeah, I know, mate, I know."

A battered little plywood runabout putters very, very slowly past, about ten feet from shore. It's crammed to the gunwales with kids. Big kids, little kids, boys and girls, barefoot, in raggedy T-shirts. The driver is a kid of about twelve in a pair of cutoff jeans and an International Harvester baseball cap. The whole boat is a mass of skinny black limbs and fat white smiles. There is maybe an inch and half of freeboard. Every face on the boat is turned shoreward, eyes wide. As the boat comes by, I notice two figures come forward from the shelter of the trees. Two big men, Melanesian, heavily built, wearing cutoff jeans and black T-shirts with the word SECURITY stenciled across the shoulders. They stand, arms folded, watching the boat go by.

"Where do they come from?"

"They're kids from the village across the bay. They'll be sending sightseeing expeditions all day."

"No, I mean the guys in the T-shirts."

"Oh, *them.* Security."

"What do you need that for?"

Charles shrugs. "We don't want stuff going missing. That village over there doesn't even have running water." I look across the bay. I can see a thin column of smoke rising from the bush and what might be houses under the trees. "See that bloke over there, at the table?" I look. There's a distinguished-looking Melanesian man sitting down, reading the paper. "He's the local chief of police. The security are all off-duty policemen."

"So who actually owns this island?"

Charles grins. "I do."

"You've bought it?"

"Ah, buying it, yeah."

"What are you going to do with it?"

"Oh, I've got plans, mate. Big plans. Yeah, the Caribbean's crowded. Fuckin' hellhole, mate. I had a little island there next door to Mick Jagger's place. Worse than Piccadilly Circus, mate.

Had to sell it. Couldn't take it, eh. Boats going by all day, bloody parties every night—other people's parties, this is. Nah, fuckin' hellhole. South Pacific. Way to go, mate, way to go."

Melissa comes back with a bottle of champagne, followed by a waitress with a tray laden with breakfast. Charles takes the champagne, winks and toddles down to the sea. Cheered by the drinking bathers he pops the cork, throws a high five to the fat woman, and slips into the water.

Melissa and I settle down to breakfast. Russell and Ella come up. Russell is lugging Brian, Ella has flippers, snorkels and masks. Russell's shorts are fluorescent, but his torso outshines them by far. They're going snorkeling and they want us to mind Brian. "Don't worry," says Russell, "there's nothing to it." He hands me Brian while Ella hands Melissa a huge carryall.

"There's a bottle in there if he's hungry—and all the gear if he fills his nappies."

"How will I know if he has?"

"Don't worry, you'll know."

"He might cry a bit at first," says Russell, "but he'll stop as soon as we're out of sight. He always does."

"If you're out of sight, how do you know that?"

"Relax. It's like the fridge light."

"Where are you guys going?" says Melissa.

"You should come," says Ella. "Frederick can manage by himself. Can't you, Frederick?"

Melissa looks at me. So does Ella. "You go ahead. Honeybunch." Melissa goes to find some flippers. Ella and Russell smile confidently and step out for the water. Brian lets them get about ten feet then he pulls the rip cord. The kid has unbelievable lungs. Ella and Russell turn, smile a little less confidently, and head for the water again.

Brian screams.

Ella turns. She is no longer smiling.

Brian howls.

Ella wavers. She takes a step toward us, her lower lip quivering. Russell grabs her arm and drags her into the waves. Now, Brian really lets out all the stops. The bathing drinkers turn to watch. The bartender looks up from his daiquiris. The security guard on the beach covers his ears. It is now that I spot the fatal flaw in the fridge-light theory. Ella and Russell will never be out of sight. Brian can sit here hollering his lungs out and watching them snorkel up and down the bay all afternoon. I'm going to have to move. "Come on, Brian." I follow the path to the lavatory block heading inland. As soon as we've turned the first corner, Brian stops. It's like flicking a switch. He looks around him, round-eyed, trying to catch at passing leaves. Below the almost deafening birdsong, I hear a distant thump-thump-thump, coming from way off in the bush, which I guess must be the generators. This place must have the power requirements of a small town.

We turn a corner. "Well, Brian, these are the lavatories. What do you think?"

"Duh."

I must say the lavatories really are a masterpiece, and they're constructed almost entirely in banana leaves. Passing through an arched opening crowned with banana leaves, we enter a large circular structure with a domed roof, built from two-by-fours, number eight wire and banana leaves. There are shower booths with banana-leaf partitioning, hot and cold water, real porcelain hand basins, mirrors, hair dryers, complimentary soap, shampoo and hand cream. Lavatories, once again with banana-leaf partitions, are, alas, not equipped with flush toilets, but teams of willing staff in face masks are emptying the buckets as fast as we can fill them. It's cool and green and leafy, and there's the soothing tinkle of running water. There's even piped music. Split Enz.

"Duh," says Brian.

Brian and I go back to the beach. His parents are now merely two dots in the bay and he pays them no attention at all. We sit in the shade of a tree. There's no sign of Sophie. Brian is sitting bolt upright. He looks around, twisting his head through a hundred and twenty degrees. He looks straight up. He points into the canopy of the tree.

"Dah."

I look up. "Yes, Brian, they're coconuts."

"Duh." Brian looks at the coconuts. I look at the sea. There's nothing really to this child-minding business after all. The bush, the sea, the sand, the sky. Blue on green on white on blue. I lie back. It's blissfully hot. I close my eyes. There's a bird trilling in the bush. It sounds exactly like my cellphone.

"Well, Brian, you might as well give up now. It doesn't get any better than this."

"Dah."

"I mean, let's face it. The best-case scenario from here on is that you get old and die." Brian doesn't answer. I open one eye. "Wouldn't you agree, Brian?" Brian isn't committing himself one way or the other. Now that I think of it, there's something pop-eyed about him. "Brian?" I look more closely. He is clutching a handful of sand. He has traces of sand around his mouth. "Brian? Have you been eating sand? Brian? Open wide, now." How do you open a baby's mouth? I know how to open a dog's. You pry it open with a stick between the gums. Turns out it works for babies too. Brian's mouth is packed solid with sand.

"Brian! Spit out the sand!" Brian looks a little worried, like he thinks I might not be entirely normal. I hook my finger in and scoop out a glob. Brian smacks his lips. "Dah." He looks around.

"Brian, don't eat the sand, okay?"

"Dah." He looks at me with intense concentration. He frowns with effort. "Duh." His face reddens. "Duhh." He relaxes and looks around again. "Dah." He points at the coconuts. I smell something. I'm going to skip the details.

Once that little job's done, I rummage around and find the

bottle in the holdall. I hold out the bottle and Brian opens his mouth. He knows exactly what this is all about. In goes the teat. I lean against the tree, he leans against me, grabs the bottle and sucks away. The fluid in the bottle sinks rapidly. When the pressure differential gets too great, Brian pauses, opens his mouth to let some air in to the bottle to equalize, and sucks again. In no time the bottle is empty. Brian sighs, leans back against my stomach and falls instantly asleep. I realize that I am extremely uncomfortable; there's a bit of tree trunk sticking in my back and my left buttock is aching. I wouldn't move for the world.

"Orange juice?" It's Sophie. She's come up behind me, from the ablutions block. She's in the same swimming costume, silk shawl across her shoulders, which parts over her belly like stage curtains. She's pretending everything's normal. She's pretty good at that.

"Yeah, ta."

She waddles over to the bar. She collects two orange juices and comes over. I think Sophie and I must be the only two on the island who are drinking orange juice. She hands me mine and sits down, leaning against my coconut palm. We're at ninety degrees. Our shoulders are almost touching but we're not looking at each other. I can smell shampoo. I can smell soap. She sighs and runs a hand through her hair. "I just saw a snake back there."

"Oh?"

"By the path. Very pretty. Yellow and black stripes." She yawns.

"You should tell someone."

"The place is crawling with them."

"Are they poisonous?"

"Deadly. But they never bite."

"What's the point in being deadly if you never bite?"

"If you're deadly, you don't *have* to bite." Sophie goes to say something else, but changes her mind. I twist my head to look at her. She takes off her sunglasses, blinks, half-rolls her eyes.

"Contacts bothering you?"

"All this sun. Dries them out." She puts her sunglasses back on.

"I saw you in *Empire*."

"Stupid photo."

"No, I liked it."

She shrugs. She hates compliments. "Sorry about yesterday."

"You don't have to be sorry."

"Just didn't expect to see you. It was a bit of a surprise."

"That's okay. I didn't expect to see you either. As a matter of fact it never crossed my mind that you might be here, not even once. Just never thought of it for some reason."

"Haven't seen you for ages."

"You've been busy."

"Yeah. I've been busy. So how are you?"

"I'm great. I'm just great."

"You've lost weight."

"I have?"

"Definitely. You're looking good."

"Congratulations, by the way."

She smiles.

"How's it going? The pregnancy?"

"I feel sick all day. I can't drink. I can't smoke. My skin's gone to shit. I can't sleep. I have fluid retention, I'm spending half my life on the toilet, my back aches and I have to get someone else to do up my shoes."

"But apart from that, okay?"

"Apart from that it's just great."

"Do you know if it's a boy or a girl?"

She shakes her head. "As long as it's healthy." She pauses. "I'm sorry it happened this way."

"Oh, hell, don't worry about it."

"I didn't plan it. It just kind of, well, happened."

There's something sad about her. I can sense it. Something is troubling her. "How do you feel about it?"

She puts a hand on her stomach. "Oh, really, really sure."

"Well, that's great."

"Oh, yeah. I've never been so sure of anything in my whole life." She pauses uncomfortably. "I was going to call you."

"Of course."

"But I didn't know you were going to be here."

"It was a last-minute decision."

"Must have been a bit of a shock. When you saw me like that."

"I already knew."

"How?"

"Oh, the grapevine. You know."

She smiles. "Tamintha."

"I can neither confirm nor deny."

"I suppose I felt sort of guilty."

"Don't be silly."

She finishes her orange juice. "Sometimes I think you're a much better person than me."

"Rubbish."

"You brought someone with you."

"Oh, Melissa? Yeah."

"Where did you meet her?"

"Selfridges. Garden furniture."

"Where you go to read?"

"Yeah."

Sophie nods, slowly. "She seems nice."

"Oh, she is. She's very nice."

"You seem to get on really well."

"You think so?"

"What does she do?"

"She's a student."

"She seems quite young."

"She is quite young but she's very mature for her age."

Sophie nods. "How long have you been going out?"

"Not that long. We're kind of pretty serious. I mean, she's crazy about me and we're very happy but we're not necessarily fully committed. Long-term. Or at least I'm not. Necessarily."

She inspects a fingernail. "I'm really glad you're seeing someone. I do want you to be happy."

"Oh, I am. I'm very happy. So how's Matt?"

"Oh, he's all right."

"He must be really looking forward to the baby."

"Well, he's had three already, so he's kind of used to it."

"Oh. Yeah. I suppose so."

She rubs her leg. "He was a bit shocked at first."

"He'd have come round by now, I suppose?"

"Yeah, he's fine."

Brian, leaning against my stomach, jerks suddenly in his sleep. His arm shoots out, fingers stiff, as if to ward off a great big hairy black spider. Gradually he subsides and the hand settles again on my leg. Sophie is drawing on the sand with her finger: a baby body with stick arms and stick legs and a little curly topknot. Brian wakes up. He sits up straight, stretches, yawns. "Dah."

"Hullo, little man," says Sophie. She holds out a finger. Brian puts it in his mouth. "Cute, isn't he?"

"Yeah, very."

"Dah." Brian removes Sophie's finger and starts to crawl toward the coconut tree. No points for style: he crawls with one leg cocked like a pissing dog, but it gets him there.

The next question is so casual I surprise myself. "So when is the baby due, exactly?"

The answer is pretty casual too. "Six weeks."

Mental arithmetic is not my strong point. I'm still working on it when Brian, who has almost reached the coconut palm, misses the ground. It's the sort of thing only a baby can do. He just completely misses and pitches forward, quite suddenly, face-first into the sand. A lot of things happen very quickly all at once. I lunge forward, my arms outstretched. Just as I reach Brian there's a white noiseless flash and a sudden wash of green, and then I'm seeing stars, but I have Brian. I have him by the waist. I pick him up and dust the sand off his face. He hiccups a few times, then turns to me. He's gone bright red but he seems to be more excited than frightened. "Dah. Dah, dah, dah!" He points into the bush, looking up into my face. "Dah, dah."

"Yes, Brian, yes, you're okay." I can feel his drool, wet on my collarbone. The kid's all right. Ugly, a little overexcited, but all right. Sophie is about six feet away, doubled up on her knees, cradling her head in her hands. We must have both lunged at the same time, and banged heads.

"Sophie?"

She makes a small muffled noise which means don't-talk-to-me-I'm-in-pain. In circumstances like this, I know exactly what to do. Nothing. I put Brian on my lap, dust him down a little more, and wait.

"Dah."

"Yes, Brian."

Sophie straightens up. "Jesus, that hurt."

"I think we banged heads."

"I *know* we banged heads. Didn't that *hurt* you?"

"Ah, a little, yeah."

"Christ, your head must be made of concrete."

"Let me see."

She takes her hand away from her eye. It's not a pretty sight. There's a small cut and it's swelling already. "Oh man, you're going to get a shiner out of that."

"Oh, no."

"Got you right on the temple, sorry."

She puts her hand back over her eye.

"Here." It's the bartender, standing over us holding a bundled tea towel. "I've wrapped some ice in it."

"Oh, thanks." Sophie takes the towel and holds it to her eye.

"Yeah," says the bartender, "you won't need stitches but keep the ice on it for at least half an hour." He saunters away. I have to say, they're *good* here.

"Dah."

"Yes, Brian."

Sophie and I move to the shade. We sit in silence, Brian on Sophie's knee. "Sophie," I say. I brace myself. My voice sounds far away. "This baby."

She lowers the icepack. She looks at me. "Yes?"

"When did you realize you were pregnant?"

"Why?"

"Could it be mine? Technically speaking? In terms of timing?"

She looks at me for a long, long moment. She shakes her head. "It's not yours, Frederick."

"Dah." Brian points at nothing in particular.

I have done a terrible thing. I have done something inexcusable. What I have done is a dirty, low-down trick. There's just no excuse, and I just can't feel sorry. I'm glad. The baby is *mine*. Somehow, I just know.

"Dah, dah, dah." Brian wiggles and jiggles.

"I really think this baby could be mine."

Sophie stares at me. Her face is stone.

"I didn't mention it at the time, but that night, the night before you left. The condom . . . there was a hole in it."

She stares at me. She can't speak.

"So . . ."

"You didn't say anything about that."

"I didn't think . . ."

"You didn't say a word."

"I didn't know you were pregnant. I didn't know. If I'd known . . ."

Sophie puts Brian down on the sand and stands up. She looks

up and down the beach. She's silent for a long, long time. Finally she speaks. "It's not yours."

"You can't be sure of that. How can you be sure? The timing. It's too close. It must be possible."

She's silent again for a long time. She's gone as white as a sheet. She opens her mouth to speak, hesitates, and closes it. She looks up and down the beach. "It's not yours."

"It could be. It could be mine. Why couldn't it be mine?"

"It's not yours, and I don't want you to say anything about this, to anyone."

"Dah," says Brian. "Dah."

"It could be mine, and if it is I have a right to know."

"I will talk to you about this later. I don't want to talk about this now."

"When will we talk about it?"

"When I've had a chance to think."

"When will that be?"

Sophie looks away, down the beach.

"And Matt, he has a right to know too."

Sophie turns on me in fury and fear, her face mottled white and red. "Don't say anything to Matt. Don't you dare say anything to Matt."

"All right. I won't."

She makes a visible effort to calm herself. "Give me some time. Just give me some time."

"How much time do you need?"

"Just leave it for now. I don't want to talk about this." She walks away down the beach. The child is mine. The child is *mine*.

"Dah," says Brian. "Dah."

## Chapter 13

**INT. PALACE BALCONY/GARDEN—DAY.**

THE PRINCE STANDS ON THE BALCONY. HE IS LOOKING
DOWN AT THE PALACE GARDENS, WEEPING. AMONGST THE
PLAYING FOUNTAINS, WHERE BIRDS OF PARADISE FLIT
LIKE JEWELS FROM BRANCH TO BRANCH, THE QUEEN IS
TAKING HER PLEASURE WITH A BLACK SLAVE OF MAS-
SIVE PROPORTIONS. THE PRINCE DRAWS HIS JEWELED
SWORD.

**INT. PALACE CORRIDORS—DAY.**

THE PRINCE RUNS THROUGH THE CORRIDORS OF THE
PALACE, HIS SWORD IN HIS HAND. MULTICOLORED
BIRDS, HUMMINGBIRDS AND FINCHES, SCATTER BEFORE
HIM.

**EXT. PALACE GARDEN—DAY.**

THE PRINCE RUNS THROUGH THE GARDEN. HE FINDS THE
QUEEN AND THE BLACK SLAVE, WHO COWER IN FEAR AT
HIS APPROACH. WITH ONE STROKE THE PRINCE SHARYAR
BEHEADS THE BLACK SLAVE. HE GRASPS THE QUEEN BY
HER LONG BLACK HAIR, AND RAISES HIS SWORD.

Queen

Mercy!

Prince

Infidel.

HIS SWORD SWEEPS THROUGH THE AIR. THE QUEEN'S
HEAD SWINGS BY THE HAIR FROM HIS HAND. WEEPING
COPIOUSLY, THE PRINCE SHARYAR KISSES THE HEAD OF
THE QUEEN AND, CRADLING IT ON HIS LAP, FALLS TO
HIS KNEES ON THE BLOODSTAINED GRASS. JEWEL-LIKE
BIRDS FLIT ABOUT HIS HEAD.

"Ouch," says Russell.

"What happened?" says Ella. They're sitting at a table in Central Square with wet hair and a fruit juice.

"We bumped heads. It was an accident."

Sophie sits down.

"That's a really nasty-looking lump," says Ella. "Are you sure you're okay?" She puts a hand on Sophie's arm.

"Yes, I'm all right, I'm fine."

Sophie hates fuss. I like a bit of fuss, myself, but no one's offering. "I've got a nasty-looking lump too."

Of course everyone crowds around Sophie. Pregnant women get all the attention. Ella goes to take Brian, but he clings to my shirt. Kids, they just love me. They adore me.

"Wow," says Russell. "He really does like you."

"Children have innate good taste."

"Duh," says Brian.

"So did you get along okay?"

"Fine, but next time don't feed him raisins, okay?" I sit down. Brian looks around perkily. He's happy.

Here we are. The four of us. All together for the first time since

Sophie and I split up. It's heartbreaking. We were a pretty special foursome, we four. Me, Sophie, Russell and Ella. They're Canadian. I love Canadians, all Canadians. Living as they do right next door to a big bossy neighbor that everyone thinks you're really just a part of anyway, Canadians *understand.*

We met in London on a Thames river cruise organized for the wrap of *Chick Fever,* which was a little TV job Sophie had. Ella did some postproduction work on it. The four of us just hit it off. Russell and I happened to be standing next to each other at the railing, watching the Thames roll by, and we got talking, standing there. It turned out we had very similar ideas about space exploration. For me there was no looking back. Russell introduced us to Ella, and away we went. We swapped phone numbers, and we rushed home and phoned them up the very next day. It was almost romantic, like our couple had a crush on their couple. Like being part of something just a tiny bit bigger than yourself. We used to do all sorts of stuff together. I don't mean anything pathological, I mean fun things. Bracing, head-clearing stuff. Walking holidays. Bike rides.

Russell coughs and clears his throat. This is tragic. This is a heartbreaker. Here we are now sitting around this table, the four of us, and there is nothing to say. It's over. It's dead. And what a terrible way to go. Russell sighs and scratches his nose. Sophie is sitting bolt upright, staring into space. Ella is staring at Brian. Brian is trying to get into my mouth. He runs his fingers up and down the gum line, searching for a gap.

I wish someone would say something.

What we had, we four, is gone, and it was good and beautiful and it deserved more. It just doesn't seem right. Someone should say something. Something elegiac.

"Well," I say. "Here we all are." I guess that about sums it up.

Russell shifts on his seat. "I'll go get some fresh ice for that eye." He heads for the bar. We sit in silence.

"So," I say to Ella, "where's Melissa?"

"Matt's teaching her to duck dive. You know she's never snorkeled before?"

"Did she do okay?"

"Oh, she's a natural."

"Doesn't surprise me in the least."

Ella smiles. "She seems really nice."

"We're very happy."

We both flick glances at Sophie. "Yes, very nice," she snaps.

"Hey, we saw a sea snake." Russell is back with the ice. "*Two* sea snakes in fact."

Ella scoffs. "The second was driftwood."

"But aren't they deadly poisonous?" I say, doing my very best to sound like a concerned lover. I risk a glance at Sophie. She's looking even more irritable than before.

Ella sips her drink. "Don't worry, they never bite."

"We'd all be dead by now if they did. They're everywhere." Russell points at the sand, at a crosshatched pattern of lines that leads under the table and away into the bush. "See those marks in the sand? Snake tracks."

"For sea snakes they seem to spend an awful lot of time on land."

"Most of it, in fact. They come out to bask."

"If they spend most of their time on land why are they called sea snakes?"

There's a shriek from the direction of the water. We all look that way. Matt and Melissa are just emerging, in snorkels and flippers. Shaking the water out of her hair, Melissa is extremely Bond girl, and Matt, I would have to say in the interests of narrative accuracy, is extremely Bond. They're both laughing at something. Sophie watches them, one-eyed. About ten yards out, Matt realizes something is wrong. The smile drops off his face and he hurries over. Everyone tries to explain at once and Matt starts fussing. Sophie loses it completely. I could have told him. She hates fuss.

"Could we all please *drop it*?" She sits at the table fuming and silent. Matt looks pissed off.

Melissa recovers first. "Anyway," she says, "that was a great swim." She chucks me her towel. "You should have come, pumpkin."

"I was left holding the baby, wasn't I?"

"Dah," says Brian.

"Of course," Russell clears his throat, "the real danger around here isn't the snakes. Or even the sharks."

"There are sharks?"

He waves a hand. "You better believe it. But it's the stonefish you gotta watch out for. They lurk in the shallows, usually on a rocky or muddy bottom. They're about so big"—he holds his hands about fifteen centimeters apart—"and they're impossible to spot. I mean, *impossible*. They're invisible. You can be staring right at one, you wouldn't even know unless it moved. And they never move."

"How come?" Melissa's looking interested. Sophie's looking disgusted. Russell's looking manic.

"They look exactly like stones. They're deformed. They're the ugliest animals I've ever seen, apart from cane toads, tapeworms and those little dogs without any hair."

"And they're poisonous you say?"

"Extremely poisonous. More poisonous even than the sea snakes. I'm telling you, these guys make cobra venom look silly."

"Eek." Melissa comes over, picks up Brian, sits on my knee and wriggles. I snatch a glance at Sophie. She's staring at her toes.

"The venom acts on the nervous system. First it immobilizes the voluntary muscles: the limbs, the speech organs. Then, as the poison spreads, it starts to affect the autonomic system, which includes the respiratory system. Imagine. You're lying there, fully conscious, unable to speak, unable to move, in mind-boggling pain. Gradually it gets harder and harder to breathe, until finally you suffocate to death." He leans forward. "And get this—guess how many spines the stonefish has." He pauses dramatically. "Thirteen."

"Wow," says Melissa. "How do you know all this?"

"I was reading about it on the plane."

"Is there an antidote?"

Russell shakes his head. "But you do have a chance. The poison is thermolabile. That means it's destroyed by exposure to heat. You have to heat the wound straightaway. I mean, boiling water, a lighted cigarette, anything, jam it straight on the wound. If you're quick enough the heat will destroy enough of the venom before it has time to propagate from the wound to the bloodstream. Once it makes it to your bloodstream, forget it, you're finished. You have maybe two or three minutes from the time the poison first enters your system." He sips his fruit juice. "You know what really gets me? Most poisonous animals are brightly colored, to warn off predators. With the stonefish it's the opposite. It's like they *want* you to step on them."

"And you've just been *swimming*?"

"But I haven't finished. There's also *Conus geographus*."

"There's . . . what?"

"It's a type of underwater snail with a very beautiful cone-shaped shell. It has *the* strongest venom in the natural world. There is nothing to match it. It captures its prey by firing a tiny poison-tipped dart out of the front of its head. So if you see one, whatever you do, keep away from the thin end. Always pick it up by the thick end."

"Pick it up? You have to be kidding."

"They're sought-after by collectors the world over. The shells are very beautiful."

"And what do you do if you're stung by one of those?"

"Don't be."

"Anything else?"

"Jellyfish, stingrays, moray eels. The eels aren't poisonous but they can take your hand off. There's a lot of them about here. I saw one snorkeling just now. I guess there'll probably be scorpions in the bush somewhere. Maybe funnel-webs, but I wouldn't really know. Giant centipedes, a strong possibility. They grow to about thirty or forty centimeters, they have a shiny dark-brown carapace, are difficult to distinguish amongst fallen leaves and branches on the forest floor and are, naturally, highly venomous. I guess that's it, as long as we don't get an eruption."

"But hey, we haven't talked about sharks!" says Melissa.

Sophie stands up. "I don't feel so good. I'm going to go and lie down." She stalks off to her tent. Matt follows her.

"Well," says Russell.

"Indeed," says Ella.

"Duh," says Brian.

"She seems nice," says Melissa.

"Oh, she is," says Russell.

Ella sighs.

I dislodge Melissa, not an easy feat, and stand up. "Excuse me," I say. I head for the ablutions block.

---

I need to think. I need to formulate a clear, robust policy. I run a basin of cold water. I wash my face. Then I make the usual blunder. I stop to look in the mirror. There's an entirely new wrinkle on my forehead. It's the stupidest forehead wrinkle I've ever seen. It cuts right across the middle of my forehead like I'm wearing a hairnet. I'm sure I didn't have it when I left London.

I have to think clearly. There is a real chance that the child is mine. A paternity test will have to be carried out, but now that I know for sure that there really is a concrete possibility that I am the father of Sophie's child, I'm reeling. One thing I know: it can't be bad news. It just can't be. I don't care about anything else. The child is mine. I've got that feeling, that gambler's hunch, when you just know. I just know it.

I have to admit I'm disappointed by Sophie's reaction. I had a vague, unrealistic hope that she might be a little more positive about it. Still, it would be a shock, naturally. She's shocked. She's reeling. She could yet come around. And of course you never can tell. The way she's clamming up and shutting down and refusing to look at me, it might be that she's wrestling with feelings of rekindled love. It could be. She could be secretly, desperately hoping that I'm right and the baby is mine, but unable to face her own feelings, or unable to admit them for fear of the implications and consequences. It's possible. She could be in her tent right now, fervently hoping against hope that I am, in fact, the father of this child—*even though she doesn't realize it.* She must at the very least have some misgivings about the thought of bearing a child to Matt Chalmers. It only stands to reason. I'm pretty sure I detected at least some ambivalence there. Anyway, the thing to do for now is to stay calm, do nothing to enrage her, and to watch for opportunities to widen the gap between them. It's a terrible thing, hope.

A beautiful gay boy walks past with a towel over one shoulder and a glass of champagne in his hand. He's probably about twenty-five. He's an inch and a half taller than me and half my weight. He's exactly the right color. He's got exactly the right hair and exactly the right shorts. He's got the right earring, the right measurements and the right sunglasses. It's official. Looks *are* everything. He catches my eye as he passes. "Amazing, eh?"

"Sure."

He fills the basin next to me and splashes his face. "Just shows what you can achieve."

"I guess it does."

"They brought half of it out by helicopter." He dries his face and sticks out a hand. "I'm Joe."

"Hi Joe, Frederick."

"Oh, you're Sophie Carlisle's husband?"

"That's me."

"I saw *Shag City*." He looks at me with a little too much interest. "That was all about you guys, wasn't it?"

"Not remotely."

He nods. "Anyway, I'm the entertainment officer. It's my job to ensure that people don't behave themselves too much."

"Sounds reasonable."

"You aren't behaving yourself, are you, Frederick?"

"As little as possible."

"Good man. Got your activities sorted?"

"I'm working on it."

He ticks off on his fingers. "Volleyball, parasailing, waterskiing, Hawaiian massage—that's booking up fast, get in early— snorkeling, you name it. You dive?"

"Well, I do have a license."

"Do the wreck dive, mate. It's brilliant. There's a whole ship down there. It's unreal."

"You've done it yourself?"

"Oh yeah, I come out here every year. With Charles." He gets curious. "Have you known Charles for long?"

"He's more a friend of a friend."

He nods, glances left and right, leans close. His skin is so perfect it's like plastic. The whites of his eyes are like porcelain. "Mate, let me tell you, when I met Charles, I was a mess. I mean, I was going the wrong direction. You know what I mean?"

"You know what, Joe? I *do* know what you mean. I happen to be going the wrong direction myself. And have been for some time."

Joe nods. My sincerity has obviously made an impression. "Okay," he says, "I hear you. So just you let me tell you this. You know what turned it around for me?"

"Dietary fiber?"

He doesn't even blink. "Charles. He turned it around for me. He *really* turned it around for me." He glances over his shoulder and shifts back to the original leg. "You know, a lot of people they only see the exterior of Charles, you know what I mean?"

"You mean, like, the outside?"

"Exactly! What's on the *outside*. The party animal. That's all some people see. The wealth, the success, the flash boats, the charter jets, the huge parties, the fun, the mind games, the drugs, the wild orgies, the mindless unending hedonistic insanity of it all . . ." He pauses for breath. His eyes cross and uncross. He stares into the middle distance.

"Hedonistic insanity . . ." I prompt gently.

"Oh, yeah. But there's a whole other side to Charles. This is what people don't realize. This guy is deep. You know what I mean? I mean, I *love* this guy, and it's not just because of the wealth, the parties, the . . ."

"The other stuff."

"Yeah. All that. It's because if you need someone to turn to, *he* is the guy to turn to. I mean"—he glances over his shoulder again—"if it wasn't for Charles, I wouldn't be here at all."

"I guess none of us would."

"No, I mean I wouldn't be *here*." He shakes his head. "No bullshit. And look at me now." He puts a hand on my shoulder. "Mate, talk to Charles. Talk to him. Nothing ever happens by chance. Whatever happens, and I mean *whatever*, there's always a reason, eh. There's always a reason. You know what I'm saying?"

"Always?"

"Always."

"Promise?"

"One hundred percent guaranteed." He punches my arm. "Wreck dive. Put your name down. Whiteboard, in the bar."

He's gone. I turn back to the mirror. Look at those eyes. These are the eyes of a father. Someone small and defenseless and not even born yet depends on those eyes. The essence of fatherhood has already become clear to me. Fatherhood is not a matter of opinion or choice. It's a simple matter of fact. By God. I straighten my back. I square my shoulders. It takes a while, but I manage it. I am the father of a child, and if I have to, I'm going to fight. Whatever Sophie thinks. Whatever it takes. Pleading, begging, letter-writing, lawyers, gossip columnists, DNA tests of fecal matter stolen from rubbish bins in the wee small hours, anything.

Anything? An evil, insane and totally idiotic scheme has just occurred to me. Business as usual, in other words.

When I get back to the table, Melissa has gone back to the tent but she left instructions with Ella for me to join her there with a margarita. I trudge across to the bar. They never mention this in the travel brochures, by the way. Trudging is the only way you *can* walk across fine white tropical sand. It's very photogenic but it's a pain in the arse to walk on, plus it's way too bright. You can't see a thing. Yellow is a much more practical color.

The enormously fat woman and a few more beautiful gay boys, one of whom turns out to be Drunken Denise, have staged a coup d'état and barricaded themselves inside the bar. There's no sign of the barman. The fat woman, whose name, I think, is Sharon, leans on the bar top. "You wanna drink?"

"A margarita and a Perrier and lime, please."

"Sorry, no alcohol-free beverages served before six p.m."

"Okay, make it a bloody Mary."

"Now you're talking."

"But hold the vodka."

I take my drinks and go over to check out the whiteboard. I run my eye down the list of activities. With horror, I note there are no slots left for the Hawaiian massage, although Melissa has booked herself for a twelve o'clock session. Failing the massage I put myself down for the wreck dive. I note that the Irish Brothers are down too. I didn't know they dived. Then I get a shock. Down the bottom of the whiteboard, in red marker with double underlining, is a special item. BY SPECIAL REQUEST, TUESDAY NIGHT SOUTH PACIFIC PREMIERE SCREENING OF AWARD-WINNING FILM SHAG CITY. I make a mental note to be hidden in undergrowth around that time.

Crossing Central Square, I notice the Irish Brothers sprawled in recliners, both reading scripts. I wave cheerily. Sean/Seamus looks up, waves back, and hastily ducks his head again. I veer left, skirt the compound and head for the tent. On the way I pass Sophie and Matt's tent. I know it's their tent, by the way, because all the tents have numbers and names and little letterboxes outside. Quite cute. Sort of Robinson Crusoe meets the suburbs. I wonder what's going on in there. I'm sure I can hear voices. If I was a little closer I could probably even hear what they were saying. I look around. No one is watching. I turn and stare out to sea, still holding Melissa's margarita, and edge a few steps backward, toward the tent. This isn't spying. It's information gathering. I can definitely hear voices. I edge another step backward. They sound tense. Possibly they're arguing. There's something wrong between them, I can feel it. That's Matt's voice, there, the deeper one. Is that a sarcastic inflection? If I could just get a little closer . . .

That's Sophie's voice. She sounds so *sad*. It cuts me. Matt is saying something, but his voice is too deep, it's just an undifferentiated rumble. I edge backward another step, then two more. More rumbling. It sounds irritable. Goddamnit. Enunciate!

Something is tickling my ankle. I kick out irritably and glance down. It's about two inches from my left heel and I'm just about to step on it. It's black with purple stripes. Hard to tell how long, all coiled up like that. It's staring at me, I guess, with its tiny black beady eyes. I'm so close I can see its eyelids. It has too many of them, and they come from below and sideways. The tongue flickers in and out, then it slips away into the undergrowth, no visible means of locomotion, just like somebody's crouching in the bushes reeling it in with a piece of invisible string.

I scream. I jump a foot in the air. I can't help it. The voices in the tent stop. Matt sticks his head out of the flap. "Snake," I say. "I saw a snake. I was just coming over to warn you. It was trying to get in. I think I scared it off."

Matt grins. "Thanks, buddy." He disappears. I really wish he could be a little less good-humored. It's quite irritating.

---

It's very orange inside the tent and it smells of hot plastic. Melissa is rummaging in her bag.

"Your margarita."

"The ice has melted."

"It's hot out there. You may have noticed."

She sighs. "Just put it on the table."

"I've been looking at the whiteboard. I notice you have a Hawaiian massage booked for tomorrow at mid-day."

"That's right."

"Why didn't you book for me?"

"Sorry, it was the only slot left."

"You took the last slot?"

"Yeah."

"As your employer, I actually think I'm entitled to take that slot."

"So sue me. Have you seen my sunblock?"

"No, I haven't seen your sunblock."

"Green tube, about so long, with a pump-action dispenser?"

I shake my head.

"Well, can I borrow yours?"

"It's in my bag."

She bends over my bag.

I sit on the bed. "I'd like to discuss a change to your terms of employment."

She chuckles. "I was wondering how long it'd take you."

"Not for me."

She looks up from the bag. She looks suspicious.

"How did you get on with Matt? This morning?"

"He's okay. He's funny."

"Do you think he's interested in you?"

"Sexually?" She shrugs. "I don't know."

"He hasn't tried anything?"

"No."

"Nothing flirtatious in his manner?"

"Sure, but for a guy like that to stop flirting he'd have to stop breathing first. What's on your mind?"

"Do you think you could seduce him?"

"Why would I want to do that?"

"If I asked you to. I mean if I paid you to."

"You're asking me to seduce him?"

"If you think you can."

"Of course I *could*. But I'm not going to." She turns back to my bag.

"Why not?"

"I'm not going to do a crummy thing like that. He's with somebody."

"The somebody he's with happens to be my wife."

"Who left you, and happens to be having *his* child."

"Correction. My child."

"You're kidding." She straightens up, holding a tube of sunblock.

"I have good reason to believe—no, I have *very* good reason to believe that the child Sophie is carrying is mine. That's why I had to come here. I had to find out the truth. And I've found it."

"I still don't see where I come into it."

"Sophie isn't actually what Matt wants at all."

"Oh, really?"

"What he wants—what he thought Sophie was—is someone altogether more like . . . well, like you."

"How so?"

"Someone young, attractive, available. Not pregnant."

"He told you all this, did he?"

"He doesn't realize it yet himself. But it's obvious. He doesn't want domesticity. He doesn't want to settle down. He doesn't want children. He's got three already and he's just deserted them. From his point of view this whole pregnancy thing is an unplanned disaster."

"I see." She holds up the sunblock. "This is mine, by the way."

"That isn't green."

She rolls her eyes. "Color-blind as well."

"That is red. Ask anyone."

"Whatever. Do my back?" She hands me the sunblock, takes off her T-shirt and lies facedown on the bed.

I hesitate.

"Hey. Come on, it's just sunblock. Relax."

Feeling slightly sweaty, I kneel down. Her skin is smooth and the color of weak tea. I drop a coin of lotion in the dip between her shoulder blades. I brace myself, and start to smooth it outward from the center. "So, as I was saying . . . he doesn't want Sophie. And Sophie, although she doesn't realize it yet, what Sophie really needs—is me. Someone who will be loyal and caring. Someone who will do the dishes. Change nappies. You know. Someone motivated. Interested. So really, you'd be doing a good thing."

She sighs and closes her eyes. "A little lower."

"Besides which, if he really cares about Sophie, he won't let you seduce him, will he? It'll be a sort of a test. What do you think?"

"I think it's the stupidest idea I've ever heard."

"Apart from that."

"Well, I guess it'd be something to tell my grandchildren about."

"So you'll do it?"

"It'll cost you."

"Of course. I quite understand."

"And what about us?"

"How do you mean?"

"The relationship."

"For the time being we carry on. In the event that anything happens we'll work something out. A scene. A passionate denunciation."

She sighs again. "Oh, all right."

"Excellent." I've finished the sunblock. I sit back on my heels.

"Thanks." She sits up, grabs her margarita, swigs it and makes a face. "Ichh. Warm."

## Chapter 14

"SEE ANYTHING?"

"Not yet."

We're all standing on the beach. The two totems stand facing the sunset, arms outstretched, silhouetted black against the flaming red ball as it slips, faster and faster, into the sea. Most of us have changed for dinner. I'm in my shiniest shirt, Melissa is in underwear. Ella is in a pantsuit and heels, Russell is in a Hawaiian shirt with giant pineapples all over it and Brian has the strangest baby outfit I've ever seen. He looks almost exactly like Henry VIII except for the beard: Brian hasn't trimmed his the same way.

The sun is down.

"Anything?"

"No. You?"

"Nothing."

We were watching for the green flash. There's supposed to be one at the moment the sun slips out of sight. I've never seen it. Now that the sun is out of the way, though, the sunset really kicks in—a Disney parade of vast salmon-pink nuclear mushrooms marches away over the horizon. You feel like applauding.

As evening settles the waiters are doing the rounds with cocktails and snacks. I order an orange juice. Darkness falls and the sand glows white, like snow at night. A mournful wailing sound comes from far down the beach. Shivers run down my spine. We all look in the direction of the sound and we see a light, dancing and wavering as it comes toward us. It pauses, and dips, and now there are two lights, and it comes toward us again, and now there are three. They're lighting torches, all along the beach. The sound comes again, a long, drawn-out note. It sounds like some mournful, dying sea creature.

"What's that?" says Melissa.

"That is the sound of a conch shell." I jump. The chief of police is standing close behind us. His voice is deep and smooth, and two tiny torch flames dance in the lenses of his sunglasses. He smiles at Melissa. The torchbearer comes closer. Stripped to the waist and generously oiled, he holds the torch aloft, jogging slowly, Olympic style. He passes us and moves on, lighting up the dark. The conch sounds again. Melissa sighs. I get a whiff of shampoo. I have an ache. I wonder what Sophie is up to. I haven't seen her all day. I spent the entire afternoon hanging around on a deck chair within sight of her tent. It was a stakeout. I hardly moved. I got so full of tomato juice my bladder must have resembled a size-twelve blood bag. While I was waiting I read some more of Gerard's script, which I have to admit is beginning to grab me. Melissa finished her entire stock of thrillers and started on my screenplays. The rate she reads at is phenomenal. Her recall is excellent too. Matt came out around lunchtime, collected some food and took it back to the tent. He wasn't smiling. Rebecca visited about halfway through the afternoon. I think I heard raised voices at one point, but I could have been mistaken.

"Well that was nice." Melissa rubs her hands together. Sinatra starts to play on the sound system. Fairy lights strung through the branches of the trees flicker on. The tables are set for dinner. We all find our places, which have been preallocated. Melissa and I are sharing a table with Russell and Ella, who has Brian on her knee and is trying to get him to eat something out of a jar that doesn't look any different from the way it'll be when he's finished with it. Also there is Drunken Denise, the old couple from next door—and, on my left, Tamintha. A cold wind blowing from that quarter. Drunken Denise has changed into a pair of skintight slacks with huge flares and ultra-low waist and a matching strapless crossover top. The five-inch stiletto heels on her rhinestone fuck-me-without-delay shoes have a dangerous habit of disappearing into the sand at every step. This is especially problematic as she keeps jumping up to go over to other tables and make a witty remark or three.

I don't know what to say to Tamintha. She's sitting tight-mouthed as staff serve the entrée: a shrimp cocktail with little umbrellas. "So . . ." I say.

Tamintha eats in silence.

"It's a lovely island."

Tamintha eats in silence.

"Have you seen the snakes?"

Tamintha puts down her knife and fork and turns to me. "Frederick," she says, in the civilized but icy tone that I've heard her using when talking to New York, "I don't want to talk to you."

"Oh."

She turns back to her shrimp.

Suddenly, the lights all go out. Thunderous drumming on the sound system. Spots hit the dance floor and eight young islanders in grass skirts and headdresses, their brown bodies daubed with white paint, carrying flaming torches, jog-trot single file into the light. The crowd roars. The dancers duck and spin, whirling their torches, passing them back and forth, catching them under legs, sideways, in their teeth. Black greasy smoke billows away into the night. Sweat pours in rivulets, staining the ground.

"Get yer gear off!" Drunken Denise has to be restrained. The dancers jog-trot off stage, looking nervous, pursued by whistles and catcalls. The sound system goes back to Sinatra.

Sophie and Matt choose this moment to make a late entrance. Sophie is looking radiant in a little black dress cut like a tent and a sticking plaster above her eye. Leaning lightly on Matt's arm, she looks around, almost shyly, as she takes her place at a table near the dance floor. She's been seated with the Irish Brothers, Charles, and other notables. She pours herself a glass of water. Matt, grinning all around, sits next to her.

It's impossible to read her expression from here, but, from the way they made their entrance, it's all too clear. There's a brittle edge to it, I can tell. They're putting on a brave face, both of them, they're getting on for the sake of appearances, but there's a rift. There's definitely a definite rift. My heart begins to pound. I can't help it. Matt glances briefly in my direction but it's a glance that betrays nothing—which is of course a dead giveaway. He's in trouble. Serious trouble, and he knows it.

The dinner proceeds. The shrimp is followed by huge slabs of cow, which, Russell explains, are delicious due to the coconut fiber in the cows' diets. I notice that Sophie is eating well, although Matt doesn't seem to be hungry. I, of course, eat with moderation: you should always get up from the table feeling that you can get up from the table.

Melissa gets up. "I'm just going to the bog," she announces. She kisses me on the nose and squeezes out of her chair.

"So who is she?" It's Tamintha. She's still looking at her plate.

"Melissa?"

"She seems nice."

"Oh, yeah, she is."

"Where did you meet her?"

"Selfridges. Garden furniture."

She lowers her voice. "She's half your age, Frederick. What are you trying to prove?"

"Nothing."

Tamintha looks at me.

"What can I say? We met and . . . wham." I punch my fist rather weakly into my palm.

"I've seen this so many times."

"Actually, I doubt that you've seen this before."

Tamintha shakes her head sorrowfully. "What do you talk about? Or don't you?"

"Lots of things. She's very bright. She's a student."

"What's she studying? Or no—let me guess. Art history?"

"Nuclear physics."

Tamintha stops chewing. She looks impressed. "That girl?"

"Hard to believe, isn't it?"

"Very."

About now, Melissa gets back, and Tamintha turns to dessert, which is something called a volcano cake, specially conceived for the occasion. It's cone-shaped and there's a lot of chocolate in it, much of it in a molten state. Chairs are pushed back. Belts are loosened. Conversation slows.

At the other table, I notice Matt wiping his lips, stretching, getting up and heading for the ablutions block. On impulse, I give it a minute, then follow. There are torches all the way along the trail but it's eerie with the shadows jumping and the distant thump-thump-thump of the generator. I try not to think of snakes.

The ablutions block is empty when I enter. Matt must be in a cubicle. I wash my hands and splash my head with water. I'm feeling nervous. A cubicle door opens and I have to stop myself from spinning around. Footsteps behind me. I glance in the mirror. It's the enormously fat woman. She goes to wash her hands, and I go back to my basin. Another cubicle door creaks. This time it's Matt. He strolls over to the basin next to mine and starts to wash his hands. "Hey Frederick, how ya doin'?" Very friendly.

I try to think of a suitably cool and cutting reply. "Good, thanks, good. And you?"

"Oh, can't complain."

The enormously fat woman finishes washing her hands and heads out. The ablutions block is now empty, except for the two of us. "So you're enjoying yourself, huh?"

"Oh, yeah, sure."

"Yeah, we're having a pretty good time." I note the "we."

"It's a very beautiful spot."

"It certainly is. Very beautiful."

We stroll for the door, Matt slightly ahead. My legs are behaving strangely. It's like they've suddenly turned into stilts. We walk down the path without speaking, me just behind. When we get to the beach Matt stops by the bar and waits for me. Sinatra is faintly audible in the background. The lighting is low. His face is in shadow and all I can see is a jutting jaw, the occasional flash of the whites of his eyes. A waiter hurries past from the kitchen, carrying a huge silver platter.

"You hungry?" says Matt. "I'm not hungry." He pulls a cigar out of his pocket. "Want a cigar?"

"No thanks. But you go ahead."

Matt sits at a nearby table. He takes his time. He hauls an aluminum tube out of his breast pocket, extracts a huge knobbly cigar. He fumbles in his left pants pocket, comes out with a gold cutter, clips the end, fumbles in his right pants pocket, stares into the flame of his rather chunky lighter. I think it's a vice that he affects. I once had the shock of my life when, walking down Jermyn Street, I looked in the window of the incredibly expensive tobacconist on the corner and saw Matt's face, wreathed in smoke, staring out at me from the cover of *Cigar* magazine with a twelve-inch Havana clamped between his teeth. Matt extinguishes the lighter with a reluctant snap. He looks at me dolefully. "You probably don't like me too much do you, Frederick?"

I remember a few months back I was standing on the tube platform. It was raining outside and everyone was damp and steaming gently. The train was approaching. There was someone standing in front of me, his toes right on the yellow line. I thought to myself that if that person were Matt Chalmers, I would probably give him a good hard shove. I would.

"Oh, what the hey. Water under the bridge and all that."

Matt pauses. He looks me in the eye, like he's searching for something—my soul, or maybe my contact lenses. He looks down at the table and slides the lighter away from him. He leaves it lying on the table like a peace offering. "For what it's worth, I'm real sorry the way it's turned out, this whole thing. I always kinda hoped you and I were gonna be friends."

"No reason why we shouldn't be."

Matt's eyes widen.

"I'm sure Sophie's a lot happier now, and I know I am, and after all, that's what really matters."

For a second he's speechless, which in itself is almost worth the effort. "Wow. You're really *together*, you know that?"

I shrug. "A lot of people say that."

"Well, let me say this, then. I really admire your attitude."

"It's only natural. After all, infidelity in a relationship is really only a sign of more fundamental problems that aren't being addressed. Sophie was seeking to end the relationship but unable to find a way to do so. I should be thanking you, really. It's thanks to you that Sophie and I were finally able to address those issues and move forward in a constructive way. We're both much happier as a result. I'm sure it's been the same for you and Anne-Marie."

He spins the lighter on the tabletop and his face sags. "Well, I don't know about that."

"Have you spoken to Anne-Marie?"

"I guess it hit her pretty hard."

"Uh-huh."

"I suppose we were growing apart for a while . . . you know, it's weird, you spend your life with someone, you think you know a person, you wake up one morning and . . . there's a stranger lying there in bed next to you." He looks up, suddenly hopeful. "I don't mean literally, a strange person, I mean . . ."

"I know just what you mean."

"And then you meet someone, and it's just . . . it's just, like, WHAM." He smacks one fist loosely into his palm. "You know what I'm saying?"

"Absolutely."

"Like a goddamn freight train, it knocks you flat. No use saying wait a minute, or . . . there's no saying anything. No time to think. Just . . ."

"Wham."

"And then there's the baby."

"A double-whammy. You must be thrilled about that."

"Oh, yeah." He nods and stares at the table. "Thrilled."

"A new baby. All the responsibilities and joys of fatherhood to look forward to."

He pulls on the cigar. "Oh yeah, I love kids. I love 'em. I mean, I've got kids of my own already."

I nod sympathetically. "Yeah, I know."

"You don't have kids, do you?"

I shake my head.

"You never wanted kids?"

"No, never. Melissa feels just the same. Just not interested for some reason."

"She seems like a wonderful girl."

"Oh, she is."

Matt nods. He rubs his chin. He looks at the ground, at the sky, at his cigar. There's no doubt about it. Here he is, he's got everything. Looks, talent, fame, fortune, Sophie. And that's just the tip of the iceberg. He's got a pilot's license, a black belt, an ancient Roman coin collection, two-and-a-half racehorses, a hand-crafted maple humidor and a personal assistant called Jerry. I know most of this because I bought that copy of *Cigar* magazine. They didn't really capture the inner person. But is Matt *happy*? Of course not. The guy's miserable. It's written all over his face. He misses his family, he's racked with guilt. Sophie is nothing to him. She's a midlife panic reaction to lost youth, lost teeth, lost hair. He doesn't love Sophie. He barely knows her. She's a fantasy. A fantasy that promptly turned around and got pregnant.

"You know, Matt, I might just change my mind about that cigar."

"Sure, buddy."

Matt slips an aluminum tube out of his breast pocket and hands it to me. I unscrew it. I breathe in. The smell of tobacco. It's one of those smells all right. Matt leans across with the lighter. I twirl the cigar in the flame until it catches. I draw. My mouth floods with saliva. I exhale through my nose and the full, sweet, musty odor blows the top of my head clean off.

"Matt, can I ask you a personal question?"

"Shoot."

"Are you happy?"

He looks at me for a long time. His eye twitches. "Who can truly say they're happy?"

I lean forward. I lay my forearms on the table. I pick up the gold lighter. It's even heavier than I expected. I flick the flame into being and it dances between us. The light reflects from Matt's eyeballs, two tiny golden sparks in the dark. "I think I can."

"No kidding?"

"No kidding."

"Melissa is everything I could ever hope for in a woman. Warm, considerate, intelligent, deeply compassionate and understanding, great sense of humor, generous to a fault . . . sensual . . ."

"Uh-huh."

"It's incredible too, the wisdom and maturity and depth of one so young and luscious and, and . . . pliant. You know, if ever I've got a problem, something on my mind, she can cut straight to the heart of it. It's amazing. Every time. You should talk to her. You should spend some time, just talking and getting to know her. Lots of time. All the time you want. You'd be surprised."

"You think so, huh?"

"As a matter of fact, she was saying just today how much she enjoyed meeting you, and how she hopes to spend some more time getting to know you better."

"Is that so?"

"Absolutely." I pause, smile at a private thought, and lay the lighter on the table. Matt picks it up.

"Can I ask you a question, Frederick?"

"Anything."

"Sophie seems to be real upset about something. I was wondering if it might be something specific."

I nod thoughtfully.

"It's just this morning she really took a dive, you know what I mean? She really, she went down. I'd have to say I'm a little concerned, and I just wondered if she'd said anything to you or if you got any indication of what might be troubling her?"

I furrow my brow. I rub my chin. "Gee, Matt, I don't know. I can't *think* of anything."

"Uh-huh."

"Of course Sophie is like that."

"Like what?"

"Well I'm sure you've noticed her mood swings already."

"She is kinda moody, isn't she?"

"Bipolar disorder is of course just a label."

Matt nods, thoughtfully.

"She's probably just having a bigger swing than usual. That happens every six months or so."

"What should I do?"

"Nothing really. Just stay calm. Try to stay between her and open windows. Sometimes I'd have to hide the knives, but only for a week or so."

Matt nods.

"I don't know if pregnancy is having any effect. The postnatal period could be a little hairy. You might want to think about hiring someone."

"What, you mean like a nanny?"

"A bodyguard. Best to be on the safe side I always think."

Matt chews his lip. "Can I ask you something straight out?"

"Sure."

"What did you guys talk about this morning?"

"Oh, nothing consequential."

"Because if there was something specific, I'd like to know."

"Well, Matt, if, without betraying a confidence, there's anything I can pass on to you, I'll certainly pass it on."

"Frederick, I really appreciate that."

"Oh, it's nothing. As Melissa was saying just the other day, it's important to remain open."

"Yeah, that's very true."

"Open to new possibilities. We must always be ready to embrace change. Perhaps on occasions, even repeated change."

"Frederick, I really appreciate this talk we've had. I feel like you've really opened up to me. You didn't have to do that, but you did."

"I believe in remaining open. As indeed does Melissa. We both feel it's important not to be jealous, or, indeed, exclusive, or possessive, in our relations with other people. We feel that keeps the relationship alive and honest, if people always feel free to express what they're feeling at any moment." I sigh and look dreamy. "Yes, I really do thank you. It's been such a huge relief. Since I met Melissa."

We wander back to the party. Matt, it seems to me, is looking preoccupied. People are standing around, now, drinking, dancing, talking. I notice Melissa chatting to the Irish Brothers. Standing on either side of her like that, they look like a pair of bookends.

"Frederick." It's Ella. "Can I speak to you for a moment?" She has an extremely serious expression on her face. It's so serious, in fact, that there's a strong possibility that she will preface whatever she's going to say with the words "it's really none of my business."

She leads me down the beach a little way. "Frederick."

"Ella."

"It's really none of my business, but I've been talking to Melissa. She told me everything. Frederick, as I say, tell me it's none of my business if you want to, but . . ."

"It's none of your business."

"I'm concerned. I don't think you should be putting any pressure on her right now."

"Pressure?"

"After all, it's been less than a year since Gary died, and . . ."

"Since who died?" I haven't the slightest idea what she's talking about.

"Gary," she repeats, as if I'm being deliberately obtuse.

Clearly someone has been allowing her overheated imagination to run amok again. This must be what it's like having Alzheimer's. "Oh, sorry, yes, of course. Gary." Wait till I get my hands on her. I'll kill her.

Ella shakes her head. "She must still be in a very fragile state."

"She is, yes. That's true."

"Imagine losing someone in that way."

"Yeah, just imagine."

"Horrible."

"Awful. Horrific. Very much so."

"I don't know why people do it."

"I've often wondered. But then, that was Gary for you." I shake my head slowly and look sorry in what I hope is the right sort of way.

"Given your ambivalence, don't you think maybe it's a bit soon? For both of you?"

"Ambivalence? Who says I'm ambivalent?"

Ella smiles. She puts a hand on my arm and gives me her

severe-but-caring look. "Don't get me wrong. I think it's great you're together. You seem really happy. Much happier than you ever were with Sophie."

"Er, really?"

"You seem much more yourself. Doesn't he, Russell?"

Russell, who has wandered over with a brandy, nods. "Yeah, definitely. Definitely. Much more. Much more at ease. More natural. More relaxed."

Ella turns back to me. "But she needs time, and so do you. Isn't that right? Russell?"

Russell nods. "Yeah. Oh, yeah. Gotta take your time, eh. Can't rush it. Can't rush a thing like this. It'll all fall over if you do."

"That almost happened to us."

"Yeah." He nods.

"When we met, we rushed right into it. We had to back right off for a month. Didn't we?" They look lovingly at each other.

It's a common misconception. The happy couple thinks they know why they're happy. In actual fact the real experts are the ones like me. We, who have taken our marriages apart, are the ones who know how it was put together. Successful marriages are based not on rational accommodation but on complementary pathology. Thus, Ella is controlling, rigid and obsessed with insignificant detail, while Russell is highly suggestible, lax, and so vague he wouldn't know a detail if it bit him on the arse. They make a wonderful team and they're very happy together. Also, just as important, are environmental conditions. Russell and Ella have an adequate combined income, a house, a baby, and—and this next really is the crucial one—adequate whiteware.

Ella squeezes my arm again. Russell narrows his eyes. "You know, Frederick, I always think a relationship is like an unfamiliar road. If you go too fast you'll crash at the first corner."

Ella beams.

"Wow. Did you think of that all by yourself?"

Ella smiles and Russell looks proud.

"Thanks, guys. I'll really think about that." I put my hands on an imaginary steering wheel. "A relationship is a road . . ." I stare into the middle distance. "Poop, poop."

I head off in search of Melissa, but I'm spotted by Charles, who is in the middle of a small but expanding circle of admirers. "Hey, Frederick! Mate! Guess what? You're the only one on the entire island who hasn't seen *Shag City* already. Be interesting to see what you think of it."

"Oh, I can tell you that right now."

A ripple of silence propagates like magic around the group. Tamintha, Charles, Sophie, Matt, Rebecca, Russell and Ella. They're all there. Other faces less familiar. Sophie turns away, quickly, to the bar. My voice is taking on a timbre it's never, to the best of my knowledge, had before.

"A tight first act draws us in, followed by adequate development and complication in the second. A punchy third act with plenty of surprises keeps us on the hook right up to a well-managed and accurately timed climax. Dénouement is to the point and leaves no loose ends. Character development, if somewhat broad, is at least consistent, with strong arcs for all major characters. Dialogue is punchy, terse and to the minute."

People are starting to relax.

"But as to the content . . ."

People stop relaxing.

"This film is utterly and unequivocally opposed to everything I stand for, believe in, and hold most sacred. The filmmaker actually seems to want us to believe that a loving relationship can be nurtured by homicidal acts. Further, while it poses as an exploratory, boundary-pushing piece, it's all in fact been done before. The tired, adolescent thesis that there is some sort of mysterious and meaningful connection between sex and death is yet again run up the flagpole, presumably on the assumption that we'll all salute. I, for one, do not. How can we show such morally-decapitated fare to our children, tell them it's art and expect them to grow up happy? What has happened to human values? What has happened to trust, mutual respect? To family? To pacifism? The cynical, unbelievably exploitative way the filmmaker trawls around the world's trouble spots, presenting the misery and poverty of others as some sort of adults-only Disneyland of thrills and danger, is so breathtakingly immoral, not to mention dense, as to surpass the very concept of irresponsibility. We would need new words to describe adequately the depths to which this crapulous insult to humanity has sunk. It contains everything that is worst about the West's neoimperialist adventure-tourism response to the third world's agony. Furthermore"—I am by now dimly aware that I am dancing up and down and wagging my index finger in a way that is strongly reminiscent of Hitler—"the repulsive notion that true love can somehow be adequately expressed by violence, that danger, lies and manipulation can lead to spiritual renewal, are so monumentally misguided, yet so universally accepted in the cinema today, as to rank with that other, greatest, of all the many, many disservices Hollywood has done civil society over the decades: the evil assumption, so pervasive in the modern cinema as to pass without comment, that irresponsible driving is cute, endearing . . . and *fun*."

I pause for breath. "Although the performances were fine." I'm panting, my legs are trembling. The entire human population of Makulalanana Island seems to be gathered around me in a semicircle, cocktails momentarily forgotten. Sophie, over by the bar, slowly shakes her head, a tight, embarrassed half-smile on her face. Matt is staring at me, stunned. I straighten my collar.

Melissa giggles.

Charles sniggers.

Matt seems bewildered. "But I thought you said you hadn't seen it."

"I haven't. But I've got the general idea."

A troupe of red satin–shirted Italian boys runs on stage, carrying an assortment of instruments.

"Are you ready to dance?"

"Yes!" roars the crowd.

"Come on!" Melissa grabs my hand, leans in close and breathy. "Tiger . . ."

———

Somewhat later, I'm staggering along the sand, just inshore of the water line, following the line of torches, straining my eyes for sleeping snakes. The band is still playing but I've insisted we call it quits. Must be about midnight. My legs ache and I'm exhausted. I can see the red and green riding lights of the *Cocksucker* at anchor, floating in the blackness. Below, there's a dim light in one of the cabins. Gilles is probably having a private party. We pass a shadowy T-shirted figure lurking under the trees. He gives me a gruff "Bon soir." It's a strange country, this. Half of them speak a little French, half speak a little English. No one seems to speak all of anything.

Melissa is schlepping along in the shallows. I've warned her about the snakes. She won't listen. "What a band! That was fantastic." Where she gets the energy I have no idea. She has a wreath of plastic ivy around her shoulders. She sidles up to me, looking like Bacchus's head nymph. "You know, you dance quite well." Well, maybe I do. Only thing is, I'm going to pay for it. I'm going to be walking bowlegged for a week.

We get to the tent and Melissa immediately turns on the lamp and picks up one of my scripts—a romantic comedy set in a space station—but I interrupt. "Now, listen. What's all this about Gary?"

"Gary? He was my boyfriend. My fiancé. But he's dead."

"Oh, for pity's sake. Melissa, you have to stop doing this."

"Doing what?"

"Making up these stories."

Melissa puts her hands on her hips and gives me a tired look. "What's wrong with that story?"

"A fiancé tragically killed? Come on. How did he die?"

"A climbing accident, actually." Her voice is like ice.

"That's such a cliché. It's too much. It's way, way over the top."

"Oh, yeah? Well, I've got news for you. That one just happens to be true."

"In fiction the fact that something is true is neither here nor there . . . I'm sorry, *what's* true?"

"It's true. The story's true."

"You really had a boyfriend called Gary who died?"

She nods.

"When did that happen?"

She sighs. "About nine months now."

"But that's terrible."

"You're telling me."

"I mean, I'm . . . sorry."

"You and me both." She sighs again, more heavily. "He would have been so thrilled to be here. To meet Sophie Carlisle too."

"He was a fan?"

"Big time. He would have loved *Shag City*. If he'd ever had the chance to see it."

The wind has been taken out of my sails.

Melissa continues "He was very talented. Critic, writer, director, cameraman, lighting, props, you name it. He did it all."

"He was in the film business?"

"That's how we met. He was the cameraman on my first film job. We were having trouble getting the right angle, and he came over and said something, I forget what, but our eyes met and it was just . . . wham." She smacks a hand into her fist. "You know?" I can tell from her voice that her eyes have gone all distant and dreamy.

"Yeah." I do know what she means.

"He really believed in me. He really gave me the confidence to get to where I am today."

"Well, I'm really sorry. What happened?"

"I told you. He had a climbing accident."

"He somehow doesn't sound like the type to go climbing mountains."

"He wasn't. He was climbing a fire escape. One of the rungs was rusty. Or to be more accurate *all* of the rungs were rusty. Anyway, I'm sorry if you didn't like the story. You said to stick to the truth so I stuck to the truth."

"Oh, forget it."

"I told Ella some other stuff too."

"What stuff?"

"I told her you proposed to me. I suppose that was another dumb idea."

"Never mind. Just try to keep me up to date."

"Do you want to know what my answer was?"

"Oh, absolutely."

"I said I thought it was very sweet and I was very touched but we should wait a bit."

"At least until my divorce comes through."

"That's exactly what Ella said."

"Anything else I should know?"

"We're thinking maybe spring, summer. Probably back in New Zealand. Nothing big, just family, a few close friends."

"Okay."

"We want the ceremony in a garden. Nonreligious and we're going to write our own vows."

"Sounds good."

She almost smiles.

"What about the honeymoon?"

"I don't know. What do you think?"

"How about Kenya?"

"Fine. We can go on safari."

A small, sad bell has been ringing for some time. "Did Gary ever work in that little sex shop round the corner from you?"

"Yeah, he did. He used to mind the shop for Ernie from time to time. You wouldn't believe how hard it is to get good staff in those places."

"God almighty, I . . . I knew him."

She half cranes her head around to look at me. Her eyes are wide.

"I went into the shop a few times. He was a really nice guy." Melissa's eyes fill with tears. "Oh, hell, I'm sorry." Now I feel really terrible. I don't know what to do.

"That's okay." She sits up and wipes her eyes with the back of her hand. She has that laboratory animal look again. She settles back again with the screenplay.

"I noticed you were talking to the Irish Brothers."

"The who?"

"The twins."

"Oh, them. Yeah. Funny little guys."

"They just happen to be the hottest producer–director team on the planet."

"Is that so?"

"They were in *Empire* just last month. What did you talk about?"

"Football."

I'm so jealous I could die.

## Chapter 15

"How did Gary feel about you being in porn movies?"

"He was always very supportive."

"Didn't he feel jealous?"

"No."

"But how could he not feel jealous?"

"He just didn't."

"But how could he really care about you if he didn't mind you doing something like that?"

"You wouldn't understand."

"Try me."

She's silent for a while. It's pitch black in the tent, although the flaps are open to let some air through, and I can hear the sea whispering, only feet from our heads. A whisper of a breeze brushes past. All the torches have burnt out, but it brings with it nonetheless a hint of wood smoke and gasoline. It's hot. We're lying on top of the sheet, limp, our bodies giving moisture to the breeze. The cigar is dry on the back of my throat. When she speaks I can smell the sweet alcohol on her breath. "Well, I guess he just understood that what he had was the real me, which is something different."

"The old separate personas trick?"

"Yeah, that's right."

"You're right. I don't understand."

"Worked for us."

"But for how long?"

"We'll never know."

"You realize what you're talking about?"

"I have a feeling you're going to tell me."

"The divorce of sex and intimacy. Citing irreconcilable differences. But then, that's your job, I suppose. Sex without intimacy."

"I don't agree. What I'm really selling, or at least what they're really paying for, is intimacy. Not sex. Sex is just the package."

"How can you sell intimacy?"

"You can't."

"Sounds like false pretenses to me."

"Come on. Someone buys a flash car, what do you think they're paying for? Transport?"

"And what about the movies you make?"

"Same thing."

"But what about you? Where are you in all this? How can you have sex with someone and feel nothing for them?"

"Don't be silly. It's the easiest thing in the world."

"But why do it?"

"Why don't I get a proper job?"

"Well . . . if you want to put it that way, okay, why don't you?"

"Hey, you're the one who's hiring me, here."

"But I'm a tortured desperate individual. I have nothing to lose. You, you're young, you're . . ."

"I have my whole life ahead of me?"

"Something like that. Don't get me wrong. I'm not judging you."

She sighs. "Oh, you're probably right. It's not the sort of thing you want to do for too long. It does kinda wear you down." She sighs and rolls over again. She seems restless. "And it hasn't been the same since Gary died. He was really very supportive. He liked me being in movies. He thought it was cool. He always said I had it in me to be a star."

"A porn star? Who wants to be a porn star?"

"Lots of people. Lots and lots of people."

"Weird."

"Not that you're judging."

"No. God, no. Did he look after you, though? Gary?"

"Sure he did."

"Did he do the dishes?"

"He did."

"Well, that's nice."

"It was nice." Melissa sighs in the darkness. "You do remind me of him, a bit."

"Of Gary?"

"You're not as attractive of course, but in other ways. Gary, he was so gorgeous."

"What other ways?"

"Oh, I don't know. I suppose it's just because we're lying here like this, talking. We used to talk and talk, me and Gary. Talk till the cows come home."

We fall silent. I can hear her breathing. I can hear myself breathing. There's a bass-voiced rumble of conversation from a few tents away, and a short, sharp burst of laughter.

"You know, what you asked me before?"

"What?"

"It's not actually impossible for a younger woman to be attracted to an older man."

"It's not actually impossible for a younger woman to be attracted to small dogs."

She snorts. "You know, you run yourself down quite a lot."

"I'm sorry, I'll try to stop. You're quite right. That's so typical of me. I'm hopeless. Just hopeless." She sits up and I can see the faintest silhouette, a hint of cheek and a dash of hair. Then she hits me with her pillow. Quite hard. "Goodness me, that must be the first time someone's hit me with a pillow for, oh, years and years and years."

"You've been asking for that for a long time, mate."

An obscure, intense, happiness.

She takes a deep, desperate breath. "Christ, it's hot in here." I pick up Gerard's script, lying on the ground between us, and fan her. "Ta. That feels great." She's silent. I can definitely make out the line of the cheek, the hair, and a bit of her shoulder. I wonder what the light source is. It can't be morning.

"Do you reckon you might be gay?"

"No, not a chance. I did try once. Total disaster."

"Huh."

"So, where do you want to live?"

"Huh?"

"After the honeymoon."

"Oh." She thinks. "I think we should go home."

"You think so?"

"Definitely."

"I didn't think you liked Auckland."

"Not Auckland, dummy, Levin."

"You can't be serious. I'm not living in Levin."

"Okay, compromise—Taupo?"

"What would we do there?"

"I dunno. A farm."

"What sort of farm?"

"Sheep?"

"No, trout. No milking time. No shearing time. No worries about sudden outbreaks of imported foot-and-mouth. Well, certainly no worries about foot, anyway."

"Kids?"

"Naturally."

"How many?"

"Oh, hell, bucket loads. An entire tribe. We'll get up in the morning, muck out the children, send them to school, round up the trout . . ."

We decide to relocate. The sand is cool. There are low voices in the dark, up and down the beach. The moon isn't yet up, but I've found my light source. We lie on our backs on the sand and stare. The stars are like nothing I've ever seen in my life. The Milky Way blazes across the sky like a viscous river of neon.

She coughs and scratches her head. She lowers her voice. "So, explain why you want me to seduce Matt Chalmers again? You think you'll get Sophie back?"

"It's possible."

"I don't see how."

"Until recently she wasn't in full possession of the facts. She's only just found out that I'm the father."

"You knew and she didn't? How did you manage *that*?"

"It's complicated. Technical. Anyway, the way I see it, in the fullness of time it's inevitable that it's going to fall apart with Matt. Either he'll dump her or she'll realize he's a waste of oxygen. It's equally inevitable that she'll realize she really needs me. I'm the keystone of her existence. But I can't afford to wait for that to happen. The birth of my child, the most important event in my entire life, is coming in six weeks. I have to be there. I don't want that child being born without me there. So I have to strike now. I have to accelerate the process."

"I guess that makes sense." She sounds dubious.

"But look, don't do it if you don't feel comfortable about it."

"No, I'll do it. If it's that important to you."

"I don't want you to feel you have to."

"I never feel that."

"But I mean, I don't want you to do it just for me."

"Hey. I'm doing it for the money."

"I don't mean I don't appreciate it, I just mean . . ."

"It's no trouble."

"I mean I'd understand if you changed your mind. That's all I'm saying."

"Forget it. It's fine."

———————

When I finally get to sleep, I dream. I'm sitting on the sofa at home with my dad. We're watching *Shag City*.

"Well," says Dad, "this is nice."

I'm rather concerned as I happen to know that the next scene has me and Matt Chalmers. I'm sucking his dick while he strikes me lightly on the back of the head with a library book. Apparently a lot of people are very turned on by library books and it's the next big thing after on-screen urination. I don't really care too much if my father sees the scene but I don't want him to know it's me. "You know, Dad," I say, "sometimes people who appear in porno movies aren't really in them at all. They just *appear* to appear."

"Is that so?" says my dad. "That's very interesting. I didn't know that."

Then at that very instant I realize I've eaten all the popcorn and I'm so ashamed and stricken with guilt that I just want to die. I want to tear my heart out and offer it to my dad. "Here, Dad," I want to say, "there's no popcorn left, but have my heart instead."

*Then*, just before the scene comes on I realize that it isn't going to be me and Matt at all, but *Matt and my mother*. I know the shock will kill my father stone dead, but there's nothing I can do to stop it. All is preordained. I know that he will see the scene and I cannot stop him. I begin to wail and to grieve extravagantly. It seems like such a terrible way to lose the father I love. I fall on my knees. "God!" I say, "oh God, turn it off! Turn it off!" "Not at all," says my dad, "it's perfectly natural." Then the scene comes on after some other stuff about the rape of Nanking that I don't remember well, but when the scene *does* come on it's not a porno movie at all. It's Jack Lemmon in *The China Syndrome*, only it's a remake and I'm Jack Lemmon, but it's been retitled *The Nuclear Family*. It's set in New Zealand and it's all being shot on location. I'm standing on top of Mount Taranaki as the shots ring out and I watch myself fall to the ground, blood leaping from my mouth in elegant spurts. I am transfixed by the innocent beauty of my own dying eyes. "What a guy," I say. "Goddamnit, what a guy! He was all right after all, that Frederick guy! Let's give him a hand!" Then Jack Lemmon comes in. "Frederick," he says, "you have achieved what I thought no mortal man could ever achieve. You have remade *The China Syndrome* so perfectly that it is *exactly* the same as the original movie. Not even Roger Ebert himself could tell the two versions apart. As a token of my esteem I'd like to present you with this pornographic library book."

I'm just about to make my acceptance speech when I wake up. It's dark—pitch dark. Melissa is fast asleep. Her breathing is slow, regular and stealthy, like someone trying to pump up a bicycle tire while a killer attack dog sleeps just around the corner. Contrary to popular belief, sand is not nice to sleep on. It's fine for the first hour but then it gets as hard as rock. I crawl back into the tent.

## Chapter 16

MATT IS ON THE BEACH, his back to us, staring out to sea. He turns and smiles an absent smile, a lot like the one he uses in *Jesus Montoya Must Die*, when he plays a father who lost his entire family in a gas explosion caused by an attempt to light one of his farts. That's the kind of stuff he does—anything at all. Matt is not quite a big star, but he's not a small one either. For a while he was always the bad guy. Now, he's just starting to get into older, craggier roles. He still does a few baddies, but there's a tendency nowadays to cast him as the aging hero, the old guy with a past. He's got a kind of dangerousness about him that is supposed to be sexy, while at the same time retaining an air of little-boy vulnerability.

He can carry a film, or he can play a supporting role. He doesn't mind too much, just so long as he's working. Working, working, working, that's all that matters. If there's a gap in the schedule, and the money's right, you can book him. Doesn't matter what the script is, who the director is. As a result, his filmography is as long as your arm, and as patchy as your oldest jeans. He's worked with the best and the worst. He'll do schlock one week, an Oscar-contender the next. He's a hired gun. People like that. He brings an air of unpredictability, of whatever-will-he-do-next, to any job he does.

Another aspect of Matt's reputation precedes him. He is famous for a string of conquests of the world's most desirable women. Somehow, through it all, he and Anne-Marie stuck together. We have some idea how. It probably wasn't pretty. Now, he's finally left her. He's fallen for his young costar. And this time it's true love. Maybe that's how he really feels. Maybe he doesn't even realize that he's the devil incarnate. After all, someone like Matt probably doesn't have people queuing up to tell him his faults. An intimate and detailed knowledge of one's own shortcomings such as I enjoy is a hard-won prize. It's taken me years of exhaustive inquiry and profound introspection, and even then I'm convinced there are one or two little lurking foibles I haven't yet spotted.

"Hi, guys." Matt smiles at Melissa, who is in her fluorescent string bikini. Oiled head to foot, she gleams with a soft and lustrous shine. She is primed, loaded and cocked. "Sleep well?"

"Oh, very well, thank you."

"So what are you up to today, Matt?"

The plan is I'm going to go diving to give Melissa a clear shot at Matt. She figures it's a morning's work. The good news, at least, is that it's as still as a millpond out there. That means I can dispense with the seasick pills. The seasick pills make diving a real chore. Falling asleep at twenty-five meters is not a good idea.

Matt, lost in thought, doesn't seem to hear at first, so I step in. "Hey, Matt, I'm going diving this morning, but Melissa can't dive so we were thinking maybe you could take her snorkeling round the other side of the island. Apparently there's a small secluded cove round there, sheltered by the rocks and invisible even from the sea, which is perfect for a bit of quiet . . . snorkeling."

Matt smiles. "Yeah, sure, we could do that. That'd be fun." A sad look crosses his face. I'm not worried. The chances of Sophie accompanying them have to be minimal. Sophie has withdrawn completely. She stays in her tent and sees no one but Matt and Rebecca. Somehow I can't see her sallying forth for a spot of snorkeling with Melissa. "Right," I say, cheerfully. "That settles that, then."

There's a distant mournful drone. A tiny black dot appears over the shoulder of the volcano.

"Ah, that'll be the croissants."

After breakfast they ferry us out to the boat. There are nine of us, including both Irish Brothers, Russell, me, Gilles and a few others. I'm still trying to come to terms with the fact that things have changed between me and the Irish Brothers. There is no longer any intimacy. I've seen them around camp, here and there, lounging, drinking. I've not had any eye contact. Eye contact is important. I've not had it and it's now clear. The Irish Brothers are avoiding me. I don't blame them. Quite the opposite, I think they're doing the only reasonable thing. If you're a person like them, you don't want a person like me. If I was a person like them, I'd run a mile across broken glass to get away from people like me. People like me are death to people like them. I should take pity on them. I should just say hey, guys, it's okay. Forget it. This is your holiday. Just enjoy it. Pretend I don't exist. I really wish I could do that. I wish I could just walk the hell up the other end of the boat and stay there and give the poor kids the space they deserve.

It's incredibly hard being incredibly successful. Ask anyone who is incredibly successful. Ask them in a moment of candor and they'll tell you why too. It's people like me. It's not the dinners with Elton John that wear you down. It's not even the distant but adoring fans, the drugs, the cars, the sex, the travel or the clothing budget that does it. It's the hopeless people. The people like me. The in-between ones, the ones just a few stops either side of mediocre, the ones with unrealizable dreams and undreamable realities. The ones who envy but flatter. The ones you don't want to know, yet seem to spend half your time talking to. The ones who are forever coming up, laughing at the jokes you haven't even made yet. The ones you pity and hate, the ones you fear and yet are fascinated by, the ones who could have been you, and vice versa: these are the ones who cause guilt, anger and frustration, internal conflict, personality distortions, delusions of grandeur, paranoia, egomania, nightmares, substance-abuse problems, even migraine.

I should turn around. I should give these young guys a break. I should stop pretending to be their friend. I should face facts, turn around and look the other way. But I'm not going to do that. I *can't* do that. Not yet.

"Hi, guys." My smile is forced, my tone excessively offhand, overloud, over-friendly, overconfident. It's wrong, it's false, it's jarring, it's hopeless and it's fucked. But that's okay.

Seamus and Sean nod and try small but distant grins. "Hey Frederick." Sean (or Seamus) looks at the waves. Seamus (or Sean) squints at his toes and then at the horizon. Poor kids. They're still desperately hoping I'll just piss off and leave them alone. If only they knew. They're not arrogant. No, not at all. They're a nice couple of kids. They're just plain scared. And who wouldn't be? They know what's coming. I'm going to hit them up in some clumsy and embarrassing way, with some crappy idea they know they're not going to be the slightest bit interested in. They're only human. They dread having to go through the same old routine of feigned interest and evasion. They're embarrassed for me. They probably even feel sorry for me. Probably at some early stage in their young but meteorically vertical career tracks they even might have felt as belligerently desperate, as impotently humiliated, as I feel now. Without the bitter overtones of age and hopelessness, of course, but still, they almost certainly have a vague notion of how I'm feeling right now. They're probably fighting with compassion at this very moment. But they can't afford compassion, any more than I can.

"So Seamus, listen . . ."

"I'm Sean. He's Seamus."

"Oh, yeah, I knew that, right, of course." A braying and insincere laugh. I hate that laugh. Why do I do that laugh? "You guys should get T-shirts with your names on. Or maybe tattoo your foreheads. That'd be good."

Seamus looks at Sean. Sean looks at Seamus. Or vice versa.

I sniff. I look at the sky. I pull a face. I "suddenly" have a "passing thought." "So, listen, by the way, did you guys ever get that proposal I sent you?" I'm going for breezy here. I'm going for casually unconcernedly confident yet at the same time detached and not at all committed to the worthiness or otherwise of the idea itself. I'm on my toes. I'm ready to duck and weave.

Seamus/Sean scratches his head.

"Oh, yeah," says Sean/Seamus. "Yeah, we did get that I think. Did we get that?"

"Yeah," says Seamus/Sean. "Haven't had a chance to look at it yet."

"We'll give it a look when we get back to LA." Sean/Seamus nods and smiles.

"Yeah, well, whatever, no hurry. Just a little idea, really. I mean that's great. I mean that's terrific, that's really, just fine and no problem there at all. Good, great. I'm happy. I'm very happy. Wow, look, a fish." I want to kill them. I want to throw them over the side. I want to see them drown. They haven't even looked at it. They haven't even read it. Or have they?

"So where's Melissa?"

"Oh, she stayed behind. She doesn't dive."

"I hear you guys are getting married."

"Yeah, that's right."

"Don't forget to invite us to the wedding."

"Consider it done."

"She's great."

"We're very happy."

Gilles meets us on deck and sorts out dive gear for us all. It's been more than a few years since I dived and I can't shake off the fear that I've forgotten something crucial.

I go forward to the pulpit again. The water is so still and clear I can look straight down between my feet to the alternating patches of coral and sand on the bottom. A sea bird skims by, flying low. A crewman comes forward to supervise the winching of the anchor. The *Cocksucker* gently eases out of the bay and swings to the north. I can see ahead of me the brilliant white line of the reef. I wonder how Melissa is getting along. They could be at the secluded cove by now. I wonder when she'll make her move. Probably she won't have to. Probably he'll make his. I have a dull ache in my chest, around where she hit me with the pillow. It must have been harder than I realized. The reef is getting closer. You can make out the individual waves now, as the Pacific swell is forced up by the coral reef into great towering white plumes, breakers the size of small houses. And yet here we are, gliding along on a lagoon as still as glass.

Gilles comes by and starts fiddling with one of the winches. He must be about to drop anchor. "Are we there?" Gilles looks up, startled, then shakes his head. "No, no. We have much farther to go." Instantly I know it's going to be bad. I'm going to suffer and it's going to be bad.

"But we're not leaving the lagoon? I thought we were diving just at the entrance."

"Yes, but not this entrance. Another entrance." He heads back to the cockpit, and the boat alters course. We're heading straight for the gap.

I'm going to be sick. I'm going to be very, very sick. The first ocean swell meets the bow of the boat at this precise moment, and she lifts, gracefully rising, faster, faster, nose to the sky. The nose hangs for a moment and my stomach hangs with it. Then down we go, smooth and fast, down into the trough with a dizzying rush, an arc of white spray flying up either side of the bow. Yes, I am going to be sick. Very sick. There will be sickness, suffering and pain. I look behind me, to land, lovely, firm, dry, solid, friendly land, so far away. I think about swimming it but I know I'd never make it. I consider going back and begging Gilles to turn the boat around but I can't do it.

I make for the railing of the boat. I grip the railing in both hands and I fix my gaze on the horizon. If I stay like this, staring at the horizon, without moving, without blinking, I might manage it. I've done it before. I might just fight it off. Either way, if we were cruising for a week, it'd be fine. It's just those first three days.

We're right in the gap now, the reef rolling by on either side. The rollers are huge. The bow rises and falls. I watch the horizon.

Now that we're through the pass the boat swings parallel to the reef. We're taking the swells on the starboard quarter so that we pitch and yaw at the same time in a complicated corkscrewing motion. First we yaw to the left, then pitch as the bow comes up, then we yaw to the right as the bow continues to rise and then once we're yawing again to the left the bow drops and the stern comes up. It's indescribable. There is no question now. I'm sick. It comes in waves, washing hot and cold from my scalp to my toes.

"Dolphin!" someone shouts and there's a stampede to the side, but I don't care. I don't care about fish, scenery, diving or any other damn thing. I'm already at the third stage of seasickness: bitterness. The first stage is denial, the second is crushing realization. The fourth stage is irrational desperation. By the time we arrive at the dive site I've reached stage four. I'm now fighting off retching impulses, and I know from previous witness accounts that I am the color of an unwashed bedsheet. People are looking at me strangely and all I can think about is getting into the water. If I can get into the water, I can get below the swell. If I can get below the swell I won't be bobbing up and down.

Gilles drops the anchor and starts the briefing. I head for the gear, but I can't put it on. If I look down long enough to get ahold of all that stuff, I'll throw up.

Gilles has finished the briefing. "All right, everyone," he says, "pick a buddy."

"Hey," says Russell, slapping my shoulder. "Let's go."

"Yeah, sure, whatever, help me with this thing."

He hoists the tank onto my back, buckles the BCD, checks tank pressure, turns on the air, checks the regulator. "Okay, buddy, now you do . . ."

I'm already in the water.

The thing about scuba diving is it's very noisy. Every time you breathe in, you sound like Darth Vader, and every time you breathe out you sound like a roomful of electric jugs on the boil. Apart from that it's very peaceful. If the visibility is good, which it is today, it's a lot like flying. Everything is in shades of blue. Right now, for example, I'm hanging above a blue valley. On the valley floor are blue corals, blue anemones, blue rocks and blue sand. Hanging below me, about halfway down, is a big school of silver-blue fish, looking something like a fleet of moored zeppelins. They're doing nothing, of course. This is the way of it, for fish. I've never once seen a fish that seemed to be doing anything.

But today we're not interested in fish. Today we're interested in getting below the swell. I fumble for the button on my inflatable vest, let out some air and begin to sink. The pressure builds on my eardrums until I pinch my nose and blow to equalize. Using the anchor cable as a guide I lose altitude, pausing to repressurize a few times. I still feel sick, and the swell is still pulling me around. Every time a swell goes by there's a big surge, tugging me out sideways from the anchor line like a fluttering pennant. I grip the line, equalize, descend, descend, equalize. Looking up I can see the other divers. The Irish Brothers, gleaming like a couple of sardines, Russell, all knees and knobs, a sea cow in his shorty wet suit, Gilles a cruising shark.

The group assembles about ten meters down on a mushroom-shaped coral plateau. Russell is eyeing me suspiciously through his faceplate. He gives me an interrogative gesture with his hand, and I give him an "okay" back. In actual fact, nothing has changed. I still feel sick, and I can still feel the swell, ten meters down. Another surge tugs at my legs, spinning me around, and we all grab for the nearest projection to stabilize. I'm going to be sick. If I throw up down here, what happens? I've never thrown up under-water before. I've thrown up in planes, cars, boats, trucks, trains, fairground rides, waterbeds, you name it, but never underwater. A lacing of panic adds itself to the turmoil in my stomach. It can't be good. It can't. Maybe I could die. I'll throw up, clog my mouth-piece and die.

Gilles signals and we begin to move off across the coral plateau, pausing to grip the bottom with each swell. I try to remember to watch out for stonefish, moray eels, lion fish, *Conus geographus*, surgeon fish, sea snakes and sharks—except, honestly, I no longer care. I no longer care about the coral. I no longer care about the fish. I no longer care about wrecked ships. All I care about is my stomach.

Next my air supply starts to trouble me. It seems unreasonably hard to pull it in, my mouth is getting so dry it hurts, and no mat-ter what I do I can't seem to get enough air. There's a panicked feeling building in my lungs, a craving for air, like the feeling you get when your older brother stuffs you wrong way around into a sleeping bag and sits on your head. You know that feeling. Right?

The second rule of diving is don't look up. The first rule of div-ing is never hold your breath. If you hold your breath and you happen to be moving up at the same time, you can rupture your lungs without even noticing—until it's too late and you're dying, that is. But the second rule is, don't look up. When tightrope walking, don't look down. When diving, don't look up. If you look up, you'll notice how far away the surface is, and once you notice that you'll start thinking about how long it would take to get there and all of a sudden you'll realize that what you are doing is crazy and mad and foolish and you are sure to die.

I look up.

The surface is a billowing, translucent ceiling of light. It's so far away. The boat, the huge, solid, dry, boat, is a tiny toy, a bullet-shaped shadow no bigger than my thumb. I am surrounded not by air but by water. It's everywhere, pressing on my ears, my face-plate, trying to get in.

This is mad.

I'm going to be sick in my regulator and die. I'm going to choke on my own vomit then drown trying to return to the impossibly distant surface.

I know what's going on. In the small detached part of my mind that is calm and clear and always aware of everything, I know perfectly well that the only thing that is really wrong is that I am about to panic, in clear violation of the third rule of diving, which is don't panic. I'm not confused about it at all. Everything is perfectly clear. I know that if I don't panic I'll probably be fine. I know that if I do panic, I probably won't. But there's nothing I can actually do about it. It's a bit like watching TV. I'm watching it all happen but there's nothing I can do to influence events. We have now swum across the reef. We are approaching the edge. The bottom drops away suddenly, getting bluer and bluer as it goes, and then it vanishes. About two kilometers down, that way, is the bottom of the Pacific Ocean.

Gilles begins to swim along the edge of the drop-off, then he stops. He turns back to the group, makes a fin-shape on his forehead with the palm of his hand, and points. This is the diver's symbol for shark. It comes up, out of the blue, gliding toward us.

It's a black tip or else a gray, I can't tell which. It cruises by without altering course, neither afraid nor interested. I can't say I'm particularly interested either. The shark having swum on by, Gilles gestures to us to continue. We're now following the line of the drop-off, and after cresting a small rise we see it: a vague blue shape, massive and angular. As we approach, the outlines of the superstructure gradually reveal themselves.

She's enormous. Even in this clear water you can't see more than half of the ship's length at any one time. There are clouds of fish everywhere, mainly one cloud of yellow, another iridescent blue. It's amazingly beautiful and mysterious, and I couldn't care less.

I think of Melissa and Matt. It's hard to imagine that somewhere, far above the thousands of tons of water pressing down on my unprotected body, far away in a land of air and sunlight, of trilling birds and flowing champagne, Melissa is up there. With Matt Chalmers. And Sophie. My child. They're all up there. My fate is being decided. Wheels are turning. What am I doing down *here*?

There's a tap on my shoulder. Russell wants to take my photo next to the ship. I check my gauge. Thank God. My air's running out. I have to signal to Gilles, who will signal to me to go back to the boat. Where is Gilles? They all look the same down here. Rubber-clad bodies, masks, air hoses. I think he had yellow fins. But then, everyone's got yellow fins. I swim forward. That's an Irish Brother, so's that. The noses are a dead giveaway. That must be Gilles. He's only five meters away, but he's swimming away from me, along the wreck, and no matter how fast I fin, I can't catch up. Again I look at my gauge. I've only got five minutes left.

Okay.

Now, I'm really going to panic. Here I go. One, two, three . . .

There's a tap on my tank. I turn. It's Gilles. He looks at my gauge, looks at me, and jerks his thumb up, toward the light.

"Wasn't that great?"

"Amazing!"

"Incredible."

Everyone is enthusing, and looking forward to lunch. Except me. Out of consideration for their feelings I'm out of sight on the swimming platform at the stern, crouched over, feeding the fish. Literally, as it happens. Beautiful violet-colored ones with yellow fins, flocking and wheeling like pigeons as I empty my stomach into the pure Pacific.

The trip back is a blank. Exhausted, I remain draped across the railing at the back of the boat, too weak to move, too weak to think, until by sheer force of will I manage to achieve a self-induced coma. Russell half carries me off the boat, drags me up the beach and dumps me under a palm tree. I'm too weak even to crawl.

---

"Frederick?"

It's Tamintha. I manage to sit up, though the world continues to swim and there's a dull ache in my stomach. I run a tongue around my mouth. One of my teeth feels funny. Slightly numb.

It's a postprandial scene in Central Square. Ella and Russell are on recliners: Ella's reading one of Melissa's crime novels and Russell is fast asleep. Brian is on a blanket in the shade playing with blocks. He's got three in already and he's working on a fourth. The bathing drinkers are drinking and bathing, the sky is blue.

"You're feeling sick, right?"

"Yeah."

"Russell said you didn't take your pills."

"I thought we were staying in the lagoon."

I squint up at her. She's looking down with mild sympathy. "You better lie down again. You're green as grass." I lie down again. She's right. She sits next to me. "I've decided to forgive you, by the way."

"Any particular reason?"

"Well, I'm glad you asked that, because there is actually. First, I was talking to Melissa, and I realized she's a really, really nice young person. If rather too young and attractive. She's bright and friendly and nice and . . . you, you're a nice person too, if a little flaky. And life is short. But then, what really clinched it, I was watching the two of you, this morning, walking across to breakfast and there was just something about the way you reached over and held her hand and the way she looked at you and I just thought, come on, these two are in love, you know? And I thought when two people obviously care about one another that way . . . how can I resent it? Human happiness is such a frail and beautiful thing. And then I thought about you, and about how amazing you've been about this whole thing with Sophie. You've been so open and unselfish and generous, and I felt ashamed."

"Thanks, Tamintha. I really appreciate it."

"Have you thought about that job?"

"I have."

"And?"

"I actually think I need a whole career change."

"What are you going to do?"

"I don't know. I'd quite like to work with animals."

"Hm."

"But if you're looking for someone to replace me, I know a really good reader. Top-notch. A born reader."

"Send him along. I'll give him a tryout."

"It's a her." I drag myself to my knees. "She's looking for a career change too. You know her. It's Melissa."

"I thought she was going to be a nuclear physicist."

"There's a glut on the market. Besides, she's really a people person." I struggle from my knees to my feet. My stomach is knotted up like a rubber band on a toy airplane. "You haven't seen her, have you? By the way?"

"I think she went snorkeling with Matt."

"I think I'll stretch my legs. A walk will do me good."

---

A walk is doing me no good at all. I trudge along the talcum-fine beach, sweat trickling into my eyes, down my back, my sides, my legs, the soles of my feet. I have to say, this whole tropical island thing is a bit of a have. It photographs well but that's about it. You get there, it's gritty, it's hot, it's sweaty, it's too bright, it's dangerous, and there's nowhere really comfortable to lie down. All that reclining with a cocktail and a sunset stuff, it's all rubbish. Those plastic beach recliners are an absolute rip-off. The fact is, these desert islands are deserted for a *reason*. Give me a skiing holiday any day.

I stop and look around. The day is getting even hotter. The sky is a strangely flat, dull, cyanotic blue, and it's suffocatingly hot and still and I continue to stream with sweat just standing here. Even the parrots in the trees sound breathless and cross. I still feel queasy and my stomach aches and that numb tooth is getting number. There's a haze gathering on the horizon.

Ahead is a rocky headland, cutting off the sand like a wall, and jutting out into the sea. I climb it. Below is the small secluded cove. It is, indeed, beautiful. Cradled in two rocky arms, one at each end of a tiny, ten-meter stretch of perfect sand. The rocky outcrops continue well out into the water, then curve around slightly, creating a sheltered little inlet like a natural tidal swimming pool.

Melissa is lying on the sand in the shade of a convenient palm, with one of my romantic comedies. There's no sign of Matt. I clamber down and go over. She looks up and sees me. "Oh, hi. Hey, this one's not bad at all. There's this couple, and they divorce for tax reasons but continue to see each other in secret."

"Where's Matt?"

"Oh, he's gone."

"What happened? Mission accomplished?"

"Yes, and no."

"What happened?"

"I tell you one thing, the guy's more screwed up than you are."

"Surely you don't allow that possibility?"

"Well." She puts down the script. She crosses her legs. "It's like this. Everything starts out fine. Sophie stays in her tent, we go snorkeling. You've got to see it, by the way, there's all this amazing coral. It's like swimming over a forest of blue reindeer horns . . ."

"Yes, yes. Matt. What happened?"

"So we do some snorkeling."

"Yes."

"Then we do some sunbathing."

"Yes?"

"Not a soul around. I spread out the towels, I lie down."

"Yes."

"I take off my top."

"Yes."

"I ask him to put some tanning lotion on my back."

"Yes?"

"So he does my back. And I roll over, and I ask him to do my front. He does my front. And then he stops. He just kind of stands there, looking at me."

"Carry on."

"So I say, 'My, let me help you with that . . .'"

"Very original."

"Incidentally, the guy is hung like a horse, I mean, I've seen a few and let me tell you . . ."

"Yes, yes, I know."

"You know?"

"The world knows. Get on with the story."

"So everything's going fine . . . and then he stops me."

"He stops you?"

"He says, 'No, stop, stop.'"

"What did you do?"

"What do you think? I stopped, of course."

"What was it? A rough filling?"

"No, nothing like that."

"Like what then?"

"Like, he begs me to consider the sanctity of the marriage vow. He pleads with me. He says I'm about to marry a wonderful man. He says, and I quote, 'Frederick is a great guy. He deserves better than this.'"

"Good God."

"He says he's made many mistakes in his own life and I should try to learn from them. He was quite eloquent."

"This is slightly ironic."

"Yeah, I thought so."

"What did *you* say?"

"I said I was sure you wouldn't mind."

"And what did he say?"

"He advised me to make a clean breast of it with you and to seek counseling. He said maybe there was still hope for me."

"What did *you* say?"

"I said I doubted it."

"Anything else?"

She shrugs. "He said he wanted to be alone. He said not to try to follow him. And he ran off." She waves the script. "By the way, have you got any more of these? They're great."

I take a deep breath. I can't quite seem to fill my lungs. "Which way did he run?" She points over her shoulder with her thumb. A little farther down the beach there's a little sign on a wooden post: THIS WAY TO THE VOLCANO.

"This one is brilliant." She's holding up Gerard's script.

"*That* one? You like that?"

"It's hilarious. I was splitting my sides all the way through. I think Sean and Seamus would love it. They're looking for a black comedy. Mind if I show it to them?"

"Be my guest. But don't mention my name. I want nothing to do with it."

---

I'm following a little winding path beaten into the coral substrate. Looks like they must have got an impacter up here. In no time at all I'm deep in the bush. Looking ahead I see nothing but tangled branches, broad green leaves, shiny and thick, hanging bougainvillea, purple and pink. Birds call, lizards scuttle. It's stiflingly hot, so hot I feel almost desperate. Sweat is pouring down into my eyes, down my sides, down the back of my neck, my knees, my ankles. My shirt is simply sopping. I take it off and hang it on a nearby branch. I'll collect it on the way down.

Suddenly the coral path ends, and the trail gets abruptly steeper. It's beaten reddish dirt, now, almost steep enough to be a climb, polished roots jutting from the ground. People must come up here quite a lot. Maybe people from the village. The path climbs steeply for what seems like forever. At last I grab a root and swing myself up a particularly steep section of track. I fling myself on the ground and lie there, gasping. I've broken free of the bush. Before me is a steeply sloping desolate land of scattered rock, mottled earth, scabrous brown, yellow, green, orange, black. Blasted earth. No life, perhaps the odd scurrying ant. The very odd lizard. The sun beats down on the back of my neck and I wish I'd brought my shirt as I begin to climb, following that same faint beaten track that winds and zigzags in front of me between sharp jagged lumps of scoria. Above the column of smoke, rising, rising, spreading.

I stop and look behind me. The entire island is laid out below me. Then across the water I can see Pakulalanana and the dotted white buildings of the village close by the shore. Beyond that the curving arms of the reef, the colors of the sea graduating from deep blue to copper sulfate. It's hotter still, and stiller still. The haze on the horizon is thickening, gathering, rising. I turn and plod on toward the summit. I've been plodding like this for more than half an hour when at last the track eases off again and begins to curve around. One more steep section and I'm skirting the lip of the crater. There's nothing there. No handrails or signs. Just a steep cornice of earth and then it drops away, steeply, then steeper and steeper, until you can't see any farther. All you can see is the steam and the smoke rising, fast, into the sky. There's a strong smell of sulfur, and a surprising amount of noise. It sounds like a rushing train. One slip and—forget it.

That's when I see him. He's standing on a little rocky outcropping that juts out over the crater. He's right on the edge. He's craning slightly forward, as if he's trying to get a view right down inside. His back is to me and he can't hear my approach because of the noise. I walk right up to him. I'm only ten feet away. Still he hasn't noticed me. He's staring transfixed into the crater.

There's that feeling you get, when you're standing on the edge of a cliff and you look down and it seems like such a short step from here to there. Just one short step, and the temptation to take it is so strong you turn away. It's like that. A genre-defining moment, no doubt about it. All it would take is one short sharp push. He'd hardly hit the sides.

"Hey, Matt."

He doesn't turn. Now that I look, in fact, there's something about the way he's standing. Something in the immobility of his neck. Something tense, something anticipatory.

"Matt?"

Still he doesn't turn. He doesn't move a muscle. He's carved from stone. But he speaks. "Pretty impressive, huh?"

"Aren't you standing a little close to the edge, there?"

"I'm on the edge all right, Frederick."

I sit on a rounded piece of baked earth. "Oh well, as they say, if you aren't living life on the edge you're taking up too much room." I feel as if I've been punched in the stomach and I'm so tired I can hardly hold my head up.

Matt snorts. "I guess you spoke to Melissa, huh?"

"Yeah, I did."

"She tell you what happened this afternoon?"

"She did."

"Don't blame her. She really cares about you, man. Please, man, don't blame her. It's not her fault. You two, you were made to be together. I swear, women, they lose their heads around me. They can't help themselves. I've seen it happen time and time again. I'm a curse, man. A curse."

"Hey, it's not important, really. Forget it." The funny tooth is still playing up. It appears to have gone completely numb. I run a finger around the inside of my mouth. He doesn't move.

"No, it *is* important."

"Whatever, come down off that rock before you fall off."

Still, he doesn't move. "You know, I'm really asking myself some questions right now."

"You and me both."

"And I tell ya, I don't like the answers I'm getting."

"Maybe you need to try different questions."

"I thought I could beat this thing."

"What thing?"

"Back in LA, I . . . I was in this program." He pauses. He hangs his head. "Sexual addiction."

"I imagine in your line of work it must be an occupational hazard."

"It is if you're a dingbat. Like I am."

"Oh, I think dingbat is a little harsh."

"I came here to this island, I told myself I could do it. I knew there'd be . . . opportunities. There always are. Wherever I go. Always. Always, opportunities. Women just can't resist me, Frederick. It's the truth. They throw themselves at me. It's always been like that. No matter what I do, they find me irresistible. Whether it's my personality or my appearance, I don't know. It just seems to be some sort of aura I carry with me." He turns his head just a little. "Can you imagine how that must feel? Always, always, to be hunted, like a . . ."

"Trophy?"

"Yeah. Exactly. But I said to myself, this time, it'll be different. I mean, Sophie, she's just so great, and . . . and she's so great, but this afternoon, I . . . I knew. When Melissa took me to that beach, I *knew*. Oh yes, I knew and yet still, I went." His voice sinks to a harsh but carrying whisper. "Yet still, I went."

"But you didn't go through with it, did you? You pulled out." As it were.

"I sinned in my thoughts, man. I sinned in my thoughts."

"Well, what better place? The no-mess, no-fuss way to sin. I'm all in favor."

"But don't you see? It's what I realized. I was standing there, looking down, and . . . it all seemed so familiar. The beach, the sun, the sea, the . . . Melissa, and I realized, I've been here before, so many times, it's like . . . I mean I don't even enjoy it anymore. It's more like, I just can't say no. I just—I can't do it. I'm not even a human being anymore."

"Oh, I don't know."

"I've let everybody down. Everybody who ever believed in me, who ever trusted me, who ever told me they believed in me. I've failed them all." He begins to sob wildly. "Man, it's like there's something dying inside me. I have no self-control, and I *disgust myself*."

"Isn't that a little melodramatic?"

"I can't do it. I just can't do it! I can't even look at myself in the mirror!"

"Look at the bright side."

"What bright side? There is no bright side."

"Sure there is. Okay, you stumbled. But you realized what was truly important, and that's why you're standing here today. You had a moment of decision. Of clarity. You should treasure such moments. They don't come along very often."

"No. I've failed. Failed!" He tenses himself. He bends his knees. He draws back his arms. He's going to jump. He's actually going to jump.

"Edmund Hillary!"

He pauses. I think it's the element of surprise that got him there.

"Sam Neill! Jane Campion! Lucy Lawless! Russell Crowe, Peter Jackson. What do all these wonderful people have in common?"

He looks at me, puzzled.

"Tell me. Look me in the eye, and tell me!"

"They're, all . . . uh, gee, I dunno."

"New Zealanders. They're all New Zealanders. Every last one of them. Do you think these people ever had moments of doubt or uncertainty in their lives? Do you think they ever felt like flinging themselves into a volcano?"

"Well, I imagine."

"Do you?"

"Frederick, I'm suicidal over here. Could you get to the point please?"

"In those moments of bleak despair, do you think those people gave up? Do you think that's how they got where they got? Because they gave up? What do you think people said the first time A. J. Hackett ever suggested it might be a good idea to jump off a . . . ah, what do you think people said when Marconi said he was going to invent the radio? Or Christopher Columbus when he said the world was round? Or Edison when he recorded sound? Or Wilbur and his brother, when he said that man could fly?"

He keeps his knees bent, but finally he turns his tear-stained face to look at me. "You're like Buddha, or Jesus or something."

"Oh, not really. Not once you get to know me."

"You give and you give. And then you give some more."

"Well . . . that's probably an overstatement."

"Me, all I can do is take. I take your wife, then I take your fiancée . . ."

"Ah, but you gave her back."

"I treat you like dirt. Like dirt, and you, you turn the other cheek. *You're* the one I envy."

"Oh, you don't envy me. I promise you."

"You've got the only thing that really matters."

"My teeth?"

"Your integrity." He falls to his knees on the outcrop. Small stones tumble into the abyss. "Help me, please, man, help me. I don't know where to turn."

"You want my advice, turn around. And get off that rock."

"But if I get off the rock, what will I do next? Where will I go?"

"Let's just take it one step at a time."

He hesitates.

"You know, I saw Anne-Marie in LA."

"You did?"

"She said to say hi. She said to say the children were missing you."

He shakes his head. "Sometimes, it's almost scary. It's like you can look straight into my soul, man."

"Talking about scary, why don't you hop down off that rock?"

"But don't you see? I'm responsible. I'm responsible to Sophie now. I'm torn, right down the middle."

"I think there's something you should probably know about Sophie."

"What?"

"Get off the rock and I'll tell you."

Matt gets off the rock.

"Now sit down."

He sits beside me.

"Listen carefully. I'm going to tell you this, and I'm going to tell you once." I look around me. Matt is listening. The parched, baked earth, the blazing sun, the distant deep blue sea. They're all listening.

## Chapter 17

FIRST WE HEAR IT: a distant lazy blowfly drone. Then we see it: a tiny black dot in the sky.

"Ah," says someone, "that'll be the croissants."

We all watch, salivating lightly, as the seaplane comes closer. Soon we can make it out clearly, the ungainly floats each almost as big as the fuselage itself. The plane drops lower, flashes of sunlight running along the wings as it turns and makes its landing approach. The note of the engine changes as the props feather and the floats hit the sea, once, twice, thrice, then settle. The plane turns and taxis in across the bay right up to the sand. The pilot kills the engine, jumps out and chucks a small anchor onto the sand. He returns to the plane, reaches into the cabin and comes out with a large basket covered with a blue-checked cloth. He lugs the basket across the beach to the kitchen tent.

There's a general movement toward Central Square. People are moving slowly this morning. It was a rough night, and the morning has dawned heavy and hot, though the haze is strong, a gauze veil across the sun. Clouds are beginning to bank in the west. As we take our seats, a figure comes out of one of the tents and crosses the beach, lugging a heavy-looking bag. Tall, lithe, with a strong jaw and little round wire-rimmed sunglasses perched on an aquiline nose. He throws his bag into the plane, climbs in after it.

The pilot returns, climbs aboard and closes the door. The plane engine fires, starts immediately, and the plane slowly taxis out across the bay, the arrow of its wake pointing to the west. The engine roars, louder and louder, and the plane picks up speed, skips once, twice, thrice, hesitates, torn between sky and sea, then begins to climb. A black silhouette, then a dot, it disappears over the shoulder of the island.

---

It is afternoon. I'm wading. The water is so warm I can't really feel it on my legs, apart from the hydrodynamic resistance. The reef is visible on the horizon as a slowly changing line of white. I round a small point and abruptly the water becomes shallower, changing color to the most exquisite copper-sulfate blue. About a half mile distant, across the shallows, is a tiny island, absurdly small, an upside-down hairbrush, araucaria pines jutting out at crazy angles. The whole thing looks like it could fall over and sink.

I come to the rocky outcrop that hides the secret cove and I begin to climb.

That's when I hear it.

Sobbing. Someone is sobbing, just over behind the rocks. Sobs are as unique as snowflakes and fingerprints, and I know this sob. It has particularly baroque complications on the in breath. Ugh, ugh, uh-uh, ugh. Unmistakable. I even remember the last time I heard it. It was in a tapas bar just behind Piccadilly Circus and it was ten past five and the place was pretty much closed only they hadn't got around to chucking us out. You can hear it yourself in the third-act climax of *Bonza, Mate*. The on-screen sob is exactly the same as the offscreen. A sob is a sob. A laugh is a laugh. These things don't change. There's really no such thing as acting. The ability to act is really the ability to be real when all else around you isn't.

I climb the rocks, coughing as I climb. She'll know that cough. The sobbing stops. I stride over the crest. Sophie is alone. She's sitting, knees drawn up, on a beach towel, wearing a bathing suit, sunglasses and a hat. I don't know how you're supposed to feel at moments like this. It's an unhealthy but invigorating cocktail of triumph, sorrow, pity, forgiveness, vindication, concern, nostalgia, nosiness, disappointment, relief and guilt. I scramble down the rocks. Sophie has composed herself by the time I get there. I stand in front of her. She compresses her lips and squints up at me.

Her belly is enormous and the most wondrous thing I have ever seen. It is gigantic, it is an entire planet. Her breasts seem to have tripled in size. Her entire body, what I can see of it, is criss-crossed with a venous network like a freeway system. She has veins in her thighs, her ankles and her calves. Veins in her neck, her arms, her temples, even in her eyelids—big fat blue ones, full of blood.

"Everyone's wondering where you've got to." She doesn't answer. I kneel before her. There's one thing I really, really want to do. "I saw Matt get on the plane this morning."

She closes her eyes.

I can't help myself. "Can I touch it?"

Her eyes remain closed. She doesn't say no. I lay my fingers on her belly, then my whole palm, resting lightly. It's cannonball hard. It's ripe to bursting. Sophie gives a little involuntary cry. I snatch my hand away. "What? What is it?"

"Baby kicked."

"Are you okay?"

"It turned over last night. Every time it kicks it gets me right in the spine."

"Ouch."

"Makes it hard to breathe."

"But you're okay?"

"Oh, I'm great. I'm just fine."

"And the baby?"

"The baby is fine." She jerks away from me, suddenly, rolls onto her side and levers herself slowly to her feet. "You told him."

"I had to."

She wheels ponderously.

"I'm going for a swim."

"Watch out for snakes."

She starts for the water, waddling, buttocks clenched, shoulders thrown back to compensate for the enormous weight of her belly. She walks like a truck driver. I follow her. At first, the water is too warm to be refreshing, but by the time we're chest deep we hit a cool layer, and it's heaven. Sophie wades farther until she's up to her neck, then leans back and floats, her stomach breaking the surface. "This is the only place I can get comfortable."

"I guess it must be pretty much like this for the baby, right now."

"What was that?" She cocks an ear out of the water.

"I said, it must be like this for the baby. Floating."

She says nothing. I lie back again. I'm happy. Absurd but true. This is the thing. I'm happy. If I could just stay like this, floating, with Sophie, I'd be happy. It doesn't make sense. But who wants to make sense?

"I don't understand you, Frederick. What do you want?"

"I want you." I feel good. I feel light. I feel like I can't lose. How can I lose? I've got nothing *to* lose. Sophie is looking at me. Her face is appalled and enthralled. She's on a knife-edge. We all find ourselves there, at one time or another. She is looking at me, now, and she's taking me in. I don't mind. I let her look. I submit to her scrutiny. I look around me. The sky, the sea, the sun, beating down, so glorious, thick as metal.

Sophie turns and swims. She lumbers ashore and heads for her towel. I follow. She turns and looks at me. She has a strange expression on her face. "Matt told me about Melissa."

"He told you about that?"

"He told me about that." She runs a hand through her hair. "I think you must be mad."

"That's a little harsh. I realize it was an extreme step."

"You realize that?"

"I love you, Sophie. We can work this out. We can have this child."

She shakes her head slowly. "You aren't the father. I told you that. Why didn't you believe me? I was pregnant before I even left you. That's why I left. I found out just before."

The ground tilts. "And you said nothing?"

She looks at her belly.

"I don't believe you."

"It's true all the same."

It's funny. You can never tell if someone is lying. But if someone is telling the truth, you can always tell.

"But then Matt is the father after all. Why didn't you say? Why did you let me think, all this time, that I was the father? Why didn't you tell me?"

"Matt isn't the father."

"What . . . what are you saying?" The ground tilts still farther. The whole island tilts. It's ready to slide into the sea. "I don't understand."

"Listen . . ." She takes a breath. I listen. The sky is listening with me, the trees and the sand and the whispering sea. We're all listening.

## Chapter 18

**INT. PALACE CORRIDORS—DAY.**

HEAVY METAL MUSIC PLAYS AS THE PRINCE RUNS
THROUGH THE BURNING PALACE. SCREAMS CAN BE HEARD
FAINTLY THROUGH THE ROAR OF THE FLAMES. HE KICKS
DOWN THE DOORS TO THE ROYAL CHAMBER.

**INT. ROYAL CHAMBER—DAY.**

THE PRINCE FINDS THE OLD KING HUDDLED IN THE
ROYAL BEDCHAMBER. HE CLUTCHES HIS YOUNGEST SON
TO HIS BOSOM, A MERE BOY EIGHT OR NINE YEARS OF
AGE. THE PRINCE STRIDES FORWARD. HE TEARS THE
BOY FROM THE OLD KING'S GRASP, AND RUNS HIS
SWORD THROUGH THE CHILD. THE BLOOD FLOWS COPI-
OUSLY. THE OLD KING, SLIPPING AND SLIDING IN THE
BLOOD OF HIS MURDERED SON, TRIES TO ESCAPE, BUT
THE PRINCE POUNCES AGAIN AND SLASHES WITH HIS
SWORD UNTIL THE OLD KING LIES STILL.

<u>Princess</u>

My son.

THE PRINCESS IS STANDING IN THE DOORWAY OF THE
INNER SANCTUM. SHE CROSSES THE FLOOR IN ONE
STRIDE AND KNEELS. SHE CRADLES THE BODY OF THE
DEAD CHILD IN HER ARMS. SHE ROCKS THE BODY
GENTLY.

Princess

He was yours.

SHE LOOKS UP, INTO THE PRINCE'S EYES. THE PRINCE
RAISES HIS SWORD.

Princess

He was your son.

THE PRINCE HESITATES.

Princess

Now, kill me.

THE PRINCE LOWERS HIS SWORD. HE TURNS AND SEES
HIMSELF, HIS DOPPELGÄNGER, STANDING IN THE DOOR-
WAY WATCHING THE SCENE. THE SWORD FALLS FROM HIS
NERVELESS GRASP.

Princess

Why do you wait? Kill me.

THE PRINCE'S DOPPELGÄNGER BECKONS FROM THE DOOR-
WAY. THE PRINCE FOLLOWS. THE PRINCESS CALLS
AFTER HIM.

Princess

Let me die with my son!

**INT. PALACE CORRIDORS—DAY.**

THE PRINCE FOLLOWS HIS DOPPELGÄNGER THROUGH THE
CORRIDORS OF THE BURNING PALACE. THE DOPPEL-
GÄNGER IS ALWAYS JUST AHEAD, AT THE NEXT CORNER,
AT THE NEXT DOORWAY. EVERYWHERE PEOPLE ARE
DYING, BURNING. PIECES OF ROOF COLLAPSE, THE
FLOOR FALLS AWAY.

**EXT. PALACE GARDEN—DAY.**

THE PALACE GARDEN IS GREEN AND SILENT. THE DOP-
PELGÄNGER LEADS THE PRINCE TO A POOL. HE GES-
TURES AT THE POOL AND THE PRINCE GOES FORWARD.
HE LOOKS INTO THE WATER, AND SEES HIS OWN
REFLECTION, WHICH SHIMMERS AND DISAPPEARS. IN
THE WATER THE PRINCE SEES A VISION OF THE WORLD
ON FIRE. DEMONS WITH ELECTRIC GUITARS STALK THE
EARTH PLAYING HEAVY METAL RIFFS AND SHOOTING
BURNING ARROWS FROM THEIR MOUTHS. THE VISION
CLEARS AND HE SEES THE PRINCESS CASTING HERSELF
UPON A SWORD. HE LOOKS UP INTO THE EYES OF THE
DOPPELGÄNGER.

<u>Prince</u>

I see now, it was heavy metal all the time.
Heavy metal has done this to me.

HE FALLS DEAD ON THE GRASS. HEAVY METAL MUSIC
PLAYS. THE ENTIRE GLOBE BURSTS INTO FLAME.

**END**

The sound of a seaplane. I open my eyes, suddenly. I'm seeing
orange. I'm thinking genre. I know the twist. At last I know the

twist. I should probably try to make sense. But how does anyone make sense? Ever?

I close my eyes again, and I watch the credits roll. It was like that. Like when you're sitting on in the dark after the film is over and everyone else has gone, and they just keep coming, so many names, more than you would ever have thought possible. What do they all do? you ask yourself. Are they really necessary? So *many*? Camera operators, sound-recordists, focus-pullers, directors of photography, actors, actresses, composers, stuntmen, editors, completion guarantors, producers, associate producers, coproducers, executive producers, legal advisers, postproduction supervisors, accountants, foley editors, researchers, stills photographers, personal assistants, assistants to personal assistants, hairstylists, standby hairstylists, dialogue coaches, set dressers, standby set dressers, assistant standby set dressers, gaffers, grips, best boys, drivers, carpenters, caterers, cat wranglers, runners, gofers, toers-and-froers, comers-and-goers.

So many.

"Oh Lord." I knelt on the sand before her in grief. "Christ," I could hear myself saying. "Oh, Lord Jesus Christ." I don't know why. I'm not even religious. There are no atheists in foxholes.

I have news, by the way. I have peeped over the border of the land of no return. I have scouted the infinite. I have looked death in the face. It's not actually that bad. I'm sort of disappointed. It wasn't so much terrifying, as a pain in the arse, coupled with a strong sense of anticlimax. Death is like the realization that you have missed that plane. To put it another way, although it's not a good thing, dying is not a bad thing either. It's morally neutral.

As I lay dying, I certainly did think about the things you'd expect to be thinking about, but I didn't think the things you'd expect to think *about* them. I thought about my family. I thought about my mum and dad and my brothers and sisters. I thought about

Sophie. I thought about the absence of an heir. I thought about my parents getting news of the sudden tragic untimely death of their son, aged *only* forty-two—still so young, so full of life and possibility, with all his own teeth—but I didn't get sentimental about it. Quite the opposite. As the darkness closed in (which was just the way the Looney Tunes cartoons end: that shrinking circle of consciousness—that's all, folks!), I thought what I thought was my last thought: "Tough, they'll all just have to deal with it." Death is a sentimental experience for the bystanders, only. The ones doing the actual dying are hard-nosed realists one and all. Death *is* the ultimate reality. Also—incidentally—I would like to report that death is *not* sexy. Sex is the absolute last thing on your mind when you hit the deck mooing, I assure you. Any sex-death link is purely in the mind of the beholder, a fetishizing coping strategy.

The only other thing I thought about was New Zealand. I realized—once again, without getting in the least bit sentimental about this—that if I die anywhere other than in New Zealand I'm going to feel like I'm dying a long way from home. That's just the way it is. It's a perception. A notion I'm stuck with. Doesn't mean anything in particular, but at least I know it's there.

The tent flap rustles in a can-I-come-in sort of way. One day someone is going to make a lot of money patenting an ultra-lightweight foldaway tent-door-knocker. Melissa eases herself through the gap. The orange light soaks into her. It infuses her. It'll leave a stain for sure. "Brought you some tea and a croissant."

"Oh, thanks."

"The plane won't be leaving for an hour or so, so you've plenty of time."

I nod.

"How are you feeling?"

"Stable."

I slurp. It's hot and very sweet. "This is great. Marry me."

She smiles. "I think you're still in shock. By the way, I've been talking to Tamintha just now. Thanks."

"Nothing to do with me. And you're fired incidentally."

"You can't fire me. I already quit."

"Fair enough." I slurp my tea and stand up.

"Where are you going?"

"To do something I should have done a long time ago."

"I'll start packing."

I stand at the entrance to the tent. It rained last night, during the wee small hours. Came down in buckets. I woke up. I've never heard rain like it. The tent staggered. I went outside in the dark and the rain was like a stick across my shoulders. This morning the sea is flat, cowed like a beaten dog. The rain has washed away every trace of everything from everywhere. The air is pure, clean and empty, the trees are polished, the sky is scrubbed, the sea sluiced, the sand sanitized. I grab a lungful. Such a strange habit, breathing. So hard to kick. I look out across the water. The sea-plane is just nosing up to the beach.

I start across the sand. I'm heading for Central Square. I walk past Sophie's tent without breaking step. I walk past the bar, past the stage, past the massage tent. The hair dryers are going at full blast, the smell of perming solution is heavy on the air. There's a spare seat at the end and I take it as a smiling staff member approaches. "What's it to be? Just a trim?"

"Radical surgery."

Years of systematic infidelity. Of calculated deception. I knelt in the sand before her as the names rolled by. I kept thinking it had to end but it just kept going. When she finally stopped, I found I had all the questions ready. It was as if I was reading off an internal clipboard. We started with the first, and we went right through, all over again, this time in detail. Names, places, dates.

"The first? How long ago?"

"A while ago."

"Exactly how long?"

"It was on *Guppy*."

"On *Guppy*? On the set of *Guppy*?"

She nodded.

"That's more than three years ago."

She nodded.

"For three years you've been doing this?"

She nodded.

The ones I knew were the worst. The director who had that special little smile for me, the leading men, but also the gaffers, the grips. Boris. God, Boris. The net was spread wide. A good cross-section, age-distribution, a cross-gender sprinkling. No small dogs, however. I got them all. I drew them out, one after the other. To start with it was like teeth. But, gradually, she began to relax. She started to speak more freely. She began to volunteer details, names and observations, until it became a continuous narrative. It all just poured out. This was a big relief to Sophie. I could see that. As she talked I could see the strain lessening. I could see the weight coming off. That's a hell of a load to carry around after all. All those lies. If you carry a lie around, you become an isolated and lonely individual. I read that somewhere in a magazine. I could see Sophie, as she talked, coming back, returning to the world. A painful but necessary re-entry.

For me it worked the other way. It was like being buried alive. She talked and talked and I slumped in the sand and listened. Sometimes she'd lose the thread and I'd get her back on track with a question. There were certain things that I knew I had to know. She stared at her hands almost the whole time, and so did I. At the long blue veins on the backs of her fingers. At the tiny, fine hairs just below the knuckle. The minute quilted texture of the skin. I lost track of time completely.

When she finally stopped talking, we both just sat and stared at her hands. Then in a rush I noticed a whole lot of little things. I was hungry and I had to go to the toilet. I heaved myself to my feet. I looked down at the stranger sitting on the sand.

"Well, I'm going back to camp," I said.

She nodded. I left her sitting on the sand. I walked like an old man. I could hardly get one foot in front of the other. It was like someone had died. I felt sorry, but I didn't know if it was for me or her. It was just this big disaster, like the wreckage of a 747. Her failure and mine, our catastrophic failure. I feel broken. I feel like I've been punched and punched and punched. There are bits of me falling off.

Over the rocks at the far end of the secret cove, it's back to a long curving sandy shoreline. I'm moving. I'm putting one foot in front of the other, in a slow, steady trudge. The sun is beating down and I'm facing pretty much due west on this stretch. I'm circumnavigating the almost-island. My eyes are screwed up even behind my sunglasses.

He's standing in the shallows, up to his knees, silhouetted against the sun. He's wearing a crumpled Hawaiian shirt. Dangling from one hand is a half-empty bottle of Piper Heidsieck. He's alone and forlorn-looking. He doesn't see me until I'm almost upon him.

"Gerard."

He turns, and holds out the champagne bottle. I shake my head. He shrugs and takes a swig himself. His beaky nose is terribly, terribly sunburnt. In fact his whole face is peeling and blistered, and he's got the beginnings of a beard.

"You can't be here."

He shrugs, and swigs on the bottle. He seems inclined to agree.

"What are you doing?"

"Fishing."

"Caught anything?"

"Not yet."

"You were wrong, by the way. It's not there."

"What's not there?"

"Sin. It's not at the core of my being at all."

He shakes his head. "It's in there somewhere. It's down, deep. Deep down."

"Maybe I'll just leave it there."

He shrugs. He seems to have lost interest. He swigs on his champagne.

Back at camp, Melissa is talking to the Irish Brothers, Tamintha is talking to Russell and Ella is playing with Brian on a beach blanket in the shade. The bathing drinkers are drinking and bathing. The sun is just gone and darkness is falling fast. Staff members are arranging seating in front of a large white screen at the back of the stage. The numbness from the day before is back. It has now spread to my entire upper left jaw.

"Hey, Frederick! Coming to the screening?"

I head straight for the kitchen tent.

The kitchen tent is full of native Vanuatuan people in white T-shirts asking how is my day and how they can make it better. It's a little hellish. It's hot as all-get-out and sweat is streaming down the faces of the cooks, waiters and kitchen workers as they bend over their tasks. A constant coming and going and to-ing and fro-ing. Someone notices me, smiles, and bustles past. I make my way through the throng. There's a big commercial-sized stainless-steel gas stove such as you might see in any restaurant, pots and dishes bubbling on the flames. On the big wooden bench opposite are the knives. Big kitchen knives, forks, spoons. A girl bent over a pile of vegetables, chopping away, frowning with concentration. Next to the wooden bench is another bench with a row of big low buckets full of soapy, steamy water.

"Okay, gimme a pair of rubber gloves, there. Size XL."

The young guy at the tub looks up in surprise, then puzzlement, then embarrassment. "Sir?" He has eyelashes like cat's claws. "The screening is just beginning."

"Yeah, I know." I slip on the gloves. Generous on the talc. A good sign. I grab an apron. All around me, the clash and clatter of bowls, the blatter and cling of dishes, pots, saucepans, plates, tureens, glasses, cups and gravy boats. I plunge my hands in up to my wrists. "Shove over, kid. I'm here to help."

Hot, soapy water. Yes. Let's get some dishes done here. After a few moments of shock-horror and a round of giggles for the staff, we all settle down to work. Dishes are all about rhythm, wrist action and timing. It's something Sophie and I never shared. We'd always do dishes separately. I wonder why that is? I remember doing dishes with my mum. I remember doing them with my brother. I remember doing them with my dad. My sister too. She had a lovely sideways action on the dinner plates.

I don't remember doing them with Sophie. I remember doing them *for* Sophie, and I can remember Sophie doing them herself. But not at the same time. Maybe I've got it all wrong. Maybe whiteware is responsible for the failure of our marriage. Maybe if we'd never got that Fisher and Paykel dishwasher none of this would ever have happened. We'd have stood shoulder-to-shoulder at the stainless-steel bench, and something deeper and more meaningful would have grown between us. Maybe convenience appliances are in fact a cancer eating away at the fabric of society. Maybe hard-core porno on pay TV and ultraviolent action movies and urban decay and the global divide between rich and poor and socioeconomic dislocation have nothing to do with it. It was whiteware. Whiteware all along.

I'm washing up a storm here.

They give up before I do. They have to. They've run out of dishes. I high-five the kid with the eyelashes and walk on out. I'm pouring with sweat and my legs are a little trembly. "Hey," the kid calls after me. "You forgot to take off your apron."

That's okay, it's fancy dress. I pick up a chef's hat on the way out.

Outside, the screening is over and the party is in full swing. Lights hang from the trees. Everyone's in costume. I grab a mask from a nearby stack, just a cheap little cardboard number like you see at kids' parties. They're all over the place. Balloons, streamers, lights. A couple of people are dressed pretty imaginatively. There's a walking fruitbowl, a pair of sharks, a coconut daiquiri and a Leaning Tower of Pizza. After that, predictably enough, are the gay boys done up in chorus-line outfits, a smattering of sailors, vamps, transvestites, and so on. The band is on stage with a sort of Latino-reggae mix that seems to be going down very well. A lot of people are dancing. I see Russell and Ella. Russell is Popeye and Ella is Olive Oyl and Brian is Swee'pea, which is sort of cute. They're way over in a small deserted corner of the dance floor, all three of them dancing, the two big ones hanging on to the little one, swaying very gently. Brian has his fist in his mouth. His head is swaying in time to the music but I don't think he's really aware of it. He's looking around him, and he's very content. They're closed off in a bubble of happiness, the three of them. They don't know the rest of the world exists.

I sit at the bar, beside Melissa, who's in a kind of Diana the Huntress outfit. Suits her too. Charles is serving the drinks. "Whiskey, thanks."

Melissa looks up. "Where have you been? You missed the screening."

"I'm aware of that."

"So how did it go? Mission accomplished?"

"Not exactly." Charles slides the drink across to me. "Happy birthday, Charles."

"Cheers, mate."

"Charles?"

"Mate?"

"Can I ask your advice?"

"Sure, mate."

"I mean, seriously."

"Seriously?"

"I've been told that you have this whole other side to you. That you can turn things around for people. Entire lives. Is that in fact the case?"

"I'm famous for it, mate." He leads me down the beach. We sit on a couple of abandoned beach chairs. The clouds are gathering, sweeping across the sky like a curtain and the sunset is going to start any minute now and it's going to be insane. It's going to be a riot. Sheer madness and it happens every day. "What's it all about then, mate?"

"It's like this. I came to this island hoping to win Sophie back. Melissa is not my girlfriend. She's a prostitute. I hired her to seduce Matt to get him away from Sophie. But I've just learnt that Sophie has in fact been cheating on me for the last three years. She's pregnant to another man, she's not entirely sure who. The only thing she's absolutely sure of is that it isn't me."

Charles rubs his jaw.

I hold up my hand. "That's just by way of background. Now. I'm forty-two. I have no job, no sense of direction in my life, no particular skills apart from the ability to spend money—money which I still depend entirely on my parents for. I have no looks, no children, no one to love and no prospect of improvement in any of these spheres. I'm dysfunctional to the point of complete inability to express or experience physical affection or emotional intimacy. I hate living in London but I'm too ashamed to go home. I'm suffering from hypertension. And my teeth are driving me nuts. Do you have any advice or any suggestions?"

Charles thinks, long and hard. He rubs his jaw. He puts a hand on my shoulder. "Sensodyne."

"I'm sorry?"

"Sensodyne. Fix those teeth in no time, mate."

"Okay. Thanks, Charles, that's good." I wait.

Charles claps me on the shoulder. "No worries, mate. Any time. Any time at all." He heads back to the bar. Rebecca walks past, disguised as the Queen of Hearts.

"Rebecca. Can I ask you something?"

She stops and stands with a hand on her hip.

"Did you know all along about all the other men and women that Sophie was sleeping with? For all those years?"

She raises an eyebrow. "So she finally told you about it?"

"She told me."

"Yeah, I knew. Sure. She confided in me regularly." I guess that explains it about Rebecca. At least she looks apologetic. "But I mean, there was nothing I could do, was there?"

"Do you have any advice to offer me?"

"Advice?" She sucks her lower lip. "Well, my advice would be to pull yourself together."

"What does that mean?"

She shrugs.

---

I return to the bar. "You look like you've just seen a ghost." It's Russell. He eyes my whiskey. "And you're drinking. What's wrong?"

"Tell me, Russell, would it surprise you to learn that Sophie had in fact been systematically betraying me for the last three years?"

Russell stares at me. His eyes get bigger and bigger. His lower lip begins to tremble.

"Forget it, I was just kidding. Bad joke, bad joke, it's okay." I put a hand on his arm. "Come on, pull yourself together."

"That's not funny, Frederick."

"No, you're quite right. It's not funny."

"You shouldn't kid around with other people's feelings like that."

"I apologize. I sincerely apologize."

That's when I feel it. There's something tickling my heel. I shift my foot, and there's a sudden, sharp, stabbing pain. Looking down, I catch sight of a black and yellow striped tail flickering away into the shadows. I reach down and feel my bare heel. My hand comes up spotted with a tiny drop of blood. I stare, stupidly.

"Hey, Russell."

"Yeah?"

"You know those snakes."

"What snakes?"

"The ones that never bite."

"Oh. The sea snakes. Yeah?"

"One just bit me."

Instantaneously I realize that I'm spaced. There's no particular sensation to it, I'm just spaced. I look at the drink. Stupidly. It's getting farther away.

The table is getting farther away.

Russell is getting farther away.

I don't feel right. I decide to stand, only I can't. I haven't the strength.

"Are you okay?" It's Russell, he's looking at me strangely. Melissa too.

"I'm not well," I say, from a thousand miles away. I seem to have cotton wool in my ears. I can't hold my head up. "I'm seriously ill."

I can't stay upright on the chair. I sink, slowly, toward the sand. My strength is ebbing.

I want a doctor. I want one, I realize, urgently.

Russell is standing, watching me. I'm now on my hands and knees. This could be serious. The process of enfeeblement is continuing and I've started to moo. I'm on hands and knees, still sinking, slowly, listing to starboard, my head arcing toward the sand. Gravity is winning and I'm mooing for a doctor. "A doctor. I need urgent medical attention." I speak slowly, fighting to enunciate, using strangely elaborate phrasing. "I am in urgent need of medical attention," I repeat. My head slowly hits the sand, chin first, then cheek, then temple. I'm lying on the sand, which feels cool and supportive. The rest of my body settles behind my head like a dying cow falling in slow motion to the ground. I moo again. "Moo. Help me. Help me."

All I can think about is medically qualified personnel. I'm so far from the nearest hospital. A helicopter. I need a helicopter. I need to be urgently evacuated to the nearest fully-equipped western hospital. I want medical staff in crisp white uniforms with stretchers and oxygen and syringes and machines that go beep. Technology. I want technology and lots of it. I want the works. Pull out the stops. Spare no expense. But it's too late. How long would it take a helicopter, even a fast one? Too long. I'm shutting down. I'm almost gone.

It's over. Forget the helicopter. Face it. It's too late. It's *all over.* I'm dying.

I think of my mother. She'll never see her boy again. I think of my father. Ditto. I think of Sophie. There will never be any sort of reconciliation. Will she be sorry that I'm gone? Of course she will. My vision is contracting. That's all, folks. Show's almost over. I can see it getting smaller and smaller. When it's all gone, I'll be dead. It's happening now. I figure I have time now for one last thought maybe. I realize that I'm not afraid. I'm too busy dying to be afraid. I suppose that'll have to do for a last thought. It's almost a relief, yes, it almost is. I relax utterly and cast myself into oblivion.

It's almost, but not quite, interesting, lying there, letting everything fade.

There's something on my shoulder. A hand. "What's his name?" There's a voice somewhere above my left ear. "Frederick. Can you hear me?"

To my surprise, I realize I can.

I'm not dead. I'm surrounded by a crowd of strangely garbed onlookers, peering down at me in the torchlight. There's Russell, and Ella and Brian too. Melissa is kneeling over me, preparing to give me mouth to mouth. Up the back, I think, I see Sophie but I'm not sure.

"Frederick, I'm a doctor." Oh, God, yes, a doctor. I have a doctor. I have hope.

"Hello. I've been bitten by a snake."

A light shines in my eye. Something cool is pressed against my back. A firm but gentle hand grasps my wrist. "Can you move your hand?"

My hand, as it turns out, is lying about seven inches from my nose. I can see it curled up loosely on the sand. "Yes. Yes, I can move my hand. I'm moving it now."

"Frederick, I think you're all right. I think you've had a bad shock but you're quite all right. We don't think you can have been bitten by a snake. They never bite."

"This one did. It bit my heel."

"We've had a look at your heel. I don't think you've been bitten. I think you've had a panic reaction. Possibly low blood sugar. Have you eaten much today?"

"But I felt it, on my heel. Does anyone have a red-hot poker?"

"All right, now just relax. We're going to get you somewhere more comfortable, give you a cup of tea with lots of sugar and we're going to see how you are in half an hour. We'll monitor the situation, don't worry. We don't think it can have been a snake."

"I tell you, it was a snake."

"If it was a snake I doubt that you'd be arguing the point."

"Could this be it?" Melissa is holding up a broken glass. "It was under his chair."

Oh, the humiliation. Hands are under my armpits, my knees, my back. I'm lifted up. I'm carried away by torchlight and laid in the tent. I'm visited by a succession of well-wishers. Melissa. Charles. Tamintha. Ella and Russell. Ella doesn't say much. She just holds my hand. Russell holds the other. Brian holds my nose.

## Chapter 19

"OH CHRIST, WE'RE GOING TO BE LATE."

"Relax."

We're sitting in traffic on the harbor bridge. We've been here for thirty minutes. Melissa is driving. Yes, Auckland has grown and it's big enough now to have all the features of a major city—traffic jams, crime, pollution, everything. You can get a snarl-up on the Takapuna off-ramp to rival any of the great congestion capitals of the world.

For the first fortnight I hid. Melissa got me on a plane, suitably tranquilized, and I came off the plane in dark glasses. They were all there to meet us. We got straight in the car and I drove straight home and that's where I stayed. Shut the door and didn't go outside at all. I sat in my room and stared at the sea and Rangitoto. They love Melissa, by the way. Absolutely love her. Can't get enough of her. She loves them too. She was up on the roof last weekend clearing the guttering.

After the first fortnight, I poked my nose out the door. I knew what was going to happen. What was going to happen was I would walk ten yards down the street and I would immediately bump into one of those people you don't really know but have always pretended to know because you always bump into them in shopping centers in Brown's Bay or Newmarket and they always look so incredibly thrilled and pleased to see you that you wonder how they've managed the two years since the last time. These people, you swear, must live on the streets of Newmarket and Mount Eden village. These people never do anything, except change their hairstyle. In other words, people like me.

In the end, though, I decided to face it. I went outside, because, eventually, you have to. I tried a few little local walks, and then a couple of outings—and nothing happened. I didn't bump into anyone. So I went a little farther, and I did a few malls and I went to the movies and I realized that they've *gone*. Everywhere I looked were unfamiliar faces. It's official. The coast is clear. Auckland is the one place on the surface of the globe where you can walk down the street and hold your head up high and know that there will be no New Zealanders. They're all in London, Paris, Munich, Moscow. I can go anywhere, I can do anything, in complete security. I am an anonymous traveler and Auckland is a mysterious new land, a land of good coffee and more Chinese restaurants than bus stops and Turkish food and Thai and Indonesian and Greek and Japanese and cheap electronic goods and incredible service everywhere. The sales assistants in this country have to be experienced to be believed. Friendly, with a no-nonsense, can-do, number-eight-wire sort of attitude, yet at the same time not remotely servile or weasely or anything else you don't want to know about. It's a bit like California, only sincere.

I've got so bold I even looked up a few old friends the other day. They've all got kids. They've all got mortgages. They've all got jobs, wrinkles, hair loss, knee trouble, plans, problems, hopes, grounds for optimism. They all seemed pleased to see me. No one seemed to mind about anything. In fact they hardly seemed to notice. It's such a wonderful relief to realize that no one really cares—well, not that much.

Yes, Auckland has grown, and Auckland has changed. But really,

Auckland hasn't changed. Say, for example, you go down the road in search of a loaf of bread and you park the car on a semi-familiar corner with a Dick Smith electronics store where the dairy used to be and while you're standing on the footpath scratching your head and looking around and wondering if you should just forget the Vogel's and go for a cappuccino and a croissant instead, you feel a sort of a tingling in the air and you breathe in.

And that's it.

Because all of a sudden, wham! there it is, your childhood, coming at you, and nothing has changed and you're ten years old again because Auckland still *smells* the same and nothing has changed that and I don't believe anything ever will and suddenly you're feeling feelings you forgot you'd ever felt, feelings you'd forgotten you even could feel, because they're feelings without names or faces, feelings you felt in the days before you had words to describe them, feelings so familiar and so strange and at the same time so much a part of you that you don't understand how you could ever have forgotten a feeling like that and still have been you, all that time, all those years. And for all that time, that smell and that feeling has been here on this street corner just waiting for you to happen by again. You breathe it in and there it is and best of all it doesn't mean a damn thing, it's just beautiful.

Takapuna has changed. The houses along the beach are all huge concrete nightmares now, every one architect-designed yet sort of the same, each with its electronic security system and halogen searchlights and eight-foot wall and central heating and plate-glass windows and built-in wall-to-wall millionaire. Truly, Auckland has made vast strides in social inequality over the last few years. It's a very impressive achievement. Why, if you look back even twenty years we hardly even *had* social inequality. It was just some newfangled idea from overseas.

But really Takapuna hasn't changed. If you stand on the beach now and you look out to sea, if you look out to Rangitoto, past the upwardly-mobile people with dogs and pushchairs briskly enjoying their morning constitutionals, past the Jet Skis and the Windsurfers — if you look out to sea and breathe in — no, Takapuna hasn't changed.

My folks have changed. My dad has changed. He's always been a worrier, but now he worries about different things. He used to worry about the exchange rate, export incentives, stock market fluctuations and the quality of locally-sourced aluminum. Now my dad worries about falling over. About his afternoon nap. My mum has changed too. Instead of worrying about the consistency of her cheese omelettes she worries about the consistency of my dad. So, no, I guess maybe they haven't really changed either.

I stand on the beach and turn and there's an old guy on the grass. I want to stop and stare and stare and I have to pinch myself and say this is my dad. This is *my* dad. I had a good long talk with my dad. We sat on the front lawn of his multimillion-dollar beach-front property on a pair of semi-rotten striped canvas deck chairs that I actually remember him buying at The Warehouse in 1992 or thereabouts for about five dollars each. We sat and we looked out across the sea to Rangitoto. We talked about a lot of things. Then we fell silent and my dad cleared his throat, which took him a little while. Then he spoke again.

"You know," said my dad, in a perfectly conversational sort of voice, "I'm going to be kicking the bucket. Sooner rather than later."

Now, as we all know this is not the sort of talk you encourage in your parents. It's just not acceptable to talk like that. So I opened my mouth to say "rubbish" or "don't talk like that" or "nonsense, you've got another ten years at least — you've got the constitution of an ox." Only I didn't say any of those things because at that moment I looked across at my dad and I saw him sitting there and he didn't have the constitution of an ox. He used to be able to bench-press two hundred pounds. But no more. He was just stating the truth, plain and simple. A dirty trick to be sure, but that's parents for you. So I shut my mouth. My dad looked across at me.

We both sat there and we looked out at Rangitoto. I wasn't sure who I was supposed to be feeling sorry for, him or me. I breathed. I took a deep breath and breathed in every moment I'd ever had in that house and on that beach and with that dad in that front garden. I took it all in, in one big breath, and I held it. I held it in there.

My dad re-cleared his throat. "I've been wanting to have a talk to you about money."

So we talked about money. My dad explained the situation. He even took me inside and we had a look at the accounts. I have to admit I was shocked. The situation was rather more serious than I'd imagined. I had no idea it was *that* much. My dad said he was sorry to have to ask but he said really he'd be very grateful if I'd be willing to accept more money, preferably large sums on a regular basis. He said he didn't know what else to do with it and it was frankly getting embarrassing, plus the family trust was facing a serious tax situation. The others were all taking their fair share. If I didn't want to take cash, would I at least consider shares or property?

Well, I didn't like it, but I had to accept it. The hard cold truth—and I'm just going to have to learn to live with this—is that money is never going to be a problem in my lifetime. Some people have money problems, I don't, and no amount of wishful thinking is going to change that. The only way I could possibly end up bankrupt and penniless would be to remain in the film business. And I'm not doing that. Not for any money.

---

I visited Gerard too. If Sittlebury is like going back to school, Paremoremo is like going back to university. The criminals are all terribly grown-up and serious—and this is just the remand wing.

Gerard's on the way through to Porirua, but they're holding him while they paint his cell and put in a flush toilet. Having said that, Gerard seems to be fitting in surprisingly well. The lifers have a certain Dostoyevskian mystique that gets them through the day-to-day. He says he feels much more at home here. He stands at the window sometimes and just breathes in the air and tells himself, this is New Zealand air I'm breathing here.

He couldn't show me his cell but they gave us a little visiting room.

I watch him as he rolls a cigarette, briskly, and puffs away. Every so often he glances at his watch. "Yeah, I've got the polishes on the second draft nailed."

"Was there much to do?"

"They wanted more joke lines." He glances at his watch again.

"Joke lines?"

He nods, eyes crinkled through the smoke.

"I thought you were supposed to be saving the world from heavy metal music and the devil?"

"Oh." He looks embarrassed. "It's really more of a contemporary satire on modern rock culture."

"I see. Have they changed your medication by any chance?"

"Yeah. I'm on lithium now. I didn't want to take it for a long time. I was scared. I'd heard all this terrible stuff about what it can do to your liver."

"I know how you feel. I had just the same problem." He doesn't seem to be listening. He glances at his watch. His foot taps nervously. "Am I holding you up?"

"No, that's cool. I scheduled this meeting in. But I have to get back to work in twenty minutes, so I'm keeping an eye on the time." He shakes his head. "So much to do, so little time. I have to have a first draft ready for next month. Seamus and Sean are flying out to talk about it."

"So what are you working on now?"

"A romantic comedy."

"What's the idea?"

"I'm not at liberty to discuss it."

"Beg your pardon."

He's got a three-picture deal. I do happen to know that much because I was involved in the early negotiations and I helped him find an agent. I also know that the Irish Brothers are paying him very handsomely, and that he's donating all the proceeds to charity. I even know which charity: my charity. Did I not mention that? I've started a charity. I'm calling it the Case Foundation. Which makes me the head Case. We already have a brass plaque, an office, a receptionist called Tara and a solicitor's firm. Even that much cost a fortune. My dad is very grateful.

Choosing an actual charitable activity isn't nearly so easy. At first I was thinking maybe something to do with animals but then I thought maybe not. Then I thought maybe something like a Distressed Overseas New Zealanders Repatriation Service. But apparently that's already covered. So I've decided in the end to keep the brief wide open and approach it on a case-by-case basis. The entrepreneurial approach to charity. One thing. The village at Pakulalanana definitely gets a water tank and a generator—if they want one, that is.

---

The traffic inches its way up and over the bridge, down the other side. It banks up again going past Auckland Grammar, but we manage to sideslip a couple of lanes and catch the Gillies Avenue exit okay. Melissa is driving. She has this insane idea that we'll find a spot somewhere in Newmarket and of course we don't and we end up in the municipal parking building above the Olympic pool where they charge a fortune but at least it's close and by now we're running out of time. We take the steps two at a time and we just make it for the title sequence.

I sit. Melissa leans across. "Feeling okay?"

"Never felt better." Perhaps something of an overstatement, but still. My hand goes to the back of my neck. It still feels pretty breezy back there, but in a good way.

The lights go out. My pulse quickens.

Music begins to play. Here come the credits. Here they come.

---

It's dark now and we're rolling down Parnell rise. Shops, restaurants, people on the street. Melissa has this insane, crazy, half-baked idea that we're going to find a park here. We end up halfway down Gladstone Road and walk all the way back in the chirruping darkness, past the rose gardens, all the way to Parnell. We've got time. The booking isn't until nine.

Melissa raises her glass. "Well, here's to it."

"To the divorce."

"The divorce."

We drink. I raise my glass. "And here's to *it*."

"And all who sail in her."

After dinner, we walk back to the car, and drive, late, to an expensive hotel in the middle of town. We cross downtown Queen Street on the stroke of midnight, and it's as dead and empty as Oxford Street on a weekday night. We check into a penthouse suite. The lift doors close. It's a long way to the seventeenth floor. I turn to Melissa. "So, listen, about payment . . . Is it really necessary?"

"Really, it is necessary."

"After all we've been through together, and I fired you and you quit, and I even came down to visit your folks in Levin and stayed the night and everything, you still insist on payment?"

"I do."

"Well, okay, if you insist."

"I do. I absolutely insist. And in advance too."

"How much would a hundred pounds be in New Zealand dollars, anyway?"

"Call it three hundred. That's a round figure."

"Okay, three hundred it is."

She unclips her purse, pulls out three hundred, in cash, and stuffs it down the front of my underpants. It was her idea. She says it's a way of restoring balance. I never saw myself as the gigolo type, but whatever. She grabs my butt.

The lift doors open and we let ourselves into the room, which, by the way, is very nice. She puts on a Miles Davis CD while I open the French doors. There's a wonderful view of the harbor, the lights on the bridge, the black shadow of Rangitoto, the sleeping volcano, felt rather than seen out across the slick water. We stand on the balcony and drink a glass of champagne, enjoying the cool night breeze. Tomorrow morning Melissa flies back to London. She has a midday flight, which I guess is civilized. She's working for Tamintha, and Tamintha is working with the Irish Brothers. They're coproducing Gerard's film. I have nothing to do with it whatsoever and I couldn't be more okay about it.

"So did you like it?"

"Actually, I did. It was okay."

"And what did you think of her?"

"She was very good. She didn't seem like herself at all. She seemed very believable—and so was he. He certainly didn't seem *anything* like himself."

"I don't know how he manages to seem so intelligent on screen."

"He takes out his contact lenses."

"Ah."

It wasn't a great film. Jazzy camera work, wall-to-wall sex, a sound track that will quickly date, a bit overt on the issues, but nonetheless, it was okay. Matt plays a war-torn journalist, and Sophie plays a tyro, both of them assigned to cover the war in Afghanistan. It's all about burnout and replenishment, sex, politics, war, guilt, sex, responsibility, honesty, sex, sex, and the media. Not a great film, but okay. It has something to say and it says it. What makes it come to life, what lifts it out of the mass, is the fact that there's a real connection there between Sophie and Matt, where it counts, on screen.

"And what did you think of the scene?"

"*The* scene?"

I sat in the dark and I watched a woman I used to know with a man I almost pushed into a volcano once. They were simulating a relationship. They were pretending to be two lonely people in a hotel room, in a place and a time they'd never been or seen. They were neither of them, in real life, remotely like the people they were pretending to be: it was fake, all of it, and they were doing it for the money. But really, they weren't, and it wasn't. They were creating something that *was* real, something alive, which passed between them at the time, which existed for that moment and now, sitting there in the dark, it was something we were all part of, all of us there, suspending our disbelief by that precious Damoclean thread. Whatever else passed between them is something else. But now, in this darkened room, it was real, and we believed.

"Actually, you know, I didn't mind that either."

"Did you think it was sensual?"

"Ah . . . yeah I guess."

"A turn-on?"

"No."

"No?"

I shake my head. "It wasn't hot. More lyrical than hot."

"I have to agree."

"When all is said and done, I suspect it's probably a chick movie."

"Maybe you're right."

"A hard-core chick movie, but a chick movie nonetheless."

I'm thinking of Sophie, as we turn into the room. For a while I missed Sophie so much I thought I was going to die. I tried to trace it back, the whole thing, where it all went wrong, why, when, how, but I could see where it was all headed. It was headed for the devil and heavy metal music. It's a girl, by the way, and her name is Esther. Sophie wrote me a very, very long letter in which she uses the word sorry forty-five times. I know because I counted. I appreciated that but I don't think I'll be writing back. Not immediately anyway. She enclosed photos. Looks like a sweet little thing. She's managed to identify the father. Apparently he's thrilled and he's suing for custody. Sophie says motherhood has changed her in a fundamental way and if I'm ever in London she'd love to see me. She wants to repair the past and build a real friendship based on honesty and mutual respect. Well, I *will* be in London, because that's where Melissa's going to be. We'll see. I'm flying out to join her in a month, then we're coming back here for the wedding, midsummer, and then off to Africa for the honeymoon. Matt's going to try to be in Kenya around February. He's going to bring the family.

It was funny how it happened with Melissa. It was when she brought me that cup of tea. She walked in the tent, all orange, and all of a sudden—WHAM. I realized. The proposal, by the way, was extremely romantic, extremely postmodern, and utterly wonderful. I took her down to the beach at Takapuna. It was the end of the day. I cleared away the seaweed and knelt before her and presented her with the severed corpse of my ponytail. (She's keeping it in a plastic bag. We're going to bury it in Highgate, next to Karl. I'm sure he wouldn't mind.) A dog was cavorting in the waves. A chill wind was blowing her hair all over the place. Rangitoto was doing handsprings in the background.

"*Now* will you marry me?" I said.

"Oh, all right."

"So much for your cast-iron guarantee about balding fattish forty-year-olds."

"You've lost weight."

As far as genre goes, it could change at any moment of course, but at present we're talking whimsical postmodern black romantic comedy, which actually suits me pretty well. I guess I'll just string it out as long as I can. And as for this whole thing with Melissa—I know, I know, it's a nightmare: a cliché of the first order, smacks of blatant wish-fulfillment of the very worst kind, but what can I do? I can't push her away from me just because she's young and gorgeous and crazy about me. That would be unwarrantedly cruel. I'm exactly what she needs and I know she'll be very happy with me. It's true I'm quite a bit older than her, but I've lost a lot of weight lately and as a nonsmoking social drinker who remembers his medication and takes regular mild exercise there's every likelihood I'll live to see my grandchildren. Even if I can't pick them up. But this is real life here, after all, and life is nothing if not a constant series of compromises. Don't forget also that I've saved her. I've saved her from a fate worse than death: squandering her youth and innocence impersonating an Australian. Also, if it makes you feel any better, we went to the opera the other night and she hated it. I wept buckets.

As for Sophie, my love for Sophie was real, but unfortunately the Sophie I loved wasn't. I don't think the Sophie I loved ever existed, or if she did, she died alone somewhere far from home in the night and nobody noticed. It hurts, and I still mourn her, but there it is, it's just something I'm stuck with, like medication. You learn to accept these things. That's what being forty is all about.

I pull the sliding doors shut and the sound of the traffic cuts out like a radio.

**INT. HOTEL ROOM—NIGHT.**

SLIGHTLY POPPY LOUNGE MUSIC PLAYS. SLOWLY SHE REMOVES HIS CLOTHES, AND HE HERS, ITEM BY ITEM. THEY STAND TOGETHER IN THE HOTEL ROOM SHOWER,

AND SHE SOAPS HIM FROM HEAD TO TOE, AND HE HER.
SHE LEADS HIM TO THE BEDROOM. THEY LIE ON THE
SHAGPILE, ON THEIR SIDES, FACING ONE ANOTHER.
MAGNIFICENT PANORAMIC VIEW OF THE CITY THROUGH
PLATEGLASS WINDOWS. THEY KISS. SHE PUSHES HIM
GENTLY ONTO HIS BACK, REACHES BETWEEN HIS LEGS.
SHE TAKES HIM IN HER MOUTH. SHE NUZZLES AND
TASTES HIM. CRADLES HIM, CUPS HIM. SMELLS HIM.
LICKS HIM. BITES HIM. TEASES HIM, CAJOLES HIM.
HE WATCHES WITH DETACHMENT, THEN GROWING
INVOLVEMENT, AS SHE DRAWS HIM SLOWLY, REMORSE-
LESSLY, ALL THE LONG WAY BACK TO LIFE.

WILLIAM BRANDT was born in London in 1961 to New Zealand parents. He grew up in New Zealand, and has lived in Australia, Russia, the UK, and Noumea. He studied acting at the National Institute of Dramatic Art in Sydney, and has appeared in many productions, from *An Angel at My Table* to *Shortland Street*. He is married and has three children.

William Brandt's collection of short stories *Alpha Male* won the Best First Book of Fiction Award at the 1999 Montana NZ Book Awards, and was highly praised by reviewers in New Zealand and the UK.